***

Death on Daugherty Creek

M·G·Lewis

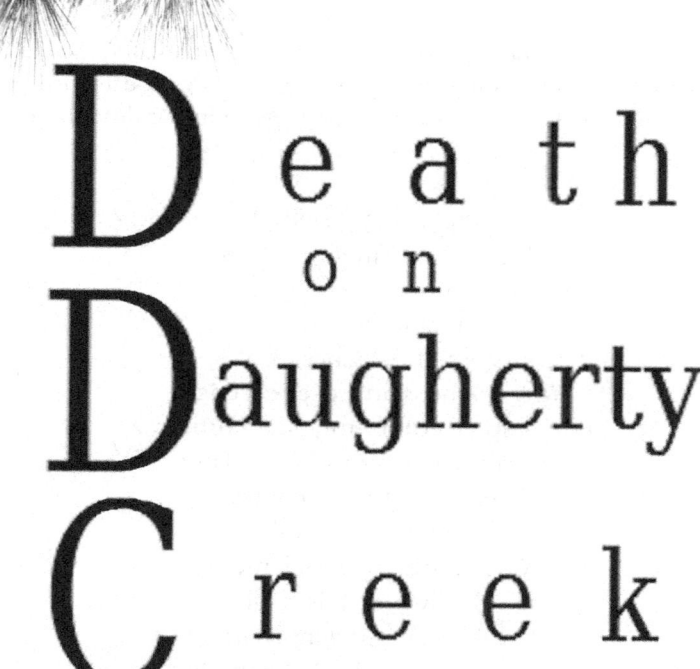

Copyright © 2016 Michael Gene Lewis
All rights reserved.
ISBN: 152344374X
ISBN-13: 978-1523443741

Cover photo by author

This book is a work of fiction. Names, characters, places, and incidents are the product of the author's imagination or are used fictitiously. Any resemblance to actual events, locales, or persons, living or dead, is entirely coincidental.

Bergeron Mystery
Death on Daugherty Creek
Foreseeable Harm
Beauty in Ashes
Deep is the Chesapeake
Mr. Boghossian Loses a Tenant
The Nuptials of Ezmeralda Gutierrez
Keypunchers & Other Villains
Bornheimer's Demise
On Farm Deadly
Waters Ebb, Rocks Emerge
Really Not His Fault
The Not So Ancient Mariner
The Detective with Dishpan Hands
The Face that Launched a 1000 Scams
Gabe & Cory's Momentous Misadventure

Other
Rune's Riddle

Nesrady Clone Series
The Clone Who Loved to Bake Bread
The Clone Who Loved to Fight
The Clone Who Loved to Swim
The Clone Who Loved Voltaire

Friday
5:45 pm

Gabe pulled into the parking lot of Janes Island State Park and came to a halt next to a boat trailer. He let the motor of the canary yellow, Ford Fiesta rental run, enjoying the AC for a few more seconds.

He could just back out and leave. Even doing the speed limit, he could be back at the airport in Salisbury in less than an hour.

A text to Neal could just say that something had come up. Neal would understand, or even if he didn't, he would never mention it. But they had been best friends since they were five and had dared each other into exploring the mucky crawlspace under Neal's house.

If it just didn't involve Neal's business partner, Eric Duncan Girard.

But maybe Neil was finally going to end the partnership? And he needed Gabe Bergeron as muscle? To kick Eric's butt? Which he could totally do. Probably.

Of course, Gabe was aware that he had never actually punched anybody. And as much as Eric deserved it, Eric was undeniably bigger than Gabe. And possibly knew how to fight?

Which wouldn't be good news for Gabriel Henri Bergeron. But Neal had called upon him.

Wouldn't it hurt a lot to punch somebody in the face; for the puncher as well as the punchee?

Gabe may have sighed, but he shut off the motor and opened the door. The heat and the humidity rushed in to hug him like a very sweaty friend with no concept of personal space.

A young guy in a tank top and shorts was launching his

outboard at the boat ramp; Eric's yacht was towering in the background. It looked bigger here at the small dock.

The "Taureau" was all gleaming white, swept back like a racing pennant even when it was motionless and mirrored on the blue water.

Layla had probably picked it out, which was only fair since Mrs. Girard had all the money in the family.

A woman was standing on the dock, talking to Eric, and she was definitely not Layla.

She had golden skin and jet black hair and a red sarong dappled with big white flowers, and appeared to have just stepped out of a full-color brochure for trips to Bora Bora.

Eric said, "Come on board, Mia? Please?"

An unbuttoned Hawaiian shirt showed off Eric's hairy chest while a red micro-speedo displayed the rest of his wares to the lovely Mia.

She was underwhelmed.

She shook her head. "No, Eric." Her smile was the chilliest thing on a July day in Maryland. "You have guests coming."

She had a slight British accent.

The young guy at the ramp failed to notice that his boat was floating away and had to lunge for it.

Mia twirled around and walked off like a Polynesian goddess, lacking only Tiki torches and big, bronzed men in body paint to complete the splendid scene.

Eric stopped ogling Mia long enough to become aware that someone was standing on the dock. Gabe gave the guy his most judgmental look. Mr. Eric looked guilty for a nanosecond before his usual hauteur took over. He raised one pointy eyebrow and went inside his boat, yacht, whatever.

How big did a boat have to be to qualify for "yacht" status? If you had to ask, you couldn't afford one.

Gabe was early for the meeting, and he didn't want to spend a second longer with Eric than was absolutely necessary so he started walking through the pine trees, looking for Neal's cabin.

The park map didn't make the place look that big, but it took ten minutes to walk to the cabin, which wasn't fake rustic, but looked to have been built of actual logs. It was set in the midst of tall pine trees which held the steamy air captive like big, green shower curtains.

No one was at home when he knocked on the door. There was supposed to be a new girl friend with Neal, but he couldn't remember her name.

Neal was a sweet guy, but he had awful taste in women...and business partners.

He walked around the park; the place was full of happy visitors in RVs, campers, and even tents. Three very blond kids were roasting hot dogs over an open fire and talking in a language he didn't recognize.

Gabe shuddered; he hated camping as much as Neal loved it.

A cloud of mosquitoes enveloped him like a Romulan force field. Even Eric's company was better than being eaten alive.

And Neal might be on the boat, yacht, by now along with this new girlfriend and Layla, and they would dilute the raw Eric.

Gabe doubled his fist. It didn't appear all that fearsome? He should have practiced hitting something soft like a pillow. Or one of those bag-things that hung from the ceilings of gyms in boxing movies? Not that he had any idea where to find one of those

The Polynesian goddess wasn't around this time.

He yelled, "Girard? Neal?" No response.

Gabe stepped onto the dock, and a gout of flame leaped from the boat straight at him. He threw up an arm and twisted, and then he was falling. The flesh-melting heat was replaced with a soothing coolness enveloping his body.

It came to him that this was because he was under water.

He thought he should do something about that, and he paddled to the top.

The fire was growling and hissing, and he could feel the skin of his face start to fry again.

Someone was shouting.

And then Gabe remembered Neal, and knew he had to get his ass out of the damn creek. Somehow.

He grabbed the nearest piling, but he couldn't figure out what the next step should be; it wasn't like he could shinny up the thing in a Tarzan maneuver.

Sharp things were cutting into his legs. He looked around for shark fins cutting the water, and then started laughing at himself.

A strong hand grabbed his arm and pulled him away from the piling, and then more hands grabbed him and pulled him out of the water.

The fire was roaring and belching black smoke into the air. The heat intensified scorching his face and arms and legs like he'd been shoved inside a very large toaster, but somebody was helping him scurry away.

But Gabe said, "Neal! You have to find Neal."

Somebody said, "Sorry, Sir, but if Neal's on board, there isn't anything we can do."

A guy was leaning over him, back-lit by the freaking, raging inferno that was the "Taureau." "Neal?"

"No, Sir, I'm not Neal. Are you in any pain? The ambulance is on the way."

The guy was big and dark like Neal, but he wasn't Neal.

"I'm Ranger Hobbs, Sir. This is Ranger Sharp."

A woman with long brown hair pulled back in a ponytail experimented with a smile aimed in his general direction as she stared at the fire. "I'm Sarah. Did you hit your head?"

"No, I'm okay." Which wasn't true. His legs hurt, and his face was burning, and his head did feel funny. "My legs."

Sarah glanced at them. "They're not too bad. Where the Hell are the fire engines, Kurt?"

There was a siren in the distance.

Kurt Hobbs said, "On their way. Wind's picking up. The mooring lines are gone, and it's drifting."

She nodded. "Shit."

Kurt looked back to him. "You had a close encounter with some barnacles, Sir, but you'll be okay. Can you tell me your name?"

"Gabe Bergeron. Where's Eric?"

"Eric?"

"He was on board. It's his boat. Or Layla's."

Sarah said, "Shit, Kurt, how many were on board? This is bad."

Kurt held Gabe down when he tried to sit up. "No, Sir, just lie there for me. Okay?" Kurt looked at Sarah. "The damn thing is moving with the tide out of the reach of the fire engines. And the wind's keeping it close to the bank. It could set the whole park ablaze."

Sarah said, "I know that, but what are you thinking of doing?"

"Get a line on it and tow it back to the dock."

"And just how are you going to do that? You feel that heat?"

"I feel it, Ranger Sharp, but it will look very bad on my record if half the park burns."

Sarah gave Ranger Hobbs a gamine smile.

A small, white boat with flashing lights and a squealing siren was bouncing across the water heading for them. It slowed as it came to the dock, which was smoldering and even still burning in spots.

Kurt yelled to the two men in uniform. "Fire engines are on the way!" There were more sirens in the distance. "But it's drifting!"

The older of the two uniformed men nodded and reached down, rummaging in the bottom of the boat.

The boat had a console like a speaker's lectern in the center, surrounded by a steel pipe superstructure supporting a cloth canopy, topped off by lights and a disk-shaped thing with "Furuno" written around it in blue.

The older guy came up with a grappling hook. He nudged the boat forward toward the floating cauldron of fire and black, billowing smoke.

He swung the hook round and round and let it fly.

It landed close to the bridge of the boat. It scratched grooves through the bubbling paint of Eric's pride and joy, before failing to catch and dropping into the creek.

The two men were shielding behind the control console. The older reeled in the hook, wound up, and hurled it at the "Taureau" again.

It caught. He reversed his boat and dragged the burning behemoth back toward the dock.

The fire engines roared into the boat ramp parking lot and began spraying water on the fire.

As a cloud of noxious smoke and steam enveloped the whole area, Kurt and Sarah got Gabe to his feet, and they all ran.

The third siren was the ambulance.

A paramedic was staring down at him. "Can you tell me your name, Sir?"

"Gabe Bergeron. My legs hurt."

And two paramedics checked him over, wrapped his legs, and loaded him into the ambulance.

"Kurt!"

"Yes, Mr. Bergeron?"

"Eric and Layla Girard, and Neal Hartmann and...." He still couldn't remember the new girlfriend's name. "And another woman could have been on the boat, yacht."

"Yes, Sir, I'll tell the police."

"Neal was here. Staying in one of the cabins."

If Neal had been on board, he was gone, and there was nothing Gabe Bergeron could do; nothing at all. He shut his eyes as the ambulance driver slammed the door.

Friday
6:45 pm

McCready Hospital was only a couple of miles away, and Gabe was expected. The paramedics wheeled him into a room, heaved him from their gurney to the ER bed, and smiled at the nurse.

"All yours, Sharon."

"Thanks, Bud. Any details you'd like to share?"

They reeled off his medical info in a practiced sing-song, taking turns.

Sharon had brown hair and gray eyes and cranberry scrubs. "Do you have any pain, Mr. Bergeron?"

"My legs hurt. My face is hot. I have some burns on my arms." The stench of the black smoke was making him sick.

"Yes, Sir. Anything else?" She was stripping him of his wet clothes as she spoke. "You fell off a dock? Did you hit your head?"

"No." His head had cleared and was about the only thing that didn't hurt.

He looked around, and it seemed he was the only customer on a Friday night. His wallet was soaked. He had never tried drying cash before.

"Shit!" Sharon looked up from his cuts. "Sorry. My cellphone is gone."

Bud, the paramedic, said, "Didn't see one. Ed?"

The other paramedic shook his head. "Probably in the creek."

They were leaving. Gabe said, "Is there any news? Of any other casualties? My friend, Neal, might have been...there."

Bud shook his head. "We haven't gotten any calls, Sir."

A bald guy in green scrubs and a white coat strolled in, and Bud and his accomplice were out the door.

Sharon said, "There was an explosion, Doctor, and Mr. Bergeron was knocked into Daugherty Creek."

The bald guy was totally hairless except for a grayish soul patch on his lower lip. He looked at the chart and then back to Gabe and then back to the chart.

"You stink, Mr. Bergeron."

The nurse, Sharon, was sticking a needle into his arm, or Gabe might have been tempted to smack the doctor upside his head. As it was, he smiled. "And you're ugly, but I can take a bath."

Which Gabe regretted as it came out of his mouth, but Sharon giggled like a tiny pixie as she hooked up an IV. She had a diamond stud piercing her left eyebrow.

The doctor smiled. "Just so. You seem to be breathing normally, so I'm going to assume for the moment that you did not inhale any noxious fumes? I'm Dr. Hahn by the way, and your life is in my capable hands."

"I'm relieved to hear it, Doctor."

Sharon giggled again. She was not in the least pixieish despite the giggle, but tended more toward your Teutonic, warrior maiden type.

Hahn said, "Any dizziness or headaches?"

"No, my head is fine, Doctor."

Sharon was removing the dressings from his legs, and Dr. Hahn was looking at the cuts that sliced this way and that on his inner thighs and calves.

Gabe said, "I tried climbing a piling...to get out of the water."

Dr. Hahn nodded. "Ah, most likely *Balanus eburneus*, or in ordinary parlance, the ivory barnacle, Mr. Bergeron. The shells are razor sharp, and you should avoid them whenever possible."

"I'll make a note. So do I need stitches?"

"A few. I don't suppose you know if you've had a tetanus shot recently?"

Gabe said, "No, I don't."

"Of course not, why would you?"

"What about my arms? They're starting to hurt. And my face.

Is my face burnt?"

Dr. Hahn looked him over. "You have an overall scorched appearance, Mr. Bergeron, but nothing serious or likely to be damaging to your beauty. I'm sure Nurse Sharon can root around in the cabinets and find something to smear on the burns. Can't you, Nurse?"

Sharon nodded. "Yes, Doctor."

Hahn then proceeded to clean and stitch the barnacle cuts. He stood back to assay his efforts, nodded to himself, and departed.

Gabe looked at Sharon. "Is he always...like that?"

She smiled. "Usually he's worse, but I think he liked you."

"If you say so? Can I get out of here soon?"

She said, "Don't see why not."

"Can I go to the men's room first?"

She pointed the way. "Don't mess up your IV."

"No problem." Gabe did his business and checked out the mirror. He looked like he had the worst sunburn of his life, and his hair and face were grimy with soot. He was uglier than Dr. Hahn.

Sharon was rooting for that burn ointment when two uniformed men marched in; the ones who had kept the "Taureau" from incinerating Kurt's park. Both were sunburnt and sooty.

They were wearing green khaki uniforms with life vests. The triangular shoulder patches read "Maryland Police" in big gold letters; "Natural Resources" in much smaller letters hugged a state seal. The badges and the guns on their hips looked very police-like.

The beefy, older one with graying, sandy hair was about Gabe's height. "Sergeant King. Up to answering a few questions, Sir?" King pulled out a little notebook.

Gabe nodded. "Did you find Neal?"

King ignored his question; the blond younger one looked like he wanted to say something, but he kept his mouth shut.

King took the only chair. "Tell me what happened, Sir."

"I was supposed to meet with Neal Hartmann and Eric Girard on board Eric's yacht. I was heading for the boat when it blew up."

"When you say blew up...?"

"Yeah. Flames and smoke shooting at me. Knocked me off

my feet and into the water."

The young guy was pacing around the room. "You were lucky! It felt like my face was going to melt off when we got close."

King glared at him. "Thank you for your help, Officer Stevens." Blond Officer Stevens wilted and sought support from the nearest wall.

King said, "Were you on board, Sir? Before the fire?"

"No, I never made it."

Sergeant King made a note and gave him a tired half-smile; the kind you gave potential perps. King rubbed a ham-hock shoulder and stretched out his left arm experimentally. "But you have been on board before?"

"Once. Months ago. When Eric bought it. For a minute or so."

King said, "Know anything about the engines? Or the state of repair of the craft?"

"Nothing. Do you know anything about who was on board? Please, I need to know about my friend, Neal Hartmann?"

"Not too concerned about the owner of the boat, Mr. Eric Girard, and his wife, Layla Girard?"

Gabe shook his head. "Of course, I am, but Neal is like a brother to me, Sergeant. I even lived with his family for almost three years when I was going through a rough patch."

"A rough patch?"

"A patch that is the opposite of smooth, Sergeant. People often encounter them in life."

"If you say so, Sir, and when was this?"

He wanted to say, "None of your damn business!" But what he said was, "I was ten. Well, nine and a half, and I'm thirty-two now."

King nodded. "Thank you, Sir. What is your relationship with Mr. Girard?"

"I used to work for his company."

King glanced at his notebook. "And that would be Girard-Hartmann Accounting? But you don't work there any longer, Mr. Bergeron?"

"No, I quit. Two months ago. To accept a better offer." He

had no idea why he'd said that? It wouldn't be hard to find out that he'd had a screaming match with Eric before he quit, and that he was still unemployed, but King was so smug.

The sergeant made another note. "Would anyone have any reason to do harm to Mr. Girard or Mrs. Girard?"

"No. I don't think so. Not Layla. She's a classy lady."

"Not so sure about Mr. Girard?"

Gabe sighed. "I don't know of any reason anyone would blow up his boat with him on it, Sergeant. It isn't the kind of thing that typically happens to accountants."

"If you say so. Who was on board to the best of your knowledge?"

"Eric. I got to the park at around 5:45. I was early so I went looking for Neal's cabin, but I saw Eric first...on the boat. But I didn't go near it."

"And Mr. Hartmann has rented Cabin #1?"

"Yeah."

"Was he in his cabin, Sir?"

"Nobody answered the door.."

"Any idea where he might have been, Sir?"

"No. And Layla. She was probably on board. I saw her and Eric on the boat at the marina. This was around 1:30 today."

King looked up. "Is that right, Sir? And what were they doing?"

"I think Eric was refueling." He wasn't going to volunteer that they had been having a fight.

Officer Stevens, who looked like the blond, blue-eyed boy next door in every classic Disney film, said, "And you didn't go on board then, Sir?"

Sergeant King gave his subordinate another look. "Officer Stevens is new to the job, Mr. Bergeron."

But Stevens smiled at his sergeant this time.

"No, I didn't, Officer Stevens. I arrived in Crisfield and got a room at the motel, and then I drove around. I found the marina so I walked through, just looking at the boats. That's when I saw Eric and Layla. I still had hours to kill so I followed these little back roads, and found a funny bridge and lots of marsh. I thought I was lost, but eventually the road brought me back to town. And I went to the park. That's all."

King said, "Nothing else you'd like to tell us, Mr. Bergeron?"

"Nope. Can't think of a thing. How soon will you be able to find out who was on board, Sergeant?"

King folded his little notebook and got to his feet. "It's still hot, Sir."

Stevens, who was back to bouncing around the room like an excited puppy, said, "It's a mess of molten, stinking fiberglass...."

King said, "As soon as we can, Sir."

Stevens said, "We'll drag the creek at first light."

Gabe said, "Right. I see. Thank you."

Stevens looked at Sergeant King. "Are you going to tell him now?"

"Tell me what?"

King stuffed his little notebook into the shirt pocket of his uniform. He considered as Officer Stevens rolled his big, blue eyes and fidgeted in a clearly, insubordinate manner.

King said, "Well, Mr. Bergeron, we don't have to wait for the boat to cool to locate Mr. Hartmann."

"Shit! You already found his body in the creek?"

"No, Sir. He's in the waiting room. He and his girlfriend...." King pulled his notebook out again and consulted it. "His girlfriend, Ellie Tyson, of West Chester, Pennsylvania. They both seem eager to see you."

All the world knew that Gabe Bergeron was not quick on the uptake so it took a second. But then he hopped off the gurney, grabbed the open ass of his gown in one hand and the IV pole in the other, and marched out of the exam room.

The ER wasn't that big, but Gabe was too pissed to search for the freaking waiting room so he yelled as loud as he could. "Neal!"

Neal and a very pretty woman popped out of a door into an anteroom, separated from the ER proper by a sliding glass door.

Neal gave him his goofy smile.

Nurse Sharon and the other nurse weren't happy, but Gabe didn't care. Sergeant King made one more note in his little book and left. Officer Stevens smiled at him.

Gabe hugged Neal as hard as he could. "I thought you were dead."

Neal nodded. "I thought you were too. I came back to the park, and Eric's boat was burning, but Ellie found me and said that somebody had been taken away in the ambulance so we came here, but Sergeant King wanted to talk to us, and the nurse said you were being treated...."

Ellie said, "He was so worried. I'm Ellie Tyson, by the way."

She had dark brown hair, enormous blue eyes, a little rosebud mouth, and a body that a million years of evolution had honed to perfection.

Gabe looked at Neal. He was tall, but there was no way to soften the blow. His eyes were tiny, and his ears stuck out. He had a great smile and a kind heart, but was that enough for an Ellie, super-dreadnought class of woman?

Gabe tamped down his suspicions as he filled out the paper work for Nurse Sharon, while trying to keep his gown closed. He had no insurance, but he'd worry about that when the bill came.

His shirt was toast, almost literally, so he exited the ER semi-nude and got into Neal's car in nothing more than a pair of damp shorts. His shoes were at the bottom of Daugherty Creek along with his phone.

The hospital, like the park, was on the banks of Daugherty Creek and had its own dock.

Neal said, "You're coming with us, Gabe. The cabin has two bedrooms, and I insist."

He was too tired to argue and needed to talk to Neal anyway about why he had summoned Gabe Bergeron to this park. He could tell just by looking at Neal that something was seriously wrong; besides the whole explosion thing.

He was trying to position his legs so the cuts didn't hit anything when he looked around. "Neal?"

"Yeah, Gabe? You okay?"

"Fine. Why am I riding in a Lexus?"

Neal giggled. It was slightly more manly than Nurse Sharon's, but only because of his deeper voice. He knew Neal's face was now as red as his own.

"I thought it was time."

Neal's former vehicle had been a 2004 Toyota Tacoma pickup with a mismatched camper top. "So you bought this new?"

Neal nodded vigorously.

"Yeah. I got a good deal."

Which couldn't possibly be true since Neal had the bargaining skills of a cloistered monk.

"Ellie helped me pick it out."

Of course she had.

Gabe exchanged appraising smiles with her. He had been preoccupied with the trip to Chicago, but as soon as he could get to a computer, he was going to find out everything that Google knew about Miss Ellie.

Friday
10:00 pm

Neal parked beside the cabin.

"Let me help you, Gabe."

"It's okay. It's just a few minor cuts and some burns."

"Are you sure you don't have a concussion?"

"Yeah." The headache and nausea were coming from the burning fiberglass stench in his hair and his shorts.

Neal said, "You want to take a shower?"

Gabe absolutely needed to wash up, but he thought Nurse Sharon had told him not to get his bandages wet, so he settled for washing his face and hands and selected other regions. He hung his head over the side of the tub and scrubbed his hair.

Neal gave him shorts and a t-shirt and a pair of boxer-briefs. Not that he kept tabs on that sort of thing, but he was pretty sure that boxer-briefs were a post-Ellie development for Neal just like the freaking Lexus.

He came out of the bathroom feeling a little better.

Ellie said, "Looking much improved, Gabe."

"Thanks. I feel better."

The interior of the cabin was just as woodsy as the outside, with pine plank walls and a little fireplace. It was light-years better than Neal's little camper.

Neal said, "Ellie made sandwiches." He was grinning at her like she had just touched up Michelangelo's mistakes at the Sistine Chapel.

But Gabe Bergeron was going to give her the benefit of the doubt.

Who was he kidding? The burden of proof was all on her. He needed to talk to Neal about Eric and the mess, whatever it was, but he couldn't do that with Ellie hovering.

Gabe bit into a toasted cheese sandwich; the bread was burnt but the cheese was still cold inside. "So how did you guys meet?"

Neal grinned again. "Ellie picked me up at a club."

She smiled at Neal like he was a naughty lapdog, one of those fidgety ones with the bulging eyes and lolling tongues. "He's such a scamp."

He waited for her to put a treat in Neal's mouth.

"Actually, Neal rescued me from a real jerk."

Scamp and rescue and Neal? Miss Ellie was going to have to do better than that.

She smiled at him. "Neal tells me that you worked for Girard-Hartmann?"

Gabe said, "I did. So what do you do, Ellie?"

"I work in advertising."

Neal was looking from Ellie to him and back to Ellie. "She's very creative, and her apartment is spectacular."

Ellie smiled demurely. "I paint a little."

"She's being modest."

Ellie said, "So what was this meeting about? I mean, you aren't with the company any longer? I heard that you were...."

She pretended to fumble for a word that wasn't "fired" or "terminated" or "kicked out on your ass."

"Eric and I had some differences. As for the meeting...."

Neal said, "Gabe's not here for the meeting. No, that was just for me and Eric; he's going to be....shit....Eric was going to be on vacation for a couple of weeks, and I needed to be updated about his clients to see if there was anything that I needed to know, because Eric hates, hated, being called when he was out of the office."

Gabe said, "So where are you from, Ellie? Brothers? Sisters?"

"Originally from Lansing. I have a brother, John, and a sister, Amber. How about you?"

"My great-aunt Flo." He patted Neal's shoulder. "And Neal."

Ellie gave Neal a look. "You're related?"

Neal shook his head. "But we grew up together in

Philadelphia, from first grade to seventh, and then we were roommates in college."

"I spent a lot of time with Neal and his family."

"So no blood relatives except for a great-aunt?"

"That's it." Gabe had no intention of getting into the whole father thing with a stranger.

Ellie said, "I see. What does she do? This great-aunt Flo?"

"She's retired." He had no idea from what. He should really visit Aunt Flo. "So you work in advertising in Philly? I know some people. Would I recognize the name of your company?"

She smiled. "Not my company, Gabe. I'm just a cog in the machinery." She massaged Neal's shoulder. "But I thought you wanted Gabe here for the meeting...."

Neal said, "No! No, I just wanted you and Gabe to meet."

Ellie didn't like being interrupted, but she twisted her little rosebud mouth into a smile and batted her lashes at poor Neal. "And now we have. Under tragic circumstances. Poor Eric."

Gabe said, "Yeah, poor Eric and poor Layla, I guess. Did you meet Eric, Ellie?"

"Yes, I met Eric and Layla. She seemed like a very interesting person; lovely, in a classical sort of way."

So they hadn't hit it off? "Maybe she still is."

Ellie said, "Let's hope so."

"What did you think of Eric?"

She smiled. "He could be very charming."

Which was probably the very nicest epitaph a real asshole could hope for. "Yeah. If it suited."

Neal was looking at him like one of his worry storms was approaching fast. "We went to a party on Eric's boat...only a week ago."

Gabe finished his sandwich and downed his diet soda and looked at Neal. "We should get some sleep. Tomorrow probably won't be any fun."

Ellie said, "No, probably not." She flitted into the first bedroom and closed the door.

Neal escorted him the six feet to the other bedroom. He smiled. "Are you sure you're okay, Gabe?"

"Yeah, I will be."

Neal sat on the bed. "How did the family thing go?"

Ah, the family thing. "It went as well as could be expected." Neal was capable of sitting there all night waiting for a real answer. "Okay. Nobody started shooting, though my half-brother and his mother were not happy about the will."

Donnie, his new-found half-brother, was just a few years older than Gabe.

Had Rhoda, his father's wife, known about her husband's extracurricular activities with Leanne Bergeron? He thought she had, which must have sucked for her. Not that it made much difference to him; they were all strangers.

Strangers with whom he shared an intimate genetic bond.

Neal said, "So how are they?"

He smiled at Neal. "How are they? They are contesting my father's will in which he left me some painting valued at one half of one percent of his estate. That's how they are."

Neal shook his head. "Sorry."

"It's okay. It sounds so funny to say 'my father.' And to have a name to go with that concept; John Teague Sullivan." He shook his head. "Think I should just throw in the towel and let them have it?"

Neal said, "Why do you think he put you in the will?"

"Just for the Hell of it."

"Really?"

Gabe had thought about it for weeks, since he'd gotten the lawyer's letter, but he'd probably never know.

"I have no idea, Neal."

"Sorry. But why leave you a painting? Do you want it? I mean really want it and not just want it so they can't have it?"

Gabe laughed. "I can't honestly say. I'd probably need years of therapy to disentangle all that bullshit."

"Okay. So what now?"

He had no idea about that either. He could call Max and ask him to recommend a lawyer who handled wills and stuff.

Neal said, "I could help with the lawyer? Or Mom could?"

"No. Thank you, but no." He let his legs sprawl so the cuts didn't rub against each other. "I sat there listening to the reading of the will and tried to figure out what kind of guy he was."

"Any ideas?"

"I think John Teague was okay. Not perfect, obviously. At least, he wanted me to know who he was. I wanted to ask for a photo, but they started in about contesting my itsy-bitsy bequest, and there was some name-calling, so that was out. That was mostly from my half-brother, Donnie."

Neal nodded.

"Which I understand. He's grieving for his father, and suddenly this stranger is sitting across from him, and the lawyer is reading this will. I could see Donnie looking at me, trying to figure out who the Hell I was. It was surreal."

Neal said, "I can't imagine."

"And the lawyer gets to the part about me and my mother and my bequest, and then Donnie's mother, Rhoda, starts crying. And this is all hitting Donnie cold. I wanted to crawl under the lawyer's desk. So I get the lashing out. I didn't know what to say so I just got out of there as fast as I could."

"That's awful, Gabe." Neal was staring at the wall. "I've been thinking. You could get a lawyer and offer a bargain. Offer to let them have the painting, if they pay you the value in cash and throw in copies of all the family stuff; photos, videos, any family history they have."

"I could do that."

Neal said, "You could. What about the rest of the family?"

"There were two ladies there; Amy and Brenda. And two guys; one was named Bob. I think they were all John's siblings. Anyway, Bob pulled Donnie aside and calmed him down."

Neal nodded.

"And before I could make my escape, Bob actually shook my hand and said, 'Give it time, Mr. Bergeron.'"

Neal's mother and father were still married and even seemed happy after thirty-five years, and Neal had an older brother, Scott, and three aunts, two uncles, and eight cousins.

Gabe couldn't imagine what that was like.

"He sounds like a good uncle to have."

"Yeah. I'll think about it, Neal. I sort of like it, and they might go for it." He patted Neal on the shoulder. "Get some rest, Nelly."

"Come on, Gabe. You know I don't like that!"

"Never again! Scout's honor." Neal had actually been a boy scout. "Go. Try not to worry. We'll talk later."

"Yeah. I need to...."

Ellie was behind Neal. "Coming, Lover?"

Neal smiled as he turned, scooped her up, carried her into the other bedroom, and slammed the door with his foot.

Shit.

What kind of freaky, sexual voodoo had Miss Ellie Tyson worked on his friend, who had always been so shy with the ladies?

Saturday
5:00 am

The groans, grunts, squeals, and indistinct, but rhythmic, comments of Neal and Ellie having marathon sex had not really been conducive to sleep, but eventually they had exhausted themselves, and the cabin had quieted down.

Gabe thought he'd slept a little, and it was getting light outside, so it was time to assess the situation in the cold light of day.

Neal was in love.

It was remotely possible that this was a good, even a wonderful thing, for his friend, and he was going to have to go with that for now.

And Eric was dead. He had been a jerk, but nobody deserved to die like that.

Gabe remembered their first meeting. Eric had been handsome; the black hair, the dark eyes, the pointy eyebrows, and the little, smirky smile. Not to mention the body.

Eric Girard had been hot. And charming.

And that had lasted for a good thirty seconds. Well, maybe a week. Before the charm had melted away in the arrogance and cunning and general shadiness. Much like Eric's yacht had melted into the creek.

The knotty pine kitchen cabinets held no coffee; not even instant. There were froufrou tea bags.

Strike one for Miss Ellie.

When the water was hot enough, he poured it into a mug, and the odor of peppermint assailed his nostrils as the bedroom door opened.

Neal wasn't naked but had on a pair of black boxer-briefs identical to the loaners Gabe was wearing. Neal smiled at him. "Sorry that there's no coffee. Ellie says it's bad for me.".

"I see."

He sat at the table. "Come on, Gabe."

"What? I didn't say anything. I'm sure she has your best interest at heart." Which sounded snippy even to him. "Okay. I'm cranky without my coffee. Would you like a cup of tea?"

"Yes, please."

Neal smiled at him again. His hair was sticking off in random directions and that paired with his ears made him look goofier than usual. His face was also scruffy in patches.

The beard growing might not be going so well, but Neal had put on some muscle, and even relaxed his abs hinted at a six pack.

"You've been to the gym, Neal. A lot. You hate the gym? We hate the gym."

Neal smiled and flexed. "I've been going with Ellie."

"She's very pretty."

Neal nodded. "She's gorgeous. Do you like her?"

"She's very pretty."

"Come on!"

"I just met her, but I like her...so far."

He couldn't keep the "so far" to himself; not even for Neal.

"Shit."

And now he felt bad. "Okay. I'm sure I will like her if you like her so much. I promise to try."

"Why do you have to try? She's wonderful."

Gabe grinned at Neal and said, "She's very pretty."

"Bastard!"

"Keep your voice down. Tell me about Eric."

Neal got up and made sure the bedroom door was closed. "I think he has been up to something...something illegal."

"No surprise there. Did I not tell you...."

"That I should dissolve the partnership. Yes, you did. Two months ago when you walked out. I know, but it isn't so easy."

"Right. You can see seventeen ways in which you lose everything and wind up homeless on the street."

Neal had this thing of seeing every possible outcome of a course of action, however remote.

"There were negatives."

"There always are. How did you meet Eric anyway?"

"Scott."

How big brother Scott and Neal could be related had always been a puzzler; of course, the humming bird was also supposed to be related to Tyrannosaurus Rex.

"How did Scott know him?"

"Scott didn't say."

Right. "So what exactly was Eric Big-Dick up to?"

"Don't call him that, Gabe! He could be dead."

"He almost surely is, but he would be delighted to be called Big-Dick. He did everything but put a full-color photo of his male member on his business cards. What was he up to? And why do you think whatever it is that you think? Explain. With details. Charts and graphs and spreadsheets would be helpful."

Neal leaned closer. "He's been seeing some clients."

"The bastard!"

"They weren't ordinary clients, Gabe."

Gabe sighed. "How were they not ordinary?"

"I think they were criminals, Gabe."

"Not everyone without a suit and tie is a criminal."

"I know that, Bergeron! But they were...rough looking, except for the woman...she was something." Neal wiggled his eyebrows. "You should have seen her."

"Right. Pass. Anything else besides uncouth and mesmerizing clients?"

"Yes, Eric didn't want me to know about them."

That wasn't good; Eric loved showing off new clients. He had dinners and parties just to flaunt them.

"Anything else?" There was obviously more, but he stopped Neal from saying anything. "Want some more of this delicious tea?"

"What?"

Gabe motioned toward the bedroom door and mouthed, "Ellie."

Neal got up and tried the door. Ellie had to jump back to

avoid getting conked on the noggin. She smiled in what she obviously hoped was a disarming fashion.

She was wearing one of Neal's white dress shirts, and her nipples were peering through the shirt like veiled eyes.

Neal said, "Hi, Honey. I'm sorry if we woke you up? Want some tea? Or we could go back to bed for a snooze?"

It was obvious which option Neal wanted her to select. She took his hand and drew him into the bedroom.

The vixen winked at Gabe as she pushed Neal onto the bed and closed the door with her foot this time.

So Gabe Bergeron donned his loaner shorts and his loaner t-shirt and went outside. It was muggy and reeked of burnt plastic, but he couldn't hear the sounds of sex.

He did a double-take as he looked toward the dock. It wasn't a bear standing on its hind legs, but a very large man in a black t-shirt with black, shaggy hair and a full beard.

The man saw him. So Gabe waved, but the guy just stared. And then the bearish gentleman started walking toward him. It wouldn't have been very manly to duck inside the cabin and drag the refrigerator in front of the door, but that was Gabe's first impulse.

The guy was six foot six, if he was an inch, with shoulders that could support a small horse; should one need to be transported hither and yon.

Gabe tried smiling again, but got nothing back as Mr. Bear closed on him. Mr. Bear halted his advance when they were two feet apart, and he had to gaze up into eyes as black as the hair and the t-shirt.

A great voice from deep within Mr. Bear's chest said, "Who are you?"

He was a scared-shitless accountant. "I'm Gabe Bergeron." He held out his hand.

Mr. Bear ignored his hand. "What are you doing here?"

"I'm staying with Neal, Neal Hartmann."

Mr. Bear snorted in disbelief. "Three's a crowd, Bud."

"Oh, you mean Ellie. Lovely woman. I'm just here for the one night. I got blown off the dock last night. When the boat exploded? And my buddy Neal was concerned about me."

"I heard about the boat." Mr. Bear noted his fire-burnt face.

And then Neal opened the door and smiled at Mr. Bear. "Good morning, Mr. English. This is my friend, Gabe."

Mr. English looked about as English as a Saudi prince; a very tall Saudi prince with unlimited access to steroids.

"Morning." Mr English gave him this Gabe Bergeron one last look and smiled. "Okay then." He took three strides and stopped to add, "There was a crazy blond kid on a bike."

Neal said, "There was?"

"Yeah. He laughed at me when I told him to clear off."

"Okay? Thank you."

Mr. English resumed walking toward his cabin.

Neal whispered, "He can be a little odd."

"A little? How do you know him? I think he took me for a burglar or something, and was pondering just which of my bones to break."

Neal giggled again. "He has the third cabin; the one next to the conference center over there." The upper story of a larger building was just visible through the trees. "He's been here a week or so. He doesn't say much. Usually."

"He doesn't have to. Can I borrow some shoes?"

Neal's feet took a size twelve. Gabe felt like he was wearing clown shoes, but it was better than going barefoot.

When he got close to the dock, he could hear lots of activity. He didn't want to look like a ghoul, but he was curious, and as an almost victim, he felt entitled.

There were a lot of uniformed personnel around Eric's boat. Two guys in white suits and breathing masks were on board; they were taking pictures and collecting samples.

A semi-circle of campers surrounded the police presence. A middle-aged, black couple were next to him. She checked out his bandaged legs and glowing face and nodded.

Gabe said, "Good morning." They both had steaming mugs of coffee. "That smells so good."

She smiled at him. "Want a cup?"

Her husband said, "We've got plenty." He turned and headed for an RV parked on one of the pads.

"I don't want to impose, but my friend only has peppermint tea."

She laughed. "That's no friend."

Gabe nodded. "Tell me about it."

Her husband came back with a mug of coffee, and the day got brighter. "Thank you so much. So have they found...anything?"

She nodded. "Yes, I'm afraid so. One body on the boat. So far. I'm Wendy Brown, and this is my current husband, Bob."

Bob grinned at her, and they shook hands all around. "I'm Gabe Bergeron."

Bob was short and stocky with the beginnings of a paunch; he was sporting a goatee and a buzzed head. Wendy matched him in the size department. She stood rock solid almost as if she were at attention.

She said, "You're the one who got blown off the dock?"

"I am. What did they do with the body? And who are all these officers?"

Wendy said, "The body is on its way to the State Medical Examiner. Most of the police here are the forensic team of the Natural Resources Police. They haven't been here that long."

The guys on the boat were taking pictures again.

"Natural Resources Police? I'm from Philly."

Bob nodded. "Yeah. They can arrest you just like any other police, but mostly they rescue people who're fool enough to fall into the Bay..." Bob looked at him and smiled. "Sorry, I meant off a boat, and they make honest citizens throw crabs back."

Wendy said, "I told you they were too small."

"Yes, Dear, you did."

"And they could have fined you besides."

"Yes, Dear, they could have."

Wendy said, "It's their job to protect the Bay from folks who'd ruin it in one way or another, and I say amen to that."

She was looking at the creek.

Gabe saw the boat then with King and Stevens. King was hauling on a rope that disappeared beneath the water of the creek..

"Are they looking for bodies?"

Wendy said, "Been dragging since first light. They haven't

found anything yet. Praise the Lord."

She looked at him. "You knew the folks who owned that boat."

"I did. Eric Girard and his wife, Layla. She was, I hope still is, a lovely woman."

Wendy said, "You think she wasn't on board?"

"I don't know, but I'm pretty sure Eric was."

Wendy nodded.

Sergeant King had spotted him among the crowd and was docking his boat.

Gabe didn't feel like answering more questions this early so he decided to split. "Thanks for the coffee. I appreciate it."

Wendy said, "Most welcome, Mr. Bergeron."

"Call me Gabe."

He turned and was face to face with a young guy with scraggly, blond hair sticking out of a black, baseball cap. The cap had two red, Chinese characters, and the brim was at ninety degrees to his face.

The guy, boy, flashed uneven front teeth at him. "Sorry, Dude. Just wanted to see what's going on."

"There was a fire. On the boat."

"Yeah. Really stinks. I'm Chuck."

"Gabe."

Chuck did a little happy dance before dropping his black skateboard to the asphalt. He launched himself across the parking lot, laughing all the way.

Saturday
6:00 am

Gabe retrieved his rental car from the boat ramp parking lot and drove back to Neal's cabin. He parked behind the Lexus, keeping an eye out for Mr. English. Neal and Ellie were still in the bedroom, which wasn't a surprise.

He wanted more coffee, and peppermint tea wasn't going to cut it, but he put some water on.

The knock on the door was Sergeant King, which also wasn't a surprise. "Morning, Mr. Bergeron."

"Come in, Sergeant, and have a seat. I don't have anything but tea to offer you."

"That's all right, Sir, I'll get coffee later." King's face was also burnt from the fire.

"You found Eric?"

"We found a body, Sir."

Gabe closed his eyes, and tried not to think about the flames, and what it must have been like. "Shit."

King said, "Yes, Sir. I was hoping you might have information about Mr. Girard's next of kin or his dentist?"

"Dentist? Oh. No, I have no idea, but Neal might."

"And where is Mr. Hartmann?"

He pointed to the bedroom. "With Miss Tyson."

King didn't smile or react in any way. "I'd like to speak to both of them."

"Sure. I know."

Gabe knocked on the door, softly at first. "Neal? Sergeant King is here. He has some questions. Neal?"

Ellie giggled and then said, "Just a minute."

Neal popped out, closing the door behind him. He smiled at King and got nothing back. "Yes, Sir?"

Gabe said, "They might have found Eric, Neal."

King said, "A body is being transported to the Office of the Medical Examiner in Baltimore."

"And Layla?"

"Nothing so far. But we'll keep looking."

Neal sat down across from King. "It's so unbelievable. I can't imagine him gone. He was only thirty-five."

King said, "Would you know who his next of kin would be?"

"He doesn't have anybody close. Except Layla. I think he mentioned a cousin once?"

"What about his dentist, Sir?"

Gabe said, "They need to know for the dental records, Neal."

Neal blinked at him. "Right. Dr. Pfrommer in Philadelphia. I have the address and phone number. He's my dentist too. Layla recommended him. And you haven't found anything...of her?"

"No, Sir. Can I have the contact information?"

Neal consulted his phone, and King noted it in his little book, before turning to him. "And when did you get into Crisfield, Mr. Bergeron?"

"Around 1:00 pm. I didn't need the GPS to find it." King was just staring at him.

"And the Lexus is yours, Mr. Bergeron?"

He laughed. "Hardly. The yellow Fiesta is mine."

"And you drove here from Philadelphia?"

"No, I had a family thing in Chicago...so I flew on to the airport in Salisbury and rented a car there."

"For a meeting with Mr. Girard and Mr. Hartmann?"

"I was coming home to Philly anyway so it wasn't a problem to fly on to Salisbury."

"I see." King cast a weary eye at Neal. "What was this meeting about, Sir?"

Neal looked like a deer in headlights. "It was about business...I told you last night."

King looked at his notebook. "You said it was about getting

29

you up to speed about Mr. Girard's clients, but why would Mr. Bergeron be at that meeting? He left the company two months ago."

Neal flashed Gabe a look he knew very well. "Well, Neal didn't say, but I think he was trying to mend fences and get me my job back at Girard-Hartmann."

King frowned. "Is that so, Mr. Hartmann?"

Neal nodded.

King said, "But you said you left to accept a better position, Mr. Bergeron?"

It was beginning to look like Eric's boat blowing up was not an accident, and it was time for some truth before King had him locked away.

Gabe said, "No, Sergeant. I just said that to salve my pride. I was fired as you guessed. So the explosion wasn't an accident?"

"I couldn't say, Mr. Bergeron."

Ellie made her appearance, looking radiant sans makeup, and wearing a short, silky kimono, which showed a lot of leg.

"Good morning, Sergeant King. Do you have questions for me too?"

"A few." King didn't return her smile either but looked back to Neal. "Where were you at the time of the explosion, Mr. Hartmann?"

Neal looked panicked again, but he couldn't help with this one. "I had to...I had to go do some errands."

"Something to do with this meeting?"

Neal shook his head back and forth like a weather vane in a gale.

"Then where were you?"

Neal said, "I went...I went to the bank, to the ATM, and then just drove around looking for a store that might have a thumb drive, but then I got lost a little."

King took a dim view of men who got lost, but he looked at Ellie. "And where were you, Miss?"

"Here in the cabin. Reading."

Which was not true. Gabe avoided looking at Neal or King as he took a sip of cold, nasty peppermint tea.

King said, "I see. Do any of you know when Mr. Girard's

yacht arrived at the park?"

There was a general shaking of heads.

King folded his notebook and got to his feet, and then he said, "How was this meeting arranged? Mr. Hartmann?"

"I talked to Eric at around 10:00 am and set it up. Yesterday."

King said, "For 6:00 pm, Mr. Hartmann?"

"That's right."

King looked at him. "And how did you find out about the meeting, Mr. Bergeron?"

"Neal called while I was still at the airport in Philadelphia."

"And after you saw Mr. and Mrs. Girard at the marina at 1:30 pm, what did you do until you arrived here at the park at 5:45 pm?"

"I walked around the marina, drove back to the motel to take a shower, and then explored the area a bit."

"Anyone verify any of that?"

Gabe said, "I don't think so."

King sighed. "Did you see anyone around the boat at the marina, Sir?"

He started to say no. "Wait. There was a guy. Skinny, almost emaciated. Medium height. Brown hair going gray, cut short."

"Anything else?"

"I think he had tattoos...on his fingers...like he had a ring on each finger."

King blinked. "And he was on the boat?"

"Not that I saw, but he was hanging around it."

King said, "Any idea of the home port of the boat?"

Ellie said, "Henry's Marina, Havre de Grace, Maryland."

"Thank you, Miss."

She said, "I know because Eric mentioned it."

Neal looked confused again, but King was heading for the door, only to stop and turn. "Why was this business meeting being held at Janes Island State Park?"

Neal smiled. "I was here. I come every year. To go kayaking and fishing. I love the place, and I wanted Ellie to see it, and we came here last Saturday. I was supposed to have two weeks, but Eric said he had to take off next week, and he mentioned he was going to take his boat out for a cruise down the Bay to the Intracoastal Waterway, to

Albemarle Sound and further south. He hasn't had it that long. And it seemed that it would be easier for us to meet up here."

King said, "I see." He folded his notebook and headed out the door.

Officer Stevens was waiting for him on their boat which was tied up at the dock in front of the cabin.

Mr. Bear, aka Mr. English, was standing watch again. Sergeant King spotted him and walked over, but Mr. English retreated inside his cabin and slammed the door. King and Stevens knocked, and were admitted eventually.

Gabe looked at Neal. "Think they called for backup? I know I would."

Neal said, "Mr. English is okay. I was catching croakers, but he showed me where to find some speckled trout too. And he caught a shark in the sound. A spiny dogfish."

Fishing might be boring, but if some drug company could bottle talking about fishing, that company would have a sleep aid to double their bottom line.

"Fascinating. Then he's a stand up guy for sure. And not dangerous at all."

Neal smiled at him.

"Okay, I'm going back to the motel. Want to get breakfast later? I saw a place called Summer Nights Cafe?"

Neal said, "Sure. Around nine?"

A shiny, red Chrysler PT Cruiser SUV pulled up next to the middle cabin, and a trio of ladies old enough to remember the Beatles' first tour of the U.S. disembarked. They hauled suitcases and bags of groceries into the cabin, milling about like a bunch of ants.

They also had a coffee maker.

They checked out King's police boat tied to the dock and put their heads together briefly to rub antennas before strolling over.

They were all blonde and powdered and rouged, wearing flowery tops over pastel shorts. The one in front, who was a fraction taller and had slightly darker hair, said, "Hello. Are you our neighbors?"

Neal was barefoot, but he walked toward them smiling. "Hello. Yes, we are." He glanced back at Ellie. "I'm Neal Hartmann, and this is my girlfriend, Ellie."

The leader blinked and glanced at her comrades. "So nice to meet you. I'm Mimi. And these are my sisters, Floria and Manon."

Ellie smiled, waved, and ducked back inside the cabin.

He said, "And I'm Gabe. Just a friend."

Neal said, "Excuse me, Ladies, but I have to get some clothes on. Ellie wants to go to breakfast."

Neal had thrown on a tank top and a pair of clingy shorts when King had arrived. The ladies had been scanning his muscles and salient anatomical features during the chat, but now they watched him walk away with rapt attention.

Floria fanned her face. "Oh, my."

Gabe smiled at her. "He's been working out."

Manon said, "He certainly has."

Mimi rolled her eyes. "You'd think you two had never seen a young man before. I'm sorry, Gabe."

He smiled. "Not a problem, Mimi. But I should get going too."

Floria winked at him. "You've been working out too."

He smiled modestly and tried not to flex his muscles or preen too much.

Floria pointed at King's police boat. "Is there a problem?"

Mimi glared at her, but Manon said, "You want to know too."

Mimi smiled. "Please forgive my sisters. I can't take them anywhere."

Gabe said, "It's okay. There was a terrible accident yesterday; a boat caught on fire. The police are talking to everybody."

Mimi said, "Yes, we heard about it from the park ranger. He said the poor man hasn't been identified?"

"Not yet."

Manon said, "How terrible."

Floria was looking at his fire-burnt face and his legs. "Were you involved, Gabe?"

"I was on the dock."

Mimi said, "How awful for you."

He said, "I'm fine, but thank you." He should run, but the sickening taste of peppermint tea was still in his mouth. "I don't want to impose, but would you ladies happen to have any coffee?"

Mimi said, "Of course, we do. Come right over, Gabe."

And he got to know much, much more about Mimi, Floria, and Manon, their absent or deceased spouses, their children, their grandchildren, and their cats than he had imagined possible.

But they had wonderful coffee and burn ointment, which they weren't shy about applying to his arms and legs.

"I think you got all the spots. Thanks."

Floria said, "My pleasure, Gabe. Would you like some more coffee?"

Mimi rolled her eyes.

"Thanks. But I need to run back to my motel. To get some clothes and wash up."

Manon, who had seemed like the shyest of the trio, said, "You could shower here, Gabe."

Floria smiled at her sister and patted her hand. "Yes indeed. We have plenty of towels; big, fluffy towels."

He headed out the door before they offered to bathe him.

Sergeant King and Officer Stevens were back in their boat. They made a u-turn in the creek and headed south as Mr. English stared at them.

Mimi, Floria, and Manon came to a halt behind him and inspected Mr. English. He whispered, "Mr. English. Been here a week. Alone. Neal thinks he's okay, because he catches trout and sharks. I'm not so sure."

Mimi said, "Thanks, Gabe."

They communed briefly, blonde silvery heads nodding close, and then Mimi led the march toward Mr. English.

Mr. English spotted them and bounded into his cabin like a startled deer.

He got into his car and drove away.

Mr. English was a big boy and could take care of himself.

Saturday
9:00 am

So Gabe drove to the motel and washed around his bandages. He changed into his own clothes, and more importantly into his own shoes.

The restaurant, the Summer Nights Cafe, looked okay except that Sergeant King and Officer Stevens had a booth near the door. He didn't think he should turn and run; that kind of thing tended to make the upholders of the law suspicious.

The floor was navy blue, vinyl tile; the wainscoting had been painted baby blue at some point, but was chipped now. The walls were covered in a bluish, nautical wall paper and supported some nautical kitsch like draped netting, but nothing over the top.

He claimed an empty booth along the wall; the booth was varnished wood and made no concessions to human anatomy.

He spotted Wendy and Bob at a table and waved. Two identical boys of about eight were eating pancakes with vigor and determination.

Next to them, a youngish man and woman were laughing and smiling at each other. They paused cooing at each other long enough to look him over, and then they smiled with teeth white enough to blind him with the reflected rays of the morning sun.

Gabe tried smiling back but it was a pitiful effort.

The waitress had a name tag with "Heather" inked on it. She was fiftyish and plump; her black hair was pinned up, but little wisps had escaped and floated freely.

She smiled at him and then registered his red face and the bandages on his legs. "You're the one who got blown off the dock?

Burr-something?"

"Bergeron. Gabe Bergeron. Yeah. Can I get some coffee?"

"Sure. I'm sorry about your friend."

"How do you know....?" He realized that every eye was on him.

She smiled. "Small town. The firemen and the ambulance boys have already been in. And King's here. Not that you'll get much from him."

She looked at the stoic Sergeant King with resignation. She had a voice that carried, but King took no note.

Gabe tried smiling at the crowd, and most of them smiled back. He looked at Heather. "I could really use that coffee. And maybe some pancakes too."

"Sure thing, Hon."

She walked by a table of four. Three of the guys had the weathered, red-cheeked look of men who worked outside; the fourth was probably twenty-five, still lean and fair.

The guy with a Ravens football cap and a camouflage t-shirt stretched over his belly spoke to Heather. "Hon." He nodded toward a young girl sitting by herself.

Heather said, "I know. She's waiting for him."

Raven's Cap said, "That boy is a wonder."

Heather said, "Jerry, you know Jace does his best. There's no harm in him."

"I'm not saying there is."

"And he told me that they broke up."

"Then why is she here?"

Heather couldn't answer that one.

The girl was probably eighteen or so. She had brown eyes, long brown hair with a pink frosting, and a knob of a chin. She was sipping a soda through a straw and chewing on her pink fingernails with a vexed expression on her face.

Gabe didn't believe that he was imagining that young Officer Stevens was gazing at her longingly?

A young guy, about her age, strolled in smiling like a five year old on Christmas morning. He was tall and slender with his shoulders being the widest part of his body. He had brown hair cut like a helmet, a patchy beard, and a wispy mustache. Brown, puppy eyes with long lashes went with a roman nose and a narrow face.

Pink frosting girl stood up. "Jace! Where have you been? I called and texted and everything."

She was on the verge of tears, but Jace's smile didn't dim by a single lumen. "Hey, Jessie. You're looking good, Girl."

She punched him in the arm. "Don't call me Jessie; my name is Jessica. So why didn't you answer?"

Jace kept right on smiling. "I was working. Ed had a rush job to finish up in Marion." He pointed to an older man with a t-shirt that read "Ed's Heating & Air." The older guy pushed past not slowing down.

Jessica said, "Is that the truth, Jace?"

"Sure is."

"You promised me you'd help me get it."

"And I will." Jace just kept smiling until her face unfroze. She pulled him to her table.

Heather was looking at the pair of them. "Jace!"

He wheeled the smile over to Heather. "Yes, Momma?"

"Come help me in the back. Right now, Jace."

"Yes, Ma'am."

They disappeared through swinging doors only to reappear before the doors had come to rest.

Jace marched over to Jessica. "Can we go for a walk, Jessica?"

"Is something wrong, Jace? Tell me now!"

"Not one single thing. I'm just going to be in an attic for the rest of the day, and I want some fresh air first."

He took her hand, and they walked out the very poster children of young love. Officer Stevens was looking vexed himself and started to get to his feet, but King said, "Down."

Stevens said, "But, Charlie...."

King pointed at his seat, and Stevens subsided.

Gabe Bergeron was no eavesdropper, but Heather's voice did carry as she spoke to Jerry. "He told me Chloe is on her way."

Jerry said, "Coming here?" The other men tried not to laugh, but they couldn't help themselves.

Jerry just shook his head; his hair was as black as Heather's.

"Jessica is going to shoot him one of these days, and I'm not even sure I'll hold it against her."

The young man, who had a Orioles baseball cap, said, "Damn, he's dumb as a clam."

Heather said, "Don't say that about your brother, Zeke!"

"But it's true."

"Just don't say it."

Zeke resembled Jace, but his hair was lighter, and he had filled out more. "He's dumber than a clam. At least a clam knows when it's in danger and closes up."

Heather shook her head and walked over with his coffee. "Pancakes in a sec, Gabe."

It was a little longer, but he had a mouthful of excellent pancakes when Neal and Ellie walked in and headed for him. All eyes followed their progress and watched them sit with him before conversations resumed.

Mr. and Mrs. Bright Teeth kept on looking and smiling until Ellie gave them a scowl.

Heather came back. "Tea for you, Ellie?"

Ellie smiled. "Yes, the Earl Gray please."

Heather knew enough to assume that Neal would have the same. Gabe shook his head at Neal, who had the decency to blush.

Jace came back having traded Jessica for a pretty Asian girl. Heather shook her head, but her son just smiled at her.

There were at least a half dozen conversations about the explosion. It appeared that the town was divided between those who believed fervently that it had been due to Eric's incompetence and those who favored a terrorist plot or a drug deal gone bad.

The Jerry and Zeke quartet were looking at one Gabe Bergeron. Heather was rubbing Jerry's shoulders. She said, "There he is. Go on and ask him. Gabe won't bite you."

The oldest guy was smiling at Heather. He had a round face and a round body, but massive forearms; they all did except for the youngster, Zeke. "Sorry, Mr. Bergeron. I'm Dan. We were just curious. A nice boat like that would have a propane tank, right? For the galley? Where was it located?"

"Sorry, no idea. It did have a galley. The explosion couldn't have come from the engine?"

Dan had a tan baseball cap emblazoned with a colorful but obscure logo. He took it off, rubbed his bald head, and put the cap back on. His cheeks were as red as any Santa Claus, but the area around his eyes was pale. "Diesel engines on a boat like that."

"And diesel engines don't blow up?"

The men shook their heads in negation or at this Bergeron guy's ignorance or both. The fourth guy never looked up from his coffee; he looked almost as old as Dan, but he had a bushy, uneven mustache.

King was staring at Gabe and Neal and Ellie. Smiling and waving got no response.

Heather frowned and said in a stage whisper, "Don't waste any smiles on him, Gabe." She stuck her tongue out at the sergeant.

They had a very nice breakfast and wonderful service since Heather was never out of earshot.

And then the Polynesian goddess entered to a moment of utter silence, followed by a long susurration of something like awe.

Gabe Bergeron had forgotten all about her.

What was her name? Mia?

She had on another sarong; this one was white decorated with turquoise and purple palm fronds.

She summoned Heather with a smile, and Heather abandoned them like week old lettuce to seat the newcomer at an empty booth. Mia sat regally and requested eggs and toast in that same slight but lovely British accent. Heather was entranced.

Jerry, Zeke, Dan, and the as yet unnamed fourth were likewise entranced, but Heather walked by and said, "You're acting like teenagers."

Elder Dan smiled at her. "She makes me remember what it felt like to be a teenager."

Heather was not amused.

Neal was trying to hide behind his pancakes. "What's wrong, Neal?"

"Are you done, Gabe? We should probably go."

Ellie said, "I'm not finished, Sweetie. What's the rush?" Ellie was looking from Neal to Mia and back again.

Mia bestowed the briefest of glances upon them before sipping her coffee and grimacing.

And then the scruffy guy with the finger tattoos entered, stage left, from the carry-out side of the restaurant. He was pushing fifty, and had on shorts and a tank top that hugged his scrawny body. The toothpick arms and matchstick legs gave him this granddaddy long legs look.

It was a damn small town.

Gabe glanced over at King; the sergeant was focused on tattoo guy who sauntered over to Jerry and Dan et al. They didn't make room for him so he had to stand.

"I saw him at the marina."

They ignored him.

"I saw the guy on the boat that blew up. The dumbass ran that fancy boat right into the dock. When he was trying to refuel."

Dan smiled. "Is that right, Lonnie?"

"Sure is! I watched it all, Dan. Some people don't deserve their fancy toys."

Jerry smiled and said, "Is that why you feel okay about helping yourself to those toys, Weasel? From time to time?"

Lonnie aka Weasel struck a pose worthy of Lincoln at Gettysburg and pointed a finger at Jerry. "Lies! All that is just lies. And don't call me 'Weasel.' I don't call you names, Jerry."

Jerry, who outweighed Lonnie by a hundred pounds, said, "You know better."

Dan shook his head at Jerry. "Leave him alone. So Lonnie, is it your opinion that this fellow blew himself up?"

Lonnie smirked at Dan and Jerry and the world at large. "No, he did not."

Jerry said, "And just how do you know this?"

Lonnie shook his head at this unbeliever. "I know."

And then Lonnie looked over at them. Neal was staring into Ellie's eyes and missed it, but Lonnie locked eyes with Gabe Bergeron and jerked his head toward the door.

And then Lonnie spotted Sergeant King and Officer Stevens, who were listening intently along with everyone else in the Summer Nights Cafe.

King said, "Lonnie? We need to talk about what you saw at the marina."

Lonnie started backing toward the door. "Nothing! I didn't see nothing. And I'm busy right now, and it's a free country anyway."

"It is."

And Lonnie was out the door without another word.

Heather shook her head as she refilled their coffee. "If they had contests for the most guilty looking, poor Lonnie would win hands down, Gabe. Even on the rare occasions when he's innocent."

But what the Hell did Lonnie want with him?

And had King seen that head toss? King was looking at him now. Shit.

And then a villain from central casting strode in. He marched over to the lovely Mia and sat. She smiled at him. "Where have you been, Gareth?"

Gareth grunted and shook his head. "Nowt."

Mia frowned and waved for Heather and ordered for the laconic one.

He had on plaid shorts, a Hawaiian t-shirt, and flip-flops, but the summer holiday effect was ruined by the shaved head, the deep-set eyes, the pale skin, and the multiple snake tattoos that writhed around his legs, arms, and neck and seemed to be feasting on one another.

Neal ran for the men's room leaving him with Ellie. "Kind of flighty, isn't he?"

"He's been like that for a week." Miss Ellie smiled and actually patted his hand. "Do you know what's wrong, Gabe? I'm starting to worry now."

Join the club. "No idea."

"No?"

And even if Gabe did know, he wasn't about to share with Miss Ellie. And then he saw Neal waving at them from outside the restaurant. He was hanging out of his car, blocking traffic.

"I think Neal is finished with breakfast."

Ellie rolled her eyes.

"I'll get the check. You should probably join him?"

She nodded. "Right. Come talk to him, Gabe?"

"I will." But it would be when Miss Ellie wasn't around so he could find out what was really going on. "Tell him that I'm going to visit with Great-aunt Flo, but I won't be long."

"She lives around here then?"

"She does. In her parents' house; my great grandparents' house." He had never met them, of course, but Aunt Flo said they had been characters and had some stories to back that up. She had also told him apocryphal tales about his grandparents, Andrew and Natalie. "It's about an hour away."

Ellie said, "You never mentioned her last name, Gabe?"

Which was a strange thing for a simple girlfriend to press for. "Barnes."

She smiled. "Have a nice visit. Bye."

Neal flung open the car door for her as she stepped out of the restaurant, and they departed posthaste.

Gabe paid the check and gave Heather a nice tip. As he walked out, he had the feeling that Mia and Gareth were watching him.

Outside, Lonnie was waiting for him. "You want to talk to me?"

Lonnie smiled, but then his face fell, and he also departed, scuttling away. He didn't need to turn around to know that King and Stevens were behind him.

Sergeant King said, "Mr. Bergeron, is that the fellow who was hanging around Mr. Girard's boat?"

"It is. He's kind of distinctive."

King said, "That's one word for him."

He waited to see if King would chase Lonnie or settle for him, but Dan and Jerry and the silent guy came out of the restaurant.

Jerry said, "Been real busy since you came back, haven't you, Sergeant King?"

Dan said, "Leave it, Jerry."

But Jerry got into King's face. "Rescuing women who fall off boats and investigating explosions and making trouble for hard working watermen. We're just real fortunate that you returned. Even if it's temporary."

Dan looked at the silent one. "Come on, Edgar."

Edgar said, "The Good Book says to turn the other cheek, Jerry." Jerry gave Edgar a nasty look "And a soft answer turneth away wrath."

"Shut up, Edgar!"

Edgar nodded, more in sorrow than in anger, and then he and Dan continued walking toward the dock and a broad-beamed workboat with crab pots piled in the stern.

Officer Stevens was fidgeting. "Well, she was lucky we found her. She was hanging on a buoy by her fingernails, and the sea nettles had got her bad."

King said, "Mr. Sterling doesn't care about that, Luke."

Jerry nodded. "My boy got a notice that his license is going to be suspended for thirty days, King."

"Not up to me."

"But you're the one who gave him five points."

"He deserved the citation I wrote."

"Damn it, Charlie! How's he going to get by if he misses this crab run? A whole month out of the summer? He's got boat payments and house payments and a wife and a daughter and another one on the way. You can do something; I know you can."

The sergeant said, "I'm not going to talk about this on the street."

Zeke was coming out of the cafe. "Leave it alone, Daddy."

"No, I'm not leaving it alone. We're going to the OAH, and if they don't give my boy justice, then the District Court. And I'm getting a lawyer. Just so you know!"

King said, "Not talking on the street, Jerry. If you want to come to the office, we can do that."

"I do!" Jerry shook his head. "But you've already made up your mind, King."

So King had other fish to fry, or crabs to sauté, so to speak, and Lonnie was long gone, which was probably a good thing.

Heather was behind her son, Zeke, watching King walk off trailed by Jerry. Heather put her arms around Zeke, who towered over her.

Zeke said, "Momma, you've got to talk to him."

She nodded. "I will. You get on home. You promised to take

Samantha to the movies before the party, and she'll be waiting for you."

Zeke nodded and walked off.

Gabe said, "I'm sorry, Heather."

"Thanks, Gabe."

"Zeke could lose his license? Not his driver's license?"

She smiled at him. "No, Hon, his commercial fishing license. And not lose it, but have it suspended."

"So he won't be able to catch crabs for a month?"

"It looks like it."

"But what's the OAH?"

She sighed. "Office of Administrative Hearings. Zeke will have to go before an Administrative Law Judge. If he fights the suspension."

"That doesn't sound good?"

She nodded. "Pure waste of time. Probably. And where does Mr. Jerry think we're going to get the money for a lawyer?"

She sighed and went back to work.

Mia and Gareth walked past him. The semi-divine Mia ignored him, but, as he passed, Gareth said, "Wanker."

Gareth got in a tiny two-seater, a black Smart Fortwo with silver trim, and glared at him as he pulled away, which was very strange since they had never met.

Not everyone loved Gabe Bergeron, and he could sorta understand with people he'd met, but he wouldn't have forgotten Gareth.

Saturday
10:00 am

Mimi, Floria, and Manon were heading for the restaurant. "I can recommend the pancakes without reservation."

Three silvery heads bobbed as they chorused. "Thanks, Gabe.".

He drove around looking for Lonnie, but he had vanished. If Eric's demise wasn't an accident, and Lonnie actually knew something, it might be good for Gabe Bergeron to know what that was, but that would have to wait until Lonnie turned up again.

He finally found a convenience store that sold prepaid cellphones, but all of his contacts were at the bottom of Daugherty Creek. He got a cheap wallet too; his old one smelled funny after drying.

He hadn't visited Great-aunt Flo for a few months; five months to be exact.

Which was bad, but they had been busy months: getting and losing a job and looking for a new one. He had an interview on Monday, which he couldn't afford to miss. Of course, the cherry on top of everything was getting the letter from the lawyer of his putative father and going to Chicago.

Great-aunt Flo lived in an old Victorian pile on the banks of the Pocomoke River. There was a cypress swamp nearby, and Neal had loved everything about the river and the swamp when he'd arrived for his first visit.

But it had seemed like another world to Gabe when he'd first come to live with her; a world that he might not fit in.

The gate was closed so he couldn't drive up to the house. The air was motionless, thick and oppressive with heat and humidity and mosquitoes. The river was flowing languidly without a ripple on its surface. A foursome of young people in canoes floated past.

It was another world compared to Philadelphia.

Great-aunt Flo had shown up at Neal's house. She had been driving a black Mercedes and wearing a business suit and pearls.

The Mercedes had been rented, and the suit borrowed. The pearls were the only real thing, and they had belonged to Aunt Flo's mother. All of which had been to reassure Claire, Neal's mother.

Aunt Flo had still been a stranger to Gabe when they had pulled into this same drive twenty years earlier, and he hadn't known a single soul for a hundred miles.

He walked past the steps that led up to the formal entrance and knocked on the side door.

Mrs. Gutierrez swept a mass of curls and ringlets from her face and peered at him through the screen; her hair was starting to gray, but he had no idea how old she was. She stared for a bit and finally opened the door. She turned her broad back and walked away into the kitchen, which was on the ground floor.

"The stranger comes for a visit." She had a Spanish accent which waxed and waned with her mood.

He took a deep breath; it didn't smell like a Mexican restaurant today. Mrs. Gutierrez wasn't Mexican and would deny vehemently that her kitchen smelled anything like that, but she had never volunteered a country of origin.

He smiled. "I'm just fine, Mrs. Gutierrez, and how are you?"

She had been with Great-aunt Flo when he'd come to stay at the house. She called herself the housekeeper, but she and Aunt Flo were more friends than employee-employer.

He had lived there full time for almost six years, and visited regularly after that, and Mrs. Gutierrez had learned to tolerate him, but that was about it.

He had asked Great-aunt Flo if there was a Mr. Gutierrez and a brood of ugly Gutierrez children somewhere, but she hadn't answered. She would talk about her childhood up to the first couple of years at college, but not about the rest of her life until she had suddenly appeared at Claire's home to claim him.

It was weird, but life with his mother, the part he could remember anyway, had been weird too, so he had always just gone with it. Aunt Flo and Mrs. Gutierrez demanded their privacy, and he figured he owed them that much and more.

He ran up the kitchen stairs to the first floor. It smelled like a field of sage. He hadn't known what the scent was called until college; sage and lemon furniture polish.

He checked the parlor and her office, but no Aunt Flo. She was probably in the garden or the greenhouse. She liked to putter around with her flowers before the sun got too hot.

She was sitting in the shade of an ancient oak, as placid as the river flowing past. The mosquitoes didn't seem to bother her.

"Aunt Flo?"

"New car, Gabriel?"

"A rental."

"Sit down. I could ask Mrs. Gutierrez to make some iced tea, but she's not been feeling very well."

Great-aunt Flo was eightyish. The uncertainty was not due to a lack of familial feeling on his part, but due to the fact that she had never shared her birth date.

"How are you?"

She smiled. "Can't you see, Gabriel?"

She had always been small and slender, but as she had gotten older, she had become waif-like, almost flesh-less, skin translucent, and hair silken wisps.

"You look good. How is your blood pressure?"

"I'm as fine as frog hair."

Which was one of her country sayings. "Right. Blood pressure?"

"Adequate to keep the blood flowing but not so high that it spurts out of my ears." She looked over at him. "What's happened? Your face? Your legs?"

Her large eyes had been blue, but now they were some indefinable mix of gray, teal, and silver.

"I got a job at Neal's partnership, Girard-Hartmann. I got fired from the job. I've been looking for another one."

She nodded.

Mrs. Gutierrez brought iced tea and dropped it on a garden table next to Aunt Flo. Mrs. Gutierrez was a foot taller and a hundredweight heavier than Aunt Flo. She tossed her somber, curly mane in his direction. "Lunch?"

Great-aunt Flo smiled from Mrs. Gutierrez to him. "Will you be staying for lunch, Gabriel?"

"Yes, please."

Mrs. Gutierrez did not snort, but there was a barely audible sniff. Aunt Flo had always cooked for herself, but she was slowing down, and Mrs. Gutierrez cooked most of their meals now.

One of Great-aunt Flo's cats strolled by and deigned to rub its head against her leg; a blue jay spotted it and screeched in blood-curdling rage.

"What else, Dear?"

"Well, Neal did not choose wisely when he selected Eric Girard for a partner."

She smiled and sipped iced tea. "Because he fired you?"

"No, I guess I deserved to get fired. Not that it was my fault. Entirely."

"It hardly ever is. Entirely."

He smiled at her. "I think he's a crook."

"A crooked accountant, how rare and unusual."

"Please, Aunt Flo. I'm not crooked, and Neal isn't either."

"I know that, Gabriel. Get on with your story."

"Well, to summarize: Eric got himself and his yacht blown up while docked at Janes Island State Park, Neal is freaking out that Eric took on some clients of a criminal persuasion, and I was too close to the yacht when it went boom."

Great-aunt Flo processed all that. "Is Mr. Girard dead?"

"Completely and undeniably."

"You don't sound upset about that, Gabriel."

"He was arrogant and conceited and not bright."

"And he fired you."

"Did I mention he was a criminal? And the bastard had no sense of humor." But the guy hadn't deserved to be blown up.

"And Neal was staying at the park?"

"Yeah."

She smiled and sipped her iced tea. They watched the river for a while. "Are you in trouble with the police?" Great-aunt Flo had been a flower child, a rebel, an iconoclast, and still had no great love for the Man.

"No. I don't think so."

"Is Neal?"

"Possibly. I think that's why he called me to come to the park, to meet with him and Eric."

"And what were you supposed to do?"

"Neal is not very forceful."

"Whereas you are. Has he talked to his mother? If he hasn't, Gabriel, he should."

"I know. I'll tell him. He has a new girlfriend. I just met her."

She giggled. "And you hate her already."

"There's something about her. I don't trust her."

She looked into his eyes. "Do you have anyone?"

"No."

She nodded. "It's not easy for someone like you."

"Someone grotesquely ugly?"

"No, Gabriel." She patted his face. "Though currently, you look like someone who's had a tanning bed accident. I mean someone who has...I think the current phrases are 'trust issues' and 'commitment issues.'" She tapped the side of his head. "As well as lots of squirrels running around in here chasing nuts they aren't sure they want after they get them."

"Thank you, Aunt Flo. Always nice to come home to the warm, supportive bosom of my family."

She did her giggle-cackle; it was a sound that the love child of one of Macbeth's witches and a pixie might produce. Her sneeze was similarly otherworldly.

Even if he did have trust issues, some of the squirrels wanted to tell her about the materialization of his father and the bequest, but a majority of them wanted to keep their little squirrel lips firmly sealed a bit longer.

She glanced at him. "Going to tell me the rest?"

"The rest?"

She nodded. "Not yet. I see. That's fine, Gabriel. I will always be here. Except I won't."

"Don't talk like that."

"Like someone who isn't immortal?"

Gabe said, "You know what I mean."

"No, I don't, Dear." She grabbed her cane and got to her feet slowly. "Lunch should be ready. Do not make any comments about the meal."

Which meant what? The dining room was one of the loveliest rooms in the house, with oak wainscoting and a coffered ceiling. The table was also oak but modern, almost minimalist, but it all went together.

Mrs. Gutierrez had made a fruit salad which wasn't bad, but then she plopped a bowl of green liquid on the damask covered table.

Great-aunt Flo ladled a gallon or so into his bowl, smiling like an imp all the while.

The soup, if that was what it was supposed to be, was room temperature and tasted fishy, oily, and sweet all at the same time. It also had lumps that were either crunchy or squishy.

Great-aunt Flo seemed to relish it. "Eat up, Gabriel. There isn't another course."

Mrs. Gutierrez was looking at him, scowling like Montezuma watching Cortes ride up to his city.

He kept stuffing bread into his mouth hoping it would expunge the soup from his tongue.

Mrs. Gutierrez looked at the empty bread basket and went to get more.

He leaned closer to Aunt Flo. "What is this?"

She smiled. "A new dish Ezmeralda is trying out."

"Week-old mackerel boiled in castor oil with Cap'n Crunch for croutons?"

"You don't have a very refined palate, Gabriel."

Which was true. He dabbed his mouth with a linen napkin.

She shook her head. "Eat some more, or you'll hurt her feelings."

He tried holding his nose as he spooned some more down before Mrs. Gutierrez came back, but that seemed to offend his aunt even more.

He managed half a bowl, and then he "volunteered" to wash the dishes. When the slimy soup bowls had been cleansed, he went up to the parlor on the second floor. Aunt Flo usually went there after lunch to have a brandy or smoke some pot and then take a nap.

A dozen years earlier, when he was still in college, she had suddenly taken to having high tea at four, complete with silverware, a linen tablecloth, and china.

Previously, meals had been a bit more informal; he had eaten in the kitchen on paper plates or directly from the pan used to warm whatever it was he had found in the refrigerator. Neither Aunt Flo nor Mrs. Gutierrez had ever felt the urge to cook for him, yet Mrs. Gutierrez resented his presence in the kitchen.

And then Aunt Flo had added silver candelabras with lighted candles.

She had looked at his face and giggle-cackled at him. "Too much?"

"Not for the madwoman of Chaillot." He had thought to say "Morticia and Gomez," but she wouldn't have gotten the television reference.

She had lost the candelabras at once, but she and Mrs. Gutierrez still continued the ritual of high tea.

Anyway, twenty years earlier, he and Neal had come home from school, from the eighth grade, to the stable life which Gabe had been enjoying, and Claire had called him into the living room.

Where Aunt Flo and her pearls were waiting for him.

Claire had said, "Gabriel, this is your great-aunt, Florence Barnes."

Great-aunt Flo had winced. "Just Flo, Mrs. Hartmann."

He had thought he had no living relatives. Claire had said so, and she was always right.

"But I don't know you. I've never seen you."

Great-aunt Flo had looked at him. "Sit down, Gabriel, and let me explain a few things? Please. Your mother, Leanne, was the only daughter of my sister, Natalie Barnes Bergeron, and her husband, Andrew Bergeron. I'm sorry, but all of them are...have passed away."

He had never heard of any of these people, except his

mother, of course.

Great-aunt Flo had looked very sad. "Leanne didn't tell you about any of us? No, I see. Well, she and her mother had a falling out, Gabriel, and then Natalie got very sick and ran out of time to rebuild burnt bridges, though she very much wanted to."

"Because she died?"

"Yes. And then Andrew died. And I lost track of Leanne. I'm sorry about that, Gabriel. I was in Latin America for a few years."

From various and sundry clues, he had deduced that the few actually numbered almost thirty years. He knew she'd been in Argentina and Mexico, and there were whisperings of Cuba.

No one had said anything about him going to live with Great-aunt Flo during that first meeting. That had come later and so subtly that he had hardly realized what was happening until he had been in the driveway staring at the house.

Great-aunt Flo said, "You were faraway, Gabriel."

"Years away but not miles."

She said, "I'd like to see Neal again. You could bring the girlfriend too? What is her name?"

"Ellie Tyson."

Great-aunt Flo smiled at him as she lit a cigarette that owed nothing to the tobacco fields of North Carolina. "Yes, I'd like to see Miss Tyson too."

Saturday Noon

Gabe had stopped in town to get a Coke to help Mrs. Gutierrez's soup stay down.

He parked the Fiesta in the same spot as the day before, and went to check out Eric's boat. The scorched shell of the "Taureau" was still tied up at the scorched dock; a Natural Resources officer was keeping watch, but no one was dragging the creek.

It had been hot and muggy in town, but a nice breeze was coming off the water so he decided to walk to Neal's cabin. He strolled through the area for campers and tent dwellers and came to a halt.

He hid behind a pine tree; he wasn't sure why, but it seemed like the logical thing to do.

Outside a beat-up RV, Mia had discarded her sarong and was recumbent upon a chaise. She had on a tiny white bikini bottom. The top was just sort of floating on her breasts all unsecured and at the mercy of any breeze.

Gareth had also discarded his Hawaiian shirt and was lifting weights. He wasn't heavily muscled like a body-builder but just ripped.

He was all tendons, veins, and muscle fibers stretched taut over a bony framework with zero percent body fat to soften, to humanize, his form.

The purple and green snake tattoos wrapped his neck and chest and ran down to his navel, disappearing into his plaid shorts to reappear on each leg.

A voice inches from his right ear said, "Enjoying the view?"

Gabe managed to keep the screech sotto voce as he whipped around.

Ranger Kurt Hobbs was smiling at him. "She is pretty, Mr. Bergeron. Or maybe you were looking at him?"

"I wasn't.... She's more than pretty, but that isn't why I was watching her...not that I was watching her. Or him. I wasn't watching either one of them, Ranger."

Gareth was way too scary.

"That's your story, and you're sticking to it?"

Gabe said, "Damn right, I am."

Hobbs had pulled his ass out of Daugherty Creek. "Thank you for saving my life, Ranger Hobbs."

Gabe held out his hand. Hobbs had a grip like the wringer on the antique washing machine in Great-aunt Flo's basement. He had been exploring, many years ago, and had thought it would be a good idea to plug the machine in. And then he had turned on the wringer.

It was a short step to getting his fingers caught between the rollers that were meant to crush the water out of clothes. He had unplugged the washer, but he'd had to yell for Aunt Flo to get his hand back. He thought she had nominated him for a Darwin Award that very day.

Hobbs smiled at him. He was tall and dark haired like Neal, but he had a square jaw and very wide-set, brown eyes. He also had a crevasse-like philtrum, that vertical groove on the upper lip.

Ranger Hobbs, or somebody, had taken the trouble to iron the creases in his green khaki uniform pants and his tan shirt.

"You're very welcome, Mr. Bergeron."

"Call me Gabe."

"Okay, Gabe, and I'm Kurt. Are you planning on staying long at our little park?"

"I don't think so."

Kurt nodded and stretched, flexing big biceps under that Maryland Park Service arm patch with its red and white trefoil cross garnished with a green sprig.

Gabe told himself to stop staring at the park ranger..

"Please try not to injure yourself again, Gabe. You wouldn't believe the paperwork I have to fill out when a visitor has an accident." He smiled. "Was that what happened to Mr. Girard, Gabe? Just a very serious accident?"

"I wouldn't know, Kurt."

"No? Well, have a good day."

And Kurt marched away, heading for three, very blond campers who were kicking a soccer ball around. The equally blond skateboarder with his Chinese cap was with them; Chuck, that was his name.

Gabe turned to realize that Gareth was glaring in his direction so he made for Neal's cabin, passing Wendy and Bob's RV.

Freelander was painted on the front, upper lip of the tan camper, which looked like it was swallowing a Ford truck, which had come too close to the hungry camper body.

Bob was working on a fishing line, but Wendy was standing, arms folded, focused on Mia and Gareth, much as he had been, but her look was more of a glare.

Gabe said, "Hello. Thanks again for the coffee."

She smiled. "Most welcome." And then went back to giving Mia baleful glances. "Just look at that."

Bob kept his head down. "I'm not falling for that one."

Wendy smiled. "You mean you haven't been looking?"

Bob shut his eyes. "I didn't do anything. I didn't even look after I saw...."

"All there was to see. That's all right. You can look."

Bob decided that silence was the best and only defense.

Wendy smiled at his bowed head. "But I can look too. That nice park ranger is quite a man." Kurt was kicking a soccer ball around. "I'll bet he looks fine with his shirt off."

Bob's placid face looked a little less peace-loving as he glanced at Kurt. One of the blond kids kicked the ball at the ranger; it took a weird hop on the uneven ground, but Kurt's foot connected with it effortlessly and sent it sailing.

Wendy refocused on Mia. "It's not right. Now, I don't care if she wants to parade around naked as a jay bird, but I have two boys, and they don't need to see that sort of thing...no telling what ideas they'd get."

She looked at him. "Don't you agree, Gabe?"

He nodded. "No telling. They're eight?"

"Ten. And old enough to know some things and imagine a whole lot."

"Ah. Do you know when she arrived?"

"Yesterday, around noon. In that thing, which is at least twenty years old. A little déclassé for someone putting on airs like her."

The Gulfstream Voyager RV had been cream and purple, but it had aged into a chalky white and slate gray now. It had the scrapes and dents and dings of a lot of miles, but the tires were new.

She looked at Bob again who kept his head down. "There's enough smut on the internet, Bob. I'm going to talk to her."

Bob continued fiddling with a lure as Wendy marched over.

Bob smiled at him. "Wendy was in the army for a lot of years and has this can-do attitude, Gabe."

"That's not a bad thing."

"No, it's not. It's just that when she thinks it's her duty to do something, it gets done. Boys, come out here."

They popped out of the RV. "Boys, this is Mr. Bergeron."

They shook his hand. "One of the twins said, I'm Edward, and he's George."

"Pleased to meet you both."

Bob said, "Who wants to go kayaking?"

They both raised their hands, but Edward said, "Daddy, why is Momma talking to the Hawaiian lady?"

"Never mind about that. Come on."

George said, "Because she's naked."

Bob said, "Hush. Both of you. You never saw the lady."

Edward and George smiled. "We saw nothing."

"Good boys."

They headed toward the kayak rental place with fishing poles and other paraphernalia.

Wendy was smiling at Mia, and Mia was smiling back, but the conversation was short, and ended with Mia going inside the RV and closing the door.

Wendy marched back, mission accomplished.

"How did she take it?"

Wendy smiled. "Dreadfully sorry. Or so she said."

"Right."

Wendy looked at him. "Are you interested, Gabe?"

He gave her a startled look. "Me? In Mia? No way, and she has Gareth."

Wendy smiled. "Does she? Maybe so, but you're a good looking man, Gabe, and he's a little young for her." She frowned at Gareth. "She's forty if she's a day."

He smiled. "Right. See you around."

She started cleaning up an immaculate campsite. "I expect so. It's a small park."

Gabe retrieved his car and parked behind Neal's Lexus at the cabin, as two speed boats roared up the creek. Ellie was on the dock, talking on her phone.

He did his best Indian guide, moccasin-footed, silent approach.

"I don't think that's a good idea, Sir." She turned away from the water.

He may have hidden behind a tree.

"No, Sir, I'm here, and.... Yes, Sir. I understand, Sir, and I'll be here. Sir? Sir?"

But Sir was gone, and it appeared she debated stomping on her phone before she shoved it into her pocket.

"Hello."

She turned and smiled. "Gabe. He's inside."

"Something wrong? I couldn't help overhearing."

"No, just a client who isn't happy."

"I see."

He didn't see one damn thing except that he had to get Neal alone and have a serious chat about Eric's malfeasance. The chat about Ellie's intentions would be trickier.

He followed Ellie into the cabin. Now that his nose wasn't full of the acrid stench of burnt fiberglass and charred wood, it was sucking up Ellie's fragrance.

It wasn't overpowering.

Or sickening.

Or anything bad except that he was suddenly very small, and

he was hiding in his mother's closet, and the scent from her clothes was as thick as a London fog.

What was he hiding from? From her? Had he been bad? He didn't think so, but he had been frightened, and there had been a reason he was hiding, but it was just out of reach.

Neal said, "Gabe? Are you okay? Gabe?"

"What?"

Ellie said, "You've been standing there for a couple of minutes with this weird look on your face."

"Have not. Have I? Never mind."

Right. He had to talk to Neal. But Neal's phone started playing Darth Vader's theme.

Neal said, "Hi. What's up? Yeah, it's true. The yacht blew up. I don't know, Scott."

Neal listened to his big brother for a couple of minutes. "They found a body, but they won't know if it's Eric until they compare the dental records."

Scott said something else. "They aren't saying if it was an accident, but it must have been. Right?"

Neal said, "Layla's still missing. They haven't found a body. Okay, I'll call you if I hear anything. Yes, anything at all."

Neal put his phone back in his pocket. "That was Scott." He looked at Ellie. "My brother. I guess he was worried about me."

Which didn't sound anything at all like big brother Scott.

Saturday
1:00 pm

Gabe was trying to figure out how to get Neal away from Ellie when she announced she was driving into town to get groceries.

Neal had his scrunched up, worry face. "I'm glad you're here, Gabe."

"Me too. We need to talk."

He looked around the cabin. The spirits of a hundred trees had made that final journey to the happy forest in the sky to construct it, and it looked cozy and non-threatening, but listening devices had become so very tiny. He was being paranoid.

Or maybe not. There was something about Ellie.

"Want to go kayaking?"

Neal smiled at him. "You? Kayaking? Where is my friend and what have you done with him?"

"I live to kayak."

"I've lost count how many times you've called them rolling death traps, Bergeron."

"People can change. Come on."

Neal smiled. "Great. I can show you all of my favorite water trails."

He followed Neal on a path through the trees, past the tiny, one-room cabins to a swath of lawn that bordered the creek, stretching all the way to the park store and the dock.

The campsites were scattered among the trees looking out at the strip of lawn and the creek.

They walked past Wendy and Bob; Bob had a net basket thing on a cord that he was lowering into the water. A hunk of anonymous meat was lashed to the bottom of the basket.

Wendy was inspecting the crabs he'd already caught. She poked a stick into the bucket and pulled it out with a crab latched on with its claw. She shook her head.

The crab decided that hanging on was no longer a successful survival strategy and dropped to the grass. Wendy lowered a sturdy boot on top of Mr. Crab's waving claws, grabbed him by the back, and tossed him into the creek.

Gabe said, "Too small?"

She nodded. Bob kept his eyes cast down upon his crab catching apparatus.

Mr. and Mrs. Teeth-so-bright-they-didn't-look-real had a creek side camp site. Neal nodded to them, but they waved him over. The glow of their smiles rivaled the sun

The guy was about Neal's height but not so muscular. He was wearing a pair of sunglasses in his black hair just as he had at the restaurant, but he had dispensed with his shirt, revealing a thick mat of coarse, swirly hair running from throat to navel. He was wearing mala beads, and a cross, an ankh, and a kalachakra mantra on separate silver chains. He jingled and clicked when he moved.

Mrs. Bright-Teeth had big, blue eyes, and boobs almost a match for Mia's, and her hair was an explosion of dark red curls. Her shorts were small enough that she could have hip replacement surgery without removing them.

The guy grabbed Neal's hand. "Hey, Neal. Are we going fishing this afternoon?"

Neal said, "Sorry, Kev, but I don't know. So much has happened."

The woman swatted Kev. "Leave Neal alone. Was it a friend of yours, Neal, on the boat? We just heard about it from Wendy."

Neal started drawing lines in the dirt with the toe of his sneaker. "Not really a friend, but I worked with him every day for almost a year. It's crazy thinking he's gone like that. He was only two years older than me."

Kev put an arm around Neal's shoulder. "Yeah. Sorry, man. I shouldn't have asked."

Neal nodded. "That's okay. This is my friend, Gabe. He's

staying with Ellie and me. This is Kev and Barb Sandusky."

Good ole Kev and Barb exchanged looks.

He shook hands with them; good ole Kev tried crushing his hand until Barb swatted him again. "Nice to meet you both. Nice RV."

Their Itasca Solei was gold and cream and barely fit between the trees surrounding the camp site.

Kev smiled at him. "Thanks. It's our little home away from home. Want to see inside?"

He stuck his head inside far enough to see a driver's cockpit like a 747's and a fireplace. "Very nice."

Barb said, "Come sit down. Can I get you something to drink?"

He wanted to kick Neal in the shin when he parked his butt in a lawn chair. Neal said, "No thanks, Barb. We still don't know what happened to Layla, his wife."

Kev sat on one side and Barb on the other.

Kev rubbed Neal's shoulder again. "Sorry, Buddy."

Barb said, "It's just awful. They haven't found...anything?"

Gabe said, "No, they haven't. I'm sorry, but we have to get going. Neal?"

Kev said, "But where could she be? If she was on board?"

Gabe said, "Don't know." It was horrible to think, but she was probably at the bottom of Daugherty Creek and just hadn't been found yet. "Neal?"

Neal looked up at him. "What? Okay." He started walking away but stopped. "Kev?"

"Yeah, Buddy?"

"I'll let you know about the fishing. Okay?"

"Sure thing."

Barb smiled again. "If you aren't up for it, maybe Ellie would like to go?"

Neal said, "Maybe? I'll ask."

Barb said, "Gabe?" She walked over and put an arm around his neck and rubbed up against him. Good ole Kev didn't even blink. "Maybe you'd like to come with us, Gabe?"

"Thanks, but I don't fish."

Barb was crushed. "That's too bad, Gabe. But that isn't all...."

Kev wasn't smiling now. "They have to go, Barb."

Barb released the head-lock she had on this Bergeron guy. "Think about the fishing, Gabe?"

Kev said, "We'll see you guys."

Not if Gabe saw them first. He marched away purposefully; one might even have said that he strode.

Neal said, "They're nice."

He shook his head. "Nice?"

Neal said, "What?"

"Nothing. How long have you known them? What do you know about them?"

Neal would happily talk to anyone not holding a bloody ax. "They got here yesterday morning."

"Anything else?"

"Kev is in real estate. I think Barb is too? They took us to lunch." Neal was smiling at him. "What is it about them? Too friendly?"

"Way too friendly."

"And Mr. English? Not friendly enough?"

Neal was making fun of him. "You call me Goldilocks, and we'll go at it right here, Hartmann."

"I didn't say anything."

"You'd better not."

Neal grinned at him again. "Think you can take me?"

"Sure do." The geek thought that his new muscles meant the balance of power had shifted, and it probably had.

"Just seems like someone is very particular about her porridge."

He chased the bastard to the kayak rental station.

The park was divided between a mainland portion and a much larger island portion, the eponymous island of Jane or Janes. And the island was pierced by dozens of small inlets that Neal called guts. The largest one meandered through the marshy, northern half of the island almost to the other side.

The four blond kids were ahead of them at the rental place. The girl was talking to Chuck.

"Come with us? It's fun. We have lunch on the beach?"

Chuck was astride his bike, which had a bulging pannier on each side of the rear wheel and a bag hung from the handlebar.

He shook his head. "Can't." He smiled at her. "Later, Girl."

She watched him ride away. The boy with the curly hair said something to her in a language which sounded like German but wasn't.

She said something back which didn't sound very friendly as she grabbed a kayak.

The other boy, whose name seemed to be Bastiaan, had buzz cut his blond hair; he and the girl looked like siblings.

The park had half a dozen water trails for kayakers. Gabe made Neal wait until the kids paddled away. He didn't want any witnesses around to see him mount the damn kayak.

The kids passed behind a tongue of marsh sticking out into the shallow water of the gut. He couldn't see anything now but the white blades of the long, double-bladed paddles semaphoring to him.

Neal said, "They're gone."

"Good. Okay, let's do this." He handed Neal his prepaid phone. "Hold onto this for me."

Neal snickered unkindly and hopped into his rented kayak with grace and aplomb. He paddled a few feet away before turning.

"Quit looking at me, Hartmann. I'm not going to capsize and fall into the water. I am not."

Neal said, "It wouldn't be the first time or even the second time."

Which was unfortunately true.

The park had a floating, kayak launch pad thing. He positioned his kayak in the slot, straddled the damn thing, and lowered his ass carefully into the seat. He used his arms to launch.

He smiled, and Neal smiled.

The creek was about a hundred feet wide and was a little rough, but he followed Neal toward the largest gut.

Neal sat like he was in an arm chair and crossed with a few, powerful strokes.

He tried to keep up, but his paddle seemed to be twisted or something. He was paddling harder when a big, black duck thing surfaced next to him.

"What the Hell is that?" Neal looked back and started laughing at him again.

He was just startled; it wasn't like he was afraid of the duck thing. He had a paddle after all. It had a body like a duck but a sharp bill with a hook on the end and a long, sinuous neck. It looked at him suspiciously until he whistled, at which it dove into the green water and disappeared.

Neal said, "A cormorant."

He watched and watched, but it didn't come up. "Shit. Did it drown?"

But then, fifty feet away, it popped out of the water with a fish in its mouth, which it swallowed, and then eyed him again with deep misgivings, before diving back beneath the surface like some prehistoric sea serpent.

Neal said, "Quit messing around and paddle, Bergeron. There's a boat coming."

The boat was roaring toward him at a good clip, and there were two guys on jet skis behind it.

They all slowed when they got to the park area, but he was still almost swamped.

And then he entered the smooth waters of the gut, and almost began to enjoy the experience as he caught up to Neal, and they paddled on the mirror bright water.

The blond kids had left their kayaks and had trekked the short distance across a sandy spit to the western edge of the island. The girl had spread a blanket on the gorgeous white sand beach and was laying out a picnic lunch. The boys were splashing in the water.

Gabe waved to the girl, and she waved back.

Neal looked at the blue water. "Tangier Sound."

Waves were rolling onto the beach; not quite ocean breakers, but not placid like the gut.

"Nice. How deep is it?"

"A hundred feet. Farther out."

Neal probably had hydrological charts of the whole bay; he loved maps and stuff.

Neal was marching south, out of ear shot of the kids. "I

asked you to come, because I thought we could talk to Eric and get it all straightened out."

Neal sat on the white sand, and he joined him.

"It?"

Neal shoved his sunglasses onto the top of his head. "The things that Eric was doing."

"Tell me what things, Neal." A horsefly bit him; he slapped it like he was trying to put down a bull rhino.

"He had these new clients."

Neal was looking across the water.

Gabe said, "Right. Clients he didn't want to show off. Rough looking clients and the hot woman."

He looked at Neal. "Shit! So Mia, the Polynesian goddess, at breakfast? That's why you rabbited? She's one of Eric's new clients?"

Neal nodded. "Mia Chandler-Hargreaves."

"And the goon? Gareth?"

"Gareth Fry."

"And they are here entirely by coincidence?"

Neal shook his head. "I think they wanted to talk to Eric too."

"Shit, Neal. About what? What was he doing for them?"

"Money laundering. I think. There are others. Not as nice looking as Mrs. Chandler-Hargreaves."

"Gareth isn't all that attractive." Not that he was ugly; scary but definitely not ugly.

Neal smiled. "Nope. He's not. About a dozen of them. That I know about, but I think Eric had big plans."

"He always did. The asshole. So you called me to do what?"

"Talk to him."

"Tell him he was being a bad boy and to please stop?"

Neal said, "Come on, Gabe! I don't know what I expected, but you know how to talk to people, to find out things and figure out what they want. I just wanted to get out of this mess and out of the partnership, and I didn't want Eric to find a way to blame it all on me."

"Was he about to get caught?"

"Maybe."

"Neal, look into my baby blue eyes and tell me why you think that?"

"Your eyes aren't blue, Bergeron. Sort of gray. Anyway, he had a meeting last week. A couple of guys in dark suits. They weren't clients or potential clients. That's what Maggie thought."

Maggie was Neal's assistant and no dummy.

"So Maggie thought these guys were police? Or IRS?"

"She didn't know, but Eric cleared out of the office as soon as they had gone, and then Maggie said I should call you."

"When was this?"

"Thursday, a week ago. And then Saturday, last Saturday, Ellie and I came here for a getaway."

"Have you told Ellie any of this?"

He shook his head.

"Are you sure, Neal?"

"I'm telling you the truth, Gabe. I didn't know anything for sure, and she might dump me, if she thinks I'm a crook and might be arrested."

Neal was worried about being dumped and not about prison. He sighed. "And when did you meet Ellie?"

"Nine weeks ago." Neal was smiling like a goof. "Friday night at that club on Halston Street. You went there once with me." Neal stopped gazing out to sea, or out to sound, and stared at him. "Why? You think she's not what she says she is? You just don't like her. You won't give her a chance, Gabe."

"I do like her. I'm just gathering data. So if you were suspicious of Eric's new clients, didn't you check them out in the computer?"

Neal knew software and computers and accounting like no one he'd ever met; less talented at people handling, but nobody's perfect.

"I did. There was nothing. No accounts set up, no hours billed for any of them. I checked every time when one of them had a meeting with Eric, and there was nothing."

"Right." Eric had hated computers. "So he was keeping a paper record, a ledger." It could have burned along with the boat. He slapped another horsefly. "Any idea where that would be?"

Neal was staring at his toes as he shook his head.

"It's okay. We'll figure this out. We can go through Eric's office. You aren't going to jail for some stupid bullshit that Eric was pulling, or trying to pull. I'll call my good buddy, Max."

Max was not really a good buddy, but he was a damn good lawyer.

They were sitting on the sand side by side, and the damn flies didn't seem to be bothering Neal, but they were eating him alive.

He got to his feet and waded into the water. It wasn't freezing like the ocean water. He turned just in time to see Neal charging.

Neal tackled him, and they both went under. He came to the surface spitting salt water, only to have Neal dunk him again.

He swam away from Neal under the water. When he popped up, Neal was laughing like an imp.

"What the Hell?"

"Sorry! You really hate getting dunked."

"Yes, I do! So why do you do it?

Neal was grinning. "You really hate getting dunked."

"Bastard." He stalked out of the water, keeping a wary eye on Neal.

Neal made a half lunge toward him, and he tripped and went sprawling on a pile of black grass stuff that didn't smell all that great. A bunch of little insect/crustacean creatures scurried away.

"You stop that! Right now!"

Neal said, "Okay. That was the last time. Promise."

He had a uniform coating of sand over most of his body. He wanted to rinse off, but he didn't trust Neal not to dunk him again.

"Neal?"

"Yeah?"

"Is there anything else you aren't telling me? Anything at all? I need to know everything."

"That's totally everything."

That wasn't everything.

"Do you know what happened to Eric's boat?"

"No, Gabe, I don't. You think he was murdered?"

"What I think doesn't matter. But, yes."

The thing was that King didn't know Neal, and know that he

would never hurt anybody. He would just see a guy who was tech savvy enough to whip up a bomb, if he had a reason. Which Neal sorta did. Which hopefully King did not know.

Neal started back toward their kayaks. "You're a good friend, Gabe, and thanks for coming, but I don't want you to get mixed up in all this. If somebody really blew up the boat and killed Eric...."

"I am a wonderful friend."

"I wouldn't have called if I'd known...." He waved a hand. "About all this. Damn, Eric."

"I'm here, and I'm not going anywhere."

"It's okay, if you want to?"

"No."

Neal mounted his trusty kayak. "There is one other thing. I think somebody got into my car while we were having breakfast."

"Anything taken?"

"No, just stuff moved around."

"Right. Okay."

Neal said, "And why did Eric tell Ellie where his boat was docked?"

Because Eric wanted to get Ellie below decks. Just like he did with every attractive woman he met.

"Neal, why do you think? You did know Eric."

It took a second. "The bastard!" Neal's hands were white knuckled as he slashed at the water with the paddle, sending the innocent water flying. "But he knew how I felt about her. The bastard! If he was alive, I'd beat his smirking face in." Neal looked over at him. "I would, Gabe."

"Yeah, I get that, and I understand, but Neal...."

"Yeah?"

"Don't share that with anyone else. Okay?"

"Right."

"In fact, if the police question you again about Eric or about this money laundering shit, don't say anything beyond what you've already told them. Ask for a lawyer and stick to that. Don't let them tell you that you have to spill everything or some kind of sweet deal will no longer be available. Listen to me, Neal."

"Right. I got it."

"Good. And try to stop worrying. You aren't going to jail. And none of the other horrible fates that are flashing through your brain are going to happen. I won't let them."

Big talk.

But Neal's face unscrunched, and he smiled.

Saturday
2:00 pm

Neal had talked him into paddling into one of the little side guts...gutlets?...instead of heading back to civilization.

The gutlet narrowed until it was the width of his paddle and then narrowed some more. From the seat of the kayak, inches above the surface of the water, the tall grasses crowded around them, and it was like they were in a different world.

There was only the sky above and the marsh below, and the only sounds were the whirs and clicks of insects and the whistles and warbles of birds in the humid air.

It could be 2015 or 10,000 B.C. The marsh just went on and on in time and space.

A startled bird was just a dark blur flapping away, but paintings from tomb walls popped into Gabe's head. Around the next bend, they might run into some long-dead pharaoh and his retainers hunting geese, standing proudly on their reed boats, or a bunch of priests making offerings to Sobek, the crocodile-headed god of the Nile.

But they were thousands of miles and years from pharaoh's Nile, and their reed boats were only fickle fiberglass.

Neal said, "Isn't this great?"

It wasn't bad. "Any reeds around here?" They were man tall he thought.

Neal twisted around. "No, not here." He leaned over and grabbed a hank of coarse grass. "But this is smooth cord-grass, *Spartina alterniflora*." Neal was so into this stuff. "And up there, where the land is higher is the salt meadow hay, *Spartina patens*."

"Very nice." It was thick and lush and green.

"And that stuff is glasswort, *Salicornia virginica*." It had fleshy stems but no leaves.

Gabe said, "And you know all this how?"

"Kurt told me."

"Park Ranger Kurt?" Handsome park ranger Kurt.

They had followed the gutlet back to the main gut. The tide had gone out, and exposed the raw banks of the tumps of marsh grass.

"Yeah. See that? That's black needle-rush, *Juncus roemerianus*."

It looked like a pin cushion with the points aimed up. It was about the tallest thing in this part of the marsh; the base of each living stem was green, but the tips were black. The rest of the marsh was some shade of green or tan, but the rushes were a grayish-black mass; a forbidding mini-forest with black, towering, limbless trees.

Neal was looking at him for some show of interest. He sighed under his breath and paddled closer to the needle-rushes. They looked sharp.

Neal said, "The salt marsh ecosystem is one of the most productive on the planet."

If the smell he was smelling was from productivity, then this patch of marsh was damn productive.

"It stinks, Neal."

"The tide is going out exposing the mud."

Gabe reached over to try to touch the needle-rushes for some reason. He had gotten cocky, because he had been upright on his kayak for almost an hour.

He felt it start to roll.

He felt it reach the point of no return, and the treacherous bastard capsized like it had been hit broadside by a tsunami.

The water might be inches deep, but the mud went clear to China. He wasn't going to think about all the creepy crawlers living in the mud.

He grabbed hold of the rushes and tried to pull himself out of the mud. His kayak righted itself and floated away. There was the sound of maniacal laughter, but that was Neal and not the perfidious kayak.

Neal caught his kayak and choked off his laughter. "Sorry, Gabe."

"You aren't. You aren't sorry one little bit. You will be retelling this story when you're ninety and in a nursing home and want to make the old ladies laugh until they spit out their teeth."

"No, I won't. I promise." Neal started laughing again. "Sorry! Come on. We have to get back."

"I'm stuck! It's quicksand, quickmud, and it's going to suck me down."

"No, it isn't."

That was easy for Neal to say. His feet and legs weren't encased in a black, rotten, decaying goo that was never going to let him go.

"It's just decaying plant material, Gabe."

"Is it really? Is that all it is?"

The methane stink was so much worse now that he had stirred up the petri dish of bacteria, creepy-crawlers, rotting vegetation, and tepid water.

Neal said, "You can't just lie there forever."

"Can to."

But he released his death grip on the rushes and tried to body surf on the mud. He dragged himself along like some hundred and sixty pound, extinct amphibian returning to the warm, shallow waters of its birth.

His hands sunk into the slime, but he clawed his way to deeper water, and finally, finally, his hands didn't hit bottom, and he dog-paddled to his kayak.

"Hold this damn thing steady!"

Neal said, "I've got it. Climb on."

"That's what I'm trying to do."

He hated kayaks, and Janes Island State Park, and Neal, and the freaking marsh ecosystem in general. He wanted a new ice age to send a glacier south to scrape all of them from the face of the Earth.

In a kinder, gentler world, there wouldn't have been anyone at the kayak rental station.

But Ranger Sarah Sharp, Sergeant King, Officer Stevens, and a camper or two were congregating.

Sarah examined him from his black goo encrusted running shoes to his grungy hair. She looked at the orange kayak which was weighted down with a load of black marsh mud.

She shook her head. "I hope you're planning on cleaning this kayak, Mr. Bergeron, because you aren't getting your deposit back until you do."

She was about his height and filled out her uniform nicely. Her brown hair was in a ponytail again, and she was staring at him with big, green eyes as he dripped ooze onto the dock.

She looked away, and her shoulders spasmed, but she managed to hold it in until a strangled sound emerged from the depths of Neal's traitorous chest.

And then everyone was laughing. It was possible that even Sergeant King smiled.

Sarah wiped her tears away. "All right. Haul the kayak out, Mr. Bergeron. There's a hose over here."

She handed him the hose and supervised the rinsing of all the mud from the orange, fiberglass spawn of Satan.

When he was done, she nodded. "And as for you...you really stink, Mr. Bergeron."

"Really? I can't tell, because I've got a nose full of toxic mud, Ranger." He even had mud in his ears.

Neal nodded in agreement. "You really do."

She said, "How about we go to the bathhouse and hose you off, and then you can take a shower?"

Neal said, "Yeah. Ellie's not going to let you into the cabin."

He walked in as dignified a manner as was possible for someone leaving a trail of black putrefaction behind him.

Sarah fetched another hose. "Stand still, and let me get the top layer off. You'd clog up the shower drains if you went inside as you are."

The bathhouse was concrete block; split down the middle for male and female visitors. Wide wooden louvers were set under the eaves, well above head height, and a fan was drawing in air for ventilation.

He took off his running shoes and his shirt. His sunglasses were lost in the primeval mud.

Sarah hosed him down, front and back.

His shorts were still dripping black, fetid water. He checked his pockets; they were filled with mud. He was glad Neal had his phone.

She said, "All right, lose the shorts."

"I beg your pardon."

"Lose the shorts. They're filthy. You've got underwear on, right?"

"I don't see that's any concern of yours, Ranger."

Neal said, "Go ahead, Gabe. I'll go get you something dry to put on."

Gabe scanned the area, and there didn't seem to be anyone staring at him. He dropped the shorts and ran inside the bathhouse.

He thought he heard giggling as the door shut.

There was a shower area with terracotta tiles and even shower curtains. He turned on the water and washed his hair.

The hot, clean, non-stinky water felt wonderful.

Sarah called, "Want some soap?"

"Yes. Please."

The door opened, and a wrapped bar of soap bounced in. He washed his hair again and then his body.

He finished, but where was Neal with those clothes?

"Neal?"

Sarah said, "Not back. How long are you going to be?"

"I'm done, but I am not running across the park naked, Ranger Ma'am."

There was more giggling.

"Okay, throw in my shorts. They may still smell, but they're better than nothing."

She opened the door and marched in. She was on the other side of the shower curtain. "Here." She shoved the wet shorts past the curtain.

"Cover your nakedness, Mr. Bergeron. I have other duties."

He took the shorts and wrung them out, and then wrung out his briefs too. He put both back on and exited the bathhouse.

"Thank you, Sarah."

She nodded. "Of course, Mr. Bergeron."

"I think you can call me Gabe now."

She gave him a look and went back to watching a soccer game. The three blond kids, who had gotten back without falling prey to the rotten, gooey marsh, a half dozen other teenagers, and Kurt had chosen up teams.

Gabe said, "So, you and him?"

She gave him a steely gaze. "I just met him, Mr. Bergeron."

"Yeah?"

"Yes. Kurt arrived a week ago; actually six days."

"Reassigned?"

"You'd have to ask him, Gabe." And she marched off.

So Gabe picked up his shirt, wrung it out, and put it back on. His running shoes were filthy, but he put them on anyway.

He caught a glimpse of Lonnie, aka Weasel, skulking behind a pine tree, but King was heading toward them, and when he looked back, Lonnie was gone.

But the sergeant was actually heading for Kurt. Gabe debated going after Lonnie, but where was Neal? He squished toward the cabin.

Wendy was waving at him. "Gabe, I think Neal could use some help."

"Yeah? What's up?"

Wendy glared at Mia's well-worn RV. "The skinhead grabbed him."

"Thanks, Wendy."

A shirtless, sweaty Gareth had Neal backed up against a tree and was poking a finger into his chest. They were roughly the same height, but Neal was no fighter.

"Gis a beuk, Wanker. Reet noo."

But when Gareth sensed someone behind him, he whirled around and landed in a fighter's stance.

"Divvin' nebby, man, or I'll fettle ye."

Gareth had a British accent, but definitely not posh like Mia's remnant. It was more urban and lower class, but Gabe hadn't watched enough Masterpiece Theater to pinpoint the gritty, possibly northern, industrial city of Mr. Fry's upbringing.

And the words might be obscure, but fist shaking was

universal.

"Let go of my friend."

"Gan hyem, man! Dee as ya telt, ya geet doiler!"

Gabe Bergeron was going to get his ass kicked. Gareth looked and moved very like the mixed martial arts guys on television and had some scars on his face too.

And then a voice just behind him said, "I do love meeting new people."

Gabe whirled around; well, he jumped, stumbled and almost fell on his ass. Fortunately, or maybe not, it was Miss Mia Chandler-Hargreaves looking lovely as always. She had put her sarong back on after Wendy's little chat.

Gareth grabbed his arm, as a first step to punching him in the face, but Mia said, "No, Gareth."

"Gie ower, Mia...."

"No. Gareth. We have company."

Wendy had walked over, and Kurt and Sergeant King had paused their conversation to look their way.

Mia smiled. "I'm Mia Chandler-Hargreaves. It's hyphenated. And you're Gabe Bergeron." She shook his hand; hers was surprisingly powerful.

"Yes, I am." He looked at Neal. "Why don't you see about those clothes, Neal."

Neal looked at him and then at Gareth.

"Go ahead."

Neal said, "Sure?"

"I'm sure. We're all friends here." At least, until King left.

Gareth snorted, but Mia said, "Exactly."

Neal walked off. "Be right back."

Mia said, "Gareth?"

Gareth was torn between ripping out this Bergeron guy's carotid artery with his teeth or just punching him to death

Mia smiled. "No, Gareth. Shake his hand."

Gareth extended a sweaty, calloused paw. "Gareth Fry."

"Gabe Bergeron. As you know. Nice to meet you both."

Gareth snorted again.

Mia said, "Would you like a beer, Mr. Bergeron."

"Thanks, but I don't care for beer that much."

"A soft drink then?"

"That would be wonderful."

Gareth was looking at his muddy shoes. "Yer trainers is aal clarty, man." He went into the RV.

Mia said, "Come and sit, Mr. Bergeron. You seem to have had an adventure." She was looking at the water puddling at his feet.

"I did."

She smiled at him with her very red lips, but her enormous, black eyes were noncommittal. She pointed to a lawn chair as she reclined on her chaise. Up close, her black hair shimmered and her face was unlined. He thought Wendy was wrong about her being forty; thirty-five maybe?

"I don't think Mr. Fry wants me here?"

"Nonsense. He's delighted."

Gareth hid it very well when he returned with the sodas.

Mia said, "You're such a dear, Gareth. Weren't you going to go for a run?"

"Nah."

"I'm sure you were."

Gareth didn't stamp his foot, but he managed to look even more enraged until he jogged away, picking up speed and disappearing among the trees.

She said, "Utterly devoted to his training regimen."

"He's very fit." He really was young for her.

She smiled again and nodded. "Yes, isn't he. He dabbles in mixed martial arts."

"Is he a friend? A close friend?"

She smiled, "Associate."

"You're British, Ms. Chandler-Hargreaves?"

"You simply must call me Mia."

He smiled back at her and sipped his ice cold cola. "Then I'm Gabe."

She said, "My father was English, Gabe. My mother was Samoan. But I've lived in the States for donkey's years."

"So you were one of Eric's special clients."

"Special clients? No, I'm sure I wasn't. Eric was very keen for me to take advantage of his accounting services, but I was still dithering."

"I see. So what does Gareth want from Neal?"

She smiled. "I'm sure I couldn't say. Gareth gets these notions, and it's very hard to dissuade him sometimes. Perhaps you should ask Neal?"

Gabe was certainly going to do that.

"I suppose I should thank you for not mentioning my little rendezvous with Eric to the police?" She pointed a bejeweled fingernail at Sergeant King.

"What makes you think I didn't?"

"Oh, I'm fairly sure, Snuggums. But I wonder why?"

She could go on wondering. He could march over to King and tell him. He might have to at some point.

"He wouldn't believe you now, Snuggums. Much too late to change your statement, don't you think?"

"You think so? I wonder. What is it you do, Mia?"

"Investments."

"Stocks, bonds, real estate?"

She smiled, "All that sort of thing, and I'm a collector. Here's our Gareth."

The guy was running full tilt, and he almost tripped when he skidded to a stop.. He leaned over panting, dripping sweat. He raised his head long enough to glare from time to time.

Gareth took a deep breath. "Gis it o'er?"

She stopped smiling. "Whatever are you going on about?" She giggled. "Do you know, Gareth, Gabe thinks that we're a couple. Isn't that amusing?"

Amusement was not one of the emotions Gareth was displaying as he pulled the Bergeron guy to his feet. "Cuddy skyetgob." They were nose to nose. "Piss off, Wanker."

Mia grabbed Gareth's arm. "Don't stand so close, Gareth. You know Americans don't like that."

She had the left arm, but Gareth could throttle him with just the right.

Mia smiled. "Go take a shower."

Gareth raised his fist. "Aal dang 'e proppa, Wanker....."

Mia, who had been looking all willowy and calm up to that point, gave Gareth a look that should have seared the skin off his face.

"Shower."

Gareth nodded and went into the RV and banged around like he was trying to punch out an opening for a new door

"Thanks, Mia."

"Whatever for, Gabe?"

Right. He knew when his ass had been saved.

She said, "Perhaps, we can do lunch? You and I and Neal and Gareth?"

"That sounds great."

"We should cooperate, Gabe. It would be in your best interest and certainly in Neal's. And I would be very grateful."

The banging in the RV stopped. Which Mia could hear as well as he could.

She said, "And I can show my gratitude in so many ways. Have a think, will you?"

Gabe waited for the RV to simply explode and rain bits of metal and Gareth over the landscape, but there was only silence, which was scarier than an explosion.

"I'm sure you could. I'll be sure to have a think. You were very lucky...to have gotten off Eric's boat before the explosion."

She smiled. "I was never on his little boat, and I had nothing to do with poor Eric's accident. Please believe me, Gabe. I was as shocked as you were. Not physically, perhaps." She patted his flushed face, still reddened from the flames. "I didn't have the misfortune to be tossed into the water. But in every other way."

She stared into his eyes. "I would hardly have been here when it happened if I had. That wouldn't have made sense at all. Would it, Snuggums?"

It actually wouldn't. But it could be that Gareth had slipped his leash?

Gareth came out of the RV with a towel.

"'E thinks we did for Eric?"

Mia just smiled at him.

Gareth appeared to have calmed down, and his English was

more like the Queen's. "'E should ask his bleeding friend what 'e were up to rummaging around bleeding boat afore it went boom."

Gareth went nose to nose with him again. " Aat's what 'e should do. Before talking shite." Gareth drew back his fist. "Gan on and leave us alurn, Wanker."

And Gabe may have jumped back; Gareth smiled.

Mia smiled. "It would be awkward to be forced to tell Sergeant King about Neal being on the boat. I do like Neal." She lost the smile. "I wonder if Neal found what he was looking for?"

Gabe walked away as fast as he could. She was just as scary as Gareth, just not as theatrical about it.

He thought about her eyes and a line of poetry popped into his head from eleventh grade English.

"Tiger, tiger, burning bright, in the forests of the night."

He walked faster.

Saturday
3:00 pm

Neal was outside the cabin, and he had clothes in his left hand, but Ellie had a death grip on the right.

They were smiling and staring into each other's eyes.

Gabe rolled his eyes. Which was just mean so he tamped down the envy.

"Neal. With me!"

Mr. English was watching them again, which was getting to be creepy.

Gabe marched to the creek which lay fifty feet from the cabin. The little dock was higher than the ground where it abutted the shore so there was a step up.

He walked to the end and sat down with is legs hanging over. The rest of his bandages had fallen off.

Neal sat beside him staring into the shallow water. There was a motionless crab on the muddy bottom; a crab or a crab shell. "Are you okay, Gabe? I was coming back. I have those dry clothes for you."

"You were about to get it on with Miss Ellie."

"No, I wasn't. I was coming back. Really, Gabe. Are you pissed?"

"Look at me. Neal, look at me. Did you go on Eric's boat before it blew up? Just before?"

Neal nodded. "Yes."

"Shit, Neal! Why didn't you tell me? If King finds out about that, you'll be hauled in for questioning or arrested."

"I was going to, but then I thought that I shouldn't get you any more involved than you already are." He tried to smile. "Sorry, Gabe. Did Mia tell you?"

"She did. Well, no, Gareth told me."

"Yeah. I saw him when I jumped off the boat. And then I saw Kurt heading for the boat too."

"Shit again, Neal. Don't tell me Kurt also saw you on the freaking boat?"

Neal shook his head. "No, I don't think so. I got to my car before he got close. I was parked in the lot near the boat ramp, and I ducked down so he wouldn't see me."

"Did you see Kurt or Gareth go on board?"

"Kurt did. That's when I left. When he went on board and into the cabin. I don't know if Gareth did. Later on."

"Was Gareth following you?"

"Maybe. I don't know. But I got out of there. Out of the park."

Gareth's little car had probably been at his campsite. Neal still hadn't told him why he'd gone on board. Or why he'd suddenly gone to the ATM, if he had.

"Neal? Were you looking for the Eric's ledger? When you went on board?"

Neal nodded, but then his phone started playing the flying monkey music from the Wizard of Oz. "Hello?"

Gabe could hear a female voice buzzing away. Neal shook his head as he mouthed the name, "Rachel."

Rachel was Scott's wife. She weighed about half as much as Scott, but she packed so much more unpleasantness per pound that one was as obnoxious as the other.

Neal said, "No, Rachel, we don't know anything more about Eric. Or Layla. Ellie and Gabe are with me."

Neal listened to the angry bees for a while. "I told Scott I'll call as soon as I know anything. Yes, it's a tragedy."

More angry bees. "Sure. Okay. Thanks for calling, Rachel."

Neal shook his head again. "She said she was concerned about me."

He laughed, and Neal joined in as a car pulled into the driveway; it was big and black and hailed from a semi-mythical time when cars were made of steel, and gasoline was ten cents a gallon.

Mr. English was watching as the driver got out and straightened her linen business suit. And then the passenger got out.

Layla Cristoforetti Girard waved at Neal.

Neal ran to hug her. "Layla! I thought you were...."

Layla reached up to wrap her arms around Neal's neck and hug him hard. "You thought I was dead."

She smiled radiantly at Neal. If Botticelli were suddenly to appear in the twenty-first century, he would use Layla as a model for one of his paintings of the Madonna; the dark eyes, the perfect cheekbones, the serenity.

Gabe said, "Hello, Layla. I'm very glad to see you too."

She smiled at him. "I'm very glad to be seen, Gabe. I suppose I am very lucky."

Neal said, "Then you know...about Eric?"

She nodded. "It was on the news." She looked over to the other woman. "Sorry, Cindi. This is Cindi, my friend and attorney. She heard it on the news and told me."

Cindi extended a delicate hand and shook Neal's hand and then his. "Cindi Lou Parker. Pleased to meet you both."

She gave them an enigmatic smile as she handed out business cards. She was probably fifty, sandy-brown hair cut short, freckles, and lawyer's eyes.

Ellie opened the cabin door, and Neal smiled radiantly at her. Gabe would have donned his sunglasses if they weren't buried for all time in the mud of Janes Island.

Neal said, "You remember Ellie, Layla."

Layla smiled at Ellie. "Of course. This is Cindi Lou Parker."

Ellie said, "Happy to meet you, and I'm so happy to see you, Layla. I was so afraid...."

"Yes." Layla added, "The handsome park ranger told us where Neal was staying. And what happened to you, Gabe."

He said, "I saw you on the boat, Layla. In the marina. Yesterday?"

"Yes, and you may have noticed Eric and I were not happy in one another's company? I left him soon after I saw you, Gabe."

She closed her Madonna eyes. She couldn't quite coax a tear, but Eric didn't deserve one. She didn't need to know about Mia, and that Eric was unfaithful to the end. If she didn't know already.

"They found a body...this morning." Gabe wasn't sure how to tell her that it was so badly burnt that it couldn't be positively identified.

Cindy Lou nodded. "Yes, sent to the Office of the Chief Medical Examiner in Baltimore. We saw the boat. Tragic. It will come down to dental records presumably."

Ellie said, "Please come in. Would you like some tea?"

Gabe Bergeron wasn't going to gag down one more drop of peppermint tea. "There's a nice restaurant in town, the Summer Nights Cafe. If you're hungry? We could get coffee at least."

Layla said, "Nothing for me. Cindi?"

Cindi Lou had been focused on Ellie and Neal. She smiled. "Can't stand tea. But I'm fine. Unless you have beer?"

Ellie made a face. "No alcohol, I'm afraid. But please come in before the mosquitoes find us."

Ellie put water on for tea anyway. Layla looked exhausted; death, violent and sudden or lingering and expected, was always a shock.

But she smiled at him. "How are you feeling, Gabe? The ranger said you were blown off the dock?"

Gabe patted his legs. "A few cuts. Nothing really."

She reached toward his face. "And these are burns?"

"I was very close."

"How terrible."

"He wouldn't have known anything, Layla. I know people say that, but he wouldn't."

"Thank you, Gabe."

A dark green, Ford F-150 truck pulled in behind Cindi Lou's Cadillac. He didn't need to see the seal on the door to know it was Sergeant King.

"The police are here."

Cindi Lou said, "Excellent."

No one else seemed to think that was so swell.

Sergeant King wasn't a huge man, but he seemed to fill the cabin to overflowing.

"I'm very sorry for your loss, Mrs. Girard."

"Thank you, Sergeant. This is my attorney, Cindi Lou Parker."

A few hairs of King's right eyebrow may have twitched at that, but he said, "Pleased to meet you. I believe that Ranger Hobbs has told you that a body has been sent to Baltimore?"

Cindi Lou said, "Yes, we know that. Has it been identified yet, Sergeant?"

King looked around the cabin. "I'd appreciate it if we could have some privacy, Folks."

Which was police for get the Hell out, and Gabe and Neal headed for the door.

Cindi Lou said, "I'll stay, Sergeant."

"Yes, Ma'am." King looked at Ellie, who was fiddling with her tea with a distracted look. "Miss Tyson."

"Oh, sorry."

They went and sat on the dock again.

Ellie was gazing into the water this time.

Neal said, "Do you think King suspects her?"

"It's always the spouse. Or the butler."

Neal made a face. "Don't joke, Gabe. I like Layla."

"I do too." But he didn't actually know her that well beyond the fact that her father had made his money in manufacturing, and that she had married Eric for some inexplicable reason.

Well, he was handsome; he had been handsome.

But if it came down to her or Neal, he could live with her going away for Eric's murder. If that's what it was.

"Anyway. I guess it will depend on her alibi, if she has one, and what King can learn about the explosion."

Ellie said, "If anything."

Gabe said, "Not a fan?"

Ellie looked up. "Oh, he's okay. Competent enough, I mean." She looked at her watch and slapped a mosquito.

They seemed so frail until they pierced skin and harpooned an artery. They seemed to like Ellie the best. Gabe wanted to rise above his schadenfreude, but he wasn't nearly evolved enough.

On the island, just across the creek, two egrets were braced on long, delicate legs, elegantly stalking their prey.

Ellie slapped again. "I'm not going to sit here and be eaten alive. Come on, Neal."

She knocked on the door and entered, only to back out as King exited.

He said, "Did you need something, Miss Tyson?"

She didn't waste a smile on him this time. "Bug spray. Or to be indoors?"

"Right. Go on in. I'm done. For now."

Layla and Cindi Lou came out. Layla said, "Will you let me know? If it is Eric, Sergeant?"

"Yes, Ma'am. As soon as I know."

Cindi Lou said, "And the explosion, Sergeant?"

"Still under investigation, Miss Parker."

"Ms. Parker."

"Right." He started to fold his notebook but stopped. "Mrs. Girard? What can you tell me about the boat?"

Layla said, "It was Eric's new toy, Sergeant. I've never cared for sailing all that much, but I know it was a Sea Ray, the Sundancer model."

"But you were sailing with him to the Outer Banks?"

Layla said, "Actually I have a friend who is coming to the park. I had been planning on visiting with her and letting Eric sail off without me."

King said, "And the name of this friend?"

"Mimi Campbell."

The sergeant nodded. "And do you know anything about the engines?"

She smiled. "It has twin Cummins QSC 600 diesels, which generate 1148 horsepower. Or had. I'm sure they must be ruined. Such a pity."

King's eyebrow twitched again. "Yes, Ma'am."

Layla said, "I love machines of all types, Sergeant, which is why I let Eric get the boat in the first place. Of course, I insisted on rebuilding the engines before I would sail on it."

"So you could attest to the fact that the engines were in running order, Ma'am?"

"I could, and I do." She gave King her Madonna smile. "And

I did nothing to alter that, Sergeant."

Cindi Lou looked like she wanted to tell Layla to shut up, but her smile only tightened.

King actually smiled at Layla. "I wasn't suggesting that you did, Ma'am." He looked over to Cindi Lou. "I would like you both to stay in the area. To make a formal statement."

Cindi Lou nodded. "We'll be at the motel, Sergeant, for a few days."

"Thank you, Ma'am."

King folded his notebook and walked back to his truck only to stop. "Mr. Bergeron? Could I have a word."

He toyed with the idea of saying no, but he had the feeling that King had no sense of humor.

"Can we get inside the truck? The mosquitoes."

King nodded. There was not a single coffee cup, gum wrapper, or errant mote of dust on the gleaming surfaces. No Bergeron vehicle had ever been this clean even rolling off the showroom floor.

"Yeah, they bother visitors."

The ones who were feeble excuses for men. "I guess they keel over and die if they bite you."

King almost smiled. "Not really, Mr. Bergeron." He pulled out his notebook. "Now that you've had some time...to recover, is there anything you'd like to add to your statement?"

Mia popped into his head. King was staring at him. The sergeant had blond, furry forearms, wrists like tree trunks, and hands big enough to make his pen look lost in his grip.

"Have you interviewed the other campers?"

"Working on it. There's a lot of them. Anyone I should focus on, Mr. Bergeron?"

"I'm not sure about this, Sergeant."

"Not sure about what, Sir?"

"There might have been a woman near the boat when I arrived."

"At 5:45? And who might that have been?"

"I don't know her name, but she's staying in the Gulfstream RV. I think she's Hawaiian. Or Polynesian."

King flipped the pages of his notebook. "Miss Mia Chandler-Hargreaves?"

"Could be. I guess."

"And what was she doing near the boat."

"Well, she had a belt hung with sticks of dynamite, slabs of C4, and a few coils of wire."

King was shaking his head.

"And a clock. One of those digital timers."

King tossed his notebook on the dash, and grabbed his arm and yanked him close. "You think this is a joke?"

Gabe had been right about that sense of humor. "No, Sergeant, I really don't, but I tend to say things...before I think."

King had a big class ring on his right hand. It would leave a mark if King punched him with it, even if the sergeant could only manage a jab in the confined space.

He had never been punched in the face, but he thought he might be able to cross that off his anti-bucket list very soon.

"I'm sorry, Charlie."

"Don't call me Charlie!"

"I am sorry. Sergeant King. I didn't blow up Eric and his boat. I don't know who did." His money was on Gareth at the moment. "If I knew anything that would help you, I would tell you."

King slowly released the grip on his arm and settled back in his seat.

"This is a big case for you, isn't it?"

"Shut up, Bergeron."

"Yes, Sir. Shutting up."

King sat there staring at the windshield.

"I really did see Mia near the boat."

King actually smiled. "Didn't know her name but now you're on a first name basis?"

"No! Absolutely not. It's just easier to say...I don't remember her last name. She may have been talking to Eric."

"Right. Get out of my truck Bergeron."

"Yes, Sir. Getting out." But he had to ask. "Was Eric murdered? Did somebody really plant a bomb on board?"

"Get out!"

He opened the door, but King grabbed his arm again. "Wait. Have you seen Lonnie?"

He could have pretended he didn't know who Lonnie was, but he thought he'd gotten on Charlie's last nerve already. "No. Well, maybe."

King leaned closer until their noses were almost touching; the sergeant needed a breath mint and skin moisturizer. "What the Hell does that mean?"

"It means that I thought I saw him lurking behind a pine tree about an hour ago. Here in the park. Near the bathhouse."

"Did you talk to him?"

"No, Sir."

"Do you know what he wants to tell you?"

"No, Sir." King thought Lonnie had seen him planting the bomb, and there was nothing he could say to change that. "I think he spotted you and ran."

"That could be the only true statement you've made."

"No, Sir. Every word I've said has been true." Well, most of them. "You should talk to Mia, or at least do a background check on them."

"Them?"

"I may have noticed that there's a guy in the RV with her."

"Get out of my truck."

"Yes, Sir."

King reversed slowly and quietly and calmly onto the paved road and drove away.

And Gabe walked back to the cabin no wiser.

Layla was standing in the doorway, looking at Mimi's red PT Cruiser.

She turned and nodded at Cindi Lou. "I think I'll go for a walk. Gabe, would you mind showing me around. I don't want to get lost."

Ellie looked like she was going to object, but Cindi Lou smiled and herded her back into the cabin. "I could use some of that tea, Miss Tyson. If you don't mind. It was such a long drive from Philadelphia."

Gabe led Layla along the forest path that Neal had shown

him earlier. "How are you holding up?"

She said, "I'll manage, but it was a shock."

"I'm sure. But you got off the boat in time."

She looked at him and smiled. "Are you saying just in time, Gabe?"

"Not implying anything, Layla."

"No? I wouldn't blame you. It's always the wife, isn't it? And Lord knows Eric wasn't a perfect husband, but I did nothing to harm him."

"But you were about to give him the heave ho? So to speak."

She smiled again. "Neal is lucky to have a friend like you. And yes, Cindi is working on the divorce and other matters."

"She seems very competent."

They had reached the lawn that bordered the creek.

"She is. We've been friends since college. More years ago than I want to remember. She was kind enough to drive down with the papers, which I gave to Eric before I got off the boat."

"Yesterday? That seems rather...spur of the moment?"

Layla said, "I hadn't really made up my mind. Eric was very handsome; the black hair, those black eyes. He could be so charming. And he'd promised me that he would behave. Cindi kept telling me I was foolish to believe him."

She shook her head. "And then I overheard him on the phone, arranging one of his little assignations. And then I called Cindi called, and I told her about Eric."

"And you did the deed."

She smiled. "I gave him the papers. If that's what you mean?" They kept walking. "And he stormed off the boat like a spoiled child."

He said, "And you and Cindi went home?"

Layla said, "You're very curious, Gabe, but yes, and Cindi was sweet enough to insist that I stay with her, so I was in Philadelphia when Eric was taken. And then, of course, we heard the news."

How damn convenient was that?

"Do you know who the assignation was with?"

"No, and I don't care." She smiled at a young boy who was running toward his mother with a tiny crab held carefully in his hand.

"But I had no reason, no financial reason, to hurt Eric. Cindi drew up a wonderful prenuptial agreement for Eric to sign."

"Very forward thinking."

"Yes, I thought so."

Why the Hell was she telling him all this?

She said, "I hope Neal won't get into any trouble."

"Why should he?"

"Oh, I don't know. I knew so little about Eric's company; Eric and Neal's company. Nothing, really."

He didn't believe that for a second.

"I left that entirely up to Eric."

"I see."

She stopped. "But was there anything...irregular at the office, Gabe?"

"I'm sure there wasn't."

"You're sure, Gabe? Of course, you would know since you worked so closely with Neal and with Eric. Wouldn't you?"

"I haven't...." He shut his mouth.

"I do hope you're right. And there is no problem. I would hate for anything that Eric may have done to get you and Neal into trouble."

"It won't. You can count on that."

She smiled again. "I hope not, but I could understand how angry you and Neal might be, if Eric had done something."

Damn her smiling face to Hell.

"Eric was always so sure that things would go his way. And that he would never be caught. It must have been trying for you both. Is that why you left, Gabe?"

He kept his mouth shut.

"I'm sorry if I've upset you. I think I'll find my own way back to Cindi. Eric was such a fool really."

And Gabe and Neal were fools too.

And the dumb Gabe fellow had been so monumentally wrong about Layla Girard. Beauty and charm were only skin deep, but ruthless self-preservation went clear to the bone.

Gabe just stood there. He stomped on an ant hill, and then he noticed the little hills everywhere filled with ants toiling away blissfully unaware.

He walked back to the cabin taking the long way.

A big, silver RV was parked two camp sites from Mia and Gareth. The owner was talking to Gareth.

Gareth said something nodding toward the Gabe fellow. Gareth said something else and laughed.

The guy was smaller than Gareth; he was wearing a black, sleeveless t-shirt featuring a coiled snake, a heavy chain hanging from his belt, and a red baseball cap. He was also sporting cowboy boots bedazzled with studs.

Gareth stopped laughing and scowled at him. Red Cap joined in the scowling like his family and the Bergerons had been mortal enemies for generations. Gabe picked up the pace.

Neal was sitting on the screen porch. A boat raced by on the creek, and after it passed, the waves slapped against the rocks piled along the bank.

Cindi Lou was leaning against her Cadillac, and Mr. English was talking to her.

Neal said, "That's funny."

"What's that?"

"Mr. English walked over and started talking to Ms. Parker. He hasn't said two words to Ellie."

Yeah, that was funny. "Where's Layla?"

"Mimi is her friend...the one she was going to stay with." Neal was pointing at the next cabin.

Mr. English lumbered away, and Cindi Lou headed for them.

Cindi Lou smiled. "I'm sure you realize, but this is a very trying experience for Layla." She focused on him. "She doesn't need any more problems, Mr. Bergeron."

"And you're telling me this because?"

"Just making sure things are clear."

"Crystal."

She smiled her thin-lipped smile. "I am glad. I hate unpleasantness...of any kind."

"Me too."

And Cindi Lou smiled and turned to see Layla coming out of Mimi's cabin. Mimi and Layla hugged, and then Manon and Floria embraced Layla too. They had all been crying.

Mimi said, "I'm so very sorry, Layla. So terrible, so very terrible."

Manon said, "He was so young."

Floria said, "Yes, he was, wasn't he?"

Mimi glared at Floria as she took Layla's arm and helped her to Cindi's Caddy. "If there's anything we can do? Anything at all?"

Layla leaned her head to the side and flashed her perfect, tear-stained cheekbones at a cruel world. "Thank you, Mimi. I'll let you know. You're such a good friend."

Cindi Lou held out a tiny hand to Mimi. "I'm Cindi Parker, Layla's lawyer...and friend."

Layla said, "I'm sorry, Cindi. This is Mimi, and her sisters, Floria and Manon."

There was more hugging but less warmth.

Mimi said, "Are you going home?"

Cindi said, "The police would like us to stay...to make statements."

Floria said, "I'm sure."

Mimi said, "Come here for dinner, Layla. Please? We can talk. And you too, Cindi?" They all hugged again.

Layla draped herself over the Caddy's seat, and departed like Cleopatra leading Caesar's funeral procession.

Mimi and her sisters bustled back inside their cabin.

Neal said, "What was Ms. Parker talking about, Gabe? What unpleasantness?"

"Where's Ellie?"

"She left too. She said she was going to get coffee. For you."

Sure she was. "I'm calling Max, Neal."

"Your lawyer buddy?"

"Yeah." He didn't know Max's number; he didn't know any numbers. "Shit."

"What?"

"I don't know his number."

Neal looked at him. "Because?"

"I lost my phone when I was almost blown up."

"I was wondering why you had that prepaid thing. We can get

all your numbers and data if you backed up your phone...."

Gabe had meant to.

He really had. Neal started laughing at him. "It's not funny, Hartmann."

"It is."

He had to do something as archaic as dial information to get Max's office number. He called Nagy & Stant and left a message for Max, which no one would hear until Monday.

"I want to talk to him now."

Neal nodded. "Is Max on Facebook or Twitter?"

Max had a Twitter account. Neal posted a tweet giving the number of his prepaid and asking Max to reply urgently.

Neal said, "Is something wrong, Gabe. Something else?"

"No, nothing."

Except that Neal's dead partner's wife and her lawyer were determined that Neal should take the fall for anything and everything that Eric had been up to.

Saturday
4:00 pm

Gabe Bergeron was sitting at the picnic table outside Neal's cabin, staring at his phone, willing it to ring, when a basso profundo voice boomed in his ear, "Want to go fishing?"

He may have tossed his phone into the air.

After catching his prepaid and spinning round, he was not met with a fugitive from the cast of *Boris Godunov* but Mr. English. "What?"

He had two fishing rods and a bucket clamped in his left hand and a basket in his right. "Want to go fishing?"

"With you?" Gabe couldn't think of anything he would be less likely to do, but Mr English was towering over him. "Uh...I'm waiting for a call."

Mr. English looked at his cellphone and raised his brows. "Bring the phone."

"Yeah, I could do that. But where would we be going to do this fishing?"

The bucket Mr. English was carrying didn't smell very good. "Not far. Three bars at least."

"So I can get my call?"

Mr. Bear was glaring at him with his bushy, black eyebrows scrunched into a uni-brow.

His mind was blank.

Neal. "Wait. Neal will want to go with us."

Mr. English smiled for the first time. "And leave Ellie?"

Which was a good point. "Wait. She's off running an errand so Neal is all alone, and he loves fishing."

Mr. English pondered and then shook his shaggy head. "Don't have to go if you don't want to, Bergeron. You looked like you weren't doing anything."

And the guy started walking toward the creek.

Which was wonderful, but he did not want to offend Mr. English. "Wait. I can go. Do I need to take anything?"

Mr. English shook his head.

"Okay. Good. Let me tell Neal where I'm going."

He ran inside the cabin. "Neal!"

Neal was napping. "What?"

"Mr. Bear wants me to go fishing with him, and I don't know how to get out of it without pissing him off, and can't you come with us?"

Neal rolled over on his back. "What? He asked you to go fishing?"

He nodded.

"So go with him. He's a good guy." Neal's eyes were closing. "He caught a shark...."

"Yeah, I know he dove into the water and caught a Great White with his bare teeth. Neal?"

Neal rolled over again.

There was a knocking on the cabin door.

"'Do not ask for whom the bell tolls....'"

Gabe took a deep breath and opened the door. Mr. English just stared at him.

"Okay. Where are we going?"

"Not far."

Mr. English handed him a rod as they walked to the lawn along the creek.

"Do much fishing, Bergeron?"

"Not that much. Call me Gabe. What's your name? Is that bait? For the hook?"

Mr. English pulled something slimy out of the bucket. "Squid. Want me to bait your hook?"

"Absolutely."

Neal had tried to teach him how to cast so he wasn't a total novice, but he let Mr. English go first; his cast arced into the air and plunked far out into the creek.

"James."

"What? Is that your name? Of course, it is."

Gabe managed to get his line into the creek without hooking himself or getting his line tangled with James'.

They stood side by side looking into the gray-green-blue water for minutes and minutes. "James?"

James looked over at him.

"What are we fishing for?"

"Whatever bites."

Which seemed like a surefire plan.

"And how long does it usually take before something bites?"

James smiled again. "Minutes, hours, days."

He'd been afraid of that.

They kept standing there.

He really tried not to fidget.

James said, "Want a sandwich?"

"Sure. That would be great."

James took his rod. "Get me one too, Gabe."

The picnic basket held sandwiches wrapped in plastic, and bottles of water, Coke, and Lowenbrau. "You shouldn't have gone to so much trouble, James."

James held out a hand for a sandwich, and they sat on the bank and ate excellent ham sandwiches while waiting for unseen, uncooperative, or non-existent fish to find the bait.

James said, "You're an accountant like Neal?"

"I am. And what do you do?"

James turned and locked eyes with him. "I'm a nurse."

Mr. Bear was waiting for him to smile or make a joke, but he wasn't suicidal, no matter what some people might think.

"That's great, James. Where do you work?"

"All over. At the ER here sometimes." Mr. Bear glared at him again. "I like Dr. Hahn."

"Oh, me too. Salt of the Earth. A shining beacon of the medical profession."

They sat for more minutes and minutes.

James smiled and tugged on his line. "I like Neal."

"I do too."

"Is Neal in some kind of trouble, Gabe?"

"No. I mean Eric was killed, and it was a shock...."

James gently patted his shoulder. "No. Before that."

"No, Neal is okay. No problems at all."

"You can go."

"I can go?"

James smiled. "Sure. You hate fishing, Gabe."

"Not hate exactly."

"You hate it."

"All right, but you invited me."

"That's okay."

Gabe got to his feet. "Are you sure? I could stay a while longer. We might even catch something?"

James said, "You're scaring the fish. Negative energy. I'm told I can be intimidating, Gabe."

"You? I don't see it, James."

James smiled again. "Good, but if I came off...scary when we first met, I didn't mean to. Well, after I found out Neal knew you. Okay?"

"Sure, but you weren't scary." Yeah, and Arnold Schwarzenegger had never played a killer robot from the future.

"Good. But Gabe, if you and Neal need any help...." He stopped smiling, and it was like a big, black, take-no-freaking-prisoners cloud passed over the sun. "I'm here and ready to help out with whatever needs to be done."

"Right. Thank you, James."

"Okay. See you."

He thought Mr. Bear winked at him.

He trotted back to the cabin, but Neal was still asleep, and Ellie was still gone so he went back to staring at his phone.

He was feeling like taking a nap himself when he heard the boat coming up the creek. It pulled up to the dock instead of motoring past.

It was ole Kev and Barb.

They were nearly naked and oiled up like Turkish wrestlers, and the boat was festooned with fishing rods.

Kev jumped off the boat heading for him. "Hey, Gabe. How's it going? Neal around?"

"In the cabin."

Kev had on sunglasses, a speedo, and boat shoes; plus his chains, beads, and pan-religious bangles. "How's he doing?"

"I don't think he's up for fishing, Kev."

"Mind if I ask him?"

"No. Be my guest."

Neal came out before Kev could go in. "Hi, Kev."

Kev hugged Neal. "How's it going, Buddy. Want to come fishing? Get your mind off things? We rented a boat."

Barb was waving like one of the guys who guide jets launching off aircraft carriers. She held up a half dozen fish.

Kev said, "We already caught some speckled trout. The guy who rented the boat gave us a map and told us where to go. How about it?"

Neal shook his head. "I don't know, Kev. It's really nice of you, but Ellie's not here."

"Well, that's too bad, but you can come. Gabe can tell her where you went."

Barb climbed out of the boat and was swaying toward them. On the nakedness scale, she had Kev beat because she was barefoot; her bikini top was barely there. "Come with us, Neal. The best fishing spots are only a half hour away, and it's nice on the water."

Neal was weakening. "Ellie wants to go to dinner, Guys. I'd have to be back by six."

Kev said, "No problem. Have you back here at six sharp; that's a promise. Okay?"

Neal looked at him. "Gabe?"

Gabe sighed. He couldn't believe he was going to have to pretend to fish twice in one day, but he was curious why these two were so freaking insistent about getting Neal on their boat.

Barb said, "Gabe doesn't like fishing. Come on, Neal."

He sighed again. No way was Neal going alone with these two. "Room for one more, Kev?"

The eclipse of Kev and Barb's smiles made it feel ten degrees cooler, but Kev rallied. "Sure! Plenty of room. Come on. We'll sail around the island. We saw some dolphins in Tangier Sound while we were fishing."

Neal smiled. "Dolphins? Really?"

Barb said, "Sure did. Six or seven of them. What's a group of dolphin's called, Kev?"

Neal said, "A pod. Think we can find them again?"

Kev said, "Sure we can."

Maybe Neal was right that he was too suspicious; maybe Kev and Barb were just really, really friendly.

"Do we need anything? Food? Drinks?"

Barb said, "No, Gabe. We've got beer on ice and sandwiches. Come on."

Barb grabbed Neal's arm and was dragging him toward the dock. Neal said, "I have to leave a note for Ellie."

And they started off on a one hour cruise with Kev and Barb on the good ship "Dottie."

It was nice on the water, and he tried to enjoy it as they sped south down the creek.

Barb helped Neal take off his shirt and started slathering him with tanning lotion. She had already coated his back and had moved on to his arms. Neal seemed to be enjoying it more than Ellie would have liked.

Kev was steering the boat, but he smiled and said, "Want me to put some lotion on your back, Gabe?"

"Thanks, but I'm fine." He wasn't sure why exactly, but he was keeping his shirt on.

"Have a beer?"

He was thirsty, but he didn't think so. "I appreciate it, Kev, but I'm fine."

Kev said, "Suit yourself, but I'm going to get one. Steer for me?"

The boat had a steering wheel just like a car. The creek was a hundred feet wide. He didn't see how he could run into anything. "Are you sure?"

Kev nodded so he took the wheel.

Kev smiled and joined Barb and Neal in the back. Barb had opened a beer for herself and Neal, and they toasted. She opened one for Kev, and they were talking and laughing. He could barely hear them over the roar of the engine as they shot down the creek.

He thought he was doing okay, but then Kev said, "Keep it in the channel, Gabe."

Just ahead, somebody had planted a sawed off telephone pole in the creek and topped it with a red light. And there were two orange buoys nearby.

It seemed likely there was a correct course and one or more incorrect courses.

There was also another boat coming. It was more barge than boat with a pile of gravel and a skid-loader on the deck. It was very large and was moving very fast.

Gabe turned around. "Kev? Which way do I go?"

Kev looked up and then dropped his beer and lunged for the wheel.

The telephone pole was looming directly ahead.

Which was a bad thing. So Gabe spun the wheel, and the boat swerved around the pole.

But they were now heading for the barge. Also a bad thing.

The barge captain gave a blast of his warning horn that made the air recoil.

He swerved the boat again.

An orange buoy was coming at them now. The captain sounded his horn again and yelled something as the huge barge roared past inches from Kev's boat.

Kev grabbed the wheel just in time to keep them from running over the buoy as they shot past the hospital dock.

Kev wasn't smiling now.

Ole Kev was shaking as he throttled back. "Shit, Gabe! Are you trying to kill us?"

"No. I'm very sorry, Kev. I've never done this before. Where is this channel?"

Kev shook his head. "Never mind. I've got it."

Another boat was heading for them. Kev slowed even more. This one looked like Charlie's boat.

Kev said, "Shit."

Charlie pulled alongside and gave Kev a stern look. "Is this your boat, Sir?"

Kev said, "I rented it, Officer. For the day."

"And have you had a boating safety course, Sir?"

Kev nodded.

Charlie was consulting his little notebook. "Mr. Sandusky, is it?" Kev nodded again. "Well, I find that damn hard to believe, Sir. Do you have a photo ID, Mr. Sandusky?"

Kev found his wallet and handed over a driver's license. "Here it is. I'm sorry, Officer, but...."

Ole Kev was innocent, and Gabe couldn't let him take the fall. "It's my fault, Sergeant King. I was driving when we zigged and zagged around the telephone pole and the barge and the buoy. I didn't know where the channel was, and I got confused."

Charlie said, "Bergeron. I might have known." Charlie glared at Kev some more. "I'd still fine you for reckless boating, Sandusky, but I'm here for Hartmann and Bergeron."

Gabe said, "You are?"

Charlie actually smiled at him. "I am. You're both wanted back at the park, Bergeron."

They climbed into Charlie's boat and headed back the way they'd come, leaving Kev and Barb looking a little dazed.

And as happy as he was to get away from them, he couldn't imagine who was waiting at the park. "Who wants us, Sergeant?"

Charlie was steering the boat and ignored him.

Neal said, "Look, Gabe."

A guy in a dark suit was standing on the scorched park dock, feet apart, shoulders back. He pointed at Charlie, and Charlie pulled in.

Neal said, "Who is he?"

"No idea."

Charlie cut the engine, and Luke tied up. "Out of my boat, Bergeron."

He said, "Thank you for the lift, Sergeant King."

The guy in the suit said, "Sergeant King? He'd like to speak to you too."

Charlie nodded and climbed out. Luke said, "Do I stay with the boat, Sergeant?"

Charlie considered. "No. Come on."

Luke smiled and vaulted onto the dock like a gymnast going for all tens.

Saturday
6:00 pm

Neal got his answer when the man in the dark suit flashed his FBI credentials at them.

"Special Agent Chernov. Come with me. Both of you."

Chernov looked like a Russian anarchist from some century old, sepia toned photo. What was that guy's name? Trotsky? Was he an anarchist or a communist, or both?

Chernov had intense eyes, magnified by tiny, rimless glasses, and the general brooding air of rage barely controlled. And muscles no suit could hide.

Plus Gabe could smell the special agent's cologne from six feet away. He may have gazed spellbound at Chernov until Neal nudged him and his brain kicked in.

He said, "And where are we going?"

"To the park office, Mr. Bergeron."

It was never good when a FBI agent knew your name without asking. He looked at Neal. He seemed calm, which was strange. Now surely was the time to freak out?

Chernov slapped at a horsefly. "Senior Special Agent Steele wants to speak to you."

Gabe realized he'd been hasty; now was the time to freak out.

They followed Chernov to the office.

Kurt was loitering in the driveway. "Get kicked out, Ranger?"

Kurt nodded but gave him a funny look.

Chernov said, "Inside. Steele wants you."

But Senior Special Agent Steele was occupied. Sergeant King was standing four-square in the center of the room; Luke was trying to emulate his superior.

Steele was also clad in a dark suit, which was like Chernov's as the coat of an Irish Setter is like a Chihuahua's.

Steele said, "And where is the yacht, Sergeant?"

"Towed to the station, Senior Special Agent Steele."

"And where is that exactly?"

"That, Senior Special Agent Steele, is in the Somers Cove Marina approximately two miles south of this location."

"And why is it there?"

"It's being held there, pending completion of the investigation of the death of Mr. Eric Duncan Girard, Senior Special Agent Steele."

Steele had a red spot on each cheek like a daub of rouge. "I want everything you've collected so far. Every photo, every scrap of evidence...you did take photos?"

"Yes, we did."

"And the body is in Baltimore?"

"Yes, it is."

"And all your notes. I want everything, Sergeant. This is a FBI matter now."

King looked from Chernov to another agent, a dark-suited, pale wraith, and then back to Steele. "I can see that, Senior Special Agent Steele."

King turned to go, pushing Luke in front of him.

Steele said, "Where are you going?"

King said, "You said you wanted everything we've collected?"

"Yes, but I might need to talk to you too, Sergeant."

King turned and took a chair next to the Pale Wraith and crossed his legs; his eyelids seemed heavy like he was about to nap. Luke was gripping the doorknob like it was a lifeline.

Steele shook his head. "Go! I want those crime scene photos. And show Chernov to the yacht. And Chernov, make sure there's adequate security." He sighed. "And get our team there."

Chernov said, "Yes, Sir."

Luke bolted as King got to his feet and walked slowly out the door. There might have been the tiniest smile on the sergeant's face.

Steele deigned to notice them. "Come with me, Mr.

Hartmann."

Gabe mouthed the word "lawyer" at Neal.

Neal nodded, and he was left with the Pale Wraith who had apparently taken a vow of silence.

Neal came out after a half hour looking frazzled but not freaked out.

Steele pointed a manicured finger at him. "Mr. Bergeron."

The office, which was Kurt's, had a nice big window looking out on the park, and photos of red and purple sunsets over what was probably Janes Island.

A dark young woman in another dark suit was sitting next to Kurt's desk. She turned on a recorder and angled the microphone at him. She had brown eyes and black hair drawn back in a bun at the nape of her neck.

She also had three scars on her face like little rilles on the pale, lunar surface of her cheek. They were too deep to be filled in by lunar dust, or in this case, makeup.

She looked him over, every bit as intense as Chernov, or maybe more.

"Our conversation will be recorded, Mr. Bergeron."

"Okay."

"Tell me what happened to Eric Girard."

Steele stopped flitting about the office and sat. He made micro-adjustments to the perfectly tailored suit to display his perfect, Ubermensch physique.

And then Steele stared out of Kurt's window the better to show off his perfect profile. He was in his late thirties or early forties.

And Gabe told Steele everything he'd told King, being sure to include Mia this time. He gave it to him in chronological order.

Steele turned. "Ms. Chandler-Hargreaves is the Polynesian woman? And did she go on the yacht?"

"Not that I saw."

"And you never went on the yacht?"

"No."

"So how do you explain your fingerprints in the galley?"

"Impossible."

"It would be better to admit it and explain now, Mr.

Bergeron."

"I was never in the galley."

"What do you know about explosives?"

"Nothing."

"Really?"

"I know I should study up, but the need for them comes up so infrequently in accounting, and who has the time?"

Steele didn't have a sense of humor either. He smiled like the big, bad wolf. "We will go into every aspect of your life, every associate, every internet site you've ever visited, Mr. Bergeron."

There were a few that he'd rather the senior special agent not see, but nothing about bombs. "I'm sure, but why?"

"Excuse me?"

"Why would the FBI care about a boating accident?"

"You and I know that it was no accident, Bergeron."

"No, I don't know anything, Senior Special Agent Steele."

Steele was still a very handsome man, but he was going to give himself wrinkles if he didn't stop glowering.

"Why did you leave Girard-Hartmann?"

"Eric and I didn't get along."

"No? So he fired you? Be aware that my team is interviewing the staff as we speak."

He smiled at Steele. "It was one of those you-can't-fire-me-because-I-already-quit deals. We both agreed I should find another job."

"I doubt it was as amicable as that."

"I knew it was coming, Senior Special Agent Steele. After the first day. He was lazy and not too bright but also condescending. And he had a real cowboy attitude toward tax law."

"Are you saying he committed fraud in preparing his client's returns?"

"No idea."

Steele said, "And what can you tell me about Mr. Girard's other business dealings?"

"Nothing."

"Nothing? I find it impossible to believe that someone as bright as you wouldn't have been aware of what was going on at

Girard-Hartmann."

"I guess I'm not as bright as you think."

"You certainly aren't as bright as you think."

"'Sticks and stones will break my bones', Senior Special Agent Steele."

The red spots on Steele's cheeks came back. "Hartmann is going to tell me everything, Bergeron."

"And I should make a deal first? No thanks."

Steele looked at the intense young woman, who was sitting like a coiled spring with her hands locked together. "Is the wife here, Reed?"

Reed left the room without a word.

Steele said, "Out, Bergeron, but don't go anywhere. We'll see how cocky you are after Hartmann confesses."

He had to stand aside as Reed escorted Layla and Cindi Lou into Kurt's office. Layla smiled at him with her Botticelli face, but the effect was forever ruined for him.

Gabe sat with Neal and the Pale Wraith.

He smiled at Neal who smiled back. He tried smiling at the Wraith, but he had also taken a vow of glumness but managed to be hot anyway.

Sergeant King returned before Steele finished with Layla. He handed a folder over to the Pale Wraith.

King said, "The photos and my notes and some preliminary forensic material as requested by Senior Special Agent Steele."

The Pale Wraith nodded as he clutched the folder in his pale hands.

King turned and left with an actual smile on his face. Gabe believed that King winked at him..

Layla and Cindi Lou emerged apparently unbloodied.

Steele said, "I may need to speak to you again, Mrs. Girard."

Layla exited as Cindi Lou said, "We'll be at the motel for another day, Steele."

Steele said, "Thank you for your cooperation, Ms. Parker. Murray, I want to speak to Ms. Chandler-Hargreaves."

The Pale Wraith was Murray? He didn't look like a Murray.

Mia gave him the barest glance as she swept past in her white sarong decorated with turquoise and purple palm fronds. She was smiling at Steele, and he was certainly smiling back.

Steele said, "Thank you, Reed." And he closed the door.

Reed looked at Murray and rolled her eyes as she plopped into a chair, and the four of them waited.

They heard Mia's laugh and then Steel's laugh. Gabe winked at Murray. "That's some brutal interrogation, Special Agent." Murray blushed, and Reed glared. "What?"

Steele opened the door and escorted Mia out of the office. They were still smiling.

Mia patted Steele's manly chest. "So sorry that I couldn't be more of a help, Senior Special Agent."

"Not at all. Thank you for your cooperation, Ms. Chandler-Hargreaves. Will you be staying here long? In case, I should have more questions for you?"

Mia leaned against Steele as she stroked the knot of his tie. "A few more days, and I'll be available whenever you need me, Senior Special Agent."

Steele realized that Murray and Reed were staring at him and collected himself. "Thank you again."

Steele pointed at Neal again. "Mr. Hartmann. And you too, Reed." The door closed, but there wasn't any laughing this time.

His prepaid phone rang. Murray, the Pale Wraith, glowered menacingly, but didn't suck the life-force out of his body, so he answered.

"It is the weekend, Gabe."

"Max! Thank you for calling. I need you."

"Do you know what my weekend rates are?"

"This call has probably already burnt through my entire life savings, but this is serious."

Max snorted. "How serious?"

"629 serious."

The Pale Wraith focused a baleful gaze upon him; his eyes were very like Gollum's, but his blond hair was nicer.

Max said, "What the Hell does that mean?"

"It's a substitution code...numbers for letters. It's very simple, Max."

Max said, "FBI?"

Murray took a bit longer.

"Yes, Max. My friend, Neal Hartmann, and I need legal representation of the highest caliber, the very crème de la crème, the apotheosis of lawyers...."

Max said, "Flattery does not affect my fee, Bergeron. So cut the bullshit and tell me what's up."

Gabe looked over at the wraith and made shooing motions with his hand. "I need some privacy to consult with my attorney."

The Pale Wraith snorted in derision just as Steele opened the door and looked at him. "Let Bergeron go."

Hallelujah.

"What about Neal?"

Steele smiled. "He's staying with us for a while."

Max said, "Is that the FBI asshole?"

"That is correct, Mr. Nagy, Attorney at Law."

"What's his name?"

He smiled at Steele. "What's your full name, Senior Special Agent Steele?"

Steele smirked at him. "Rodney Alexander Steele IV."

Holy, entitled, old-money shit. "Of course, it is. Did you hear that Mr. Nagy?"

"Got it, Gabe. Tell Neal to keep his mouth shut."

"Neal? Your lawyer says to keep your mouth shut."

Neal said, "Okay, Gabe."

Steele pointed at him. "Get him out of here, Murray."

Murray shoved him out the door and into the warmth of the sun.

"Thanks, Max."

Max said, "So tell me what you and your friend have gotten yourselves into."

He told Max everything as he walked back and forth along the creek.

"Shit, Bergeron. You're probably okay, but this Neal is not so lucky."

"But you can get him out of this?"

"Out of blowing up this Eric or out of laundering money for

unsavory Polynesian types?"

"Both."

"Both could be tricky. Let me see what I can find out about Rodney Alexander Steele IV. I'll get back to you."

"You're a prince, Max."

"The hourly rate is still the same."

"Call me back soon. Tonight? Okay?"

"Okay, Bergeron."

King was also talking on his phone outside. "Yes, Lieutenant. I understand that, Sir. I'll call if there are any developments."

King pocketed his phone and looked at Stevens. "Which we will never hear about. See? You were scared about nothing."

"I wasn't scared; it was just a big case. But this isn't right, Charlie...."

"What did you expect?"

Stevens said, "That we might get to help a little?

Sergeant King said, "Never going to happen, Luke. Best we can hope for is that we aren't arrested ourselves for impeding a FBI investigation."

"Shit."

"Yes, Officer Stevens, but this is now federal shit." King looked over at him. "And I'm betting Mr. Bergeron could identify the precise kind of federal shit for us. If he wanted to?"

"I know nothing."

King smiled again. Getting kicked off the case seemed to have loosened him up. "King? Did you question Mia?"

"I did."

"And?"

"I can't discuss the case, Mr. Bergeron. Especially now that the feds are here."

Saturday
7:00 pm

How much longer was Steele going to question Neal? Gabe wandered some more.

Gareth's new buddy with the red baseball cap and bedazzled boots was heading toward him and looking even less pleasant up close.

"Bergeron!"

"That's me, Gabe Bergeron." He held out his hand. "What can I do for you?"

The guy stopped and adjusted his red cap, as he glared at all the unmarked sedans and SUVs surrounding the park office before finally noting the outstretched hand.

It was like shaking with a wet dishrag, and there was zero eye contact. "Randy."

Mr. Randy was about forty and heading down the pudgy trail, but still trying to look tough.

Randy continued to glare at the cars. "Shit. They state? Or feds? Not local."

He nodded. "FBI."

Randy shook his head. "Shit. This is you? The boat explosion?"

Randy was very curious if verb adverse. "They questioned me, but it's all just a misunderstanding."

Randy smiled at some clever remark the tree next to him made. "Always is. They leaving soon?"

"I don't know. I hope so."

Randy turned toward his dirty, silver Fedco RV.

"Randy? You know Gareth?"

Randy asked his tree pal. "The Brit?"

No, the other Gareth in the park. "Yeah. And Mia?"

Randy took off his sweat-stained cap again at the mention of Mia's name; his black hair needed a close encounter with some shampoo. He just shook his head.

Randy kept walking with his chain swinging. It looked like it was attached to his wallet. Was that a biker thing? But Randy had no tattoos on his skinny arms?

Randy unlocked the RV door, but did a one eighty sweep of the terrain before opening it. Ole Randy gave him one last nasty look before slamming the door.

Gabe Bergeron hadn't made a new buddy, but he was okay with that. The RV had Florida tags, but Randy wasn't a native of Florida. He couldn't place the accent.

He wandered some more; he should invest in some hiking boots. There was a party at the picnic pavilion, which was just a concrete pad with a roof and picnic tables, but someone had decorated it with pink streamers and balloons.

Gabe saw the "Happy Birthday" signs and then spotted Heather.

She had shed her jeans, work smock, and name tag for a nice, dark pink dress. A little girl of five or so was hanging onto her hand.

Heather spotted him and waved him over.

Heather said, "No, darling. We cut the cake after you open your presents."

"But when, Grandmom?"

"Soon. Zeke! Get over here. Take Samantha for a walk."

Zeke had his hair slicked back. He was dressed in dark pants and a white shirt and looked like a Mormon or a mortician. "Where, Momma?"

"I don't know."

Gabe suggested, "The observation tower?"

Zeke nodded at him and grabbed Samantha's hand. "Come on, Baby Girl. We're going for an adventure."

Samantha looked doubtful but went along.

Heather said, "Don't let her get dirty, Zeke!"

Zeke smiled at his mother, grabbed Samantha up in his arms, and spun her round until she squealed with joy.

Heather said, "Stop that! You'll make her sick." Zeke laughed and ran off.

Heather waved at the birthday party paraphernalia including the cake with a candle in the shape of the numeral "5"

"I don't know why I agreed to do this, Gabe. I must have been drunk."

"Her fifth?"

"Yes. Think she'll remember it when she's old?"

"I remember mine." It was one of the few good memories with his mother. "And it was wonderful."

Heather smiled at him. "Thanks for saying that, Gabe. Where is that daughter-in-law of mine?"

"She isn't helping with the party?"

Heather snorted. "Think we have enough balloons?"

"Plenty." He wasn't about to be drafted as a balloon blower-upper.

An auburn-haired lady was shoving sodas into a tub of ice. She said, "You can never have too many balloons."

Heather said, "That's Donna, my cousin. This is Gabe Bergeron, Donna."

Donna was younger and tinier than Heather. She wiped her hand on her apron, but it was still cold and clammy. "Sorry, about your friend. Terrible thing."

"Thanks. And yes it was." Eric wasn't his friend, but he was dead.

Donna said, "Have they found the wife?"

"She just turned up as a matter of fact."

"She did?"

Which made it sound like she had just bobbed to the surface. "No, no, she's fine. Not a scratch on her."

Heather and Donna exchanged a look. Heather said, "Well, that's good."

Donna said, "Where's she been all this time?"

Gabe had to smile at Donna. "With her lawyer."

Another look was exchanged. Layla had already been tried,

convicted, and sentenced in the court of Crisfield public opinion.

And then he spied Jace and the pretty Asian girl walking hand in hand toward the pavilion.

Heather and Donna followed his gaze. Donna giggled and went back to setting out food.

Heather said, "My Lord."

He said, "And that would be Chloe."

Heather turned. "You don't miss much, do you Gabe?"

"Scads of stuff. I'm virtually blind. And deaf. I feel obliged to ask the location of Jessica, and if she might possibly be armed?" He knew she was dangerous.

Heather shook her head. "Jace!"

There was a guy called Stentor, who lived a long time ago, a Homer and the Trojan War long time ago, and who was reputed to have a voice that could be heard for miles. Stentor had nothing on our Heather.

Jace broke into a canter. "Yes, Momma?"

Heather said, "Jace, didn't we have a little talk at lunch?"

Jace's recall didn't stretch back that far. Chloe was smiling at Heather.

"You told me not to forget Sammie's party?"

Heather shook her head and grabbed his arm. "Chloe, talk to Gabe for a second sweetheart. Or blow up some more balloons for me."

Chloe just kept smiling as Jace was dragged away.

He smiled. "Nice party. I'm Gabe."

She nodded and kept smiling, perfectly comfortable standing mute next to the strange man. She held a present in delicate, sculpted hands; she fluffed the cascades of pink ribbon and smiled on.

Gabe was about to abandon her and Heather when Zeke came back with Samantha.

Zeke was a forthright young man. "Jesus, Chloe, what the Hell are you doing here? Jessica will shit a brick if she catches you with Jace. And where is Jace?"

Chloe just kept smiling.

"Ah, he went with Heather. That-a-way." Gabe directed Zeke's attention to the dock where Heather was having a reasoned discussion with her younger son.

"I'm going to put my foot so far up his ass he will taste shoe polish."

Zeke's dress shoes had recently been buffed to a mirror brightness.

Samantha put a hand over her mouth. "You said two bad words, Daddy."

"Yes, I did, Baby Girl, and Daddy is very sorry." Zeke looked over at him. "Who the Hell are you again?"

Heather was dragging Jace back to the pavilion. "Gabe Bergeron: an innocent bystander present at a moment of high drama."

He probably should have walked away, but it was kind of fascinating in a traffic accident kind of way.

Jace hugged his niece. "Happy, happy birthday, Sammie. Here."

Chloe handed over the present, and Jace presented it. Sammie hugged her uncle, and Jace picked her up and spun her around just as Zeke had done. And then Jace hugged Heather.

Zeke said, "Jessica better not show up."

Jace shook his head and hugged Zeke who shoved him away. "Be happy, Big Brother. Be happy for your beautiful girl."

And he and Chloe floated away like birthday balloons set free.

Zeke said, "If Sammie wasn't here, I'd...."

Heather said, "You wouldn't touch a hair on your baby brother's head."

Zeke said, "But Momma...."

"I know, but he swears that Jessica is fine with him and Chloe. He said she has somebody new."

Zeke oozed doubt, disbelief, and incredulity. "Who'd be stupid enough to get hung up with her? Besides my brother?"

Heather said, "He wouldn't lie to me, Zeke. Anyway, isn't it about time for Samantha to open her presents?"

Samantha was sure that it was.

While Zeke was helping Samantha with that, he leaned closer to Heather. "Does Chloe speak?"

Heather said, "Not all that much."

"Is she as spacey as..."

"My darling son?"

"I was going to say 'as she seems' though...." He smiled at Heather. "I should get back."

Ranger Sarah was heading toward them. "Hi, Heather. Need anything else? Or some help?"

Heather surveyed the scene. "Thanks, Hon, but you've done enough already. Unlike a certain daughter-in-law I could mention. I think we're about set."

Heather pointed at the tub full of ice and brown bottles and soda cans. "Want a beer?" Sarah nodded and received an ice cold beer. "Gabe?"

"Thanks, but no."

Heather looked at him. "I've got plenty of soft drinks?"

"A coke would be very nice." He took a long sip. "Thanks."

Sarah said, "You don't drink?"

"Only on very special occasions. I have zero tolerance for alcohol."

Heather was looking at all the dark cars and dark suits swirling around the park office like a fed-nado. "Is Neal in trouble with the feds, Gabe?"

Gabe shook his head, but Heather was no dummy. "Let's just say that we have retained legal representation."

"Sorry to hear that. Did he...."

"Blow up Eric? No, he did not."

Jerry, Heather's husband, came up, fished a beer from the tub, and chugged half of it. He was wearing a white, dress shirt and a nice tie, but the collar was doing a constrictor number on his throat.

Jerry looked over. "The FBI wouldn't come all this way for just a murder?"

Heather said, "Don't pay any attention to him, Gabe."

"No, he's right, but that doesn't mean that my friend is guilty of anything. Or that I am."

"Didn't say you were, Gabe." Jerry smiled as he tugged at his collar. "But where there's smoke..."

"...there's fire? Not in this case. Although, there was actual smoke and actual fire."

Jerry had shifted his attention to Sarah. "How would I get in touch with your Justin?"

Who was Justin?

Heather said, "Are you sure about this, Jerry?"

Jerry said, "Damn sure! Zeke is going to have a lawyer."

Sarah pulled out her phone. "Here's the office number, Jerry, but I'm not sure Justin handles DNR cases?"

Heather said, "And how much is he likely to charge?"

Sarah shook her head. "I don't know, Heather, but he'll tell you at the consultation."

Jerry shook his head and grabbed another beer. "I'm calling him first thing Monday, Heather. I don't know what else to do."

He said, "So what happened, Jerry? Why did King give Zeke the citation?"

Jerry gave him a nasty look but turnabout was fair play.

Heather said, "Zeke says it wasn't his fault; he was rushing to get in before the weather turned bad, and I believe him." She smiled. "But then I'm his mother. Anyway, he got five points to add to five he got last year."

"And ten points is enough for a suspension? But what did he do?"

Jerry said, "None of your business." Heather gave Jerry a look. "What? It's not."

She said, "Why don't you give Sammie our present."

Her husband nodded. "All right. And I'm not talking to him anyway."

Jerry stomped off as Sergeant King marched over, but Heather remained rooted to the spot.

King nodded and touched his cap like Gary Cooper in *High Noon*. Aunt Flo loved his movies.

"Heather. Your granddaughter?"

"That's right, King."

"Sorry to intrude, but Gabe, you might want to get back to the office."

Shit. "What's up?"

"I think that Senior Special Agent Steele is going to take Mr. Hartmann away for further questioning."

"Shit! Thanks, Charlie."

"Don't call me Charlie."

"You called me Gabe?"

"I guess I did. It's been a long day."

Heather said, "You look worn out, Charlie."

"But you're looking good." He smiled at her. "It's been an interesting twenty-four hours."

"I'll bet. Want a beer?"

"Why not? But how is Jerry going to take that?"

"I bought this beer, and if I want to give my first husband a beer then I will."

King smiled at her. "All right then."

She let him take a sip. "Can't you help Zeke?"

"Jerry seems to think I targeted Zeke, but that isn't the case, Heather. I hope you know that?" King looked at him. "And why are you still here, Mr. Bergeron."

"Sorry. I'm already gone."

Sarah said, "Come along, Bergeron."

But as they walked away, Charlie said, "I recommended a five day suspension, Heather."

Sarah said, "Keep moving, Bergeron."

"Ma'am, yes, Ma'am. So what did Zeke do?"

Sarah couldn't figure out whether she wanted to roll her eyes or smile. "I did not ask, but a commercial fisherman can get points for having too many undersized crabs, for having too many female crabs, for having too many crabpots or non-regulation crabpots, for fishing restricted areas...."

Sarah stopped as they watched Neal being hauled out of the ranger office.

"Hey! What's going on?"

Murray, the Pale Wraith, was pushing Neal into the back seat of one of the black sedans. "He's being held for further questioning, Mr. Bergeron."

"Where are you taking him?" Murray was loathe to give aid and comfort to the enemy. "Come on, Murray. I need to call his lawyer."

"The Philadelphia office, Sir."

Neal was still holding it together. "Neal, I'll let Max know. And I'll be right behind you. I have to get the car. Okay?"

Neal nodded. "Ellie won't know what happened to me, Gabe."

"I'll find her and let her know."

"Thanks, Gabe."

And the Pale Wraith slammed the door of his black, funereal vehicle and drove off.

He had no idea where the Philly FBI office was, but he'd find it. First, he had to get his car. And he had to call Max.

Max answered. "What now, Bergeron? I am about to get frisky with a gorgeous brunette."

"Eww. I didn't need that mental picture, Nagy." Max was a hairy gnome. "I hope that's Stephanie?"

Max said, "Of course it is!" Stephanie was his wife and far lovelier than her spouse. "What do you want?"

"Steele's taking Neal away to the Philadelphia FBI office."

"Is he under arrest?"

"The Pale Wraith said he was being held for further questioning."

"I'm going to assume that the Pale Wraith is your cutesy name for a FBI agent. Calm down, Bergeron. I'll get somebody there. Or I'll go myself."

"That would be great, Max."

"After all, I am the crème de la crème."

"You are. Absolutely. Thanks, Max."

And Gabe set out on the forest path that led to the cabin. The sun was low in the sky now, and the horizontal rays were slashing through the trees.

He was doing a jog-walk, trying not to trip over forest stuff, when he heard a noise to his left.

A dark, back-lit shape came from behind a tree and hit him.

And Gabe Bergeron went down hard.

He tried to yell for help, but he wasn't sure he actually made a sound before somebody jumped on his back and looped a cord around his throat.

The cord was cutting into his throat, cutting off his oxygen.

A voice said, "Where is it? The bleeding ledger?"

The cord slackened just a little bit.

He croaked, "I don't know. Gareth?"

The cord was yanked taut again. He tried to get his fingers under it and pull it away, but it was too tight.

He was going to pass out, and then he was going to die.

The voice said, "Last chance, Wanker. Where is it?"

When the cord loosened this time, he yelled for help and got two fingers between it and his throat before the guy slammed a knee in his back and really started pulling.

He tried clawing at the guy's hands, but he felt like he was falling now.

And then he was on his back looking up at the canopy of tall trees swaying gently.

The cord was still around his throat. Somebody was beside him. He threw a punch, but he missed, and the guy laughed at him.

Kurt was looking down at him, and just behind him, Sergeant King, was surveying the scene with his gun drawn.

"Did you see him, Hobbs?"

"Just a shape. He ran west toward the creek. The sun blinded me. He was fast...but maybe not too big."

King knelt down and pulled out a handkerchief which he used it to finish unwrapping the cord. "You touch this, Hobbs?"

Kurt said, "Had to. He was choking."

King was staring at him, shaking his head. "Amazing."

Gabe had been trying to speak, but all he could do was croak at first. "I was walking along in a state park overrun with police and FBI, minding my own business, when I was brutally attacked, and you say, 'Amazing'? What the Hell?'"

King smiled. "Nine lives. Are you hurt anywhere else, Bergeron?"

"My head." He touched the back of his head and came away with bloody fingers. "Shit. The bastard hit me with something."

Kurt pointed at a branch, a log really. "He probably used that. I touched that too, Sergeant, as I was turning him over."

King nodded. "You feel like getting up, Gabe?"

He thought so until he tried it.

Kurt got him vertical. "I'll take him to the ER."

Gabe said, "I'm fine. I have to follow the FBI to Philadelphia." But he was swaying like a hula dance.

King said, "Did you see anything, Gabe? Anything useful at all?"

Gabe shook his head, which he realized was a mistake when a pain shot to the top of his head. "Ow! No. He came from behind me. I just saw him out of the corner of my eye before he hit me. He might have had a hood? Or a mask?"

"Did he say anything? Did you recognize his voice?"

He had thought it might be Gareth, but he wasn't so sure now, and he couldn't mention the ledger, and his head really hurt. "No."

King said, "Take him to the ER. I'll let Steele know what happened."

Kurt pulled up to the ER and walked him in. Nurse Sharon looked at him. "A repeat customer. What is it this time, Mr. Bergeron?"

Kurt said, "He got hit on the head with a branch and throttled with a clothesline cord."

Sharon looked them both over. "I see, and who are you?" She was smiling at handsome Kurt.

Kurt flashed the pearly whites at her; his were almost as bright as Kev's, plus they looked real. "I'm Ranger Kurt Hobbs from Janes Island. Sergeant King, or other police officers, are probably on the way."

Sharon flashed a light in his eyes and checked out the back of his head. "Any trouble breathing or swallowing, Mr. Bergeron?"

"No. I'm fine." It still felt like he was being choked; he had to keep touching his throat to be sure the cord was gone. And his head was throbbing, but he didn't want Nurse Sharon to know how bad his head hurt.

"Let me get Dr. Hahn."

Dr. Hahn had on cranberry scrubs this time. He checked him over. "What did he use?"

Gabe said, "Clothesline cord."

"You're very lucky to be alive. Just a little more pressure

and...." He snapped his fingers.

Sharon was cleaning the wound on the back of his head. "Stitches, Doctor?"

Dr. Hahn nodded and then looked at him. "I don't suppose you know if you've had a tetanus shot recently?"

"Why yes, Dr. Hahn, I had one yesterday. In this very ER."

Dr. Hahn stepped back and looked him over; he spotted the cuts on his legs. "Ah, *Balanus eburneus.*"

"No, Gabus Bergeroneus."

Dr. Hahn smiled at him. But when he'd finished with the stitches, he said, "You could have a concussion. You have to stay overnight."

"No."

Dr. Hahn blinked. "No?"

"No, get those AMA forms ready, Doc."

Dr. Hahn felt his head with both hands. "You do have a very thick skull, but I still advise you to stay."

"Me and my thick skull are leaving."

Dr. Hahn looked at Kurt. "He shouldn't be alone."

Kurt said, "I'll see that he isn't, Doctor."

"Excellent." And Dr. Hahn exited stage left.

Nurse Sharon was bandaging his head when Charlie pulled up. "How's the patient, Sharon?"

She smiled at Charlie. "Not willing to stay here overnight like he should."

Charlie shook his head as he pulled out his little notebook. "Not surprised. Gabe, you know you could have a concussion?"

"I'm fine. Really. Did you catch anybody?"

"From the description you and Hobbs gave me?"

"Right. Sorry about that." He had been thinking about it, and was almost certain it hadn't been Gareth; the accent had been way off.

Charlie said, "Is there something you didn't tell me?"

"Nope. So you and Heather were married?"

Sharon smiled.

Charlie said, "We were." Charlie shook his head. "If you're not telling me something, Bergeron?"

"Nope. So what happened? Do you have any kids."

Charlie folded his notebook and was walking out when Special Agent Chernov rolled up in his FBI-mobile.

Chernov said, "I got this, King."

"Sure this is part of your case, Special Agent?"

Chernov said, "It is until we say it isn't, Sergeant."

Charlie was never going to be a fan of Special Agent Chernov. He nodded as he exited. "If you say so."

Chernov wheeled and faced him; the dark eyes boring in as the rest of him exuded a virility as potent as his cologne. "And who would assault you, Mr. Bergeron?"

"I have no idea. Everyone loves me."

The Anarchist smirked and went for the obvious. "Not everyone. And you didn't see anything at all?"

"Have you ever been Ninja-ed in the woods with a log?"

Chernov said, "No, Sir. I learned how to defend myself, Sir, at a very young age."

So Gabe Bergeron was a blockhead and a wuss? He wasn't even sure he could disagree with either.

Gabe had taken a self-defense class a couple of years ago. It had not gone well even though he had really tried. He kept getting thrown around like he was the class teddy bear.

Bill, his instructor, had passed through all the stages of teaching. Enthusiasm and encouragement had lasted a long time because Bill was a good guy. Irritation and discouragement had lasted long enough for Bill to try hoisting him high into the air before slamming him into the mat to see if maybe self-preservation would kick in; it hadn't. Resignation and defeat were sad to see. He had felt like hugging Bill and claiming some kind of genetic deficiency.

But now he could name all the moves that someone might use against him, but stopping them...not so much. No inner warrior. Or a very-slow-to-react inner warrior which was about the same thing. Of course, Bill had never hit him with a log.

Chernov said, "You might want to cooperate, Bergeron."

"I am. I didn't see his face."

Chernov shook his head. "How is this connected to the bombing?"

"I really don't know."

Chernov knew he was holding back, but what could he do? The special agent was just as pissed with Kurt's answers.

Sharon had finished bandaging his head, which was killing him, and he wanted to find Neal.

"Chernov, am I under arrest?" The special agent's cologne was making him sick.

"No, Sir."

"Then go away. Kurt, will you drive me back to the park so I can get my car."

Kurt said, "My government vehicle is totally at your disposal."

"Right. Bye Sharon."

Sharon smiled. "Don't come back, Gabe."

"Do my very best."

They walked out of the ER to face a western sky with massed clouds, purple and red, and a golden sun sinking into the black tree blobs on Janes Island.

Chernov was leaning, muscles rampant, against his car, which was blocking Kurt's truck. "What? For the love of God, what?"

"I need to know where you'll be, Sir, in case Steele has more questions."

He scrunched his eyes shut. "I will be driving to Philadelphia, Special Agent Chernov."

Chernov was shaking his head. "You might want to rethink that, Bergeron."

Kurt said, "Look at you. You can hardly stand up, Gabe. And I promised Hahn I'd keep an eye on you." He looked at Chernov. "He'll be at my house in the park."

He was fine, but his eyes didn't seem to want to work in tandem anymore. "Okay. I guess. I'm sorry for yelling at you, Chernov. It's been a bitch of a weekend."

Chernov smiled. "It isn't over yet, Bergeron."

He looked at Kurt. "Who writes his material?"

And then he almost fell down, but Kurt caught him.

Saturday
8:00 pm

Ellie had popped into Gabe's head on the way back to the park. Kurt was kind enough to go with him to the cabin. The door was wide open.

Chairs had been tossed around, and the mattresses dumped on the floor. The contents of the refrigerator and of every cabinet had been tossed, smeared, or splashed onto the floor.

Neal's clothes had been scattered, but Ellie's bras and panties had been hung around the cabin like garland in a perv's idea of Christmas.

They went outside and searched around the cabin. He went to the dock; Kurt was behind him. "How deep is it?"

Kurt said, "Deep enough."

How was he going to tell Neal this? They went back to the cabin.

Kurt was pissed. "Bergeron, things like this don't happen in my park."

"Well, I didn't do it. Did they kick in the door?"

"No. Did Neal leave it unlocked?"

"No, and he's anal about that sort of stuff. He locked it and then checked it when we left with Kev and Barb. Where the Hell is Ellie? You don't think she was here?"

Kurt shook his head. "No. We have no reason to think that."

He righted the chairs and sat at the kitchen table hoping Kurt was right. Ellie's peppermint tea was scattered across the sink. She was just off somewhere looking for the right kind of coffee; Guatemalan or Brazilian. Or something.

She wasn't his favorite person in the world, but still.

"I don't even have a number to call her."

Kurt said, "Her number will be on the cabin rental form."

"Yeah?"

"Should be."

Sarah was at the ranger office. Kurt smiled at her. "You're here late?"

"I heard about him. I wanted to see if he was...if we needed to fill out an accident report." She was checking him over. "You look worse than ever, Bergeron."

"Thanks for that, Sarah, but it was no accident. Some villain smacked me with a log."

Kurt winked at her. "It was a branch; more of a twig."

She reached out to touch his throat. "Does that hurt, Gabe?"

"A little." He gave up on the macho. "I will pay you ten dollars for a single aspirin, Tylenol, acetaminophen, or ibuprofen."

She really smiled. "Coming up."

Kurt sat behind his desk, and tapped on the computer keyboard. "Let me pull up Ellie's form."

Sarah said, "What are you looking for?"

"The cabin has been trashed. Looking for a number to call to see if Ellie Tyson is okay."

"She is. Or at least she's with the FBI, if that counts? I saw her get in a car with Steele and drive off."

"When was this?"

"Around seven. Before you got clobbered, Gabe."

He let out a breath. "Good. I don't have to call Neal. Or at least not about that."

So why did Ellie get transported by Senior Special Agent Steele himself? She was either FBI or a villain; of course, it was possible she was both.

Sarah brought him a bottle of acetaminophen. "Bless you. You are a vision in green khaki and black leather. A veritable green goddess. So who is Justin? A boyfriend?"

She said, "I will take back the pills."

Kurt said, "Justin Gray, lawyer. Drives a Porsche."

"Really?" He downed three tablets without water.

"Compensating much?"

She glared at him. "Shut up, Bergeron. Didn't the doctor want you to stay in the hospital?"

Kurt said, "He did."

"And you left anyway? Typical."

Kurt said, "I'm going to watch him. To make sure he doesn't die on us."

"Good idea. The paperwork would be awful. Good night."

And Gabe sat very quietly in a comfy chair and waited for the acetaminophen to kick in just a little.

Kurt was doing something on his computer.

Gabe was also getting more pissed with each passing second; people were trying to blow him up and choke him to death.

Kurt said, "Sleepy?"

"Nope. Got any coffee?"

"I can make some?"

"Please. Sorry to be such a pain."

Kurt smiled. "I can honestly say I have never had a park visitor like you."

"My life isn't usually like this. Believe it or not?"

"No?"

"No, of course it's not. I'm not a criminal. I'm a freaking accountant; paper cuts are the big hazard in my line of work. That and boredom. It's an endless repetition of tasks; daily, weekly, monthly, quarterly, and yearly. Like the freaking Mayan calendar with its cycles of kins, uinals, tuns, katuns, baktuns, cycles of thirteen and twenty days, and Venus cycles, all stretching from the unbounded past into the infinite, but deadly dull future."

"That sounds boring, Gabe, and I barely understood a word."

"It is."

Kurt went to make coffee, leaving his computer on. Gabe wanted to think that it had been deliberate. He checked out every camper and jotted down addresses and numbers for Miss Mia Chandler-Hargreaves and anyone else he could think of.

The three blond kids were Dutch students from Eindhoven in the Netherlands; Bastiaan Kuiper, Aafje Kuiper, and Ruurd Oosting. Wendy and Bob were from Atlanta.

He checked out Mimi, Floria, and Manon; Mimi was Mrs. Campbell, as he knew, Floria was Mrs. Berg, and Manon was Mrs. Stevenson. They were all happy residents of Miami, or so they had reported.

Mr. James English was from Salisbury, Maryland. Kev and Barb claimed to be from Pennsylvania.

There were dozens of other campers, but he couldn't assign faces to the names; they were from all over. They all seemed legit; every single one was a fine, upstanding citizen. Or so it appeared.

He and Kurt were drinking their coffee when a knock came on the door. It was Mimi, backed up by Floria and Manon.

They were flustered, but Mimi said, "There's an animal in our cabin!"

"Can you describe it, Mrs. Campbell?"

If a camel is a horse designed by a committee, then this creature was not of this Earth; hopefully. The sole area of agreement among the sisters was that it had rows of teeth like a velociraptor and had hissed at them.

Kurt nodded. "I'll come and take a look, Ladies. Give me just a second."

Kurt looked at him. "I'm fine. Go."

Kurt got a pole with a loop on the end and a cage that looked small for a velociraptor and marched away; poor Kurt.

Gabe knew he should sit still and let his head stop pounding, but he was tired of being on the receiving end of shit. He wanted to know what was happening, and he didn't trust the FBI to find out.

He took another acetaminophen and sallied forth. The Dutch kids and Chuck had set up ramps in the parking lot under the lights. He watched as Chuck hurtled himself and his skateboard into the air trying to jump over an upended trash can.

The landing was less than perfect, and Chuck slammed into the blacktop and rolled, but the guy just laughed as he picked himself up.

Gabe Bergeron marched up to Mia's RV and rapped smartly on the door.

Gareth opened it glaring.

And then Gareth smiled for the first time.

The glare was preferable as it disguised the shortcomings of Gareth's dental history. He turned and said, "It's the wanker, Mia."

Her voice floated from within. "Which wanker, Gareth? You do call everyone that."

"Bergeron."

"Really? Well, invite him in, Gareth."

Said the spider to the fly.

Gareth smirked and waved him in as if his Gulfstream was Buckingham freaking Palace, and he was Queen Mia's footman.

There was a small kitchen and a table with banquette seating and a lumpy sofa. It was all clean but worn.

"Sorry, your billy got nicked." Gareth smirked again.

"No, you aren't." He thought the tattooed bastard was talking about Neal.

Mia came out of the bedroom which had a regular sized double bed. "Don't be cross with Gareth." She got a look at his throat and the bandage around his head. "Oh my. Do sit down, Gabe. You don't look like you should be visiting. Does he Gareth?"

He plopped down on the lumpy sofa with gratitude.

Gareth was six inches away, staring at his throat. "Howay, man! Aabut put paid to yer, 'e did."

"Yeah. Was it you?"

Gareth grabbed his t-shirt and hauled him back to his feet; he toyed with the idea of popping Gareth in the face.

"Nowt to do with us, yer bleeding, clarty Wanker."

Mia said, "Stop. Gareth. Let go of Gabe."

Gareth shook him a little and then released him.

Mia said, "I can assure you that Gareth had nothing to do with attacking you. He was with me." She smiled. "And you can trust me, Gabe."

He wanted to stay on his feet facing Gareth, but his legs had other ideas. "I actually don't think it was Gareth, not that I trust either one of you, but someone wanted me to think it was."

Gareth said, "Bollocks!"

Mia said, "Please explain, Gabe."

He leaned back into the sofa; he closed his eyes and tried to focus.

"Are you all right, Gabe?"

"Yeah. The guy who choked me said, 'Last chance, Wanker.' And he also said 'bleeding.' Now how many people in the park say 'bleeding' and 'wanker' in every other sentence?"

Gareth looked at Mia, who was focused on him and him alone. "Nivvor did, Mia! You said to do nowt with the bleeding FBI round..."

Mia relaxed her lovely face and held out a hand. Gareth took it and sat beside her. If he had been smaller, he would have climbed into her lap. How old was he?

Mia said, "I see. And obviously you didn't share this with the FBI. I wonder why? I'm quite sure I would have, if the positions were reversed."

"I didn't because I'm fairly sure it wasn't Gareth's voice, and the accent was off."

Gareth's face had a look of child-like innocence.

"Now, who wants to put the blame on you, Mia?"

Of course, it wasn't impossible that Gareth was a master of accents and fiendish misdirection, but he really doubted it.

She looked well and truly vexed.

"Mia?"

"I'm sure I don't know."

"I'm sure you have a very good idea."

Gareth said, "Nowt an' all. Yer gannin' micey."

She smiled and squeezed Gareth's hand. "Do be quiet, Gareth. Is that all he said, Gabe?"

"That's it."

Mia said, "Really, Snuggums? I don't think that's quite true."

"What else do you think he said?"

She stopped smiling. "I think he demanded a certain item from you."

"I don't know what you could possibly be referring to, Ms. Chandler-Hargreaves."

Mia said, "I see. Well, Gareth and I are on holiday. We had nothing to do with Eric's tragic accident or with the attack on you."

"I'd like to believe the second half of that. But I think we can stop calling what happened to Eric an accident, don't you? The FBI would hardly be here."

She smiled. "Steele is a very handsome man."

"And did you tell Senior Special Agent Steele that you lured Eric off the boat?"

Gareth scowl returned redoubled.

Mia laughed. "I don't lure gentlemen, Gabe. They sometimes pursue me. Eric certainly did."

"But he was here with you?"

She glanced at Gareth. "Well, Eric may have come to visit with me for a little jouissance, which would mean that his little boat was completely unattended in the interval."

She smiled. "But I didn't plant any bomb or cause any bomb to be planted during that time, Snuggums."

"You didn't go on board? The FBI is very good at finding fingerprints."

"None of mine, Snuggums, are on that accursed boat. I am guilty of nothing more serious than poor judgment. Dear Eric was such a disappointment. In every way."

"But you are one of Eric's special clients? And you're here because you knew the FBI was circling Eric? You certainly aren't campers."

"Gareth is." She patted his hand. "And we truly are not clients of Eric's, but I will say that we came here to explore a possible business arrangement, which I quickly realized was impossible."

He looked at Gareth, "And you didn't go on board?"

Gareth looked confused, but Mia said. "No he didn't."

"How did you know Eric would be here?"

"He telephoned. Several times."

One of which Layla overheard. "So you ran out and rented or bought this rattrap of a RV and drove here, heart all aflutter?"

"Don't be unpleasant, Snuggums."

Gareth said, "Cost a canny wad. The coach. A love it, me. Yer cakky, ill-fard bastard."

Gabe thought Gareth had said nice things about the RV and bad things about him. "Right." He looked back to Mia. "If you know who killed Eric, it might be in your best interest to share."

Mia said, "But I don't. We don't. But we could still cooperate on resolving any problems Neal might have with the FBI?"

"I think you have more problems than we do."

She smiled. "But I'm not the one in FBI custody, Snuggums."

Which was absolutely true. "But the bastard who clobbered me knows who you are, and you don't know who he is? That isn't so good for you."

Mia and Gareth said nothing.

He managed to get to his feet.

Mia followed him out and shut the door so Gareth couldn't follow.

"Gabe, if you or Neal should come across any items of Eric's...."

"Like what?"

She waved a hand. "Business records, Snuggums."

"If you aren't a client, why would you want these business records?"

She just smiled. "It's nothing to do with me personally, Snuggums, but if you were to hand them over, there would be a reward."

"What kind of reward?"

She rubbed up against him. "Any kind you fancy. And you don't need the records, do you? It isn't as if you're in custody or were involved in Eric's little contretemps. You left Girard-Hartmann at just the right moment."

"Did you make an offer to Eric?"

She laughed. "Eric was as thick as two short planks. He was handsome, but sex with him was so adolescent. The ninny seemed to think he need only get an erection, and his job was done. I require a little more than that." She kept smiling at him. "I could send Gareth away, and we could go in the RV? You wouldn't be adolescent in bed, would you, Gabe?"

He may have cringed and shuddered and stepped back but he said, "As tempting as the offer is...."

Her smile dimmed a bit. "As I thought. Or I would pay handsomely."

"I'll keep that in mind."

Gabe wandered away from Gareth's RV trying not to fall

down. He saw Wendy, who was hiking the green lawn that bordered the creek. She waved but didn't slow down.

The blond kids had stopped trying to smash their brains on the parking lot blacktop. One of the Dutch boys, Ruurd, was doing a handstand on a pier. He jumped down to the dock and pointed at Chuck and then at the pier.

Chuck laughed, but then Aafje was looking at him, and the unmet challenge wasn't so funny.

Chuck looked at the dark water and shook his head. He whirled around and then spotted the four-story tall observation tower next to the park store. He ran up the spiral staircase all the way to the top.

Chuck tried a handstand on the rail. He laughed as he wobbled back and forth until he locked it in. His cap with the red Chinese characters fluttered to the ground.

Chuck yelled, "Come on, Ruurd! Get up here! Does my good pal, Ruurd, have no balls? Bastiaan? How about you? Bunch of pussies."

Aafje said, "Come down, Chuck. You fall."

Chuck laughed as his arms started to shake.

Gabe joined the Dutch kids. "Chuck! You're going to kill yourself." He was high on something, or he was just crazy.

Chuck got down from the railing. "Hey, Dude. How's it going." He shook his head. "What a rush."

He ran down the spiral staircase and retrieved his cap. "They towed her away." He pointed at the dock. "The yacht."

"Right. To the marina."

"Think she can be fixed up?"

"Maybe. But how much would it cost?"

Chuck nodded sagely. "Yeah, that's true, Dude."

Aafje walked over. She put a hand on Chuck's bony shoulder. "We ride to town?"

"Yeah. Okay." The kid looked at him. "This is Aafje, and I'm Chuck."

Gabe held out his hand and said, "I remember, Chuck. Nice to meet you both. I'm Gabe Bergeron."

Chuck had a real grip. "Yeah, we know."

Aafje shook his hand too. "I am Aafje Kuiper." She turned and waved to the Dutch boys.

They trotted over. The one who looked like a brother to Aafje held out his hand. "I am Bastiaan Kuiper, and this is Ruurd Oosting. He doesn't have much English."

Ruurd was the one with the curly hair. He smiled and nodded and said something in Dutch. Bastiaan said, "He says that he's sorry about your friend. On the boat."

Aafje said, "Yes, we all are."

"Thank you. Are you students here in the U.S.?"

Bastiaan said, "Aafje and I. In the autumn. We ride around now." He looked at his sister. "We ride in town?"

She said, "Yes. Chuck comes?"

Chuck nodded. "Yeah. In a bit. Be right behind you guys." The Dutch boys took off, but Aafje stayed put. "Go with them, Girl. I'll catch up to you."

"Yes?"

"For sure." He smiled at her and smacked her bottom as she turned to go. The boys came back with the bikes, and they all waited for Chuck.

Gabe thought he could just make it to Kurt's place if he paced himself.

Chuck said, "Are you okay, Dude? Need some help?"

"It's been a rough day, Chuck."

"Yeah. I get that. Sorry the cops took your friend away. Neal's an okay guy. He didn't kill that Eric guy, the dude on the boat. No way."

"You know Neal?"

"We went fishing a few days ago. Freaking FBI thinks everybody's a terrorist now."

"Neal wouldn't hurt a fly."

"That's right, Dude. He's no pyro."

Just what did an arsonist look like and how many of them had Chuck ever seen?

The kid looked at him like he knew what was going through his mind. "I can spot a bad guy. Or a troublemaker."

Maybe he could.

Chuck said, "So did the FBI dudes arrest him?"

He shook his head which made the headache worse. "I don't think so. He has a good lawyer now."

"So he might get out? Hope so. Take it easy, Dude."

And Chuck ran off toward the Dutch kids who were still waiting for him.

Saturday
9:00 pm

A boat was coming up the creek from Crisfield. Weren't boats supposed to have lights?

Gabe had turned to head back to Kurt's when a voice said, "Mr. Gabe?"

It was more hissed than spoken, and it was coming from the little boat. It was Lonnie aka Weasel visible now in the dock lights.

Lonnie cut the motor and pulled the skiff close to the dock. "Get in."

"Not happening."

Lonnie was nonplussed that he wasn't eager to jump on board. "Why not? We have business."

"And what would that be? Exactly?"

Lonnie smiled, sharing all of his ocher teeth. "I saw things, Mr. Gabe."

"Well, I saw you too hanging around Eric's boat at the marina."

Lonnie said, "So? It's a free country. Ain't it? I just thought he might need some help...running the boat and all. From someone who knows the area."

"Very commendable. What do you want, Lonnie? Did you really see something?"

Mr. Weasel smiled again which wasn't as reassuring as he thought it was. "Get in the boat. I don't bite, and this should be private."

He wasn't sure what Lonnie was suggesting, but he shook his head. "Here's fine."

Lonnie's hiss was more of a whine. "Not out here in the open. Somebody might see."

The guy was as robust as a mosquito, but still he wasn't about to trust him. "I'm not getting in the boat. If you saw something, tell me; right here and right now."

Lonnie stared at him. "You're a damn fool, Mr. Gabe. I can help your friend."

He had thought that Lonnie was going to try a spot of blackmail by claiming that he'd seen that Bergeron guy plant something on the boat. "So tell me."

"It's going to cost you."

"Get lost."

"Listen to me! I saw the guy with the bomb!"

Lonnie's eyes kept sweeping the area, but the moon hadn't risen yet, and outside the little oasis of pseudo-day created by the dock lights, lions and tigers and bears and humans could be roaming.

"And why should I believe you?"

"Cause it's true."

"Who was it?"

Lonnie cackled. "A thousand bucks, and you can spring your friend Neal from the feds."

"Fifty bucks."

Lonnie was mortally offended by a low-ball offer. "No, Sir. Five hundred dollars and not a penny less. What kind of shit are you trying to pull?"

"A hundred. Maybe. If this information sounds plausible...if it sounds like it might be true."

Lonnie said, "No deal. I'm taking a risk even talking to you. Five hundred, and I'll tell you who put the bomb on that dumb asshole's boat. I saw the...the perp as clear as I'm seeing you."

He smelled like a brewery, and was probably seeing two of everything, but he might know something. "I don't have five hundred on me."

Lonnie smirked at him. "That's why God created ATMs, Mr. Gabe. Get the money. I'll be back."

And he pushed off from the dock. He didn't start the engine, but poled the little boat away heading south back to town.

A voice two inches from his ear said, "He a friend of yours?"

Gabe was exhausted and felt like shit, but he managed a pirouette followed by a respectable grand *jeté*.

"What the Hell, Kurt. You've got to stop doing that."

Kurt just smiled at him.

"Think of all that paperwork, if I have a heart attack."

"Right. Forgot about that. So you and Lonnie?"

"No, he just sort of sidled up to me. Never did figure out what he wanted."

Kurt said, "Don't you trust me?"

"There are many levels of trust, Ranger Hobbs."

"Right. A word of advice: Lonnie is not someone with whom a respectable, law-abiding gentleman should be consorting."

He smiled at Kurt. "Nobody has ever called me a gentleman before."

Kurt nodded. "Ever wonder why?"

"Asshole." He was reasonably respectable and reasonably law-abiding. "How do you know about Lonnie?"

Kurt said, "Sergeant King advised me to keep an eye on him. You didn't ask what fearsome beast was in Mrs. Campbell's cabin."

"Based solely on the indigenous fauna, I'm going to guess opossum or raccoon? Or maybe a squirrel on steroids?"

"Possum. Want to see it?"

He was beat, but he'd never seen one in the flesh. The cage was in the back of Kurt's truck parked next to the house.

The white face was decorated with black marble eyes, a pink nose, and round, black, Mickey Mouse ears.

It might have been almost cute, but it kept its mouth open to show lots of teeth as it swayed side to side, hissing and growling at Kurt.

"Not happy, is he? She?"

Kurt said, "She, and no she's not, but she'll be all right." He turned off his flashlight. "We'll let her calm down."

They went back inside. Kurt was staring at him. "Look at you."

"What?"

"You look like shit, Gabe. Maybe we should put you to bed."

"Ordinarily, I would ask you, Sir, to declare your intentions, but I'm too beat."

Kurt said, "You look it, but guess who was with Mrs. Campbell?"

"The Dalai Lama?"

"Layla Girard."

"The Hell you say!"

"Every word is true." Kurt grabbed his arm when he stumbled. "And she had a 45 Colt revolver that took both of her hands to hold."

"What?" Gabe wasn't processing words very well.

"She was going to shoot the possum, but Mrs. Campbell wouldn't hear of it."

"Good for Mimi."

What was Ms. Girard doing with the three good witches of south Florida, armed for bear? Or armed for cheating spouse? "I wonder if Eric's body had any extra holes?"

Kurt shook his head. "That's a thought. We could ask Sergeant King?"

"Charlie wouldn't tell us."

"No, probably not."

And then he remembered that Mimi had invited Layla to dinner.

Kurt helped him into the front room. There was a jumble of boxes piled where a living room should be, but there was a couch.

He pointed toward it. "Mine? I need to sit down, Kurt."

"I can take it. You could have the bed?"

"Nope. The couch is fine. Just position me so when I fall I hit the cushions."

He and the couch embraced.

Kurt said, "Sorry, but the AC isn't working."

Kurt was saying something else, but he couldn't make it out. He hoped Kurt was just a park ranger and not in the hire of misdoers who wished him harm, but he was too tired to care.

He remembered he was supposed to go to the ATM, but that would have to wait until the rosy dawn or possibly later.

Kurt woke him up once and demanded that he count

backwards from a hundred. He might have said some bad things to Kurt, but Kurt just laughed.

Sunday
1:00 am

Gabe woke up. He didn't know why exactly, but something was wrong? He saw a shadow across the room. Was it moving?

He froze and held his breath until he just had to have air. He sucked in sweet oxygen while watching the shadow. He kept expecting it to lunge for him.

He waited and waited, but it didn't move. Had it moved at all? Or had he been dreaming? He waited another minute and then sat up on the couch.

The shadow was a box with a pile of clothes on top of it. He got to his feet. Where was he?

And then he ran into more boxes; Kurt's house. Where was Kurt? Probably in his bed asleep.

He needed water so he tiptoed to the kitchen; he couldn't find a glass so he bent over and slurped water from the faucet.

The windows were open, and sounds were louder at night, but it was quiet now.

And then he saw Kurt walking toward the dock, jogging really.

He stumbled around until he found his shoes and found the door. Kurt was pulling away from him and was already past the park store and had reached the lawn next to the creek.

He tried jogging to catch up to the ranger, but he hadn't taken time to tie his laces, and he came close to falling on his face.

He sat down on the grass, probably on an ant hill, and tied his jogging shoes. The gibbous moon gave just enough light to see Kurt disappearing into the woods ahead.

A voice said, "Hello?"

It was Aafje. "Hello, it's Gabe, Gabe Bergeron. You're out late?"

Bastiaan was behind her. She said, "We look for Ruurd."

"Haven't seen him. Is something wrong?"

Bastiaan said, "No, Aafje and Ruurd are..."

Aafje said something in Dutch that didn't sound too sisterly, and Bastiaan shut up.

"I'm sorry, but I want to catch up to Kurt, to the ranger. If I see Ruurd, I'll tell him you're looking for him." Which would be difficult since he had zero Dutch. He thought the German for "search" was *suchen*, but that probably wouldn't be helpful.

He started jogging, but he'd never find Kurt now.

Bastiaan and Aafje caught up to him. "Is something wrong with the ranger? We like him."

"Yeah, I like him too." A lot.

There was a scream.

And then another one, louder and more terrified.

Gabe slowed down, but Aafje and Bastiaan blasted past him. Well, they hadn't been blown up, clobbered, and choked..

And they were kids. He yelled, "Be careful! Slow down!"

The screaming was getting a lot closer. They were about to run out of lawn, and the dark, freaking forest primeval lay ahead.

There was a gunshot which sounded like a howitzer in the silence of the night.

Somebody was crashing through the woods ahead.

Aafje and Bastiaan finally stopped. There were two more shots, each louder than the one before. Gabe tackled the kids, and they all fell to the ground in a pile.

Somebody came crashing out of the woods running for his life. There was a final shot and a groan, and the dark form plunged into the creek.

Bastiaan was getting up. Gabe tried to hold him down, but Bastiaan was a big boy. He whispered, "Not yet."

They stayed prone as lights in campers and tents across the scattered campsites winked on.

Someone was coming out of the woods. A ten thousand

lumen flashlight blinded him, and now he was going to be shot.

Kurt said, "Gabe? Aafje and Bastiaan? What the Hell are you doing out here?"

Gabe said, "I was following you, Kurt. What are you doing out here?"

Aafje said, "We were looking for Ruurd. Who was shot?"

Bastiaan said, "He went in the water."

Kurt flashed the light at the creek, but there was nothing but still water. He shook his head.

"Kurt?"

"I heard a boat. I thought it was...." He stopped and flashed the light at the water again. "Did you see anybody?"

"Nobody but the guy who did the swan dive."

Gabe walked over to the spot where the guy had gone in. "Shine that freaking light here, Kurt."

"What are we looking for?"

"Shine the light, Ranger, please."

The dark spots weren't hard to find.

Bastiaan said, "Blood."

There was an obvious trail from the edge of the woods to the creek.

Kurt said, "Damn it all to Hell!"

And then Ruurd came bounding out of the woods. Bastiaan hugged Ruurd; Aafje patted his shoulder. But after the reunion, Ruurd kept saying something.

Aafje shut him up too.

"What is he saying, Aafje?"

She frowned. "He is silly."

Wendy was marching toward him. "What's going on Gabe? Who the Hell was shooting? And at what?"

"I don't know who the shooter was, but the shootee is in the creek."

Kurt said, "Shut up, Gabe! Just shut up for once."

And then he saw Layla with her backup group, Mimi, Floria, and Manon. She wasn't holding a pistol, but she had a big purse.

They were still dressed, but dozens of people in every stage of semi-nudity were gathering around them.

Gareth was there in leopard print briefs, staring at him. Randy, fully accoutered from bedazzled boots to carnelian cap, was standing next to him.

Kurt was on his phone, and then he turned to the crowd. "All right, Folks, please go back to your campsites. There's nothing to see here."

Wendy said, "Who the Hell was shooting, Kurt?"

Kurt said, "The police are on their way. I can assure you that there won't be any more shooting, and that you are in no danger."

Wendy looked deeply unconvinced, but she turned around, gathered up Bob, Edward, and George, and departed.

Gareth said, "Bleeding Yanks."

Kurt was looking at one Gabe Bergeron.

"I didn't do anything, Kurt. I certainly didn't shoot anybody. You can ask Aafje and Bastiaan."

Kurt said, "Sergeant King will be doing that. I'd appreciate it if you all had a seat until he gets here."

Gabe sat down, exhausted again. The Dutch kids sat in a circle chattering like catbirds about to swarm a cat. Ruurd was doing a lot of pointing at the creek and at the woods, but it all seemed to leave Aafje unimpressed.

Kurt was standing over him. "Are you okay?"

He looked up; it was too dark to see Kurt's face. "Yeah, except when I was forced to dive for the ground to avoid being shot, I believe I landed on a pine cone."

Kurt snorted and walked back to the edge of the creek.

He could hear sirens now.

Sergeant King arrived first, and then city police and state police and even the Coast Guard; every branch of law enforcement except for the FBI.

Charlie was sitting at Kurt's desk, shaking his head. "Take me over it one more time, Bergeron."

He sighed. It was now four in the morning, and he had told Charlie his story three times. He thought Luke was asleep.

"I got up. I saw Kurt jogging off. I followed. I have no rational explanation why I did that. I am obviously suicidal."

Charlie was staring at his notebook. "And nosy. Pathologically nosy."

"I take issue with the 'pathologically' part. To continue, I met up with Aafje and Bastiaan. We heard shots. We ran toward the shots; that suicidal thing again. But the shots were coming toward us. We cowered on the ground. We saw a dark shape, which could have been anyone, run out of the woods and fall or jump into the creek. There was a splash. We cowered some more. Kurt came out of the woods. Ruurd appeared. Layla Girard showed up. Gareth Fry and a host of others gathered. You came. Finis."

Charlie said, "All right."

"All right what?"

"The Dutch kids back up your story, so go away. For now. But don't go far."

A city cop followed him back to Kurt's house and took up a position at the door. To guard him or to prevent his escape? He didn't care, if it meant nobody would shoot him.

He was wired up, but he was also bone tired. He paced around Kurt's dusty abode. He debated making coffee, but he couldn't find where Kurt kept his coffee. He slurped more water instead.

He found Kurt's couch and renewed his relationship therewith.

Sunday
8:00 am

The sun was shining, and birds were singing when Gabe's eyes popped open again. Said sun and birds did nothing to make him feel even a tiny bit less shitty.

He was done with Janes Island State Park.

He was going to retrieve his car, check out of the Chesapeake Motel, and drive north as if his ass was being nipped at by all the orcs of Mordor, and their dire wolves too.

He might wedge a shower in there somewhere; he didn't smell so good.

He looked around; Kurt needed to dust with a shop vac, and the place had a definite locker room smell that wasn't coming exclusively from the Bergeron guy.

Where was the bathroom?

He found a likely door, but he heard the sound of running water. He needed the bathroom *tout de suite*.

He knocked. Kurt said, "Gabe?"

"Yeah. Sorry."

"Come in." Kurt was naked in the shower with hair and muscular body soaped up. "What's up now?"

Gabe averted his eyes. "Nothing! No gunfire. No explosions. Nothing criminal or violent. As far as I know. I just need to use the bathroom really bad."

"If you need to drop a bomb, Bergeron, you can hold it until I get out of the shower."

"No bombs."

"Then go ahead."

The seat was already up. He pissed enough to turn the bowl water a marigold yellow.

Kurt shut off the water and grabbed a towel. "Damn! You weren't kidding about needing to go."

Kurt walked out of the bathroom drying his hair. The ranger was comfortable being totally naked, but Gabe made himself look away. Well, after a cursory full-body scan.

Gabe focused on washing his hands and then stared at himself in the mirror. His fire-burn was fading so that he felt worse than he looked.

He tried to look at the back of his head, but Kurt's bathroom had a razor, a toothbrush, a bar of soap, a bottle of generic shampoo, one roll of toilet paper, and a roll of paper towels with two sheets left on the roll, but no hand mirror.

A box with "bathroom" scrawled across the top was beside the lavatory, but he wasn't going to rummage.

He washed his face with the bar of soap and used a paper towel to dry off.

He needed to retrieve his car.

Kurt was in the kitchen in his briefs looking exceptionally fine. "Gabe, we need to talk."

"About?"

"I hate to do this, but I think you need to leave the park; you and Neal. I'll pack up Neal's stuff and store it until he can pick it up or whatever."

"I could take it."

Kurt wasn't looking at him. "No, I'd rather store it. And tomorrow, I'm having his car towed. I have visitors coming who've rented the cabin."

"I see. You want us gone; I get that."

"Sorry." Kurt smiled at him. "But I can offer you a cup of coffee before you go."

"You know I didn't blow up Eric and hit myself over the head or shoot anybody. You do know that?"

"I don't think you did."

Gabe laughed and looked away from Kurt. "There was just a bit too much emphasis on the 'think', Buddy. So you're not a hundred percent about me. I get it. But what about you?"

Mr. Park Ranger wasn't smiling. "What about me?"

"Where were you going last night? Where were you when all the shooting was going on?"

Kurt was really not smiling. "I was awake because I was checking on you. I heard a boat on the creek, but it had no lights so I went out to investigate, Bergeron."

"Okay. So you've been here at Janes Island, for what, six days?"

"A week actually."

"Damn, a whole week. Where were you before that, Ranger Hobbs, if that's your real name? And why did you go on Eric's boat before it blew up?"

Kurt smiled, but his teeth were locked together by the bunched up muscles of his square jaws, and the dark brown eyes lacked a certain warmth. "I don't have to explain myself to you."

"No, you don't, but I wish you would."

"No. You should go."

Kurt might truly be just an innocent park ranger, but he was absolutely a muscular, angry guy, who had three inches and thirty pounds on Gabe Bergeron, and was giving serious thought to some ass kicking.

"I am sorry, Kurt. Did they find a body?"

"Leave, Bergeron. Now."

"About that coffee?"

"Out!"

No coffee then. Shit. He really hoped Kurt was just a ranger. He really did.

There was activity on the creek. He saw boats from the Natural Resources Police and the Coast Guard, but no sign of King.

He didn't care. He strode purposefully toward the damn cabin and his car. He stayed in the center of the paved road and kept looking behind him and around him. He thought about picking up a stout branch to quarterstaff attackers, but he opted for speed over armament.

He made it to his car without being ambushed. One of the sisters was outside; either Floria or Manon, but he couldn't remember which was which.

She locked onto him like a Raptor drone. "Hello, Gabe. Any news? Who was shot?"

"I don't think they've found out yet."

"Are they still looking for a body?"

"Think so." He was realizing just how beat he was. "And I've been kicked out of the park."

She nodded. "Oh, sorry, but you shouldn't be surprised? This..." She waved a heavily ringed hand in the air. "...is not the kind of PR that a park wants. I'm Floria, by the way. People are always getting me and Manon confused though I don't see why?"

"Sorry, Floria. I know, but I haven't done anything."

"I know, Honey."

Mimi's red PT Cruiser wasn't in the lane. "Is Layla still visiting with you?"

"No."

Manon popped out of the cabin. "Gabe? Has anything else happened?" She smiled at him. "And how are you feeling?"

"I've been better."

Manon patted his shoulder. She and Floria were carefully made-up already. "Oh, where are my manners? Would you like some coffee, Gabe?"

He would, more than life itself, but he really needed that shower. "Thank you, but I need to get my car and scram. And get cleaned up."

Manon and Floria stood shoulder to shoulder; the silver blonde hair, the noses, and the shape of the faces were identical, but Floria's cheeks were sunken in a bit more, and their eyes were subtly different.

Floria said, "He's been kicked out of the park."

Manon said, "That's so unfair."

He tried again. "Where is Layla?"

Floria said, "Mimi took her to the motel. Thank God. I think she's having breakfast with Madame Girard and the lawyer."

Manon frowned ever so delicately.

He said, "Not a fan?"

Floria smiled at her sister. "Mimi likes her. I don't know why, but maybe because they shared a husband?"

Manon said, "Not simultaneously."

Floria winked at him. "No, Mimi wouldn't go for that. Now, I can see Layla with multiple husbands."

Manon said, "Mimi's third husband...."

Floria said, "Who was much too young for her. Just as Eric was too young for Layla."

Manon sighed. "Mimi's third husband became Layla's second. Briefly."

"Did he die? Unexpectedly."

Floria and Manon looked at each other and tittered like chickadees hearing a bawdy joke.

Floria said, "I wish. She divorced him, but it would be such a good story if he had died mysteriously. Now that Eric's gone. You think she did it, Gabe?"

"Eric? I think it's not impossible."

Floria looked at Manon. "See? I'm not the only one."

Manon said, "But why would she? He signed the prenup."

Floria sniffed. "Layla says he signed a prenup."

He said, "Eric was unfaithful to her."

Floria frowned at him. "Everybody knows that, Gabe. The man had the morals and discretion of an alley cat."

"And there could be other reasons."

Floria and Manon exchanged a glance. Manon said, "The business?"

He nodded. "Did Layla leave the cabin? Before the shooting started?"

Floria said, "She did. To go for one of her walks."

Manon said, "But she didn't have the gun with her."

Floria interrupted. "She had her purse, Manon." Floria looked at him. "If you want to play detective, Gabe, then I'd get that nice Sergeant King to check Layla's gun."

Manon said, "To see if it's been fired recently."

"Thank you, Ladies."

The red PT Cruiser pulled into the lane, and Mimi walked over. She looked at her sisters. "What are you up to?"

Floria said, "Nothing. Chatting with Gabe."

Manon flushed just a little, "Nothing at all, Mimi."

He smiled and backed away. "Very nice to see you again, Ladies."

He hopped in his car and headed for the park exit. He was gone; he was history; he was a song fading on the wind.

The barrier was blocking the road. He pulled off the road and honked his horn, which was something that people in Crisfield didn't seem to do..

Kurt and Sarah were standing in the park office doorway, but Sarah walked toward him.

"Sorry, Gabe, but Sergeant King wants to see you."

"But I don't want to see him."

The barrier was no match for however many horses were underneath the hood of his mighty Fiesta. Maybe. He raced the engine in a threatening manner.

Sarah smiled at him. "If you break my gate, I will kick your ass, Bergeron."

"You'll have to catch me first."

"Just how old are you?"

Kurt had a phone to his ear. He yelled to her. "Let him go, Sarah. King says to open the gates."

He didn't want to think that handsome Kurt was a villain. He waved, but Kurt stomped back inside.

Sarah lifted the barrier. He realized he hadn't seen a single officer, and the boats were gone too.

"Where are the police?"

Sarah said, "They pulled out, and I don't know why, Mr. Bergeron."

"Okay. So I guess I won't see you again, Ms. Sharp."

"You never know, Mr. Bergeron."

He smiled. "That's true. When my friend asked me to come here, the worst I expected was to be eaten alive by bugs."

"See. Keep that positive attitude."

"Right. Tell Kurt sorry for me?"

"He's inside. You may tell him yourself."

"Yeah. Bye, Sarah."

He hit the little button to seal the window and applied steady pressure to the accelerator.

He cranked up the AC and turned on the radio; a country singer wept over every note. He made it to his motel without having to dodge a mortar attack.

He got in his shower, scrubbed his body, washed his hair, and then let the hot water run over him until it was as tepid as the creek water.

The bandage on the back of his head washed off. He would worry about medical supplies at a later date.

He dried off, and sat on his bed naked.

To sleep or to get food? That was the question.

A knock on his door was likely the death knell to both options. He threw open the door.

It was Charlie and Officer Stevens, whose first name he couldn't remember. He wondered about that concussion thing for a second.

Charlie ignored his undressed state. "Good morning, Mr. Bergeron. May we come in?"

"I am not at home to visitors, Sir."

Charlie flexed his right eyebrow and smiled. "I see."

Charlie turned and walked away. Officer Stevens looked at his boss, shrugged, and followed.

Charlie was descending the flight of stairs from the balcony. "Charlie?"

He didn't stop.

"Sergeant King?"

Clank, clank, clank went his boots on the metal rungs.

"All right, if you want me to chase you naked, then I will." Gabe stepped boldly onto the balcony.

Charlie said, "I'd have to arrest you for indecent exposure, Sir."

"You'd love that, wouldn't you?"

Officer Stevens winked at him. "He would."

Luke; that was his name.

"Come back. Please. You obviously came to tell me something? Come on." He felt something on the back of his neck; it was blood. "Wait. I'm bleeding!"

Gabe held up a bloody finger when they turned, but Charlie said, "You'll never live long enough to make it to the ER with a gusher like that."

Luke snickered.

"Please come back and tell me what the Hell has happened now? Please?"

He went back inside and pulled on a pair of briefs and some shorts. He wasn't chasing anybody across a parking lot naked. He had a little self respect.

Charlie darkened his doorway again. "May we come in?"

"Yes. By all the saints and martyrs, come in, and shut the damn door." The bright light was giving him a headache.

Charlie said, "Turn around."

Gabe thought, for one awful moment, that Charlie was going to cuff him, and it must have shown on his face. Charlie and Luke giggled in a very unmanly fashion..

Charlie controlled himself. "No. Let me look at your head." He prodded. "It's nothing. Do you have any bandages? Antiseptic?"

"Sure. And a tracheotomy kit and three pints of O negative blood in my carry-on over there."

Luke snickered again. "I'll get our kit."

Charlie said, "Do that, Officer Stevens." Charlie sat and waited.

He stood it as long as he could. "You are a cruel, cruel man, Sergeant Charles King."

"I've been told that before."

"Tell me!"

"We found a body in the creek, close to where it went in." Charlie rubbed his eyes. "They don't usually travel very far."

Charlie paused again, which was just mean. "It was Lonnie."

"Shit! Shot?"

"Twice. Through the upper back. One of them looked like it might have nicked the heart."

"Damn. I guess he was telling the truth."

"About?"

Luke came back, and Charlie splashed antiseptic on the back of his head and applied a couple of band-aids.

Gabe wanted to make Charlie wait a little, but he had to tell him. "Lonnie told me he saw who put the bomb on Eric's boat."

Charlie was not pleased.

Which he could understand.

Luke's eyes were showing white like a horse about to bolt. "When?"

"Last night." Was it only last night? "After nine. He was in a boat, and said he could help me spring Neal from jail for five hundred dollars."

Charlie was going to punch him; repeatedly. "And you didn't call me?"

"I had a headache like my brains were going to run out of my ears, and I wasn't sure I believed him, and I didn't have any cash, and I was too beat to drive into town to get any, and I thought you were off the case, and the FBI had departed for Philly, and I didn't have your number."

Charlie gradually stopped looking like Vesuvius in 79 A.D., and said, "Stupid fool. I thought he was bullshitting like he always did."

Luke said, "You didn't know, Charlie."

"That doesn't help Lonnie."

Which was true.

Charlie said, "You saw Lonnie at the marina. So that's the most likely place for him to have spotted the bomber. Who else was around? Think, Gabe."

"I don't remember anybody, Charlie. There were people but nobody stood out enough for me to remember. Have you talked to the marina staff?" Charlie glared at him again. "Of course, you have, and they're no help?"

"Almost as useless as you."

"As bad as that?"

Charlie was pacing. "Somebody has committed two murders under my nose, and nobody saw a damn thing?"

"So it was a bomb on Eric's boat?"

"Yeah. Very sophisticated according to the techs. There wouldn't have been anything left to find if the propane tanks hadn't been empty. The boat would have been blown all to Hell."

"How do you know about the propane tanks, Charlie?"

"Mrs. Girard."

"And you believe her?"

Charlie stopped pacing. "About that. Anything you'd like to tell me, Bergeron?"

Gabe said, "I don't know anything more about her except that she was divorcing Eric, but she and her lawyer, sweet Cindi Lou, had made him sign a prenup so he wouldn't have gotten the family jewels in the settlement."

"And how long have you known that?"

"Since yesterday. Sorry."

"You are a piece of work, Mr. Bergeron."

That didn't sound like a good thing. "Charlie? Just as a matter of curiosity, why are you telling me all this now? You've decided that I'm innocent?"

Charlie said, "I'm pretty sure you didn't hit yourself on the head; not a hundred percent, but close. But I know you didn't shoot Lonnie. And if you'd tried to blow up Eric's boat, you would have blown yourself up."

"Would not."

Charlie said, "If I'm wrong about you, Gabe...."

"You're not."

"Then tell me what else is going on? Why blow up Girard?"

This sharing of confidences and general bonhomie was all well and good, but Charlie would be obliged to tell the FBI about any money laundering.

"I don't think I can do that. I'm very sorry, Charlie."

Charlie wasn't pleased again, but he got a call. He listened for a second and stepped out of the room.

Luke said, "You should tell him the truth, Gabe."

"I want to. If it was just me."

Luke nodded. "Your friend, Mr. Hartmann, got into something with Mr. Girard?"

Luke wasn't as blond as he appeared to be.

"I don't know why you would think that, Officer."

Luke laughed and went back to looking as dangerous as an angora rabbit. But there was something about the laugh?

It was a cross between a hiccup and a bark, and Gabe had heard it before. At the marina while he was watching Eric and Layla quarrel.

Charlie came back. "Yes, Senior Special Agent Steele, I will tell him. Of course, Sir, you can expect our full cooperation. We'll be only too happy to provide any assistance that the Federal Bureau of Investigation may require."

"Tell me what, Charlie?"

"That's Sergeant King to you, Mr. Bergeron."

"Don't be like that. I don't know who planted the bomb."

"But you know why."

"I have suspicions."

Charlie said, "So share those."

"Can't. But I'm pretty sure that Senior Special Agent Steele knows even more than I do."

"And what good does that do me, Bergeron?"

"I take your point. Sorry." Charlie and Luke were leaving. "Luke?"

"Yeah, Gabe?"

"Were you at the marina Friday?"

Luke shook his head vigorously. "No! I was at Jenkins Creek." Young Luke was studying the strange painting that featured muscular, toothy deer bounding across what looked like fields of marijuana. "All afternoon. Like you told me, Charlie."

Charlie grunted and walked out. He had clothes on this time so he could follow them. "Charlie?"

He got nothing. "Thanks for bandaging my head."

Charlie got in his truck. Luke had to run to avoid being left behind as Charlie pulled out of the parking lot.

Charlie stopped on the street and lowered his window. "Mr. Hartmann is being released. He's returning to the park. You are to make yourself available to Special Agent Chernov who is en route."

"Thanks, Charlie."

But Charlie had roared away.

Well, he couldn't tell him about Neal.

Charlie should understand. He probably did, but he didn't like it. Gabe put on his shoes and went to get breakfast before he passed out.

    Heather was on duty. She examined him. "Damn, Gabe." She was drawn to the rope burns on his neck like a bloodhound to a fresh trail. "Can I touch it?"

    "Get me coffee, and you may make a plaster cast."

    "Coming up."

    "And pancakes! Lots of pancakes. And bacon. And aspirins?" What had he done with the bottle of acetaminophen that Sarah had given him?

    Mr. English, James, was just finishing his breakfast; they exchanged friendly waves as James got to his feet and ambled over.

    "You okay, Gabe?"

    "Fine. Well, not bad. I have a headache." James kept staring at him. "And to tell the truth my throat still feels funny."

    James peered at his throat and noted the back of his head. "Somebody actually tried to garrote you?"

    "Right. They did. Yesterday, after the FBI came. But I'm okay now."

    "They catch the bastard?"

    "No, not yet. Sergeant King is still looking."

    Mr. Bear scowled. "Shit. Went to a friend's house and just got back in town. I didn't know. Sorry."

    "That's okay, James, and thank you for asking about me."

    "Sure. My vacation's over."

    "Is it? They never last long enough, do they?"

    James kept staring at him, but finally, he nodded. "Okay. Nice meeting you, Gabe. Take care of yourself." He smiled. "Take better care of yourself."

    "I will. And nice meeting you too."

    And Mr. Bear walked out of the Summer Nights Cafe filling the doorway quite completely as he exited. Much too large.

    Heather brought aspirins and his pancakes and bacon. He drank lots of coffee and ate until he couldn't swallow another bite. And he asked Heather what people were saying about Lonnie.

    She sat down. "They don't know what to think, Gabe. There aren't that many murders in Crisfield. It's been years and years. Most folks think it's something to do with the boat blowing up, and with

Neal and you, Hon."

"I didn't shoot him."

"We know that. Or most of us do." She glared at an ancient man who was giving him the evil eye. "You were almost killed yourself."

"I was, and I'm sorry about Lonnie." Gabe wanted to tell her that he'd brought it on himself.

"Are you leaving?"

"As soon as I can."

She smiled at him. "It might be for the best, Hon."

"Yeah."

He stepped out into the dazzling sun. It was going to be hot, sweat-running-down-your-back hot. He went back to his motel room to take a nap.

His phone launched into a samba. He had no idea who was calling, but he answered anyway.

Special Agent Chernov said, "We need to talk, Bergeron."

"Yeah, King told me."

"Are you at the park?"

"No, I was kicked out. I'll be at the motel."

"Not there, Bergeron."

"Well, of course, your wish is my command, Special Agent. Wait. Did you let really Neal go?"

"We did."

"Great. Why?"

"There's a Denny's south of Princess Anne. Meet me there, Bergeron."

And Chernov was gone. So he was supposed to jump in his car and burn rubber? He snorted in derision and flopped on his bed. The painting was starting to creep him out.

He had no reason to doubt Chernov, but he called Max, and Max confirmed that he had talked Steele into springing Neal from durance vile.

"Thank you, Max."

"It was easier than it should have been, which makes me uneasy, Bergeron, but my bill will be in Monday's mail anyway."

"Right." Neal was going to have to handle that. "I'll try not to call you again. At least not today."

Max hung up on him.

He tried calling Neal again, and he answered.

"Neal!"

"Hi, Gabe."

"Where are you?"

"In a car with Ellie heading back to Crisfield. They let me go."

"Great! Why?"

Neal hesitated. "Well, the lawyer, Max Nagy, came."

"I see. And Ellie is with you?"

"Sure is." He didn't need video to picture Neal's smile. "Are you okay, Gabe. You sound funny."

"Funny humorous or funny bizarre?"

"Funny not feeling good."

"I'm as right as rain. As fine as frog's hair."

Neal laughed. "What does that even mean?"

"You would have to ask Aunt Flo. See you soon, Buddy."

Gabe got in his car and drove north. The Denny's was doing a brisk business. He didn't see any black sedans, but he parked.

He might have jumped when the Anarchist rapped on the passenger side window. The agent was wearing tight shorts, an even tighter, black tank top that showed off his chest and the eagle tattoos on both shoulders, and he had traded the rimless glasses for mirrored, wrap-around shades. He hadn't shaved for a while.

Special Agent Chernov looked scruffy and muscular and dangerous and damn proud of it.

"Open up, Bergeron."

Gabe stopped memorizing Chernov's body and complied.

"Why the get-up?" Not that he was complaining.

Chernov said, "What get-up?"

Chernov proceeded to question him, going over and over the ground that Charlie had already covered.

"And you saw nothing? Again?"

"It was very dark, and I was very prone."

Chernov's lip curled a millimeter. "Sure he wasn't shooting at you?"

"Yes, Chernov, I'm sure." The special agent looked away. "Are we done?"

"For now."

Chernov answered his phone. "That's affirmative." And the call was over. But Chernov didn't move. They sat another five minutes.

"What are we waiting for?"

"For your partner in crime."

Like he was dumb enough to admit knowing who that was. "I'm sorry? I am a virtuous man. I am the direct descendant of Marcus Aurelius. On my mother's side. I don't have any criminal associates."

Chernov's lips made a curling motion before the agent strangled the smile mid blossom.

"Hartmann and Tyson will be joining us."

"Great. Why here?"

It was as if he had never spoken.

They sat and waited. He tried out Denny's men's room and purchased coffee. He didn't get Chernov any.

They sat some more.

A silver, Jeep Liberty Sport SUV with tinted windows parked next to them. Chernov exited his vehicle as Murray exited the Jeep.

They exchanged manly grunts.

The Pale Wraith had shaved his head and was outfitted in ripped jeans, a camouflage t-shirt, and a baseball cap with a twelve point buck rampant. He looked surprisingly robust, even hot. But not as hot as Chernov.

Neal and Ellie got out of the Jeep and into his car. Ellie got in the back, and Neal took the front seat.

Reed was sitting in the Jeep with her hands folded in her lap. She looked like a mousetrap ready to snap shut on the first mouse dumb enough to approach.

She had on a flowered top, pink shorts, and a hat adorned with red, plastic crabs and netting. Gabe would have giggled, but she was too damn scary to chance it.

Gabe said, "What is going on?"

Ellie said, "The FBI released Neal."

"I got that part."

Chernov rapped on his window. "Back to the park, Bergeron."

"I was kicked out." He waved at Neal and Ellie. "We were kicked out, and the cabin has been rented to other visitors."

"Not any more." And Special Agent Chernov walked over to a blue Hyundai. "Remember I told you the weekend wasn't over?"

Murray and Chernov pulled out of the parking lot and sped off.

He looked at Neal. "What?"

Neal said, "It's okay, Gabe. You don't mind giving us a lift back to the park?"

"No, of course not, but...."

Neal said, "Are you okay? Your throat?"

"I'm fine."

Ellie said, "Then we should get going."

"I live but to serve." Neal smiled at him. "Is anybody going to explain what's going on?"

Ellie said, "Nothing's going on, Gabe. We're just going back to the park to finish our vacation."

Sunday Noon

Gabe Bergeron sat there and looked from Neal to Ellie and back to Neal. They smiled. Oh, Hell no.

"I have a stop to make."

Ellie said, "And where might that be, Gabe?"

He ignored Miss Ellie and called Aunt Flo and got the okay to bring himself and two other lunch guests.

Neal said, "You'll like her, Ellie."

Ellie was sure she wouldn't. If there was any justice in the Universe, Mrs. Gutierrez would serve more of that green, lumpy soup to Ellie.

Neal got out of the car and surveyed the Victorian pile with its porches and balconies and turret. "It looks just the same."

It had five trim colors now instead of six. "Pretty much." Gabe looked at the river and told himself to calm down. "Come on."

The first summer after Gabe had come to live with Great-aunt Flo, she had said it was okay to invite Neal to come for a week.

He had been afraid that Neal and Aunt Flo might not hit it off, but they had bonded over a television special about Jupiter, and he had learned that Aunt Flo was as much an astronomy geek as Neal.

And one week had stretched into a very happy month.

A space probe had been zooming around Jupiter at the time, taking photos and measurements, but he couldn't remember the name.

"Neal, what was the name of that Jupiter space probe?"

Neal smiled at him. "The orbiter launched in 1989?"

"Yeah. The one that took the neat photos of the moons?"

"Io, Europa, Ganymede, and Callisto. That was Galileo. It was one of the first probes to have a CCD camera. What made you think of that, Gabe?"

"I don't know."

And that was when he had also discovered that Neal had been studying Spanish. Meals, which had become a little more organized with company present, were conducted in that language for the rest of the visit, and Mrs. Gutierrez had been won over.

Unfortunately, Gabe had decided to take French, but only because Aunt Flo had told him that the Bergeron clan was French Canadian.

Great-aunt Flo met them at the side door. Mrs. Gutierrez was behind her giving him a look that would freeze an orc's heart.

Great-aunt Flo said, "How wonderful to see you again, Neal. And this must be Ellie. I've heard so very much about you."

Neal hugged Great-aunt Flo while also giving Gabe Bergeron a suspicious look. "It's wonderful to see you too, Ms. Barnes, and, yes, this is Ellie Tyson. Isn't she beautiful?"

Ellie went for modesty as she fluttered her eyelashes at his great-aunt. He may have snorted, but everyone ignored him.

Great-aunt Flo said, "Very lovely. And you look good too, Neal. All these muscles." She patted his chest and biceps. "They look good on you."

Ellie said, "He's my big, strong man."

Gabe managed to roll his eyes and gag at the same time.

But Ellie smiled at him. "I'm sorry that Gabe forced us on you."

Great-aunt Flo smiled. "Not at all. We were hoping to see Neal. And you too, Miss Tyson."

Mrs. Gutierrez hugged Neal and said something in Spanish, and then it transpired that sweet Ellie was also fluent in Spanish. She got a nod, before Mrs. Gutierrez lumbered back into the nether regions of the kitchen.

Which was just peachy.

Still, noxious fumes and a clattering din dominated the kitchen so maybe Ellie wouldn't enjoy lunch. But, much to his chagrin, the meal was identifiable and even edible. Not that he felt like eating.

And the conversation was entirely in Spanish, and Mrs. Gutierrez was beaming at Ellie. Well, not glowering.

And Ellie was just so cutesy with Neal. Like Neal's first college girlfriend, Charlene something, had been. It was Charlene's fault that Mrs. Gutierrez hadn't spoken to Gabe for a whole summer.

Neal had been describing Aunt Flo's house and living arrangements, and Charlene had just blurted out, "Are they lesbians?"

Which was something that naive Gabe Bergeron had never considered; not once. So when he'd gone home for the summer, he had tried to keep his mouth shut, but he couldn't do it. He had thought he was exercising delicacy and finesse, but Aunt Flo had figured it out almost at once and burst out laughing.

He would never know just how Aunt Flo had phrased it when she'd blabbed to Mrs. Gutierrez.

It had been in Spanish, but Mrs. Gutierrez had said some things to him that hadn't sounded very nice along with vivid facial expressions.

And then she had said nothing at all.

For the rest of the summer.

Charlene had also wondered about Aunt Flo's income, but he hadn't been stupid enough to bring that up after the lesbian thing. He had secretly rejoiced when she'd dumped Neal.

Aunt Flo was looking at him. "Why are you smiling, Gabriel?"

"No reason."

Neal said, "Oh there's a reason."

Gabe shook his head, and they went back to Spanish until the meal was almost over, and Aunt Flo brought up Pluto.

Aunt Flo said, "Have you seen the latest photos, Neal?"

"A few, but we've been fishing and kayaking at the park."

Plus having marathon sex with Ellie.

Aunt Flo was looking at him. "The latest ones are truly amazing."

Ellie wanted to get moving, but Neal was hooked.

Aunt Flo had a computer; a nice computer with a monitor larger than Gabe's TV.

So a nuclear-powered space probe called New Horizons had screamed past Pluto doing thirty thousand miles per hour while snapping pictures like a maniac.

Ellie oohed and aahed at the pinkish heart shape, but Aunt Flo said, "Look at this colorized closeup. That's the Sputnik Planum and the al-Idrisi Montes."

And Neal and Aunt Flo had babbled science stuff while his eyes glazed over, but the pictures were interesting even to an accountant.

The peaks were snow covered like any mountains, but the jumbled valleys looked like they had been dusted with cocoa. "What kind of rocks are those?"

Neal and Aunt Flo smiled at him. Neal said, "Not rocks, Gabe. Those are blocks of water ice."

"Ice? Mountains of ice?"

"Water ice."

He wasn't going to ask what other kind of ice they could be.

Neal said, "And the plains are mostly nitrogen ice."

The plains were divided into weird polygons. He tried again. "So it's nippy on Pluto this time of year?"

Aunt Flo said, "Nitrogen freezes at minus 210 Celsius, Gabriel, and this is Pluto's summer."

"Right. Cool." Neal laughed.

Aunt Flo said, "Why don't you take a look at the other photos, Neal? There are some interesting ones of Charon too."

Aunt Flo got up and let Neal take her place. She said, "Walk with me, Gabriel."

They took the path to the river and sat on a bench. "What happened to your throat, Gabriel."

He took a deep breath and was almost overpowered by the cloying scent of honeysuckle. "I was attacked."

"Did you really annoy someone that much?"

He told her about the FBI arresting Neal, and Lonnie's death, and the FBI releasing Neal to go back to the park.

"And you think that Ellie is FBI?"

"Don't you?"

She smiled. "There is something about her. You believe they

are using Neal as bait?"

"Of course. I tried talking to him...."

"He's a grown man, Gabriel, and he loves her."

"Yeah. But does she love him?"

Great-aunt Flo shook her head. "What about your throat? And the lump on the back of your head?"

"Someone really wanted to know where this freaking ledger is, but Kurt scared them off. And Sergeant King."

"Someone hit you and then garroted you?"

"With a log. Well, a branch anyway. And Kurt said it was clothesline. For the garroting part."

She patted his face. "Gabriel, I think they've rattled your brains. Your story has no narrative structure at all. What ledger?"

"Oh, yeah. The money laundering ledger that Eric was keeping."

"I see. A ledger that would incriminate himself and his clients. Eric wasn't very bright."

"Which I have been saying since the very first day I met him."

She smiled at him. "And who is Kurt?"

"The park ranger at Janes Island. He's a good guy. I think. I'm pretty sure. He's handsome."

She smiled again. "I see. Anything else you haven't told me?"

"No. Well, there's Mia and Gareth, and Sergeant King of the Natural Resources Police, and Kev and Barb. It's complicated."

"Obviously." She took his hand. "Gabriel, you aren't a detective."

"I know."

"Then why don't you drop Neal and Ellie off at the park, and come back here to stay with me?"

He shook his head. "I can't. Too much is going on right now."

"You can't control things, Gabriel, no matter how hard you try." She patted his face. "And it isn't your responsibility to save people."

"I'll be careful. Nobody is going to sneak up on me again."

"Gabriel."

"They aren't."

Ellie was walking toward them.

"'Something wicked this way comes.'"

Aunt Flo giggled. "Has Neal ever had a girlfriend like her before?"

"No way. Look at her."

"And is she banging his brains out?"

Which might not be something most great-aunts would ask, but Aunt Flo wasn't all lace and potpourri. "I guess so."

"Gabriel."

"They almost demolished a stoutly built cabin. The vibrations triggered seismographs up and down the East Coast. So you're saying that I should accept her?"

"For the time being, Gabriel."

Great-aunt Flo got to her feet and met Ellie on the path. "He's coming, Miss Tyson. It was lovely to meet you."

Ellie smiled back. "It was nice to meet you too, Ms. Barnes. Amazing house you have. Neal said it was your parents' house? So you've lived here all your life?"

Great-aunt Flo gave him a wink. "Not really. I'm sorry, Ellie, but I need to lie down for a bit."

Ellie said, "Of course. I'm sorry."

"No need to be sorry, Dear." And she waved at Neal and went toward the house.

Ellie said, "Come on, Bergeron. We should have been at the park two hours ago."

"Right. So very sorry to hold you up."

Aunt Flo was talking to Mrs. Gutierrez.

Mrs. Gutierrez nodded and pulled a phone from her flowered apron.

Sunday
2:00 pm

So Gabe drove Neal and Ellie back to the park. He didn't know what the land speed record on the straight stretch of Rt. 413 from Westover to Crisfield was, but he might have broken it.

His headache was back.

He pulled up to the park office. "You might want to find out if the cabin is really available."

Ellie smiled and hopped out.

He turned in his seat. "What the freaking Hell, Neal?"

Neal said, "There's nothing to worry about, Gabe. Ellie and I will be here for a few more days, and then I'm going home. We'll be going home."

"Well I'm going home now."

Neal nodded. "Okay. That's a great idea. Is your throat really okay?"

"Someone tried to garrote me. In this park. But I'm not the one they really want."

Neal said, "I'm sorry, Gabe."

He waved that away. "You do know that the one they really want to murder is you!"

"Yeah."

"Is that all you're going to say?"

"That's about it."

"What about Ellie?"

Neal frowned. "What about her?"

"Is she FBI? Or is she working for the people who are willing to do whatever it takes to get this freaking ledger?"

Neal shook his head. "You're wrong about Ellie, Gabe. She loves me."

The rental was too small for him to climb over the seats, wrap Neal's seat belt around his throat, and give him a taste of what being choked felt like.

"Come on, Gabe. Don't be pissed."

"Get out of my car, Hartmann! Now!"

Neal looked at him like he'd just set fire to his favorite teddy bear.

Neal's phone rang. "Hi, Mom. No, I'm fine. Yes, Eric's boat blew up. Yes, right here in the park. I don't know, Mom, but they think it might have been the propane tank."

Neal shouldn't lie to his mother.

"Yes, Ellie's here with me. We're both fine. Gabe? He's here, and he's fine too. Oh, well he dropped his phone into the creek. That's right. You know how he is."

"Ms. Barnes called you? She shouldn't have worried you, Mom. Yes, I'll be home soon. Tuesday at the latest, and I'll tell you all about it. No, I don't know why the FBI is involved. Really. Please don't worry. I have to go, Mom."

Neal said, "She was worried about you."

"What do you mean by 'you know how he is'?"

"You break things, Gabe."

Ellie bounced out of the office smiling.

Neal said, "Gabe's pissed. He told me to get out."

She gave him an inscrutable look as she took Neal's hand. "We can walk, Sweetie."

He sat there and watched them skip down the road to that cursed cabin like Hansel and Gretel, or Dorothy and Toto on the yellow brick road. Well, they didn't really skip, but they looked happy and excited, or at least Ellie did.

Gabe envisioned running over her. He raced the engine experimentally; she'd never see it coming.

Kurt knocked on the passenger window.

He lowered it. "It's okay. I just dropped them off. I'll be out of your park in ten seconds."

Kurt said, "Stay as long as you want, Bergeron."

He cut off the engine.

He walked around the car and headed for Kurt.

Kurt looked a little bit alarmed, which was nice, but certainly unfounded. Sarah ran out of the office.

"Whoa, there."

He couldn't hit a girl. Well, he could, but it wasn't right, and there was the awful possibility that she might kick his ass.

She said, "We are not the enemy, Bergeron."

He knew that.

Kurt said, "We weren't given a choice."

Gabe could feel the veins in his head throbbing like a drum solo. He took a deep breath and tried to calm down before he had a stroke.

"Weren't given a choice about declaring us persona non grata or declaring us grata?"

Kurt said, "Neither. Both. I got a call...two calls."

"From your boss?"

Sarah said, "From more rungs up the ladder than that."

"So the FBI called the head of the parks department?"

Kurt said, "No one specifically told me that."

A silver Jeep SUV with tinted windows shot past them into the park.

"The Pale Wraith. Shit."

Kurt said, "What the Hell are you talking about, Bergeron?"

"Never mind." He still liked Kurt, even if he wasn't sure he could trust him after last night. "Forget I was here. Have a nice life. May you never fall into marsh mud, and may all your visitors live to write glowing reviews."

He got back in his car and drove to the motel. He jammed his stuff into his carry-on. He sat on the bed and tried not looking at the painting.

The deer were looking at him.

What the Hell was Hartmann doing?

Neal was doing what Ellie had convinced him to do. Neal was the brightest person he knew, but he was also suggestible and thought the best of people even when he wasn't besotted.

Gabe knew he shouldn't leave. He had sort of promised

Neal's mother that he'd look out for him. But that had been years ago and what the Hell could he do?

There had to be something.

He could go apologize.

He drove back to the damn park. Chuck was on his bike near the park office and gave him a big wave and a smile.

He had to apologize to Kurt too, but first he had to see Neal. He banged on the cabin door, and sweet Ellie answered.

"Gabe. I didn't expect to see you?"

"Yeah. About that. I'm sorry for losing my temper." She was standing in the doorway. "Is Neal here?"

"He's taking a nap. He didn't get much sleep last night."

"Join the club. Can I come in?"

Ellie said, "I don't think that's a good idea, Gabe."

"Why not?"

She smiled like a female praying mantis about to decapitate her mate. Not that insects smile, but if they did, the smile would be just like hers.

"Neal and I need some time alone. We think you should go home. I'm sure you understand."

"No. Who are you? Really?"

She held out her hand and smiled again. "Ellie Tyson. I thought we'd already met, but I could be wrong."

"That might be your real name, but I doubt it."

"Bye, Gabe."

She shut the door. He had never tried to break down a door; it probably hurt a lot more than it looked like it did on TV.

As he walked away, he caught a glimpse of Neal peeping at him through the curtains, before the doofus ducked down.

He said, "I'm sorry I got angry, Neal, but a lot has happened, and my head hurts. Talk to me. Please?"

But the door remained firmly shut. He walked to the dock and back.

Mimi's red PT Cruiser was parked in her lane.

New people were moving into the third cabin now that James Mr. Bear was gone.

The new guys looked like hunters, or maybe what the FBI

thought hunters should look like? The two guys had camouflage clothing head to toe, neon orange vests, and a Ford F-150 pickup truck with a fully loaded gun rack. He didn't get the camouflage and the orange together?

He didn't spot Chernov or Murray so he left.

He parked outside the park office. He had intended to knock on the door very meekly, but Kurt came out.

Kurt spotted him and came toward him looking fired up. "Come to go a few rounds, Bergeron? Step around to the back of the building, and let's go."

"No. I stopped by to apologize." Kurt looked skeptical. "No, really. I don't know what the Hell is going on, but bad things keep happening, and I'm acting a little stupid."

Kurt said, "And you know I could kick your ass, right?"

"No way. I'm a master of multiple martial arts."

Kurt smiled at him. "Name one."

Gabe went totally blank for seconds and seconds, but then he said, "Judo. Karate. Tae Kwon Do. Brazilian Jujitsu. Krav maga."

"Bullshit."

"I did take a self defense course."

"And how did that work out?"

"Bill, my instructor, who was a burly, battle-hardened man, wept openly at my ineptitude." Kurt smiled even more. "Apology accepted?"

"Yeah. I guess."

"Want to get a late lunch?"

Kurt shook his head. "I'm on duty now."

"Maybe tonight?"

"Can't. I have a previous engagement. Tomorrow?"

"Okay. Lunch at Heather's?" He thought of the Summer Nights Cafe as Heather's. "Around noon?"

"See you there, Bergeron. And Bergeron."

"Yeah?"

"I'm going to be out of town." He smiled. "Don't do anything stupid in my park between now and then."

Like he would do that.

Kurt or no Kurt, he was really hungry again, but he went to

the marina first. Charlie's boat was at the dock, but no Charlie.

He cruised around the restaurants and fast food joints and spotted Charlie's truck in MacDonald's parking lot. He pulled alongside and waved at Charlie and Luke in a friendly fashion.

Luke gave him a nod and a smile.

He went in and got a burger and then stood beside Charlie's window until he lowered it.

"Go away, Bergeron."

"How are you doing, Sergeant King? Officer Stevens? Isn't it a lovely day? What is the FBI up to?"

He was wearing Charlie down; he knew it because Charlie smiled. "Get away from me. Even if I knew, I couldn't tell you."

"They are using Neal as bait to catch Lonnie's killer. Right?"

Luke nodded.

Charlie smacked Luke in the gut with an open hand, and Luke coughed up a french fry.

"What did I do?"

Charlie said, "Don't tell him anything, and you know what you did."

So Luke had been at the marina? "It's hot out here. Can I get in the back seat?"

"No."

He took a bite of his burger while leaning against Charlie's spotless truck. "I think that the FBI thinks that whoever blew up Eric and shot Lonnie is still around." He leaned closer to Charlie and took a big bite out of his squishy burger.

Charlie looked at him. "Get ketchup on my truck, and I will arrest you."

"On what charge?"

"Premeditated pain-in-the-ass-ery."

He smiled. "If that was a real thing, I would have been in jail a long time ago."

Charlie said, "Leave it alone, Bergeron. Better yet, go home. There is not one damn thing you can do. Or should do." Charlie rolled up his window.

The black top was so hot it was sticky. He got in his car and cranked up the AC.

He wasn't ready to accept that he couldn't do anything.

Step One to getting Neal out of the park and home to Philly was to get him away from Ellie.

And Step One in cleaving them in twain was to find out who she really was. He got out and tapped on Charlie's window again.

Charlie gave him a look, but it wasn't the Vesuvius look. "Charlie? I know you can hear me. Who is Ellie Tyson? Is she FBI? Tell me that, and I promise never to bother you again."

Until he had to.

Charlie engaged the automatic transmission of his vehicle and motored away, but he saw Luke looking back at him in the passenger side mirror, and sweet Luke nodded his head.

Of course, that was better than the alternative, but still there was twain cleaving to be done.

But stealth was called for so he parked in the boat ramp lot. He considered a disguise, but he wasn't shaving his head, and it was too hot for a wig, so he settled for dark sunglasses and a hat.

When he was close to the cabins, he slipped into the forest like a ghost. Sort of.

He crept close to Neal's cabin. The damn forest was too quiet, and it was impossible not to step on something that snapped, crackled, or popped, but, surprisingly, no one spotted him or tapped him on the shoulder or tried to bludgeon him, so he waited. He wasn't sure what he was waiting for exactly.

Neal's Lexus was in the driveway; Mimi's PT Cruiser was missing.

The mosquitoes found him. Killing the little monsters quietly took some of the fun out of it. He decided to look into the window, but he made sure it wasn't Neal and Ellie's bedroom. Some things can never be unseen.

He saw Neal! And he was in one piece.

Gabe Bergeron was moderately gratified.

He heard the cabin door open and close. He curled in a ball and waited until he saw Ellie striding off.

He could talk to Neal, but he wanted to know where Special Agent Ellie was going.

She stopped and did a three sixty before proceeding to the

third cabin which had been Mr Bear's.

She tapped on the door and was admitted.

He approached the cabin, crawling for the last few yards; he made a note that long pants were called for when crawling on hands and knees in a forest.

He huddled underneath a window and could hear voices. He decided to peek in.

Special Agent Tyson, if that was her name, was plotting with Special Agents Murray and Reed, and one of the faux hunters.

Ellie said, "Are you set up for tonight?"

Murray, the Pale Wraith, said, "Yes, Ma'am."

And he heard Reed speak for the first time. Her voice was as deep as he'd imagined, but she didn't have the Russian accent that he'd been hoping for. "Do you think he's still around?"

"He was last night."

Reed said, "But the park's been searched, and the backgrounds of the visitors are clean?"

And then somebody big tackled Gabe Bergeron to the ground. He landed hard and felt the air whoosh out of his body. A hand grabbed his right arm and pulled it behind his back.

He felt the handcuff lock around his wrist as he got a whiff of cheap cologne.

He took a breath. "Chernov?"

Special Agent Chernov hauled him upright and marched him into the cabin and kicked the door shut. He was wearing camo gear and a hat pulled down to his eyebrows.

Ellie smiled and shook her head. "Gabe, you just aren't very bright, are you?"

"Bright enough to confirm that you're FBI."

"Congratulations. Get rid of him, Anderson."

Anderson was in his hunter costume. He was young and had a wispy beard; the pale gray eyes widened a bit. "What should I do with him? Ma'am?"

She frowned. "I'd like to toss him into the creek, but get him in a vehicle and out of the park. Don't let anybody see him. Call for transport to meet you and then get back here."

Chernov said, "Impeding a federal investigation, Anderson."

Anderson nodded.

Ellie smiled at him. "Good bye, Gabe. Let's plan never to meet again."

But then Neal said, "Let him go, Ellie." He was standing in the doorway.

Ellie said, "What are you doing, Neal? Did anybody see you come over here?" She pulled him into the cabin. "Anderson, you and Dunning check out the area again."

Anderson nodded and went.

Ellie said, "He needs to be locked up, Neal. He's going to screw up the plan."

Neal said, "There is no plan if I'm not here."

Ellie said, "You don't want to do that."

"Sorry, Ellie, but that's the way it is." Neal looked at him. "Promise me, Gabe, that you'll leave the park and won't come back? You have to promise me, or I'll let them lock you up for your own safety."

"But she's FBI."

"Yeah, I know. Promise me."

"What about your safety?"

Neal smiled at the four FBI agents. "I'm safe enough."

"Okay, I promise to leave."

"And not come back?"

"I promise."

Ellie wasn't pleased, but Neal wouldn't budge. "Damn it, Neal. He's about as trustworthy as a two year old."

"Let him go."

She hated it, but she nodded at Chernov to release him.

Chernov spun him around. After the cuffs were off, he spun him back and leaned in close so he could really see those black, anarchist eyes. He felt a chill zip up his spine, half terror, half not terror at all. "Go away, Bergeron."

He walked back to the cabin with Neal as FBI Ellie and her merry men continued their plotting.

"Neal? When did you realize she was FBI?"

"A few days ago."

"Shit, Neal! Why didn't you tell me?"

Neal looked like the wheel had come off his toy truck. "I wasn't a hundred percent sure...and I kept hoping I was wrong. You know?"

"Yeah, I get that."

Neal smiled. "And you aren't very good at keeping secrets, Gabe. Or hiding how you feel."

"Am to." Neal was right. "Wait. Has she told you about Lonnie?"

"Who's Lonnie?"

The evil, treacherous, manipulative succubus.

"Lonnie is the local guy who said he saw who put the bomb on Eric's boat."

"He did?"

"That's what Lonnie said, and he offered to tell me who that was if I paid him...he asked for a thousand originally, but I got him down to five hundred."

"Did you pay him?"

"He was shot through the heart before I could."

"Shit, Gabe. So the bomber shot him?"

"Who else? So let's rethink your participation in the FBI's stupid plan."

"No, I told Ellie I would help, and I'm going to do just that."

"Why?" He had never wanted to punch his friend in the balls before. He gritted his teeth and tried to think how to ask the question. "You don't still think that she...."

"Yes, I still think that she loves me, but even if she doesn't, I love her."

Wasn't that just marvelous?

He shook his head at Neal as he scanned the area looking for FBI agents with parabolic microphones or drones hovering in the tree canopy, but all he saw was young Anderson doing a grid search of the area in a totally casual, non-FBI manner.

"But you told Max about the rare book?" Neal nodded. "And you haven't told Ellie, or any of them, anything?"

"No. Not a word."

He hugged his friend. "Excellent. But you really did tell Max about the rare book?"

He nodded. "Yes, Gabe, I really did. He said to keep my mouth shut."

"Max is very wise." He looked at Neal. "So you've been here for a week? Anyone seem odd?"

He shook his head. "Everyone's been really nice, Gabe. That's part of the reason I love this place."

Right. "One of them is a hit-man, Neal. Or hit-person." No need to be sexist even in desperate times.

Neal shook his head again. "I have no idea, Gabe, and if I did, I wouldn't tell you. Go home. Like you promised. Please."

"Come home with me. There's no reason to stay here, Neal."

Ellie was approaching. "Get moving, Bergeron. If I see you again, no force on Earth will keep you out of prison."

"It's been a pleasure getting to know the real you, Miss Tyson. It truly has. Neal? Keep your head down, and don't take any risks no matter what they tell you."

Neal should be okay. There were at least six FBI agents watching over him.

But he didn't really trust them. Not even a little.

But he kept walking.

Sunday
3:00 pm

Wendy was tidying that immaculate campsite.

She smiled. "Gabe. I saw your car in the lot. How are you doing? Want some coffee?"

"You don't have to twist my arm, and I'm okay."

He felt the rope burns on his throat; it was still hard to believe that someone had almost choked him to death.

She poured coffee into a mug, and the aroma wafted around them. "Have a seat, Gabe."

He sat in the shade and sipped.

She said, "Does it hurt?"

"Some. Where are Bob and the twins?"

"Gone fishing again. They don't even like fish. But as long as they don't expect me to clean the things, they can catch as many as they want."

He didn't have any reason to trust Wendy any more than anyone else in the park, but he sorta did.

"You were very lucky, Gabe. Just a little more pressure..."

"I heard. Did you have hand-to-hand combat training? In the army?"

"I did. The basics. I like to think I was pretty good."

She probably still was. "I need your help, Wendy."

"With what? Exactly?"

"You walk around a lot. You see things."

She smiled at him. "Have I spotted the killer? Is that what you're asking me, Gabe?"

"Or just anything suspicious?"

"If I knew who the killer was, I would tell Sergeant King. I wouldn't hesitate one second."

"No, I'm sure you wouldn't. You'd tell Charlie and not the FBI?"

She rolled her eyes. "The FBI has a different agenda. From the questions they asked."

He didn't say anything.

She smiled again. "You don't have to tell me what's going on with Neal."

"He didn't blow up Eric."

"I know." She was staring at him. "I saw him and that Ellie walking back toward their cabin? Just a while ago?"

"I know. I asked him to come home."

"But he won't listen to you? He's not going to, Gabe. Don't you know that?"

He did. "Right. So nothing suspicious? Nobody lurking around?"

She laughed. "I didn't say that. I wouldn't trust half the people in this park. And as for lurking, a whole lot of that's been going on."

"Who and where and when?"

"Gabe, you aren't a cop." She cast a gaze at his throat. "And you aren't exactly...equipped for that line of work, so I'm not going to say anything, and you should probably go home yourself."

He sipped his coffee. He could see Kev and Barb's golden RV through the trees. They had slathered their nearly-naked, golden bodies with oil and were taking the sun. Barb waved at him.

"Right. I hear you. But what about them? Something's off with those two?"

Wendy gave the Sanduskys a glare. "Those two! Don't get me started." But she wouldn't say anything else.

And then they saw Jace and Jessica knocking on the door of the silver RV.

Randy opened the door. "Not now! Get lost!"

Jace smiled and nodded, but Jessica folded her delicate arms over her strangely ample bosom. "What are you scared of? They're gone, and I paid half already, and I want it. Now."

Randy shook his head. "Keep your voice down."

Jessica said, "Now! Tell him, Jace."

Jace seemed a little not-Zen for once as he looked from Jessica to Randy, but he just shrugged.

Jessica said, "I want it. Now!"

Randy wanted to slap her, but he said, "Then get in here, and shut up!"

Jessica hopped up the stairs into the RV of the man who was going to dismember her youthful body, turn her skull into a drinking cup, and bury the rest of her in the woods.

Good enough for her.

But then Jace followed her inside, and the door slammed shut.

"Shit. And there's something about him too."

Wendy said, "You know them, Gabe?"

"Jace is the son of Heather...waitress at the Summer Nights Cafe, and Jessica is his girl. If I knew Heather's number, I'd call her."

Wendy said, "Drugs?"

That was his first thought too. "I don't know."

"Get the ranger, Gabe. I'll keep an eye on the RV."

Sarah was in the office; he didn't see Kurt. She said, "What now, Bergeron?"

"It may be nothing, but Jace and Jessica are in Randy's RV, and I think he's up to no good."

Sarah smiled at him.

"No, really, Sarah. You know who Jace and Jessica are?"

"Yes, Gabriel. This is a small town, and Heather is my friend as you may recall."

"Okay. And do you know who Randy is?"

She frowned. "Randy is not a friend, but he's never caused any trouble. He stops here every so often."

"And does he strike you as a great soul come to commune with nature?"

"No. Jace and Jessica went inside his RV?"

"I believe that's what I just said. She said something about already paying half."

Sarah said, "Stay here."

But before she could ride to the rescue, Jace and Jessica drove past them. Jace waved and smiled at Sarah.

Little Jessica was beaming so she had obviously gotten her way. Something about the smile gave him a chill.

Wendy was walking toward them. "They came out with a good-sized box, Gabe. Jace was carrying it for her."

"Thanks, Wendy. I guess I'm suspicious of everybody, and maybe a little jumpy."

"With reason, Gabe."

Sarah said, "I'll have a chat with Mr. Randy Green."

He and Wendy followed her to Randy's RV. Sarah knocked and then banged on the RV door, but Randy didn't show.

Sarah said, "I'll keep an eye out for Green."

Wendy went back to her camper, and he and Sarah walked toward the park office.

She said, "Neal and Ellie are safely in their cabin?"

"They are. And I have no other crimes or accidents to report, Ranger Sharp."

"Good to hear."

"So where's Kurt?"

"Ranger Hobbs is in Baltimore on personal business."

"Really? What kind of personal business? A girlfriend?"

She smiled at him. "I never told you, Bergeron."

"Of course not! What's her name?"

"No. Go away."

"Sure. But have you seen any suspicious behavior recently?"

She laughed at him. "Besides your behavior, you mean?"

"Yeah, besides mine."

"Gabe, I think you mean well, but do not play sleuth. This is not a lame murder mystery party. This is not a game."

"I do know that."

"Do you really?"

"Yes, I really do."

She smiled. "Excellent. Now I have work to do, and I promised Kurt that the park will still be here when he gets back from Baltimore." She grabbed his arm. "So don't do anything. Understand?"

"Right. Absolutely."

He got in his car. Neal and Ellie were walking hand in hand along the creek, waving and chatting with all the happy campers.

She should paint a target on Neal's back. One of the "hunters" was loitering nearby, and nobody was going to shoot Neal in broad daylight.

Still.

But Wendy was right.

And Sarah.

And Great-aunt Flo.

Gabriel Henri Bergeron was not a cop. But he knew two cops.

He spotted the boat with the radar saucer on top coming into the marina and was loitering casually on the dock when they pulled in.

Charlie ignored him as Luke tied up the boat.

Luke said, "All done, Charlie?"

He nodded, and Luke drove off.

Charlie finally looked at him. "What now, Bergeron?"

"I want to pick your brain."

"Never going to happen."

"Please? I need your help."

Charlie said, "You need professional help, just not my profession."

"Don't be like that."

Charlie covered the electronic gizmos on the boat and climbed out. "I am going home now."

"Right. I understand. I just wish Neal would come home to Philadelphia. He's in danger."

"Where is he?"

"At the park."

"Alone?"

"No, Charlie. He has five FBI agents watching over him; six if you count Ellie."

"But that's not enough? In your professional opinion?"

"Nope."

"So why are you keeping me from going home, Gabe?"

"Wait. The FBI thinks that Eric was involved in money laundering."

Charlie said, "I don't care." The sergeant walked to his truck and got in. The door locks clicked home, but Charlie didn't drive off.

He stood beside the truck looking hopeful until he heard the door click again. He got in.

"Thanks, Charlie."

"I shouldn't talk to you."

"But you're curious?"

"I am. Do you know who blew up the boat, Gabe?"

"No idea. I was hoping you knew? Or suspected? After your investigation and the forensic reports and the background checks and all the other stuff you know that I don't have access to?"

Charlie smiled at him. "And what would you do, if I suddenly lost my mind and gave you a name?"

Which was a very good question.

"You have no idea. If I knew anything, I'd tell the FBI. Now get out of my truck and go home to Philadelphia."

"Okay." He got out but he couldn't go home.

Charlie looked at him. "Here is my number. Call me before you do anything crazy. Before, Bergeron. Not after. Not during. Before."

"Absolutely. Not that I'm going to do anything crazy."

Charlie looked very tired. "I'd arrest you right now, but I'll leave that up to the FBI. I'm sure they'll take care of it."

"They wanted to."

"So Girard was involved in money laundering?"

He nodded and smiled at Charlie. "But I have no evidence to prove that he was."

Charlie said, "Does Neal have any evidence?"

"I have no evidence that he has any such evidence."

"Asshole." Charlie was looking at him. "If he really hasn't told you, you might want to ask him about that, Gabe. Are you sure he's innocent?"

"Yes, I'm sure."

"I hope you're right." And Charlie pulled out of the parking lot.

Sunday
6:00 pm

Gabe hadn't found out anything useful. He was an accountant and no detective, but he knew Neal was innocent; innocent in many ways. Charlie would know that if he knew Neal.

He was starving, but the restaurant was packed. Heather was dashing back and forth, but she spotted him.

"Sorry, Gabe, but we're full up. Can you wait a few minutes?"

He would have left, but he was hoping to see Neal. "Sure, I can wait."

And then a voice at his ear, said, "Hey, Buddy."

He was going to have to invest in a motion detector, if people were going to keep sneaking up on him. At least, he didn't jump.

Kev wrapped an arm around his shoulder. "Crazy busy in here. Want to come sit with us?"

Ole Kev hadn't buttoned his shirt, and what Gabe really wanted to do was to drive his elbow into Kev's hairy gut.

Heather rushed by. "Are you sitting with Kev and Barb?"

Barb was smiling at him; Kev was smiling at him. He didn't want to be a jerk, and he was too tired to come up with even a half-assed excuse."

"Okay. Thanks."

Kev helped him over to the table. They hadn't been served yet so he was going to have to spend a whole meal with them.

"I'm sorry about the boat, the steering of the boat. I'm a bit of a klutz."

Kev said, "You did get the old heart racing, Gabe, but no harm done."

Barb was looking at his throat. "Are you okay, Gabe? Lots of excitement at the park, right?"

"More than I like actually."

She nodded. "Scared me half to death...the gunshots, I mean. They found a body in the creek."

Kev said, "I don't know if we'll come back here again. Know the guy, Gabe?"

"I think he was local."

Kev said, "Really? But I thought you were talking to him?"

He smiled at Kev, but Heather came back before he could tell Kev to take a long walk on a short pier.

"Ready to order?"

Kev and Barb made a big deal of it, making Heather recite the specials and dithering around when everybody knew they were going to order seafood.

Heather kept smiling through it all and bustled off.

He said, "Not really talking, Kev; the guy just asked about Eric's boat. But where were you guys? After the gunfire? I don't remember seeing you, and it wasn't that far from your monster RV."

Kev finally stopped smiling. "Sorry, Buddy. I wasn't implying anything."

Barb said, "Kev just runs his mouth when his brain's not in gear sometimes."

Kev gave Barb a look. "I'm not the only one. You scared off poor Neal."

"I did no such thing!"

"Guys? Scared him off how?"

Kev and Barb turned to him like sunflowers tracking the disk of the sun. Kev said, "Sorry, Buddy. It's just that we're friendly people..."

She cut in. "And sometimes people are a little overwhelmed. We just wanted to get to know Neal."

"And Ellie."

She smiled at Kev. "And definitely Ellie. But Neal seemed a little shy."

"Yeah, he is until he gets to know you." He patted Kev's hand. "So where were you guys?"

Kev smiled at him. "We were busy when the shooting started. Really busy." Ole Kev winked at him.

She said, "We really were." She grabbed Kev's hand and giggled. "And by the time we got some clothes on, Gabe, the ranger was shooing people away."

She smiled as she rubbed her foot up Gabe Bergeron's calf and on to his thigh. Her legs were long enough that she could rest her foot against his crotch with ease.

He glanced at Kev who just smiled at him as Barb started massaging some very sensitive areas. He was about to run for the men's room, when Heather brought their order.

Barb had to retract her ovipositor.

Kev and Barb had hearty appetites, which wasn't a big surprise.

Gabe ate as fast as he could.

Heather was seating Wendy and Bob and the boys. He waved at Wendy, who gave him a funny look.

Barb said, "I don't think Wendy likes us, Kev."

Kev said, "Everybody likes us, Honey."

Not true. So not true. He asked them about real estate; they seemed very interested in Eric and Layla.

He inhaled the rest of his crab cake and moved his chair back out of Barb's reach.

Kev rubbed his forearm. "You aren't going, are you, Buddy?"

He tried to smile at Kev. "No, just stretching my legs."

Mia and Gareth entered, and behind them, Neal and Ellie. Barb had spotted Neal too. She tried to wave him over, but Ellie just waved back and steered Neal to a booth.

Barb and Kev broke their eye-lock on Neal and refocused on him. They seemed to be ignoring Mia and Gareth completely.

Kev said, "Dessert?"

Barb said, "Sure. This is a vacation, and we deserve to enjoy ourselves. Isn't that right, Gabe?"

"Absolutely. But I think I'll skip dessert, Guys."

He felt Kev's foot touch his thigh and start exploring. "Come back to the RV with us, Gabe. The night is young."

It would never be that young. "I'd love to, but I'm not feeling that well." He patted the back of his head. "But it was great getting to know you better."

Barb said, "Are you sure?"

Kev was getting into massaging him under the table. "We've barely started getting acquainted, Gabe?"

He scooted back and headed for the door. He nodded to Mia and grinned at Gareth, who muttered under his breath.

He stopped by Neal's booth. "We need to talk, Neal."

Ellie said, "Not here, Bergeron. And not tonight." She smiled sweetly. "Why don't you just go away."

Neal said, "Please, Gabe. I'm okay."

"Right."

So Gabe sat in his car and waited until Ellie and Neal finally appeared. They thought they could ignore him, but it took a lot more than that to make him back off. He leaned against the Lexus until they acknowledged his presence.

Ellie said, "What do you want now, Bergeron?"

He said, "I'm going back to the cabin with you. I don't trust you to protect Neal."

Ellie smiled like they were having a pleasant conversation. "Like Hell you are."

"If you don't let me tag along, there's no telling what I could get up to."

She wanted to shoot him with the gun she surely had in her purse. She looked at Neal, and he nodded.

"All right. I should keep an eye on you, but if you interfere in any way, I will arrest you, no matter what Neal says."

"I promise to be on my best behavior. You'll hardly know I'm around."

"I don't believe that for a second, Bergeron."

He smiled at Neal and gave him a thumbs up; Neal shook his head.

He was cranking up the AC in the Fiesta when he saw a guy who looked a lot like Raúl drive past him in a white van with "Dalton's Plumbing – Quality Service" lettered on the door.

Raúl was one of a handful of young Hispanic men who had appeared at Aunt Flo's home over the years and been introduced as a "nephew" of Mrs. Gutierrez.

They had stayed for a week, or a month, or longer in Raúl's case, before vanishing again. They had generally ignored him and pretended not to speak English.

It was true that Gabe had no evidence that Raúl, Carlos, Luis, Yoel, and Tomas weren't her nephews, but there was something about the smirk they all shared. And they looked nothing like Mrs. Gutierrez, except for Raúl, who did a little.

But he didn't want to give Ellie time to reconsider her decision so he didn't chase Raúl, or his doppelganger.

He pulled in behind the Lexus at the cabin. Mimi's red PT Cruiser was in her lane. Every light in her cabin was on, and antique rock music was taking liberties with the forest silence. The lyrics seemed to be about Jeremiah and some bullfrog? The third cabin was dark.

Ellie turned on the lights, and Neal headed for the bathroom.

He said, "So what is the plan? You tie Neal to a tree with a spotlight on him and wait for someone to shoot him?"

Ellie said, "I knew this was a mistake."

"You didn't tell him about Lonnie."

She looked a little guilty. "He didn't need to know."

"Says you."

Neal was standing in the bathroom door. "Gabe? Shut the Hell up."

"Yeah?"

"If you want to stay here." He walked into the bedroom and slammed the door.

Ellie pointed at the other bedroom. "Go away."

He was being sent to bed early. No one had ever done that to him...that he could remember. Great-aunt Flo had thought he should decide for himself.

"I want some coffee."

She had grabbed a book and claimed the one comfortable chair. "It will keep you awake."

"That is kind of the idea, Special Agent."

"Well, I don't have any."

"How well I know. Be back soon."

"Where do you think you're going?"

"Over to visit with Mimi and Floria and Manon, who know how to treat guests."

Ellie stared at him. "You aren't a guest. You are a pain in the ass with a big mouth."

"I am. But tell me this, do you even like Neal? I'll bet you have a husband and a houseful of children somewhere?"

"Go get your coffee, or I will shoot you. Or tell Chernov that he can do whatever he likes to you."

"Where is the Anarchist?"

"Is that what you call him? What about Murray? Got a cute name for him?"

"The Pale Wraith."

She nodded. "I can sort of see that one. What about me?"

"No."

"No name?"

"No cute name anyway."

Gabe left seeking more congenial company. The current selection from the Top Ten of Some Year Before 1990 began with "one, two, three," and then "good lovin'" was shouted with youthful, horny vigor over and over again.

The music paused as Manon opened the door.

She smiled. "Gabe. Do come in."

Manon was tipsy. And handsy.

But then so were Mimi and Floria.

"I hate to impose...."

Floria said, "Anything for you, Gabe. Anything at all."

"Can I make a pot of coffee?"

Mimi said, "Of course. Or you could join us?"

There were two empty wine bottles on the table, and the level in the third was dropping fast.

"Thanks for the invite, but I have to stay alert."

Floria focused on him. "Why? Is something going to happen?"

He did have a big mouth. "No, I have some work that has to be done by morning." They looked very disappointed. "So may I make a pot of coffee?"

Manon made it for him and rubbed his ass as he left their cabin.

Ellie was holding a pistol when she opened the door to let him in. "What is that?"

"A semi-automatic pistol."

"I knew that." He knew the pistol part anyway. It was black and squarish; a knob bumped out of the bottom of the handle.

She smiled at him. "A Glock 22."

"Can I hold it?"

She laughed.

"How good a shot are you?"

"Good enough."

"I'm glad to hear it."

He took his pot of coffee and retired to his bedroom. It was only nine o'clock, but he turned off the light and opened the curtains.

Ellie went into the bedroom at eleven, and the cabin was dark. He hoped Chernov and Murray and Reed and the "hunters" were watching over them. He wasn't going to sleep anyway.

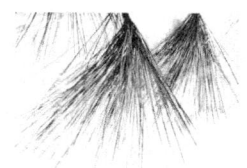

Monday
2:00 am

And Gabe had nodded off. Some watchdog he was. The next time that Neal got into trouble, if there was a next time, he should probably hire somebody.

He looked outside and didn't see anything, but there was a smell. It was so faint that he couldn't place it.

He opened the window, and it was like having a gasoline soaked rag shoved into his face. He caught a glimpse of a dark shape running around the cabin.

And then there was fire, lots and lots of fire.

"Neal! Neal, get up!"

He barged into Neal's bedroom.

They were naked and asleep and naked.

"Get up! The cabin's on fire!"

Ellie sat up in bed covering her breasts with her hands. "Get out, Bergeron! What did you say?"

He pointed to the window where the cheery glow of firelight was rising to the sky. "Fire! Move your ass, Special Agent."

Gabe tossed clothes at them. "Get dressed!"

He ran to the door. He wasn't really thinking about anything but getting out. He flung it open and then jumped back.

The door was on fire, and a wall of burning brush was blocking the doorway. The smoke was filling the cabin.

Ellie and Neal were behind him now. He slammed the door.

"Shit! Where's Chernov and your guys?"

Ellie was screaming into her radio. "Chernov! Murray! Anderson!" She looked at him. "Can we jump through it?"

"I don't think so." The flames were too intense.

Neal said, "The porch?"

Each cabin had a screen porch facing the creek. The flames didn't seem as bad on that side. "Maybe."

He opened the door and stepped onto the porch with Neal behind him.

Ellie's radio crackled to life. Murray said, "Tyson! We're coming. There's a guy...."

Gabe saw the guy.

Well, he saw a black blob with shiny eyes and a shiny gun in the woods.

And then somebody knocked him down.

The sound of the shot wasn't that loud what with the roar of the fire, but he heard somebody grunt and fall on top of him.

Neal.

And then Ellie was doing her best to pump the black blob full of lead. And there were shots coming from the dock too.

The black blob merged back into the black forest. Ellie vaulted over him and Neal and gave chase.

He grabbed Neal and carry-dragged him out of the burning porch and away from the cabin.

There were more shots fired, and then Anderson ran past him following Ellie.

The cabin was burning fiercely.

He grabbed Neal and dragged him toward Mimi's cabin.

Murray was suddenly there helping him lift Neal. Mimi and Floria and Manon were standing in their doorway in their nightgowns.

Murray yelled, "Inside! Now! Move it! Move it!"

He and Murray carried Neal inside pushing the three sisters along as they went.

Murray slammed the door. He was wearing camo gear and had night vision goggles pushed up on his head. "Get down! On the floor." He grabbed his radio. "Chernov? Tyson? Anybody? Shit."

Murray looked at him. The Pale Wraith finally had some color in his face. "Stay here, Bergeron. Bolt the door after me!"

"Right! Bolt the door."

And the not so Pale Wraith was gone.

He bolted the door. Mimi grabbed the sofa. "Help me, Gabe."

They barricaded the door.

Floria was beside Neal. "How is he?"

Manon was on the phone to 911.

Floria said, "Tell them GSW to the left upper quadrant of the abdomen, Manon. I need something to stop the bleeding."

Mimi handed her a towel, and Floria applied pressure to Neal's wound. He sat on the floor. "Neal? Can you hear me?"

He patted his best friend's face. "Neal?"

"Gabe?" His eyes popped open. "The cabin's on fire! Where's Ellie?"

"We're safe, Neal. Ellie's fine. Stay down." He had no idea if Ellie was fine or not.

"Somebody shot me."

"They did, but the ambulance is on the way. You're going to be fine." Neal's eyes closed. "Neal?"

Mimi said, "He passed out, Gabe."

He looked at Floria. "Are you a doctor?"

Mimi smiled at him. "She's just watched too many hospital and cop shows on television."

Floria said, "I took that first aid course, Mimi." She looked at him. "Neal will be okay, Gabe."

"You think so?"

She nodded. "He's young and strong. They'll take the bullet out, and he'll be up in no time."

He wanted to believe her, but Neal didn't look very good.

Manon patted his shoulder and pointed out the window. "What happened, Gabe?"

Flames were shooting out of the roof of the cabin. What was the phrase; fully involved?

"Some sick bastard tried to burn us alive."

Mimi said, "The same bastard who blew up Eric's boat?"

He nodded. "That would be my guess. I knew this was a stupid plan."

Floria was looking at the bloody towel and at Mimi. He didn't have to be tuned into their sister frequency to know that Neal was bleeding a lot.

"Where is that ambulance?"

Mimi said, "On its way, Gabe."

He thought he heard a siren.

Somebody started banging on the door.

He looked around for a weapon of some kind. Manon handed him a poker from the fireplace. He motioned for them to get down.

Ellie said, "Bergeron! Open the damn door."

"Are you alone?"

"What do you mean, am I alone? Yes, I'm alone. Open the door."

"Hold on."

They dragged the sofa away from the door, and he unlocked it. He scrunched up against the wall as he opened the door.

Ellie stepped in.

He didn't brain her with the poker.

He so wanted to.

She was covered in soot and dirt. She had mud or something in her hair. She was nearly naked and barefoot, and her legs were bleeding..

"Put the damn poker down, Bergeron."

He still wanted to brain her, but Mimi took the poker.

"How is Neal?"

"As if you care."

She shoved the muzzle of her Glock into his face. "I care."

Floria said, "He's bleeding quite a bit. We called for an ambulance."

Ellie knelt beside Neal. "Neal? Can you hear me?"

Mimi went into the bedroom and came back with some clothes. "I'm sure he'll be fine, Ellie. I think the ambulance is here." She held out the clothes. "You might want to put these on. They'll hang off you, but needs must."

Ellie kissed Neal on the forehead. She looked at Mimi. "Thank you."

She got dressed as Mimi called the paramedics in. He

recognized them. "How is he, Bud?"

Bud said, "He's been shot."

Ed nodded. "In the upper, left quadrant of the abdomen."

"Yeah, but what the Hell does that mean? He's going to be all right, isn't he?"

Bud said, "We'll do everything we can, Sir."

Ellie said, "Bergeron, come with me." And she dragged him outside. She looked like a little girl playing dress-up in her mother's clothes.

"Did you see anything?"

The flames had all but consumed the cabin, and now were chowing down on the trees and getting close to Neal's Lexus. He could hear another siren. It had better be a fire engine.

"Did I see anything? You mean the guy?"

"What else?"

"I saw a shape. You didn't catch him? Where were Chernov and Murray and the rest of them?"

"They were surrounding the cabin."

"So how did the guy get past them?"

"I don't know." She closed her eyes. "And we can't find Chernov."

This was bad. If Neal came through this okay, Gabe thought he might almost feel sorry for her.

The fire engines pulled in, and they sprayed the burning trees and then hit the cabin and the Lexus.

And then there were people everywhere as the whole park turned out to see what was going on. Again. There were even boats on the creek. He saw Sarah pull up to the dock and jump out.

Anderson appeared through the smoke and steam. Ellie said, "Have you found him?"

Young Anderson shook his head. "I searched the area. His gear is right where it should be, but no Chernov. Reed is still looking."

"And the perp?"

Anderson shook his head.

She grabbed her radio. "Chernov! Answer me!"

The paramedics were bringing Neal out. "How is he doing?"

Bud said, "Stable enough for transport."

Gabe crawled into the back of the ambulance with Neal. Ed looked at Bud, but Bud just nodded.

Ellie stopped Bud from closing the door. "I'll call you, Bergeron."

"Right."

"I can't leave."

"Yeah, I understand."

He saw Murray and Reed heading for Ellie as Bud reversed. They had to wait until one of the fire engines moved before they could negotiate the narrow road.

They carried Neal to Peninsula Regional Medical Center in Salisbury. The ER team took Neal and shooed him toward a waiting room.

But one of the nurses said, "Do you need treatment, Sir?"

"I'm fine."

"You have some burns, Sir."

Gabe checked out his arms. They hadn't hurt until the nurse mentioned them. They didn't look too bad.

"I'm okay."

The nurse said, "Let a doctor check you over. Did you inhale any smoke?"

"I don't think so."

An ER doctor inspected him, noting the stitches on his legs and on the back of his head, and his general scorched appearance.

They wrapped the worst burn on his right forearm and called the police. He was trying to explain his weekend in a thousand words or less, when Ellie and Reed arrived. Ellie had changed her clothes and combed her hair; Reed was still in her camo outfit.

"Where is Neal?"

"In surgery. They won't tell me anything."

Ellie left to find a doctor.

Reed took a seat across from him. "Mr. Bergeron?"

He tried smiling at her. "I didn't think you talked to anyone but FBI personnel?"

She didn't call him an idiot. "Yes, I do, Sir. Tell me what happened from the beginning, please."

"'In the beginning God created the heaven and the earth. And the earth was without form....'"

Dumb Gabe stopped because Reed looked upset, and it wasn't impossible that she had tears in her eyes. "I'm sorry, Reed. I can be a smart-ass. I can see you're upset."

She cleared her throat and glared at him. "Not quite that far back, Sir. The last four hours." Or she was going to reach down his throat and yank out his lungs.

"I fell asleep. But I woke up, and there was a stink. It was gasoline, and then there was a lot of fire. I woke up Neal and Ellie, and we tried to get out. And Neal got shot saving my ass. And Ellie chased the guy who shot Neal, and I carried Neal out of the cabin, and Murray helped me get him into Mimi's cabin, and...."

"Did you see the arsonist?"

"I saw the shiny gun. I saw a black shape. I saw his eyes. I think they were pale."

"Nothing else? How big was he? Or she?"

"I don't know. Not huge. Not like Mr. Bear."

"Who?" Reed's dark eyes had widened just a little.

"Sorry, Mr. English. The guy who had the cabin that Anderson and the other agent are in now."

Ellie came back.

"Anything?"

"He's still in surgery. They'll find me as soon as they know anything."

"Right." His arm was hurting. "What about Chernov?"

Chernov wasn't a buddy and never would be, but Gabe didn't want anything bad to happen to him.

Ellie said, "He's here." He looked around the apparently empty waiting room. "In the ER, Bergeron."

Reed said, "Murray found him."

"How is he?"

Ellie said, "He'll make it."

"Shit. What happened to him?"

Ellie and Reed pretended he hadn't spoken, which seemed to be an FBI thing.

They sat and waited for hours, but eventually, the doctor

came to speak with Special Agent Tyson.

"Mr. Hartmann came through the surgery fine, and barring any unforeseen complications, we expect him to make a full recovery."

She said, "Thank you, Doctor. Can I see him?"

Gabe said, "Can we see him?"

The doctor said, "He's in recovery. For a minute or two."

Neal was wired up to machines, and had IV's in both arms, and had tubes running into his body, and was swaddled in bandages around his torso.

Ellie leaned close. "Neal?"

His eyes fluttered, but he didn't respond.

Gabe said, "You're going to be okay, Neal. You're in a hospital, and they've taken the bullet out. The surgeon says you're going to be fine."

More eye fluttering, and then Neal said, "I'm glad you guys are okay."

"Ellie and I are fine. You just rest."

He and Ellie were shooed out of recovery. She was on her phone arranging for security for Neal in the hospital. She made another call, but not before she walked away from him. She probably had to call Steele.

Gabe went into the first men's room he found. He faced the mirror. He had looked better, and he started to shake. He tried a few deep breaths and washed the dirt and soot off his face and arms. He stood there taking more of those deep breaths.

He had to think of something else besides Neal coming so close to being dead, but the images of Neal's blood soaking the towel kept popping into his head.

He washed his face again, and walked out. He had to call Neal's parents. That's what he should be doing.

They were shocked and upset, but at least he could tell them that he would be okay. They said they would be in Salisbury in a few hours.

He went back to the waiting room; his feet and legs were grimy, and he stank of smoke. Again.

Ellie was there by herself. He wouldn't hate her quite so much if she'd been crying over Neal, but he couldn't tell.

He sat across from her.

"Go away, Bergeron."

"People are always saying that to me."

"Are you surprised?"

"A little. I am great company. Neal's parents are on their way. Can you make sure they're on the approved visitors list? And me too?"

She nodded.

"Thanks. Now what happened to Chernov? And why was the freaking killer able to douse the freaking cabin in gasoline in preparation for a freaking human barbecue?"

"Chernov's a good agent."

"Obviously."

"Shut up!" Her face had been red, but it turned a very scary white. "He is. The arsonist pepper sprayed him, and then kicked him to within an inch of his life, before dragging him into one of the little cabins."

He wasn't going to ask how the arsonist had gotten close enough to Special Agent Chernov to pepper spray him. "But he's going to be okay?"

"Yes. Don't pretend you care."

"I do care." He really did. "Where were all the other agents?"

"At their assigned posts." She got up and started to walk away. "Remember I was in that cabin too, Bergeron. If I thought anybody had screwed up...."

She resumed exiting the waiting room.

He sat and watched early morning infomercials until Neal's parents arrived.

Neal's mother, Claire, rushed over to hug him. "Gabriel! What happened to Neal? And to you?"

He hadn't seen them for over six months, but she looked exactly the same; still outfitted in matron chic, with her hair permed and tinted.

She hadn't really changed that much in twenty years. It had been strange to live with her after his mother.

"It's a long story."

Neal's dad, Richard, had bags under his eyes and was oyster white, which might be an okay color on a wall, but not so much on a face. He was bent over a cane. Neal had said he'd been sick.

Richard was wheezing. "How is he? Can we see him?"

"I'm sure you can. Come on."

Neal was no longer in recovery, but they tracked him down. There was a police officer outside his room, and he was checking IDs. The nurse would only let one person in at a time so Claire went first.

Richard lowered himself toward a chair and fell into it. "What the Hell is going on, Gabe?"

He wasn't sure how much Neal wanted his parents to know. "There was a fire at the cabin, and Neal got shot."

"But why? And who would shoot Neal? And Eric was blown up on his boat?" Richard was giving him the eye just like he had twenty years ago when he'd come to live with them. "What is going on, Gabe?"

"I don't know. I think Eric got involved with some very bad people."

Richard closed his eyes and took a deep breath. His face had red splotches now. "And these people killed Eric?" He took another breath. "And tried to kill Neal?"

"I think so."

"What about you?"

"What about me? I left two months ago, Richard."

"Neal told me you were fired."

"I was, but I told Neal he should get out too."

Richard was wheezing. "Neal doesn't run away...." He started gasping.

"You should try to calm down. Are you okay?"

Richard wasn't looking okay at all, and he was about to yell for a nurse when Claire came back.

She took one look. "Take one of your pills, Richard. Right now."

Richard swallowed the little white pill without any water.

She patted her husband's arm and leaned in to kiss his forehead. "Now slow your breathing down, Ricky. Neal is awake and talking. Do you want to see him?" He nodded. "But you have to calm down."

He and Claire helped Ricky to his feet and into the room.

They sat in the orange plastic chairs. Claire said, "So what exactly did Eric get Neal into?"

Claire had been a corporate lawyer for a lot of years and knew how to ask questions.

"He took on some clients, some very bad clients, Claire."

"I see. And the FBI was investigating Eric and his clients?"

"Yeah."

She took his hand. "And Neal called you when he became suspicious?"

"Yeah, I was coming back from Chicago when I got his call. I told him he should get out of the partnership two months ago, Claire."

She nodded. "He told me." She didn't ask what he'd been doing in Chicago, but Neal had probably told her.

"But Eric is dead? Why are they coming after Neal?"

"I don't know."

"Gabriel?"

He wanted to tell her about the ledger, but Neal should be the one to do that. And about Ellie and the FBI.

Richard came back looking better. "Neal is going to be okay. The doctor told him so." Richard frowned at the Bergeron guy. "He says he wants to see you."

He slipped in. Neal was alert. "Gabe! Are you okay?"

"I'm fine. Thanks to you." He squeezed his hand. "But we need to have a serious talk about the fine art of bullet dodging."

"You're the one who needs lessons."

"Probably true. I'm a klutz as we both know. Did you see the bastard?"

"A glimpse. You carried me out of the cabin, didn't you? Thanks, Gabe."

"The very least I could do. Neal? Do you have this freaking ledger? Tell me the truth."

Neal closed his eyes. "Can I have some water?"

"I'll find out, but answer me first. I'm already in this up to my chin."

"I don't have it, but it's safe until I can get to it."

"Are you sure? Tell me where it is, Neal."

Neal's eyes were closed.

"Neal? Come on, Neal. Talk to me."

The nurse pushed past him. "Mr. Hartmann needs to rest."

"Right. I know."

She stopped checking the monitor to look at him. "And you need to leave."

"Right. Leaving now."

Gabe sat with Claire and Richard for a while, but Richard wanted him gone even though he tried to hide it from Claire. And Richard shared that Scott was on his way.

So Neal had Claire and Richard and the police officer, and big brother Scott was due soon. Scott hadn't wanted him living with the family any more than Richard had.

He needed to get cleaned up, but he went looking for Chernov first.

Ellie was pacing outside Chernov's room on her phone again. She said, "Yes, Sir, I understand, but I still want to do a complete sweep of the area. Yes, Sir, I agree that we have a solid suspect, but why would he say something like that? Why would he speak at all?" She spotted him. "Excuse me, Sir. Sir?"

"Sir Steele is gone again?"

"What do you want, Bergeron?"

He could see Chernov in a bed with Reed sitting next to him. The parts of his face and body that were visible were bruised and abraded. His nose was covered with a bandage.

"Shit! Is he going to be all right?"

"Yes."

"I'm sorry. About what I said."

"Go away."

"Who is your solid suspect?"

She actually smiled at him. "Unbelievable. You are like a freaking wall of lava coming down the side of a volcano."

"A pyroclastic flow? That sounds a little bit harsh."

"Go away and stay away."

"I will. Neal's parents are here. I didn't say anything about you. Do they know about you? Have you met them? Do you want to?"

She shook her head. "Yes, no, and not now. I have to get back."

Reed squeezed Chernov's hand and joined them in the hall.

Ellie said, "Reed, I want that park searched. I don't care what Steele thinks. I don't want a blade of grass or a pine needle to be overlooked. And I want everyone questioned again."

Ellie walked away.

Reed was staring at him with those dark, dark eyes. "He wants to talk to you."

"Who? Chernov?"

Reed shoved him into the room. Chernov had been kicked in the face along with everywhere else. He hadn't been exactly handsome before but it was hard to see him like that. Would his face be scarred? Maybe he wouldn't mind that?

Reed and Chernov were staring at him. He should say something. "Hi there. How are you feeling?"

Chernov was gritting his teeth; either from pain, or the unfulfilled urge to punch him, or both.

Chernov said, "Sorry."

"What? You're sorry? For the screw-up?"

Reed got in his face. "He didn't screw up, Asshole. The bastard slipped by me too. Somehow."

Chernov grabbed her hand. "No, Reed. I let him get right on top of me."

Gabe said, "So did you get a look at him?"

Chernov groaned. "Reed? Can't you shoot this bastard for me?"

Reed considered carefully. "Sorry. No. But I can take him out of your sight."

"Do that. You need to get back to the park anyway."

"Wait." He took a seat. "Chernov, I am truly sorry that this happened to you, but...."

Chernov sat up and put one leg out of the bed. "Reed!"

Reed grabbed his arm. "But only because Neal's going to be

fine. I have this burn on my arm, but it's nothing really. Did you see or hear anything?"

Special Agent Reed hauled him out of the room as Chernov settled back and shut his eyes.

Gabe said, "And what is that cheap cologne he wears?"

And then he found out how scary Special Agent Reed could really look. She fingered her gun obviously reconsidering shooting him. "It's Achilles by Cinq Mars, and it's not cheap...." She stopped herself.

"You bought it for him? Oh. Oh! Does Steele know about you two?"

Her hands balled into fists, and he could tell she was mentally reviewing all the ways she could hurt him. But she turned and walked away. He followed her until they were outside.

"Reed?"

"What?"

"I need a ride back to the park."

"And why would I give you a ride?"

"Easiest way to be sure that I don't visit Chernov again and annoy the Hell out of him."

She rested her hand on her gun. "All right. But if you open your mouth once, I will kick you out and leave you on the side of the road."

"Got it." They got in a silver Jeep SUV. She adjusted her seat and the mirrors. "And that cologne's not so bad."

"How old are you?"

"Thirty-two. Why?"

She pulled out of the parking lot. "That's about what I thought, but it doesn't add up."

"Again why?"

"There's no way you could have survived for thirty-two years without somebody taking you out."

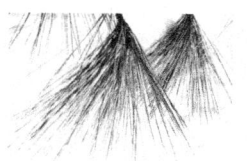

Monday
11:00 am

Janes Island was an armed camp with every branch of law enforcement present, and he would never have breached the perimeter without Reed.

She stopped behind his car. "Get out."

"Yes, Ma'am. Thank you for the ride. I hope Chernov recovers quickly."

She looked at him. "We're going to nail you and Hartmann."

"But what if we're innocent?"

She laughed diabolically and sped off. Well, she didn't laugh at all, but it was implied.

His Ford Fiesta was okay, but Neal's lovely Lexus was tragic; the heat had shattered the windshield, scorched the paint, and made anything plastic sag like the face of a centenarian.

And Kurt's cabin was a pile of smoking timbers and ashes.

Kurt himself was talking to Mimi and Floria and Manon. "I'm sorry, Ladies, but the FBI isn't letting anyone leave the park until they've been questioned."

Floria shook her silver blonde head. "But we don't know anything, Mr. Hobbs."

Mimi said, "We were sleeping soundly."

Manon said, "We'd had a little wine."

They had downed three bottles at least.

Kurt said, "I'm sure they'll interview you soon."

Mimi said, "Gabe, how is Neal?"

"He came through the surgery fine, and they expect a full recovery."

Manon said, "That's wonderful news, Gabe. Wonderful, but I don't want to stay here another night."

Mimi said, "We aren't going to." She handed Kurt a key. "Thank you. I'm sure it's not your fault, but we've never had a camping trip like this before."

Kurt shook his head as the three of them got into Mimi's PT Cruiser and pulled out.

Kurt looked at his destroyed cabin. "Gabe, I leave the park for one night and get back to find this? I'm not sure how I feel about you right now."

"You want to kick someone's ass, but you realize that I am not responsible for burning down your cabin. Or for the other stuff."

"But you're here, and if I punched Steele, I would wind up in federal prison."

"That's true. Okay. My left arm is pretty much undamaged so if you...."

Kurt punched his arm hard enough to stagger him.

"Ouch! What the Hell, Hobbs! I was kidding about my arm."

Kurt sat down at a picnic bench which had somehow survived the fire. "Sorry. But this is an awful, shitty mess, Gabe."

"It hasn't been much fun for me either."

"But Neal is okay?"

"He's wired up like a Christmas tree and has tubes running from his body into plastic bags, but they say he'll be okay. His mother and father drove down, and they're with him now."

"Good." Kurt smiled. "Well, I guess I might as well start thinking about career options; my limited career options."

"They won't fire you. None of this was your fault."

"You're wrong." Kurt waved at the trees and the creek. "This is what I always wanted to do, Gabe."

"Well, I was good with numbers, and Aunt Flo shot down my wilder career ideas. I don't hate accounting. I think I'm good at it." He wanted to tell Kurt not to worry, but that would be stupid. He punched his shoulder gently and said, "I'm sorry, Kurt."

Kurt twisted to look at him. "You look like shit. Again. Why don't you take a shower and get some sleep?"

"Those are wonderful suggestions. What are you going to

do?"

"Keep reassuring the visitors that they are not going to be roasted alive in their beds. Or shot through the heart and dumped into the creek."

"You might want to phrase it a little differently."

"Good point. See you around?"

"Yeah. This has become like my second home."

Kurt laughed at him.

He rubbed his numb left arm as soon as Kurt was out of sight. And that's when he remembered the job interview. In Philadelphia. Which had been scheduled for an hour ago.

Shit.

He called and tried to explain, but they weren't interested in hearing about Gabe Bergeron's problems.

Shit.

He went to the bathhouse and splurged on hot water. At least, he had stashed some clothes and toiletries in the trunk of the Fiesta this time.

He felt almost human except that he was starving. And still profoundly unemployed.

The park was on lock down so he parked and considered who might feed him. It was a pity that Mimi and the gals had packed up for departure.

Sarah and Kurt were both talking to skittish campers so he wandered. The sun was too bright, but he'd lost his last pair of sunglasses to the fire.

Wendy might give him coffee.

But he spotted Mia looking upset first.

He said, "Still here?"

"Unfortunately. I had hoped to leave this morning, but now all this...." She waved at the forces of law and order. Everything was packed up except for one folding chair; Gareth's little Smart Fortwo was hitched to the RV.

"Where's Gareth?"

"Went off on a run." She sat down in her chair. "Gabe, you may not believe me, but Gareth and I had nothing to do with anything which has happened here."

"You didn't set fire to Neal's cabin last night?"

"No, of course not. I would never; Gareth would never." She smiled at him. "He's not as ferocious as he would have you believe. We went to a club in Ocean City and had a little fun. We were dancing when someone tried to kill you and poor Neal."

"Gareth dances?"

She smiled. "After a fashion. But the salient point is that we didn't return until after the fire."

He had no reason to believe her, but if he were to part those palm frond eyelashes and gaze deeply into those dark, tropical eyes, he didn't think he'd see the crazy peering back; not burn people alive crazy.

Of course, he'd have to squint his eyes just right to block out the glare off all that hot, tanned flesh.

She said, "And how is Neal? I should have asked."

"He's going to make a full recovery."

"Excellent. And I do mean that."

They both spotted Gareth returning, but Gareth was cuffed, and Murray had a grip on his arm.

Ellie was just behind them; gun and badge hanging from her belt, FBI cap and Kevlar vest all proudly displayed.

Mia gave her a look before turning to Murray. "What is the meaning of this, Special Agent Murray? Are you all right, Gareth?"

Gareth had a bruise on his face and looked like he'd rolled around in the dirt a bit.

He smiled at Mia. "Mint." He smiled at Murray. "Slop had a go at me s'all."

Mia was staring at Murray. "You assaulted Mr. Fry, Special Agent."

Ellie said, "I'm Special Agent Tyson, Ms. Chandler-Hargreaves, and Mr. Fry had to be subdued when he refused to surrender as requested."

Mia looked Ellie up and down and found her lacking. "I see. I wonder if poor Neal knows what you are? Do tell me why Mr. Fry has been taken into custody? Any particular reason? I'm sure my attorney will be curious."

Ellie looked at Reed. "Mr. Fry was arrested because he was

trying to dispose of that."

Special Agent Reed was carrying a plastic Food Lion bag and a small camping shovel in her blue gloved hands.

"Are you sure, Special Agent Tyson? I've never seen those items before, and I'm quite certain Gareth hasn't either."

Gareth shook his head, but his heart wasn't in it.

Ellie said, "That's strange since Agent Murray and I saw him put that bag into a hole and try to bury it."

Mia said, "One bag looks very much like another."

Ellie said, "You'll have to do better than that. We need to talk, Ms. Chandler-Hargreaves." Ellie looked at Gabe. "Someplace a little more private."

Mia said, "Gareth and I will have nothing to say without our attorney being present."

Ellie said, "Of course."

But before she could take Mia away, Senior Special Agent Steele arrived.

He had forsaken his expensive suits for field attire. Was it possible to tailor Kevlar vests? Apparently, it was.

"You have them, Tyson?"

Ellie was so very, very unhappy. "Yes, Sir."

"Excellent." He smirked at Mia. "You're in a great deal of trouble, Ms. Chandler-Hargreaves."

"Is that so? We'll see about that, Steele."

Ellie was standing with her arms folded. Steele looked at her. "You can wrap up all this, Tyson." He waved a hand at the police presence.

"Sir, I think we should complete the interviews and the search of the area."

Steele smiled. "Hardly necessary." He pointed at Reed still holding the bag. "Let me see, Reed."

She dutifully marched over. He took the bag and looked inside. He held out a hand and said, "Gloves."

Reed handed him a pair.

Steele withdrew a honey-colored, cowboy boot. He examined it from all angles and held it up for Mia and, more importantly, Ellie to see. Brown stains covered the toes. Steele looked over at Gareth, who was trying for stoic but not quite pulling it off.

"Is this yours, Mr. Fry?"

Mia said, "Say nothing, Gareth."

Steele said, "It doesn't matter. I'm sure Mr. Fry's DNA and fingerprints can be recovered. And the brown stains are blood; Special Agent Chernov's blood, Ms. Chandler-Hargreaves."

Gareth was shaking his head. "Aah shite. Nar man, I nivvor."

Mia said, "Gareth." Poor Gareth nodded.

Steele admired the boot some more and then carefully returned it to the bag. He held it out without looking at Reed, who grabbed the bag, while giving Steele a look that should have ruptured his aorta.

Steele, ever oblivious, said, "Bring them."

Mia gave the classic villain line. "You're making a big mistake, Steele." He smiled at her again. "Someone is using those to incriminate Gareth. We didn't return until almost three this morning, Senior Special Agent."

Steele marched away with his retinue and Mia and Gareth in custody.

Ellie was still standing there.

"Is he the solid suspect?"

"Not now, Bergeron. I'm really not in the mood."

"She says they have an alibi, Tyson."

"They'll need one."

Ellie wasn't just upset because Steele had taken charge. "You don't think they did it."

She turned to him. "You have no idea what I'm thinking."

And she departed, and Gabe was left standing beside Gareth's RV all alone in the noon day sun.

He watched the FBI vehicles roll out and right behind them, Mimi's red PT Cruiser. He should go too. There wasn't any reason for Gabe Bergeron to stay now.

But he saw Wendy watching him.

He strolled over. "Wouldn't have any coffee?"

She smiled at him. "Always. Come inside." Wendy's RV had a range with a genuine, old-school coffee pot. She also had a very comfy sofa. "Did they arrest them, Gabe?"

"They did." She poured him a mug of coffee. He took a sip and smiled. "Are you leaving too?"

"Tonight." She sipped her coffee. "How is Neal? He's okay? You wouldn't be sitting here drinking coffee and smiling if he wasn't."

She was right about that; he didn't know what he'd be doing. "Came through the surgery fine and expected to make a full recovery. His parents are with him."

"Mighty glad to hear it. So what's spinning round in that head?"

"I don't think they did it; Mia and Gareth."

"Why?"

"She says they have an alibi, which may or may not be true, but I get this feeling." He looked at Wendy. "I get this feeling that she's been one step behind the whole way...just like me. We've all been running very fast to stay in the same place."

"*Alice in Wonderland.*"

"Yeah."

Wendy said, "So you think the killer is still here?"

"I don't know. What do you think?"

She smiled. "Well, I admit I'm curious. I knew Ellie was up to something, when she got into Fry's RV."

"When was this?"

"Friday, a couple of hours before the yacht exploded."

"But you didn't say anything?"

"I figured she was law enforcement. Something about her. And she didn't take anything out of the RV."

"Anything else?"

"Pretty sure that Fry got into Neal's cabin, Friday night, again after the yacht exploded, before you and Neal got back from the ER."

Gareth had been looking for the ledger.

Wendy said, "That doesn't surprise you. You know what he was looking for?" He shrugged, and she giggled. "You don't play poker, do you, Gabe? Or you lose a lot if you do."

"Okay, I have an idea. Anything else?"

She shrugged. She was probably a great poker player, but he

thought there was something else.

"So you do a lot of walking around."

She nodded. "Can't sleep. I'm lucky to get four hours a night, which leaves a lot of time to fill." She smiled at him. "And I like to walk, and I am a curious person. Like you. But you should just go home, Gabe, before anything else happens."

He wanted to; he really did.

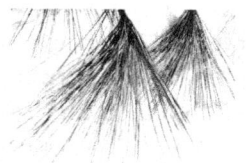

Monday
1:00 pm

Aunt Flo called while he was getting lunch at Denny's on his way to visiting Neal. "Are you all right, Gabriel?"

"I'm fine. How are you?"

She said, "I can understand why someone would want to take a whack at you. There was a news report of a cabin burning down at Janes Island State Park, and my thoughts naturally turned to you."

He couldn't lie to her. Well, he could, but she'd know. "On television? You hate television."

"Gabriel."

"Yeah, it was Neal's cabin, but he's okay."

"Gabriel."

"Okay, he got shot, and he's in PRMC, but the doctor said he'll be fine. And Claire and Richard are with him."

"And did you get hurt? I know you were nearby."

"A tiny burn on my arm."

She sighed. "Mrs. Gutierrez also saw the FBI arresting a couple on television."

"Mia and Gareth, but I don't think they did it."

"And why is that?"

"Somebody is trying too hard to set them up. And they have an alibi."

"I don't want to know how you know that. Come see me, Gabriel?"

"I will, but I have to go check on Neal first."

"Yes, do that. And then come here. I'm worried about you, Gabriel."

Which was the first time she'd ever said something like that out loud. "Thanks, but I'm okay."

"I still want to see you."

"I'll be there soon."

Ellie was outside Neal's room.

She was chatting with Claire and Richard; Richard was gushing over her like a teen fan girl.

"How is Neal doing?"

Claire smiled. "He's sleeping now, but we spoke with the doctor, and he's doing very well."

"I'm glad to hear that. I see you've met Ellie."

Richard said, "Neal told us that he had a new girl friend, but he never said how lovely she was."

Ellie had the charm turned up to toxic levels. "Richard, you're a scamp just like Neal."

Sadly, that worked on Richard.

Claire was smiling at them both, but she caught his eye and winked at him.

"Can I see him? I won't wake him if he's sleeping."

Claire said, "Of course, Gabriel."

Neal had his eyes closed. He whispered, "Neal?"

"Gabe?"

"Yeah, it's me. How are you doing?"

"Okay. I hurt some." His eyes opened. "Probably going to get a lot worse before it gets better."

"If you need pain meds, sing out. Don't be macho."

"Never. How is my car?"

"Well, it didn't burn, but it needs work. A new windshield and grill, and a paint job at least."

"Damn. I really love that car."

"Neal, the FBI arrested Mia and Gareth for the fire."

"Shit! I never thought Mia would do something like that?"

"I'm not convinced she did."

Neal looked at him. "Then who did?"

"No idea."

"Gabe, let it go. Okay? I wouldn't have called you if I'd known any of this was going to happen."

"Don't be stupid. I wouldn't have missed it for the world. Okay, I might have wanted to skip the part where the cabin was burning with us inside. Hey, Ellie is here. She's met your folks. Richard seems to be a big fan already."

"She's here? Can you ask her to come in?"

"Sure can."

He stepped into the hall and pointed at Special Agent Tyson. What was she going to say to Neal?

"Neal would like to see you, Ellie." As she walked past, he whispered, "Could you not give him the heave ho until he's stronger?"

She ignored him, and he took a seat by Claire.

Scott and Rachel were coming down the hall; it was like watching a St. Bernard and a Terrier try to stay in step.

Neal looked like Richard, or at least, he had the floppy ears, but Scott looked more like the pictures of Claire's father. He was bigger and thicker and blonder than Neal or Richard.

Scott had on a nice suit, but his tie was askew, and he looked rumpled as he always did. Rachel had on a suit too, but the skirt part of her ensemble was mid thigh, and the blouse under her jacket was tissue paper thin. Her boobs were rocking and rolling as she tried to keep up with Scott's long legs. The three inch heels couldn't be helping.

Scott hugged Claire and patted Richard's shoulder. Rachel and Claire hugged like two icebergs passing in the North Atlantic.

Rachel took the only empty chair. "Such a tragedy. How is Neal? I've been so worried, Claire."

Claire's face tightened up into a rigid mask. "He's doing well. We expect a full recovery."

Scott was pacing. "Well, that's good." Scott rubbed his eyes and combed his hair with his fingers. "I guess this means that somebody offed Eric? Right?"

Claire said, "The FBI hasn't confirmed that or anything else so far."

Rachel said, "That doesn't matter now, Scott."

"The Hell it doesn't. You say some of the dumbest things, Rachel."

Rachel said, "I say dumb things? Is that what you just said to me, Scott?" She smiled at her husband, but her little red-nailed hands were curled into talons.

"Hi, Scott. Long time."

Scott was looking at the burns on his arms. "Gabe. It has been a long time. Three years?"

"About that. Neal will be happy to see you."

"Yeah, this isn't a good time for me, but Dad wanted me to come."

Richard said, "Your brother needs you."

Scott was eight years older than Neal and had never had time for him.

"That's why I came, Dad. Gabe, walk with me."

"Sure, Scott."

Rachel said, "Scott?"

"Be right back, Honey."

Rachel said, "Well, I'd like to see Neal." Scott kept plodding on.

He heard Claire. "Ellie, his girlfriend, is with him now, Rachel. Give them a few minutes?"

Rachel said, "Sure. I'm only the sister-in-law."

Scott groaned and kept moving forward until he found an empty lounge.

Scott sat down and patted the chair next to him. He smiled, but it wasn't very convincing even for him. "So what's my little brother gotten himself into this time?"

"This time? He isn't exactly an international criminal."

Scott smiled again. "No, he's never screwed up like this before. Did he listen to you about this partnership with Girard, Gabe?"

"No. That's funny, Scott. I thought you introduced him to Eric?"

"Me? Hell, no!"

Denial thy name was Scott.

"Well, Neal didn't ask me about this partnership, Scott, and he isn't a screw up, unless that means that he doesn't take your advice from time to time."

Scott was in real estate and owned a dozen or so parking garages. He gave every appearance of doing well, but if anybody was likely to screw up, it was Scott. He was pretty sure Claire and Richard had bailed him out of scrapes before.

Scott said, "I don't buy that. Neal always listens to you and tells you everything."

"No, he doesn't. If he did, he would have dumped Eric months ago."

"Sure. Well, let's see if we can fix this mess. All right?" He got up and started pacing again. "Tell me what Eric was up to."

"You should talk to Neal about that."

"Come on, Bergeron! I know you know."

"Talk to Neal."

Scott said, "I should have known better than to expect anything from you. Dad tells me you got Neal a lawyer. Who is this Nagy?"

"He's one of the top criminal lawyers in Philly, Scott."

"Is that so? I'll check into that, if you don't mind. But even if that's true, understand this: Nagy, or whoever I get to replace him, is Neal's lawyer and not yours."

"I understand."

"Just so we're clear, Bergeron."

"Crystal, Scott. Just like always."

Scott smiled again. "Hey, congratulations."

"For?"

"Dad says that some guy has owned up to being your father?"

Gabe should have punched Scott in his round, fleshy face, but by the time the shock had receded from his tired brain, Scott was walking away, and the moment had passed.

He got up and walked calmly back to Neal's room. Ellie was coming out. Rachel had popped out of her chair and taken Scott's hand.

Claire was smiling. "This is Scott, Neal's brother, and his wife, Rachel." She was staring at Scott and Rachel as she continued. "Ellie's with the FBI. I'm afraid I don't know her position?"

Scott looked like someone had kicked him in the balls, and Rachel was smiling like she was having a seizure.

Ellie smiled at them. "I'm actually a special agent, assigned to Philadelphia. White collar crime."

Rachel said, "Isn't that fascinating. How did you meet Neal?"

"We met at a club."

Scott sat down in Rachel's chair and started rubbing his eyes again.

Rachel said, "Don't just sit there like a lump, Scott. Say something to Ellie."

"Hi."

Rachel said, "He's upset about Neal."

Claire said, "We all are. Thank you for coming to see Neal, Ellie. Will we be seeing you again?"

Ellie smiled. "Not for a little while. My job, you understand."

Claire nodded, and sweet Ellie walked away.

He said, "I'll be back tomorrow, Claire."

She nodded. "Thank you, Gabriel."

And he jogged after Special Agent Tyson. "Hey, wait up."

"I don't have the time or the patience, Bergeron."

"I can imagine. Steele doesn't seem like a very nice boss."

She stopped. "What do you want?"

"Two things really."

"I shouldn't be talking to you."

"Right. Okay, what did you tell Neal?"

She closed her lovely eyes. "I told him that we couldn't see each other for the foreseeable future."

"Does that mean until you stop trying to put him in federal prison?"

She actually smiled. "Yes, Mr. Bergeron, at least that long. And your last question?"

"Why did you arrest Gareth?"

She said, "Why shouldn't I? But actually Steele arrested him."

"I don't think Gareth did it."

"Why?"

There was no good, no solid, FBI-evidence-based answer to that. "Just tell me this. You suspected him even before you caught the idiot burying his blood-stained boots. Why?"

"I can't tell you that."

"Was it evidence from Chernov?"

"No comment."

"Wait. I heard you talking to Steele. You said 'why would he speak at all.' Right? So did the guy who was kicking Chernov call him a wanker? Possibly, a bleeding wanker?"

She just looked at him, but her eyes grew two sizes larger.

He said, "Damned impressive. Most people would have blurted stuff out. I know I would have."

"Tell me how...tell me why you think that, and I may not arrest you here and now."

"No need for threats, Special Agent Tyson. Because that's what the guy who choked me said, but I knew it wasn't Gareth."

"How?"

"The accent was off. Have you talked to Gareth? His accent is kinda distinctive and hard to fake. Has Chernov even talked to him? No way that even Gareth would be stupid enough to talk when he didn't have to."

"Why are you sharing this now?"

"Because I could rest easier if you had the bastard who wants Neal dead locked away. Not to mention personally feeling a little safer too."

"You should have told us, Bergeron."

"Maybe, maybe not, but I'm telling you now. Are you going to tell Steele?"

She snorted. "Even if you're telling the truth, the case is closed as far as he's concerned."

"So if he's wrong, it will make him look bad? I don't know how things work in the FBI, but in my world, that's usually how it goes."

Malice danced in her lovely eyes. "Shut up, Bergeron."

"Yes, Ma'am."

"And go away."

"Going away now, Ma'am. One last thing...if you are still stringing my friend along to use his love for you to entrap him in some way, I will find a way to hurt you just as much as you'll hurt him."

And then he did go away.

Monday
5:00 pm

Back at the motel, even the carnivorous deer looking at Gabe from the painting couldn't keep him from taking a two hour power nap.

That Dalton's Plumbing van was in the motel parking lot, but he didn't see a Raúl lookalike anywhere as he pulled out.

He had no reason to go back to the park except that he thought the killer was still there.

Somewhere.

Sergeant King's truck was at the park office. Sarah looked less than thrilled to see him when she answered his knock on the door.

"Hello, Ranger Sharp, may I come in?"

She took a moment. "Why?"

Kurt was behind her. "God! What now?"

"I am neither a prophet of doom nor an evil omen, Rangers. I came to invite you both..." He raised his voice. "...and Charlie to dinner. To say I'm sorry though I am blameless and much maligned."

Charlie was behind Kurt. Their continued silence was just hurtful.

Kurt said, "I could eat. You're buying, Bergeron?"

"I am. Anything you want." His credit card would probably not be declined. "Sarah? Charlie?"

Charlie said, "This should be good."

Sarah said, "I'm in. But only to keep an eye on you."

"You wound me, Madam...Mademoiselle? Do the French have a word for Ms.?"

Sarah said, "I'll inquire the next time I'm strolling on the

Champs-Élysées."

All of them would have fit in his Fiesta, but they seemed reluctant to ride with him.

The restaurant wasn't crowded for once.

Heather smiled. "And what will you all have?"

Kurt actually took the anything you want bit seriously.

Charlie was smiling.

"What?"

Charlie said, "We're just waiting for the shoe to drop, Gabe."

"I have no idea what you're talking about, Sergeant."

Heather brought out their food, and he let Charlie swallow a bite before he said, "You know Senior Special Agent Steele has arrested Mia and Gareth?"

Charlie glowered at his plate. "I am aware, Gabe."

But Gabe needed the sergeant's help so he soldiered on. "And what do you think about that?""

Charlie smiled and sipped his iced tea. "No, what do you think about that?"

"That Steele is an idiot."

Charlie said, "I am unwilling to agree or disagree with your assessment at this time."

Kurt said, "Gabe, do you know who's responsible? Who burned my cabin to the ground?"

"I don't know. Not yet."

Charlie sighed. "I knew it."

They were staring at their crab imperial or steak, in Charlie's case, and not looking at him. "Don't you want to know who's done all this shit?"

Charlie wanted to punch him again. "Yes, Gabe, I do. I'm sort of paid to solve little puzzles like this. Along with a lot of other shit."

"I know, Charlie. Sorry."

Charlie said, "But the case belongs to the FBI."

"I know. But I don't want this bastard to get away."

Sarah said, "But you have no idea who it is."

Which was unfortunately true. "I know that he must have a good cover identity, and that he really seems to hate Gareth and Mia."

Sarah said, "I know I'll regret this, but do tell us why you think that, Gabe."

"Sarcasm isn't attractive, Ranger Sharp. But the FBI has talked to everybody, right? And checked their identities?"

Charlie said, "They certainly had the manpower. I know I talked to everybody...." Charlie paused and sipped his iced tea again.

"And? But?"

Charlie smiled at him and cut into his rare steak; the blood oozed.

Sarah said, "And you think he hates Gareth and Mia?"

Charlie was going to be unhappy with him. "Let Charlie finish his steak first."

Charlie stopped chewing. "I can get it to go, Bergeron. Tell me what else you kept to yourself."

"When the guy choked me, he said some stuff."

"What stuff, Bergeron?"

"He called me a 'bleeding wanker'."

Charlie had a vein in the center of his forehead that was standing out and throbbing.

"I didn't tell you because I knew it wasn't Gareth...the accent was all wrong and the voice. And I was afraid that you might focus on Gareth and not look for anybody else."

"You stupid asshole."

"I'm sorry, but I didn't know you that well. Now, I know that you wouldn't have done that."

Charlie got to his feet.

"Please sit down. The killer tried the same trick on Chernov, and Steele fell for it hook, line, and sinker."

Charlie was looming over him. "Did you tell the FBI?"

"Yes, I told Ellie, Special Agent Tyson."

Charlie said, "Is that the truth?"

"Yes, Charlie, I told her. You can call her. I don't know what she'll do with it. Mia and Gareth have an alibi anyway."

Sarah shook her head. "How do you know that?"

"I talked to Mia."

Charlie said, "Of course, you did."

"Please sit down and finish your steak, Sergeant King."

Charlie walked out of the restaurant. They watched him walk to his truck, open the door, stand there, and then slam the door. He came back, sat, and picked up his knife and fork. "This is a very good steak."

"Charlie?" The sergeant was chewing and didn't see Gabe Bergeron's very best smile. "So the killer wore Gareth's boots to kick Chernov to make sure the FBI focused on him."

Kurt nodded. "Gareth came to me on Saturday saying somebody had 'twocked' his boots; that apparently means stolen. So not Gareth and Mia. But who?"

"I don't know. Could somebody be hiding in the woods? Or on the island?"

Charlie said, "No."

They ate in silence for a while. The food really was good, but they weren't going to help him, and he really didn't know what to do even if they were game.

He ate another french fry, and considered the dessert menu.

Wendy and Bob and the twins came in and grabbed a booth.

He waved.

Charlie had almost finished his steak, and Kurt and Sarah were getting ready to leave. It appeared that Gabe Bergeron had one shot left.

He could ask one more time.

He walked over, and Wendy said, "We're heading out after we eat, Gabe."

"Right. Back to Atlanta?"

Wendy raised an eyebrow at that, but Bob said, "After a few stops on the way."

"Have a safe trip."

George or Edward looked at Wendy. "Ask him, Momma."

Edward or George said, "Please! We want to know what happens."

"Ask me what?"

Wendy said, "I thought I said no?"

Bob said, "What would it hurt, Wendy?"

She frowned. "George, slide over so Mr. Bergeron can sit down."

The boys scooted over, and he sat and waited like a rock in a Zen garden.

Wendy finally said, "The boys...." She patted Bob's face. "...all the boys want to know what happens...about Mrs. Chandler-Hargreaves and Neal. And you."

"Okay?"

She wrote an email address on a napkin, and handed it over.

"Ah. You want to be updated about the denouement? Crime scene photos and forensic details? Not a problem. But about that, Wendy, I get the feeling there was something else you know about all this?"

Wendy shook her head.

He pointed at Charlie. "I promise to tell Sergeant King, and that's all." He had his fingers crossed under the table.

Bob and George and Edward were exerting all their mental powers to persuade her to comply.

"I don't know anything."

"But you suspect something?

"Not even that." She glared at her menfolk. "Stop staring at me. All right. Has anybody really looked into the background of that blond kid? The one who has been hanging around with those nice Dutch students?"

"Chuck?"

She nodded.

"I don't know. I thought he was gone?"

"He keeps popping up. And disappearing. And that laugh. There's something about him that's just off."

Chuck was a little crazy and reckless, but he didn't look like a contract killer and arsonist.

But maybe that was the point?

She said, "I'm pretty sure he was watching you and that local man, Lonnie, talk at the dock. A few hours before he was shot."

"Really?" She nodded. "I don't know if they checked him out, but I'll ask Sergeant King. And Ellie. Thank you, Wendy."

"Send me an email telling me you're safe when all this is finally over. A few details wouldn't hurt."

"Absolutely. Okay. Have a safe trip."

George and Edward were smiling at him. "Please don't forget, Mr. Bergeron." And they trooped out to the Coachmen RV and set off on their homeward journey.

He went back to his own table. "Charlie?"

Charlie shook his head. "Am I going to like this, Gabe?"

"What do you know about Chuck?"

Charlie wiped his mouth and enunciated each word. "Who the Hell is Chuck?"

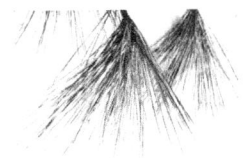

Monday
6:30 pm

Kurt said, "Chuck is that blond kid who's been hanging around with the Dutch students. You must have seen him?"

Sarah said, "I think Aafje likes him."

Kurt said, "Yeah. But Ruurd doesn't."

Sarah smiled. "Because Ruurd's jealous."

Charlie still looked pissed. "You've all seen this guy?"

They all nodded.

"Is he staying in the park?"

Kurt said, "He could be bunking with the Dutch kids, but I don't know that for sure."

Charlie sighed. "Does this guy have a vehicle?" Kurt and Sarah shook their heads. Charlie looked over. "Gabe?"

"I've only seen a bike, Charlie. Loaded down with bags and gear."

"And when did you see him last?"

"Uh. Yesterday. Sunday. Just before I saw you and Luke at MacDonald's. He was on his bike near the park office."

Kurt said, "I saw him Saturday, I think."

Sarah said, "I don't know. Probably Saturday too, but I'm not sure. Why?"

Gabe said, "Wendy thought he was suspicious."

Charlie snorted. "Like you, Bergeron?"

"No, not like me. Do I need to get a t-shirt with a big 'V' for victim emblazoned across the chest? And she thought he was watching me and Lonnie talking at the dock."

Charlie said, "Before Lonnie was shot? She could have shared that."

"So you never questioned him?"

"Never saw him." He looked at Kurt and Sarah. "And no one mentioned him."

Kurt said, "A lot has been going on, Charlie."

Charlie's phone went off. "King."

"All right. I'm on my way, Luke. Be there in five."

Charlie got to his feet. "I have a missing boater on the Big Annemessex River." Charlie stuck a stubby finger into his face. "Do nothing, Gabe. Do not go looking for this Chuck. I will follow up on this, and find you later."

"Absolutely, Charlie."

Charlie looked at him. "I should cuff you to the table."

But Charlie didn't.

Gabe looked at Kurt and Sarah. "Finished? Why don't we just head back to the park then?"

It had cooled off due to the lovely breeze coming off the creek. They strolled down to the scorched dock where it had all begun just three freaking days earlier.

The white, Dalton's Plumbing van pulled into the lot, and Raúl got out. He was twenty-five, big and dark, with a Roman nose and black, almond-shaped eyes. He was actually looking more like Mrs. Gutierrez as he filled out.

He ambled over. "Gabriel, Mrs. Barnes wants to see you."

"Hi, Raúl. Did she send you? I'm sorry she put you to all this trouble."

"No trouble. Not for her. Coming?"

Raúl glanced at Kurt. He thought Raúl was trying to gauge how Kurt would react if more physical measures were required to get the Bergeron idiot to come along.

Raúl shifted his gaze to Sarah, and they stared at each other.

Raúl was large and intense, and he had never had any doubts that not upsetting Raúl was the proper course of action, but not this time.

"Look. I have to take care of something, but I won't be long, and then I'll be right there."

Raúl smiled, but it was just an excuse to bare his teeth.

"Can't it wait?"

He shook his head. "No, I don't think so."

"Can I help?"

He didn't know Raúl any better than he knew Mrs. Gutierrez and her other relatives. He didn't even know if Aunt Flo had sent him. "No, but thanks. Give me an hour. Two, tops. Nice seeing you again, Raúl. When did you become a plumber?"

Raúl squeezed his hands together, obviously imagining crushing stupid Gabe's skull between his extra-large mitts. "Who said I was a plumber?"

He pointed at the van.

"Maybe the former owner, he was a plumber."

Probably best not to ask what had happened to Mr. Dalton. Raúl stared at him for a few more seconds before shrugging and getting back into the van. He didn't drive off but sat there glaring at the little Bergeron guy.

Kurt said, "Who's your friend?"

"I wouldn't say Raúl is a friend. He's the nephew of Mrs. Gutierrez, my great-aunt Flo's friend/housekeeper."

Sarah smiled. "Is that all he is?"

"I'd be very surprised. Back to the matter at hand."

Kurt was looking at him. "You want to talk to Aafje? Don't you, Gabe?"

He said, "No. Ruurd is the one."

Sarah said, "How is your Dutch, and Sergeant King will arrest you, Gabe. You don't know him."

"Charlie and I are tight."

Kurt laughed. "Come on, Sarah. It can't hurt to talk to Aafje."

She shook her head. "If I had a penny for every time a man has said something like that..."

"You'd be a very wealthy woman, and fighting off more suitors than Penelope."

Sarah said, "I wouldn't fight all of them off, Gabe." She was definitely smiling at Raúl, and Raúl took a short break from radiating menace at stupid Gabe so he could smile back at her.

And she sashayed toward the campsites with a very un-ranger-like gait.

Aafje's unlined face tightened up, and her translucent eyelashes fluttered in alarm. "Why ask about Chuck, Mr. Bergeron?"

Which was a perfectly reasonable question. "It's just that he seems to have disappeared, Aafje."

"He comes, and he goes."

Sarah said, "He hasn't registered and shouldn't be staying in the park. Regulations, you understand."

Bastiaan nodded. "Yes, of course, but we don't know where he is."

Gabe smiled. "What's his name? Do you know when he got here?"

Bastiaan shrugged. Ruurd asked something in Dutch, and Bastiaan brought him up to speed.

Aafje said, "Thursday. I saw him then."

Kurt said, "Has he been staying with you?"

Aafje shook her head. "I ask him, but he says no."

Ruurd said something which included "Chuck", but Aafje told him to shut up. It wasn't necessary to speak Dutch to figure that much out.

"Aafje, what did Ruurd say?"

"Nothing,!" She glared at the stupid Bergeron guy. Ruurd always says things about Chuck. He never likes him."

"Please Aafje, what did he say?"

She set her jaw and hunkered down behind the bland, alabaster walls of her face.

But Bastiaan said, "Aafje likes Chuck. Very much. Ruurd says that he saw Chuck riding his bike north, on the road to the log houses."

"When was this?"

Bastiaan said, "The last time was yesterday...early in the afternoon."

Ruurd started saying something else, but Aafje laughed at him. "He is so foolish."

"What did he say, Bastiaan?" Bastiaan looked from Gabe to Aafje. "Bastiaan? Please tell us?"

The boy shook his head. "Aafje is right, it is time we should go, Mr. Bergeron."

He said, "The police officer, Sergeant King, is coming to talk to you soon. If you go, he will find you. You should tell us what Ruurd is saying, Bastiaan. If he knows something about the bad things that have happened here...."

Aafje twisted her childish features into a respectable sneer. "He doesn't. He is a foolish boy. Chuck is a man."

But Bastiaan wasn't so sure that Ruurd was foolish. He said something in Dutch to Aafje; she shrugged and turned away. "Ruurd says that he saw Chuck following the skinny man, the man who was shot."

"He saw Chuck following Lonnie?"

Bastiaan shrugged. "The man with the...." Bastiaan pointed to his fingers. "...the man with the *tatoeage* on each one. You know, yes?"

He knew. "The tattoos."

Bastiaan smiled. "Yes, tattoos."

"Is that all Ruurd saw?"

Bastiaan translated. "He followed, along the creek, but Chuck was into the forest. He went away."

Gabe shook Bastiaan's hand. "Thank you, Bastiaan." He shook Ruurd's too. "Thank you, Ruurd."

He looked at Aafje. "Bastiaan, tell Ruurd he can do better." She might be Bastiaan's sister, but it was still true.

Kurt said, "Sergeant King will want to talk to you."

Sarah said, "But it will be all right. You aren't in any trouble."

Bastiaan said, "No?"

Sarah smiled at him. "No, you aren't."

Kurt and Sarah wandered back to the dock, and he followed. The sun was going to be setting soon.

Sarah said, "That doesn't prove anything."

Kurt said, "But Charlie will want to talk to him."

She nodded.

Gabe said, "But I don't get it. The FBI searched the park."

Kurt said, "They searched the island too. They had drones."

"Really? How cool is that?"

Kurt smiled. "Very. So Chuck's not here. He must have taken off Sunday afternoon after you and Ruurd saw him."

Sarah said, "Good. He's gone, and it's up to King to track

him down, Gabe. Or the FBI."

Which was very true. "But if he really is the guy, if he set the fire, then he didn't leave Sunday, or he came back. Anyway, how did he get away before the FBI had the park sealed?"

Sarah said, "This place isn't a fortress, Gabe. He slipped out through the forest."

"Or, maybe he has a hiding place?"

Kurt said, "But the FBI searched."

Sarah said, "There's King."

Charlie and Luke were sailing past, heading up the creek to look for the missing boater. They waved; Charlie nodded.

"Chuck has to have a hiding place."

Kurt said, "I've only been here a week." He looked at Sarah.

She said, "Oh, no. I'm not getting drawn into Gabe's craziness, and you shouldn't either, Hobbs."

"It's only crazy, Sarah, if I'm wrong."

"No, Gabe, it's crazy to want to find a killer. Sane people run from them."

Which was a good point. "Okay. We'll wait for Charlie to get back."

Kurt said, "But it will be dark by then."

Sarah was staring at the water and fidgeting. "Sarah? What are you thinking?"

She said, "I'll tell King when he gets back."

"Come on, Sarah!"

She said, "No way. I don't trust either of you."

Kurt said, "So if Chuck was heading toward the cabins, the only other structure is the conference center."

He said, "But the FBI must have searched it?"

Kurt nodded. "They must have, Gabe."

"But maybe they did a half-assed job of it?"

Kurt said, "We could go look around?"

"We could."

Sarah said, "Guys? You don't want to do this."

She was very wrong about that. "We'll be careful."

"Typical." She shook her head. "If I had a half penny for every time a man has said that..."

Kurt said, "We can take the boat."

The boat, which had "Park Ranger" on the side, was a scaled down version of Charlie's NRP boat, but the Mercury engine looked as powerful as Charlie's Evinrude. It didn't have the canopy or the radar dish.

Kurt jumped onboard, and he managed to follow without falling into the creek.

Sarah was standing on the dock, arms folded. "You aren't going into the conference center. Tell me you aren't."

"We...I might peek."

"No, Gabe. Chuck could be inside."

"Where? You have an idea, Sarah, I can see you do."

She shrugged. "There's an elevator. It's out of commission, but there could be hiding places above...or maybe below...the cab? Or in the attic space where the machinery is?"

Kurt said, "And Chuck is not very big. It wouldn't take much space."

He said, "Thanks, Sarah."

"You still shouldn't go."

"Kurt, wait. I made Charlie a promise that I'd call him before I did anything."

Kurt nodded. "And you should do that."

It wasn't Gabe's fault that Charlie didn't pick up, but he left a message on his voicemail, a detailed message.

Kurt turned the key, and the Mercury roared to life. Sarah cast off the bow and stern lines. Kurt throttled back, and they putt-putted into Daugherty Creek and headed north.

Sarah watched them go. She was on her phone.

Kurt said, "Are we going in guns blazing?"

It wasn't a comforting metaphor since they had no guns, and Chuck certainly did. Or might. He shook his head. "No. I don't think that's a good idea. Wait. So I'm in charge?"

Kurt smiled. "It's your idea."

It was, but he wasn't a leader of men. "How about we share responsibility?"

"Okay with me. Here." Kurt handed him a pair of binoculars.

The sun and its reflection in the still water were above and below the dark strip of marsh. The sun's rays were slanting into the forest and painting trees, cabins, and the conference center in golden light. He didn't see any movement at all.

Kurt slowed down even more and then cut the engine, and they glided up to the rip-rap just south of the dock in front of Neal's cabin, or the ash heap formerly known as Neal's cabin.

"See anything, Gabe?"

"Trees." Kurt punched his arm again. "Ow! No, Ranger Hobbs, I do not see Chuck, the perp."

They sat there and took turns scanning the center and the surrounding forest.

This had seemed like a much better idea back at the dock. Kurt handed him the binoculars.

He looked at Kurt. "So you have a girlfriend in Baltimore?"

Kurt said, "Now?"

A swarm of gnats had found them. "Why not?"

But Kurt shook his head. "Later. Or never, Bergeron."

"Right. So I think we need to get closer to the conference center. Or I do. Can you hold this thing steady so I can jump onto the rocks?"

"And I do what? I stay in the boat?"

"Yeah. How fast can this thing go? If we really needed it to?"

Kurt looked at him. "Fast, but it won't outrun bullets."

And fiberglass wasn't bullet proof either.

"Just stay here, and if you hear anything, motor away as fast as you can and call for help."

"Got it. Hear what exactly?"

"Gunfire. Screaming. Anything like that."

Kurt smiled at him. "You sure about this?"

"Absolutely."

Gabe did his best crawl-run-scamper across the rocks to the dock. He still didn't see anything. Well, if Chuck were hiding inside an elevator shaft, he wouldn't; not having x-ray vision and all.

And then Kurt whispered in his ear. "See anything?"

He was wasting time worrying about being shot, because he was going to have a heart attack.

He gave Kurt a not-so-gentle elbow to the solar plexus; Kurt gave a satisfying grunt. "Stop sneaking up on me!"

Kurt said, "Sorry."

He wasn't sorry at all. "Where's the boat?"

"At the dock." Kurt had his hand out for the binoculars. "Let me look. I don't see anything."

"No. I didn't either."

"Do you want to get closer?"

Gabe didn't, but he said, "Sure."

They crept up to the conference center and peered into the windows.

There was nothing stirring, not even a mouse.

He sat down on the ground with his back against the building; Kurt sat next to him, shoulder to shoulder, all comrades in un-arms.

"So do we go inside? Kurt?"

"Sure."

He was pretty sure that Kurt didn't want to go inside either, but Kurt had a key, and they didn't have any excuse not to, except for the getting shot thing.

The door wasn't locked.

Kurt looked at him. "Shit."

"Yeah." He opened the door a crack.

The kitchen was directly in front of them, down a few steps. They peeped in very cautiously. There were stairs to the left going up to the second floor.

"Which way is this elevator?"

Kurt whispered, "That way."

They slipped inside and found the elevator; the door was closed. They looked at the elevator. He turned to Kurt and whispered, "You know what?"

Kurt nodded. "We should probably...."

"...get out of here..."

"...while we still can."

They tip-toed back to the door and let themselves out. Kurt grabbed his arm. "Sarah was right."

"Yeah?"

"This was a very bad idea, Bergeron."

It was, but Kurt had been gung ho, and they had both been very brave so far. "Any particular reason, Hobbs?"

Kurt pointed. "Well, I was wondering if that's Chuck's bike?"

It was leaning against a tree. "Holy shit!"

Kurt said, "I'll take that as a yes then."

Monday
7:00 pm

The tide was high, and the water was making a soothing lapping sound against the dock. The sun was an orange candle flame with a yellow heart as it disappeared into the purple clouds beyond the island.

It was all lovely and serene and postcardy.

Kurt said, "We should really get out of here."

Which was undeniably true. "We should. Where do you think he is?"

"Don't care."

"Right. I was just thinking about which way we should go?"

Kurt grabbed his arm. "To the boat."

"Right."

They crept like little forest animals toward the dock. Kurt smiled at him. "I have to give you points for sang-froid."

"Yeah, you too. Of course, Sarah would say it's stupidity."

"Or a bad combination of the two."

And then Gabe saw Chuck sprinting for them, holding a very large, hunting knife in an overhand grip.

Chuck was smiling, and his cap with the red Chinese characters was still sideways.

And his sang lost all its froid.

Chuck slashed at Kurt, but Kurt twisted his body, falling back in the process. Chuck leaped on top of him.

Gabe kicked Chuck in the gut hard enough to lift him off Kurt and send him sprawling.

He grabbed Kurt's arm and dragged him to his feet. "Boat!"

Chuck rolled to his feet in one lithe motion. He tossed his knife from hand to hand.

"Well, hey Dude." He laughed. "First time I saw you, I knew you were going to be trouble, more trouble than the big, bad FBI, and here you are again."

"You saw them, didn't you, Chuck? From the conference center?"

"Right again, Mr. Gabriel Bergeron. I watched them set their positions from the attic. It was almost too easy to take out the big one."

"Chernov; his name is Chernov."

Chuck was smiling and slashing the air. "You've had a damn good run, Bergeron, but your stupidity has finally trumped your luck."

"The police are on the way, Chuck."

Chuck giggled and slashed at him, coming just close enough to his face to toy with him. "But you'll be dead before they get here."

Gabe was backing toward the dock.

Chuck slashed again. Gabe felt pain across his chest; more like a sting than anything else.

There was a branch on the ground. It crumbled in his hand when he grabbed it, but he threw a handful into Chuck's face anyway.

It bounced off his nose and disintegrated into dust, coating Chuck's face and getting into his eyes.

Chuck was wiping his eyes as he slashed with the knife. "Bastard. I'm going to cut you into little pieces, Bergeron."

There was nothing else more deadly than a pine cone so he ran for the dock pushing Kurt ahead of him.

Chuck was right behind them.

But Chuck still couldn't see that well, and there was this weird step up to get onto the dock.

Chuck missed it and went boom, flat on his face.

And Gabe Bergeron stomped on Chuck's knife hand.

Chuck screamed and got to his knees and managed to pull his hand free but lost his grip on the bloody knife.

Gabe kicked it and sent it skittering across the dock. It dropped into the creek with a lovely little plop.

Chuck said, "Bergeron, you bastard! I'll kill you!"

But Kurt had a paddle in his hands now, and Chuck was at a disadvantage even if he had mad Ninja skills.

Chuck took one step back and smiled before sprinting through the trees toward his bike. Toward his gun?

Kurt said, "What the Hell do we do, Gabe?"

"No idea!" Kurt jumped into the boat and put the key in the ignition, but there was no way they could get out of range before Chuck got back.

"We'll never make it, Kurt!"

"Then we run for it?"

And then he gave up any pretense to rational thought as a bullet hit the dock.

He had never claimed to have good reflexes. Kurt, obviously better equipped to handle the vicissitudes of life, jumped off the dock and spun behind a tree in one balletic move.

"Get your ass down, Bergeron!"

He found his own tree. "Which way do we go?"

Kurt had his head down trying to avoid splinters of bark as a bullet hacked at his tree. "Don't know!"

Chuck could chase them down in the forest and shoot one or both of them. But he had an idea. He thought he did. "Come on."

Gabe dragged Kurt away from his tree, and they ran back onto the dock.

He ran as fast as he had ever run in his life. This was no time to hold anything back.

He plunged into the creek and sank beneath the surface of the tepid water; something he really hated. Kurt landed, or watered, inches from him and sank into the depths beside him.

They surfaced.

Chuck was coming for them. Gabe started to swim around the boat, but jumping into the creek no longer seemed like such a good idea even if Chuck was afraid of the water.

Kurt was swimming toward the dock. "Come on, Bergeron!"

Gabe had no idea why but he reversed course. The tide was high enough to be lapping against the beams on which the planking rested. Kurt ducked under the water.

And then Kurt pulled him under.

He came up under the damn dock and bumped his head in the dark. He could just breathe through his nose if he tilted his head.

Chuck was stomping on the dock above them.

"Assholes. I'm going to shoot you, and hack your bodies into little tiny pieces, and then use you for crab bait."

Chuck fired at the dock.

The planks were too thick.

"Bastards!"

Chuck tried firing between the planks, but they were set so close together that he was firing blindly.

"I'm going to kill you. Don't think that I'm going to give up and just go away."

And then they heard Chuck run away.

Chuck was a very strange, young man.

"Is he running for it?"

Kurt said, "Somehow I doubt it."

"Should we swim across the creek?" It was just marsh on that part of the island with not a single tree for cover.

"If he comes back before we make it across, we're dead. How fast can you swim, Gabe."

"Like a freaking dolphin. Okay. It's sort of a dog paddle...I can never get my legs in sync with the rest of my body."

Kurt sighed.

But it didn't matter because they heard Chuck stomping on the dock. There was a sort of clank and then silence.

Chuck said, "Now, I've got you." He had to be kneeling on the dock whispering into a crack between the planks. "I have a couple of gallons of gas left, Gabe, and do you know what I'm going to do with it? Come on, guess? No? Well, I really like fire."

They could smell gasoline now.

"You may have noticed? I should have just shot you and Neal and the lovely Ellie instead of trying to burn the cabin down, but that wouldn't have been so beautiful. It wasn't as nice as the yacht, but I had time to do that one right. And I told myself that if Hartmann had the ledger hidden in the cabin, it would go up with everything else. Where is the ledger? It isn't going to make any difference to you.

Gabe? Come on be a sport and tell me?"

Like that was going to happen.

Gasoline was dripping into the water around them.

"Okay, be that way."

Gabe thought he was imagining the siren, but then Chuck said, "I hate this damn park. I really do. I should have charged double. Triple."

Chuck jumped into Kurt's boat and started the engine. "And I hate freaking boats."

The sirens were getting louder.

Kurt whispered, "The cavalry is riding to the rescue."

Chuck was still in the boat. "Shit! Shit! Shit!"

Chuck started shooting again.

One of the sirens cut off, and somebody returned fire.

Chuck screamed something, and the gasoline ignited as the boat roared away from the dock.

Kurt grabbed him and dragged him under the water again. They swam from under the dock and surfaced like that cormorant but not so elegantly.

Chuck was no seaman.

The boat was lurching right and left as it picked up speed heading north. The dock was a sheet of fire for a few seconds as the gasoline flamed, but then settled down to a smolder.

People were running through the woods, toward the creek, firing at Chuck as they came, but he was getting away. One of them was Ellie.

Gabe saw Sarah, and then Raúl stepped in front of her, shielding her. Raúl had a gun; maybe he should have accepted the guy's offer of help?

Kurt swam to the dock. He splashed water on the few tongues of flame still burning, and popped out of the water.

"Gabe?"

He felt exhausted, and the dock seemed so far away. He kept treading water as he watched the spray from Kurt's boat as it sped northward.

And then the spray collapsed. There was a new siren.

And the boat spun round, almost running into the bank, as it slalomed from one side of the creek to the other.

Chuck was heading back.

From his vantage point, an inch above the water, it appeared to Gabe Bergeron that a larger boat was chasing Chuck.

Both boats were heading in his general direction at high speed and were exchanging gunfire.

Kurt said, "Get your ass over here, Bergeron."

Ellie was on the dock too, and some of the local police.

He was tired. But the freaking boats were coming.

Chuck's boat swerved toward him until Ellie fired a few rounds in its direction.

The boat veered away and shot past him. Chuck was standing up and laughing.

Ellie fired again.

Chuck dropped, and the boat skidded across the creek, leaving the water for the moist marsh. It kept going even after the propeller started chewing marsh mud and grass roots instead of water.

Chuck turned the wheel hard, trying to get back into the creek. The boat turned obediently until the propeller dug in.

The boat rolled on its side, skidding across the inundated marsh before finally coming to rest.

The other boat was slowing. Charlie and Luke both had their guns drawn as they closed with the boat resting in the marsh.

Chuck's blond head popped up behind the boat. He spotted Charlie and Luke, and ducked.

Chuck screamed, "Freaking boats!" And then he must have found his cap, because he was wearing it as he ran into the marsh, dragging a life vest behind him like a security blanket.

Chuck was still laughing as he disappeared into the purple dusk.

Charlie pulled up alongside him. "That is one crazy asshole, Gabe."

"That's Chuck."

"Need some help?"

He nodded. "Please."

Charlie and Luke pulled him out of the water. His t-shirt was ripped across the chest.

Gabe sat in the bottom of the boat leaning against the center console.

Charlie said, "You're bleeding, Bergeron."

He was. He had a gash across his chest from above his left nipple to below his right. It was bleeding a lot and dripping onto Charlie's boat.

Charlie handed him a rag.

He didn't really feel like wiping up the blood, but he knew what a neat freak Charlie was. "Sorry."

Charlie started laughing at him.

"What?"

Charlie knelt beside him. "The rag is to stop the bleeding, Gabe."

"Oh. Okay. Thanks then."

Luke said, "Let me do it, Gabe."

And then he must have passed out.

A bright light was shining on him, but he wasn't ready to go toward it yet.

Someone said, "Mr Bergeron? Gabe? Can you hear me?"

Nurse Sharon and Dr. Hahn were looking at him.

"Yes, I hear you."

Dr. Hahn shook his head. "I don't really need practice, Mr. Bergeron."

"No?"

"No, I'm already quite good at suturing wounds."

"Practice makes perfect, Doctor. Idle hands are the devil's playthings. And a stitch in time saves nine."

Nurse Sharon said, "I could call the anesthesiologist, Doctor, and we could put him under?"

Dr. Hahn smiled. "No, I like Mr. Bergeron's babble. It reminds me of a parrot my dear mother had."

Dr. Hahn began stitching up his chest. Sharon was smiling at him. "Are you always here?"

She said, "Overtime. I should be off today. But then I would have missed seeing you again."

"Wait! Did they catch Chuck?"

Dr. Hahn paused mid stitch. "Chuck?"

Nurse Sharon said, "The guy who's whacked, choked, burned, and slashed Mr. Bergeron." She smiled. "So far."

Dr. Hahn said, "Ah, the perp. No idea. Hold still."

He had no problem in holding still since he had never ever been so tired before.

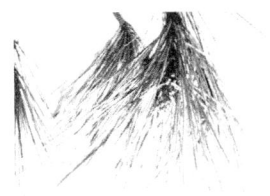

Tuesday
8:00 am

Gabe opened tired eyes. He had no idea where he was until he caught the odor of sweaty socks and saw the unpacked boxes and the ankle high dust bunnies. Kurt had offered his couch again.

He had bled through the bandages a little, but his chest didn't hurt very much.

He found Kurt's bathroom and then headed for the kitchen. Kurt was sitting at a beat-up table with three mismatched chairs, but the room was redolent with the aroma of coffee.

There was also an ironing board and a freshly pressed uniform hanging from a door knob.

Kurt said, "How are you feeling?"

"Hale and hearty." Gabe sat down and patted the table, which rocked, and was a yard sale find if he'd ever seen one. "I see you've...acquired a table for your stylish abode."

Kurt smiled and held out his hand. "Thank you, Gabe."

"For?"

"For? For stopping Chuck from stabbing me full of holes."

He smiled back. "Are you sure about that? That doesn't sound like something I could do?"

"I remember very clearly."

"Well, it was my fault you were in harm's way to begin with, and you've saved me twice that I can recall off the top of my head, so you don't have to thank me."

"Well, I am thanking you."

"Wait! Did they catch him?"

"Not yet."

"Shit!"

Kurt smiled and poured him a mug of coffee without being asked. "Only a matter of time. The FBI has a helicopter chasing him."

"On the island?"

"Yep. Running around like a madman."

"Sounds right." He sipped his coffee. "I'd like to watch."

"You feel up to that?"

"Oh, yes, Ranger Hobbs. Most definitely. But I need clothes." He was in his briefs. "In the trunk of my car. But I have no idea where my keys are?"

"I've got them. Be right back."

He got dressed, and they walked to the dock. Kurt was heading for a small, inflatable boat, which had an unassuming yet raffish engine.

Gabe assumed a sorrowful air. "Sorry about your other boat, Kurt."

Kurt closed his eyes and shook his head. "You mean the very expensive boat which the State of Maryland entrusted into my care?"

"Yeah. I am sorry."

"It's okay. It isn't damaged that much. Come on."

Kurt was fibbing; he didn't want to know how much outboard motors cost. "Do you know where Chuck is?"

"I've been following the chatter."

They motored to the southern end of the island and joined a flotilla consisting of two Natural Resources boats, two Coast Guard boats, and most of the watercraft home ported in Crisfield, Smith Island, and points nearby.

They sailed past a work boat; Jerry, Dan, Zeke, the quiet guy, Edgar, and Heather were on board. Heather smiled and waved when he waved at them.

Chuck had somehow crossed most of the island with his life vest and made his way through marsh and mud all the way to the extreme southern tip of Janes Island.

He was motionless in front of a tall brick chimney stack that was standing, for no apparent reason, on a sandy finger of land sticking out into the Little Annemessex River.

Chuck waded into the water until he was hip deep. He still had his cap.

He had been shaking his fist at the NRP boat, at Charlie's boat, but he spun in a circle looking around him at the deep water and the dozens of boats, and then he dropped his fist, and his shoulders slumped.

Chuck offered his hands to Charlie who cuffed him, and then he and Luke hoisted Chuck on board to a round of cheering from the assembled multitude.

Charlie was still some distance away, but he appeared to be blushing.

Charlie shook his head as Kurt maneuvered them alongside. Luke was trying to be professional, but he couldn't stop grinning.

Charlie glanced over. "Gabe."

"Charlie."

Chuck had welts over his face and arms and legs where the flies and mosquitoes had feasted, plus a liberal coating of marsh mud. He wouldn't look up.

Charlie said, "Is there something you wanted, Gabe?"

"One thing. Chuck? Hey, Chuck. Who hired you?"

Chuck shook his head.

"Okay, be that way. But what do the Chinese characters mean?"

Chuck smiled inscrutably at the bottom of Charlie's boat. "Flame."

Black suited Ellie and Murray and Reed were waiting at the city dock, lined up like mortuary attendants, along with news crews from Salisbury and one from Baltimore.

Charlie and Luke presented Chuck to Ellie. Smiles and handshakes were exchanged, photos taken, video captured, and little speeches made.

Charlie mentioned one Gabe Bergeron, and then proceeded to point him out.

Kurt whispered, "Shit. Want to get out of here?"

"No. I have an idea."

Kurt looked at him. "Oh my God."

Gabe Bergeron had been thinking about all the trouble he

had caused Kurt so far, and the possible trouble to come. He waded into the scrum of reporters smiling.

He hated public speaking, but needs must. He gave them a spirited, mostly true, convoluted tale of murder and intrigue and derring-do.

They adored him. He was golden.

"But the hired killer would never have been caught if it hadn't been for the brilliant insight of Ranger Sarah Sharp and the matchless courage of Ranger Kurt Hobbs. They are both true heroes, and the park service of the great State of Maryland is fortunate to have them."

Ellie rolled her eyes at him, but Charlie and Luke were smiling. Luke started to hug Charlie, but the sergeant gave him a shove. Charlie started the boat, and he and Luke set sail for calmer waters.

Kurt was now the focus of every eye and lens.

If he had been golden, Kurt was platinum; laconic, square-jawed, the very archetype of the classic hero; like Aunt Flo's Gary Cooper. She had his movies on DVD, and they had watched a lot of them together.

Shit. He should call her and tell her he was okay.

Kurt ran for his boat and almost left him behind in his becoming modesty.

Kurt said, "What the Hell was that, Gabe?"

"Just let them try to fire you now, Ranger."

"Oh."

They sailed along in silence to the park. Sarah was at the dock. She smiled as they disembarked and headed for the office.

She said, "I'm glad you're okay. Both of you. But you are idiots. You both should be dead. And that bullshit that you just poured over the media, Gabe..."

"Amazing, wasn't it?"

Kurt said, "But I can't keep pretending to be a hero."

"You aren't pretending, Kurt. But you won't have to say anything for long. By tomorrow, something else will have happened, maybe something good but more likely something horrible, and the reporters and their viewers will forget that some guy called Hobbs and a place called Janes Island ever existed."

Kurt said, "So what good did lying today do?"

"Ah, well, there is going to be a grass roots campaign to get you awarded a medal...what kind of medals do rangers get? We'll figure that part out later."

Sarah said, "And what about me, Bergeron?"

"Well, of course there will be a medal for you too! It was your idea. And once you have your medals, you're set. Unless, of course, something else happens in the park, but that's on you, Hobbs. There's only so much I can do."

Sarah and Kurt looked at each other and rolled on the floor breathless with laughter. Well, not really but they did chuckle at this Gabe and his silly ideas.

Which wasn't very nice, but he was going to rise above it. He had stuff to do so he went back to the motel to get cleaned up.

He called Aunt Flo. "Hi. I'm fine."

She said, "Yes, I saw your performance on television. I saw the assassin, and I saw Ellie among the FBI agents. I saw your Kurt too."

Alas, would that Kurt were his Kurt. "See! I told you I had a feeling about Miss Ellie."

"You did."

"So did you send Raúl to save me from myself?"

"I did. He's very upset that you ignored him, Gabriel."

Raúl wasn't the boss of him. "I had things to do, Aunt Flo."

"I know. But you should apologize to him, Gabriel, the next time you see him."

Right. He would do that. Would Raúl appreciate a gift? A small token? "I'll come see you tomorrow. Okay? And I'm sorry if I worried you? I had to see this through."

"Of course, Gabriel, I understand."

Which made him feel like a very bad nephew.

And then he went to see Neal.

Claire was talking to Layla. Lawyer Cindi Lou was coming out of Neal's room, and Neal's security was nowhere to be seen.

Claire said, "Here's Gabriel now. Thank you so much for stopping by to see Neal, Layla. I know he appreciated it."

Layla aimed her Botticelli Madonna smile at him, but Gabe was too worldly wise now to be deceived. "Help you with something, Mrs. Girard?"

Claire frowned at him, but she didn't know Layla, the real Layla.

Layla's smile was undimmed. "I'm sorry to bother you. It's terrible, I know, to think about things like this with Eric still not returned to me, but the business is going to need someone, Gabe. At least until Neal is back on his feet?"

"Me? Not a chance." Why was she asking him? She could find another captain to go down with the ship.

Layla was hurt but ever resilient in the face of outrageous fortune. "I am sorry to have bothered you then." She turned her glistening eyes to Claire. "If there's anything I can do for Neal, don't hesitate to ask, Claire."

"Thank you, Layla."

And Layla and Cindi Lou shouldered their purses and marched away.

Claire said, "What's wrong with you, Gabriel? You were so rude to her, and she's just lost her husband...."

He held up a hand. "She may or may not have arranged that loss, but I know she's trying to pin Eric's crap on Neal."

"Exactly what kind of crap, Gabe? I think it's past time that you told me everything, don't you?"

"How is Neal? Is he awake?"

She nodded. "He's doing much better."

"Come on then."

Neal seemed to have just a single IV now. He hugged his best friend carefully. "How are you?"

Neal smiled. "Feeling better."

"That's great. I have news."

"Yeah?"

"Do you remember Chuck, the blond skateboarder?" Neal shook his head. "He hung around with the Dutch students?"

"Oh, the crazy guy on the bike. What about him?"

"Chuck was the guy who shot you. He also blew up Eric and killed Lonnie, and smacked me on the head."

"Him?"

"Yes, nasty things can come in slender, smiling, zany packages. Well, Sergeant King arrested the sucker this morning and handed him over to your...to Ellie and the FBI."

"How did they figure out it was him?"

"Well, modesty forbids me from telling you of my small role, but when he stole Kurt's boat and tried to shoot Charlie and Luke, it was a dead giveaway."

Neal said, "That's great, Gabe."

Claire said, "This man was a professional? A hit man?"

"He was."

Claire's face tightened. "And you suspect that Mrs. Girard hired him? Do you have any evidence, Gabriel?"

Neal smiled at him. "You're in for it now, Gabriel."

He shook his head. "No, young master Neal, I think you are. Where is this freaking ledger?"

Neal frowned at him. "Shut up, Gabe. She has enough to worry about...."

Claire said, "What ledger? Neal, you tell me right now."

Neal closed his eyes. "I'm not feeling so well. I need to rest."

Gabe said, "The ledger, which I haven't seen, but your son has, is a record of money laundering transactions carried out by Eric Girard. And that, plus a good lawyer like Nagy, may be enough to keep Neal out of federal prison. At least, I hope so. You'd know better than I would?"

Claire said, "Money laundering? For mobsters and drug dealers? Neal!"

"I didn't do anything, Mom. And I only started to suspect Eric a few weeks ago." Claire was staring at him. "Maybe a little longer than that, but I didn't know what to do."

"So you called Gabriel?"

"Yes. I shouldn't have gotten him involved...."

"No, you shouldn't. But I'm glad you did." She was staring at the IV bag. "So where is this record?"

"It's safe."

Claire said, "But does anyone know you have it? Besides Gabriel"

"No."

He said, "But people suspect he does, Claire."

"Of course. Then the sooner it's in the hands of the FBI, the better. I called some friends, and Mr. Nagy is a first rate attorney. Can you call him and see if he'll come down here, Gabriel? Today or tomorrow. To go over our options in dealing with the FBI?"

"I'll call."

"As soon as possible, Gabriel." She looked at Neal. "And we need to talk about Ellie."

"She loves me."

She smiled and stroked his hair. "We'll talk, but I need to...to see how Richard is doing now."

And she left without another word.

Neal really was tired. "Rest, Neal. I have to call Max."

Gabe found a waiting room in the rabbit warren of corridors and buildings and levels of PRMC.

He was dialing Max when Cindi Lou walked in, all smiling and freckled and business like.

"We need to speak, Mr. Bergeron."

"No, we don't."

"Yes, we do. I'm sure you are aware of Eric's business dealings."

He scrunched up his face in thought. "I think he was an accountant."

She smiled. "He was, but he had a side line."

"About which, I know absolutely nothing, Ms. Parker."

She laughed. "We both know that isn't true. I have been talking to Layla, and we feel that the firm needs to present a united front to the FBI."

"Really? Well, that really shocks me, Counselor, since Mrs. Girard informed me only two days ago that she knew nothing about the business, and implied that any shit would be falling solely on Neal and me."

Cindi Lou really tried to keep that smile in place. "Well, while it is demonstrably true that Layla was not involved in the business, still she is one of the partners, and...."

"And the FBI has been huffing and puffing at her door. Who?

Ellie Tyson or Rodney Alexander Steele IV?"

"Please be serious, Mr. Bergeron."

"This is as serious as I get; take it or leave it."

Cindi Lou said, "We really could help one another. Obviously, the FBI would like to net as many of Eric's clients as possible, and if Neal or you should have any documentation...."

He was tired and hungry, and he didn't like Cindi Lou. "You're wasting your time, or I guess if you're billing Layla, you're wasting her time. Go away, Cindi Lou."

Her expression of mild annoyance morphed into a grimace. And as the color drained from her face, he flashed on his mother's lifeless face. Shit. He didn't need that.

She handed him another card as she got to her feet. "If you should change your mind, Mr. Bergeron."

He made sure she was gone before he called Max and updated him. Neal had already told Max about the ledger.

"But I can confirm that there is a rare book that should be of interest."

Max snorted. "A rare book. God, Bergeron, do you think the FBI listens to every conversation?"

"Yes."

Max made a strange sound that might be described as a chortle. "Paranoid, but sometimes paranoid is good. Tomorrow? Yeah, I think I can make it down there. Let me call you back."

"Great, Max. I'll be waiting. Call me or Neal's mother, Claire Hartmann."

He found Neal's room without getting lost again, but Neal was asleep. He was heading for his Fiesta when he saw Claire talking to Scott in the parking lot.

Scott was getting reamed out. Gabe didn't know for what, but he surely deserved it.

Claire spotted him and waved him over. "Did you speak to Mr. Nagy, Gabriel?"

"Yes. He thinks he can make it tomorrow, but he'll call to confirm in a bit. I gave him your number too."

"Thank you, Gabriel."

Scott was staring at his shiny, expensive shoes..

"Okay, I'll be at the Chesapeake Motel just outside Crisfield, if you need me."

Claire said, "Can you be at the meeting with Mr. Nagy tomorrow, Gabriel?"

"Sure. If you want me."

"We do. And thank you, Gabriel."

And after that, he was going home to his tiny studio apartment, order pizza, and not come out for a good month.

Tuesday Noon

Gabe had one leg in the shower when somebody started banging on his motel door.

If he had been wet, he would have ignored them no matter what they did, but he found his briefs and shorts and went to the door.

He looked before he opened and sighed.

"What do you want, Scott?"

"Just want to talk, Gabe. Let me in. Please?"

"Are you alone?"

Scott said, "Who else would be with me?"

"Rachel."

Scott laughed. "No, she's getting something to eat. Come on, Gabe, I really need to talk to you. This is serious."

He opened the door.

Scott had lost the tie and the jacket; his dress shirt was sweat stained. He marched in and plopped on the bed. "Thank God, you have AC. I hate summers. Got anything to drink?"

He had one lukewarm Diet Coke, but Scott wasn't getting it. "No. You said there was something serious?"

Scott let himself fall back on the bed. "Damn, Gabe, you must have something to drink?"

"Nope."

He stayed supine. "I need to talk to you."

"I'm right here."

Scott was looking at the ceiling. "Yeah. It's about Eric."

"I thought it might be."

"Can I trust you, Gabe?"

"No."

Scott rolled over to look at him. "No? Why the Hell not? We grew up together."

"Neal and I grew up together."

Scott flopped onto his back again. "I was there too, not that anybody noticed."

"Scott, what do you want?"

"You have to promise me that you won't repeat anything I say to anybody, Gabe. Not to Neal or Mom or anybody."

"Not to the FBI?"

Scott jerked like he'd been slapped. "Of course not them! None of this is my fault, Gabe."

"None of what?"

"Do you promise not to tell?"

What did he want? A pinky swear? "Sure, I promise." But he crossed his fingers so the promise didn't count.

Scott said, "I never wanted to do it, but Rachel said it was easy money. She said her friends had it all set up, and she introduced me to that dumb bastard, Eric. He thought he was so all that. And I didn't like the way he looked at Rachel either."

"Eric was a prick."

Scott rolled toward him like a beached whale. "Yeah, he was! And I'm pretty sure he was going to skip the country. Or make a sweetheart deal with the FBI."

"Where would he go?"

Scott smiled, happy to be able to impart knowledge. "Costa Rica, of course."

Scott remembered the explosion. "But now he's dead, Gabe, and some of the stuff he was doing could come back on me."

"So you were part of a money laundering ring?"

Scott shook his head. "No way."

"So you have nothing to worry about then."

He sat up again. "But you don't understand, it might look like I was part of it."

Scott didn't smell very good, and Gabe was tired. "So why are you here? In my room? On my bed?"

Scott laughed. "Well, you're pretty sharp, Gabe. Always were. And I figure that if anybody knows where that damn ledger is, it would be you?"

"Why me?"

Scott fell back. "Because I asked Neal, and he says he doesn't have it. And Rachel's friends don't have it, and it isn't at the office. Some people who've been looking into some stuff for me checked there and on Eric's boat, and they can't find the freaking thing, which Eric was stupid to have anyway...."

"Maybe it went up with the boat?"

Scott heaved himself upright. "That would be great! But Rachel says we can't assume that, and I guess she's right. This time. So do you know where it is?"

"No, Scott. I've never seen it and don't know where it is. And that's the truth."

Scott was frowning. "I was hoping that you would know. Shit. Now I don't know what to do. I can't go to prison, Gabe. I can't."

"Sorry, Scott, but I can't help you. How about you go find your wife."

Scott said, "Kicking me out?"

"Yeah."

"Can't I stay until she comes back? She's got the car."

He didn't want Scott in his room. "Tell me this: did you get Neal involved with Eric knowing about the money laundering?"

Scott shook his head. "No way!"

"But you introduced them?"

"Yeah, well, Rachel said to invite Neal to a party we had. And once he was there, Eric was all over him."

Eric had needed a legitimate front, and Neal, innocent, former boy scout Neal, had been a dream come true.

"And you didn't warn your brother off?"

Scott was staring at his shoes again. "I was going to, but Rachel said to leave them alone."

"So it's all Rachel's fault?"

"Yeah. All of it."

And that was probably sixty, seventy percent true. "So who are these friends of Rachel's?"

Scott shook his head. "Why do you want to know that, Bergeron? You promised to keep your mouth shut." Scott got to his feet, glaring at him. "Just remember that."

"I'll remember. So these people who been looking into stuff for you, could they have gotten carried away and blown up Eric?"

He thought Scott was going to pass out. He fell back onto the bed. "No! No way! She isn't like that."

"You'd better hope not."

Somebody laid on a car horn. Scott nodded and heaved himself vertical again. "That must be Rachel. Later, Bergeron."

"Sure, Scott. Any time."

The guy lumbered out, but as the door closed, Scott mumbled, "Sarcastic little bastard."

He locked his door.

And then the freaking knocking started again.

It was Rachel this time.

He put the chain on the door and opened it a crack. "What?"

She smiled. "Is that any way to talk to a lady?"

He kept his mouth shut. "What can I do for you, Mrs. Hartmann?"

"You can let me in for a start. It's a hundred and ten out here."

"No."

It was a good thing she was petite, or she would have kicked the door open and beaten him to death.

"All right then! If Scott isn't the dumbest man on Earth, he's near the top of the list...."

"Or the bottom."

"Shut up, Bergeron! He actually thought you would just hand over the ledger if you have it." She smiled. "Fifty thousand."

"Fifty thousand dollars?"

"All right! A hundred thousand, but that's it."

"Rachel? Listen to me very carefully: I do not have the ledger. I do not know where it is."

She didn't believe him.

"Who are these money laundering friends of yours?"

There was a moment's silence. "Damn, stupid bastard! Scott!

What the Hell did you tell him!"

"Goodbye, Rachel." He shut the door.

She didn't say anything but kicked his door a couple of times before she gave up. That must have scuffed her three inch heels.

He made sure they pulled out of the parking lot before he went back to the shower.

He got clean, and the AC gradually got rid of the eau de Scott. He was hungry, but he didn't feel like talking to anybody.

He was paying the pizza delivery guy when he spotted the Pale Wraith.

Murray was wearing shorts, a tank top, dark sunglasses, and a hat suitable for the Australian Outback. He was trying to hide behind a boat on a trailer.

Gabe walked down the stairs and strolled over.

Murray just stood there sweating in the noon day sun looking hot in every sense of the word.

"Want a slice of pizza?" He had ordered a two liter bottle of Coke too. "And a drink? I have plenty. And there's an ice machine."

Murray lost the glasses and wiped the sweat out of his eyes.

"Could you just go back to your room and pretend you never saw me?"

"I could do that." He shook his head. "No, I couldn't. So just as a matter of curiosity, is my room bugged?"

Murray smiled at him. "Were you thinking of that when you pumped Hartmann and the wife?"

"Of course. I am a chess grand master, always six moves ahead of my opponents."

Murray smiled again. "So that was just you being you. That's what I figured."

"So are you going to arrest Scott and Rachel?"

Murray said, "And why would I answer that?"

"You wouldn't, but it was worth a shot. Neal is not a crook, Murray. What's your name anyway?"

"Murray."

"Ah, more FBI humor. Okay, it's hot out here so I'm going back to my cool room. You could come and question me in the AC for a while, or you can stay out here and keep pretending you know which end of a boat is which."

"I'm a good sailor, Bergeron."

"On boats with motors? Or the ones with sails that look like way too much trouble?"

"Both."

"Really? The sailboats always look like they're going to capsize."

"The idea is to learn how to stop that from happening."

"I guess." He turned and headed for his room.

He heard Murray on the steps behind him. "So shouldn't you be tailing Scott and Rachel?"

"Not my assignment."

"Oh. Right, somebody else is following them. Anybody I know?"

"Shut up, Bergeron. I need a cold drink."

"Sure. I'll get some ice." Murray went with him to get the ice. "I'm not running. My keys are on the dresser."

Murray said, "Trust but verify."

He nodded. "Ah, quotations from Chairman Reagan."

Murray relaxed enough to take off his Crocodile Dundee hat and sit in the one chair.

"Murray, you can believe me when I say that Neal is not a crook. He's never broken a rule in his life."

Murray was pink now rather than pale. "I know you believe that."

"Because it's true. You're sunburned, Murray."

"Yeah, I know."

His shoulders seemed to be reddening by the second. "The tank top was a mistake."

"Yes, Mr. Bergeron, I know."

"Don't get huffy. You want to go get something to rub on that before it really starts hurting? I know where the pharmacy is? I could go with you? In case, you think I'm a flight risk."

Murray shook his head. "I wish you were a flight risk."

"Are you married, Special Agent Murray?" He had the tan line of a wedding band, but no ring.

Murray sipped his Coke.

"How do you like working for the Glorious Fourth?"

Murray smiled into his Coke. "I knew this was a mistake. Good day, Mr. Bergeron."

And the Pale Wraith grabbed his hat and vamoosed.

Wednesday
8:00 am

Semi-secure in the knowledge that Murray or another agent was watching his room, Gabe had slept through a whole night.

No one had tried to do a single fatal or even unpleasant thing to him. He was glad Charlie had caught Chuck.

Charles and Charles; if Chuck was his real name.

Probably not.

He packed, said goodbye to the carnivorous deer romping in fields of marijuana, checked out of the motel, and drove into Crisfield.

Charlie and Luke were at the dock, cleaning a spotless boat. "Gabe!"

"Hi, Charlie. You know that boat is already clean? Any bullet holes to be patched?"

Charlie pointed out a smashed light above the canopy. "Sorry. So how are things?"

Charlie glanced at Luke. "Pay up."

Luke shook his head. "He hasn't done it yet."

"Done what? Ask what you know about Chuck? Ask if he's confessed or said who hired him? Ask if the FBI knows who he really is?"

Luke handed over a ten dollar bill.

"A measly ten?"

Luke smiled at him. "It was a losing bet, but I took a shot."

Charlie said, "How is Neal?"

"On the mend, I am happy to say."

Luke's phone beeped. He looked at the screen and then at

Charlie.

Charlie said, "Go, but be back in fifteen minutes, or I'll leave without your sorry ass."

"Thanks, Charlie. But she's coming here."

Luke sprinted for the parking lot.

"A girlfriend?"

Charlie nodded as a red Volkswagen Beetle pulled up alongside Luke, and Jessica got out. They hugged and kissed like starving piranha.

"Shit! Not Jessica?"

Charlie shook his head in bewilderment. "Can you explain why a reasonably intelligent young man...."

"Our Luke?"

"Yes, our Luke. Why he would get involved with a young lady with the brains and personality of a sea nettle?"

"What?"

Charlie said, "A stinging jellyfish."

"Ah. I see. Very apt."

Charlie shook his head again. "I don't know anything about Chuck."

He sat on the dock letting his legs hang over the edge. It was already hot. "Come on, Charlie?"

"No, Gabe, the FBI has not seen fit to share any information with me. I did get a snippy phone call from Special Agent Reed asking for a report of the events of Monday evening and yesterday."

"They never learned to share."

"No, they did not. I do know they recovered Chuck's gun from the marsh. How about Neal's other problems?" Charlie smiled at him.

"Okay. I know that Eric was into money laundering and probably a spot of tax evasion."

"And Neal knew nothing?"

"Nope."

"And you knew nothing?"

"If I had known, I would have punched him in his stupid, smirky face many, many times."

Charlie frowned. "I hope Neal has a good lawyer?"

"He does. And Claire, his mother, is a lawyer too."

"Handy. Do you have a lawyer?"

Which was a good question. "Not really."

"You should look into that, Gabe." Charlie stopped polishing a gleaming instrument panel. "I know you and Neal are close. You've proved that over and over by doing some really dumb stuff."

"But?"

"But people tend to do things they might not otherwise do when facing federal prison, Gabe."

He shook his head. "Neal would never throw me to the wolves. Never."

"He hasn't had to. You done that without him asking as far as I can tell. Look, Neal seems like a good guy, but you need a lawyer who is on Gabe's side and only Gabe's. Understand?"

"Absolutely. I know what you're saying, Charlie, but they saved me; Claire and Neal. They rode to the rescue when I called them."

Gabe hadn't talked about this with anyone, not even Aunt Flo. "I knew my mother was dead when I called 911. I was only ten years old, but I knew. She was cold. And her face...was white and twisted. You know?"

Charlie nodded still polishing the panel. "What happened, Gabe? Or shouldn't I ask?"

"No, it's okay." He paused to watch a tiny crab the size of his thumbnail swimming just below the surface of the water. "I don't know. I never asked. She drank a lot...that's really all I know."

"And Mrs. Hartmann took you in?"

"Yeah. Until my great-aunt Flo popped up three years later."

"Popped up?"

"Yeah. One day I didn't know I had a great-aunt, and the next she winked into existence like she'd beamed down from a starship. But she told me about my grandparents, and my great grandparents; she lives in their house. It's not far from here...on the Pocomoke River." He smiled at Charlie. "And, you may find this hard to believe, Sergeant King, but I am not the craziest member of my family, of my mother's family. Not even close."

Charlie laughed. "If you say so, Sir."

"It's true, Charlie. Anyway, thanks for not arresting me or stopping me from doing stuff you knew I shouldn't."

"I should have, but it's been an experience, Mr. Bergeron. And no matter what Neal and his mother did for you, you've paid them back."

He shook Charlie's big paw. "Thanks. Well, goodbye."

Charlie smiled. "Goodbye, Bergeron."

Luke was walking back to the boat. "I have to go, Jessie."

She said, "But you were supposed to be off today. You promised. And don't call me Jessie!"

"I'm really sorry, Jessica, but I have to work."

Charlies said, "Officer Stevens? Whenever you're ready?"

Luke tried to kiss her, but she pushed him away; he ran to the dock and leaped into the boat.

Jessica pulled out her phone. Luke said, "Bye, Jessica. I'll be back soon."

"Don't care." Her eyes never left her phone as her delicate fingers flew over the surface. "You're no fun."

Charlie looked at him. "Was there anything else, Mr. Bergeron?"

There was one thing. "Hi, Jessica."

She didn't even glance at him. "I don't know you."

"I'm a friend of Heather's."

"Oh. Her. I'm not Jace's girl any more."

"Right. I can see you're with Luke now, but I saw you with Jace at the park on Sunday. Buying something from Randy Green. I was wondering what that was?"

Gabe was aware that it was none of his business, but he liked Luke.

Her fingers froze. She looked at Charlie and then back to her phone. "Did not. You're lying! I never went there, and I don't know any Randy."

She ran to her Bug and drove off barely missing a couple of parked cars.

Charlie said, "Gabe?"

"I don't know. Just another mystery."

Charlie was staring at Luke, who was seeking enlightenment

or salvation from a blank radar screen.

The boat still hadn't moved when he drove away.

Gabe stopped for breakfast and went to the park, which was calm and serene as campers engaged in their blameless outdoor activities.

He knocked on the office door, but there was no answer. He didn't want to leave without saying goodbye to Kurt. And Sarah too.

He wandered; the place was all but deserted. Wendy and Bob, Kev and Barb, and the Dutch students were all gone.

And Randy's RV was pulling out of the camp site.

But Gareth's shabby RV was still there, and the door was open. Mia's voice was as lovely as always. "No. We've talked about this."

Gareth said, "Too bloody late anyways. Buggered off, 'e has."

"Excellent. He was a right minger. I don't know why you wanted one?"

"Proppa canny, that, like."

"No, a dog is a proper pet."

Gareth said, "Like us then?"

Mia said, "I don't think of you as a pet, Gareth. Don't be silly."

"Disappointment, I am. Told me mam?"

"You're being just too silly now. You've done very well. Do you want to go for a run or lift your weights before we leave this accursed place?"

"A love it, me."

"I know you do, but we have to get back to civilization and find a paying job."

"'E won't pay?"

She laughed. "Not likely. Not without the ledger. The whole affair has been a right royal cock up."

"Sorry, Mia."

"Not your fault, Gareth. Someone was just too clever."

He backtracked and declaimed in a clear voice, "Hobbs? Anybody seen Ranger Hobbs?"

The trees were mute as was their wont.

Gareth burst out of the RV, sinews, thews, and tattoos

rampant, and headed for him, fists raised. "Hi, Gareth. Have you seen Ranger Hobbs?"

Gareth was overwrought as was his wont and threw a punch. "Reet, nebby bugga!"

And Gabe Bergeron ducked and punched Gareth in the nose as hard as he could.

Gareth hit the ground and lay there.

He wasn't sure who was more shocked.

Mia's sarong of the day was salmon with voluptuous, white flowers; he couldn't imagine her in winter. "Gareth! Are you all right?"

Gareth was bleeding.

Gabe just stood there, rooted to the spot, but Gareth did not leap to his feet and beat the crap out of him. Mia fetched a towel and pressed it against Gareth's nose.

Gabe casually admired his right hand and sent up a silent prayer to Bill. He would have to tell his former , self-defense instructor that all his efforts had not been in vain. But he was pretty sure that Bill had said something about not leading with the right? He'd leave out that part.

Mia helped Gareth into the RV and made him lie down on the sofa. She turned to glare at him. "What is it, Bergeron?"

He stood in the doorway. "Nothing! I was looking for Hobbs."

Gareth muttered something; the towel did not help his diction. He repeated, "Yer nobbut a nebby wanker."

Mia said, "You were eavesdropping, Bergeron."

"Was not. Look I'm sorry, but he tried to hit me."

Gareth muttered darkly.

Mia smiled. "Gareth has never hit anyone."

"He hasn't?"

She took the towel away, but his nose was still bleeding. "No, Mr. Bergeron." She got some toilet paper. "Now, do be still, Gareth." She stuffed his nostrils with wadded paper while Gareth moaned.

Now, he really did feel sorry for the guy.

"Lie still. I'm very much afraid your nose is broken."

Gareth said, "Brokken?"

"You should take him to the ER."

It seemed unnatural that he was sending someone to Dr. Hahn and Nurse Sharon and not being sent himself.

Mia said, "I'm perfectly capable of seeing to Gareth, Mr. Bergeron."

"Right. I'm sorry, Gareth."

Mia let him walk away. "Gabe?"

He turned. She stepped out of the RV and closed the door over Gareth's protests.

She strolled over. "They captured the culprit?"

He nodded. "Chuck. A blond kid. You must have seen him around?"

"Perhaps. And he killed Eric?"

"He did."

She ran a silky hand up his arm and over his shoulder.. "I understand you played a part in his capture? It's possible that you aren't quite as useless as one had assumed."

She was stroking his cheek.

"Thanks. I guess."

He had been afraid of the wrong member of the Mia-Gareth duo. She thought she could Black Widow him; mate, suck the life out of him, and hang the desiccated Gabe carcass from her web. "Where is the ledger, Gabe?"

"I don't have it, Mia."

She smiled. "But you know where it is. Name your price."

Gabe shook his head. "I don't know. I'm not even sure it exists."

She flicked the shimmering black hair back over her shoulder. "Such a disappointment. Well, I had to have a go, but I can't faff around with you all day."

"Sorry." What was he sorry for? "So you and Gareth are going to jail? If the FBI gets this ledger?"

She laughed at him. "No, Snuggums. Gareth and I have nothing to do with silly Eric's silly schemes."

"Then why.... Wait. Someone else wanted the ledger?"

"I'm sure I don't know what you're talking about."

"You were hired to get the ledger. By Neal's brother, Scott?

So is that what you do? You're a private eye, a Sherlock, a gumshoe, a sleuth...."

She smiled and walked back to the RV. He kept waiting for her to spin and shoot him dead. He couldn't imagine where she might have concealed a weapon, but still.

She slammed the RV door, started the engine, and drove away into the rising sun.

Wednesday
11:00 am

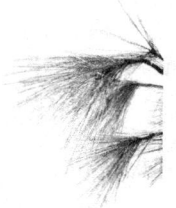

Gabe's hand was starting to hurt. Was he supposed to apply ice to his knuckles after a bout of fisticuffs? He had no idea.

He walked along the creek and finally spotted Kurt and Sarah. They were towing Kurt's boat, the park's boat, with the inflatable.

He waved.

They were covered in mud. They waved back, but the greeting lacked a certain warmth. He walked back to the dock anyway.

"Hi. Just stopped by to say goodbye."

Kurt said, "We could have used you an hour ago, Bergeron."

Sarah said, "When we righted the boat and hauled it out of the marsh."

"Right. I see. How is it?" It had three bullet holes he could see, the compass gizmo and the windshield were smashed, and the engine was lying in the bottom of the boat.

Kurt said, "Not great. But it floats." He jumped out of the inflatable. "How is Neal doing?"

"Better every day."

Sarah said, "Well, that's good. Take it easy, Bergeron." She walked away.

Kurt said, "So it's back to Philadelphia for you?"

"Yeah. And I have to find a job."

"And how are the activities of Mr. Girard going to impact you? And Neal?"

"It should be okay."

Kurt smiled. "I hope so, Gabe."

"Me too."

Sarah was backing a trailer down the boat ramp. She got out and headed for the damaged boat.

He looked at them. "If I wanted to come back? Maybe rent a cabin?"

Kurt and Sarah looked at each other and laughed.

He said, "So I'm persona non grata again? I mean I understand."

Kurt said, "No. Come back any time. Be happy to see you."

Sarah said, "But if one camper gets a splinter in one finger, you're out."

"Right. Totally understandable."

He held out his hand to Sarah. She smiled. "It's been an experience, Bergeron."

"People are always saying that to me."

Kurt smiled. "Do you wonder why?"

"After the last few days, not so much."

A beat-up pickup truck hauling a white and green Viking trailer was parked in front of the office. The trailer was one of those that opens up into a tent like a kernel of popcorn exploding.

And behind the Viking was Randy's silver RV. He was laying on the horn.

Sarah was smiling for some reason. "Mr. Randy seems to be in a hurry."

Kurt said, "You want me to...."

"No, let me."

Sarah said something to Randy and went inside the office.

He said, "I should get going too."

"Take care of yourself. I have a boat to get repaired."

"Right."

Gabe was starting the Fiesta when three police vehicles entered the park, all screeching tires and screaming sirens; two were Natural Resources Police and the third was a Maryland State Police.

They tried to box Randy in, but Randy had other ideas. He rammed one of the police cars and pushed it aside, but they shot out his tires.

The silver RV lurched across the road and then tilted and slipped into a ditch, coming to rest on its side.

The officers surrounded the RV, guns drawn, yelling at Randy to come out. Charlie and Luke were among them.

Randy muscled the door open and climbed out of the RV.

Charlie handcuffed Randy and dumped him in the back of his vehicle.

Kurt was looking at one Gabe Bergeron. "I had nothing to do with this. Honest, Kurt."

Kurt smiled. "I know, Gabe. Sarah called them about Randy a few days ago."

"What is he selling? Drugs?"

Kurt smiled. "Nope."

Kurt was walking toward the RV.

"Then what?"

"Come see."

A city police car pulled in behind the others. An officer got out and lifted a cardboard box from the trunk. She carried it very carefully and set it down on the road, stepped back, and smiled at Charlie.

"All yours, King."

Charlie said, "Thanks, Wright."

Charlie nudged the box with his boot.

The box made a strange hissing sound as something inside thrashed about.

Charlie shook his head and walked over to talk to Randy. "How many snakes are in the RV?"

Randy smirked. "Go in and find out."

Charlie said, "Don't think so. Wright? Get her out."

Jessica was in the back seat of Wright's vehicle, and she was handcuffed.

Luke was shaking his head. Wright said, "She resisted, Luke. She kicked me and scratched me." Wright had welts across her cheek.

Charlie looked at Jessica. "It's illegal to own a cobra, Jessica."

She shook her pink frosted head and glared at him, her face a mask of rage. "Says you! I paid for it, and it's mine. It's a free country, and I have rights, and you can't take it. And it's not just a cobra, it's a spitting cobra." She looked like she wanted to spit at Charlie herself.

"You were in the RV. What else has he got in there?"

"Cobras and rattlesnakes and alligators, some baby ones and some not so little."

"Well, we're confiscating the snake, and there will be a fine. Plus whatever Wright wants to do about the assault."

She stomped her foot. "I didn't hurt her. She's just a baby. And the snake is mine. I will get it back. I'll get a lawyer. You'll see."

She shifted her fury to Luke. "You told him. I know you did. I know it!"

"I had to, Jessie. It's illegal and dangerous."

She tried to kick Luke in the balls, but his reflexes saved him by the width of a pubic hair.

"Traitor! Chicken! We're done. I know how much you want me! You'll be begging for me to take you back. But I won't!"

She tried to kick Luke again, but Wright grabbed the handcuffs and held her.

"And my name is Jessica!"

Charlie looked at Luke who wouldn't meet his eyes.

Kurt said, "I'd appreciate it, if you would get these critters out of my park, Sergeant."

Charlie said, "An animal control specialist is on the way, but if you want to round them up yourself, Ranger, be my guest."

Sarah said, "No, I think we'll wait."

He said, "Do you think they're loose?"

Kurt waved toward the RV. "Have a look, Gabe."

He smiled at Kurt. "I will, if you will."

Sarah said, "You two are certifiable! Nobody is having a look." She glanced at King. "You know he's been stopping at the park on his way north for a couple of years, Charlie."

Charlie said, "I've caught transporters of all kinds of drugs, and cash, and untaxed cigarettes, but this is a first for me: reptile smuggling."

Sarah said, "But I wonder if other people, other locals, have purchased reptiles from him?"

Charlie said, "I'm not going to think about that."

Wednesday
1:00 pm

Gabe didn't wait for the animal control specialist but left Crisfield and headed for the hospital.

He held the elevator for a big, hairy guy in blue scrubs. The door closed before he realized it was Mr. Bear.

James had a name tag that read "English." He nodded. "Hi, Gabe."

"Right. Hi, James. And you work here?"

He nodded again. "All over the Shore, like I said. And you're here to see Neal."

He elevator door opened and as he got out, James said, "Read about the fire at the park. And about Neal getting shot. Want to tell me what's been going on, Gabe?"

"I'd like to."

James smiled at him. "I understand. Tell Neal, I hope he's feeling better soon."

"Okay. I will. Thanks, James."

James smiled. "I caught some nice fish...after you left."

"Really? Well, that's good." He smiled at James.

Big James leaned closer and stroked Gabe's arm and along his shoulder until a big hand was gently cradling Gabe's neck. "So are you going to be around, Gabe?"

"No, we'll be heading back to Philly soon. Maybe today."

"I see. Bye then." And Nurse English walked away.

Gabe may have felt tingly all over but Jimmy Bear was still too large and scary. He scampered to Neal's room.

Claire and Nagy were outside and the meeting seemed to be

over.

"Hi guys. Pow-wow concluded? Plan to thwart the misguided machinations of the FBI formulated?"

Max was giving him the lawyer smile as he scanned and recorded his faded, Beethoven t-shirt, ragged navy shorts, and worn leather sandals. Max's suit and sparkly cuff links and equally sparkly tie tack probably totaled more than his net worth, but he was much prettier than Max.

Max said, "Hi, Gabe. I think we're good." He looked at Claire. "I'll call and set up a meeting."

Claire nodded. "Thank you, Mr. Nagy."

Max snapped the locks of his spiffy attache case, and departed.

Claire walked into Neal's room. "Sit down, Gabriel."

What the Hell now?

"Neal told me you were called to Chicago by your father's attorney."

"For the reading of the will. And I wanted to see what his family was like. And to see if they would share any tidbits about my casual sire and my ignoble birth."

Claire frowned. "Your birth was no different from anyone's, Gabriel, and he wasn't like that."

"No? Wait. Did you know him? Know who he was?"

She looked as un-placid and un-Claire as he'd ever seen.

"Claire? Please tell me."

Neal said, "If you don't want me to hear this, Gabe, just say?"

"No, it's okay."

Claire said, "Your mother left a note among her papers, Gabriel."

"Which said?"

"It named John as your father."

"John? Not Mr. Sullivan? That really sounds like you knew him, Claire?"

She nodded. "Yes, I knew him."

He shook his head, a bit baffled

"Not well. I didn't know he was your father until we found the note in the apartment."

"Do you have any photos?"

"No, I'm sorry, Gabriel."

"What did he look like?"

She smiled. "Like you in many ways. You have his hair and certainly his smile, but your eyes are your mother's."

"And you never mentioned any of this because?"

She frowned. "I contacted John after your mother passed away."

"Oh. And good ole John T. Sullivan said that bastard is no son of mine?"

"No! He never said anything like that. He said that he would come to see you as soon as he could and would tell you himself; he asked me not to say anything."

"But he never came, Claire."

"No, but I think he wanted to."

Which was so much bullshit. "Planes, trains, and automobiles, Claire. He didn't have to scale the Himalayas on a yak."

"You're right. I'm sorry, Gabriel."

There was no point in second guessing a decision made twenty years ago, and he had been ten. "No, it was a sticky situation, and I'm sure you did what you thought was best for me."

"I did."

And Gabe Bergeron had never asked about his father. He had also never asked exactly how his mother had died. Claire knew more about that too. He shook his head again to cast off the demons.

Claire said, "I'm glad he mentioned you in his will. If you want me to, I'd be happy to handle that for you. Have you heard from the attorney for his family?"

"No, but I lost my phone."

"Do you want me to act for you?"

"Yes."

"Give me the name of the attorney, and I'll get in touch. Neal told me his suggestion. Is that something you'd like to pursue?"

"Yes. I'm not sure I want a painting. Other than to know why he left it to me?"

He thought Claire was going to say something about that, but she smiled. "Of course. I should go see how Richard is doing."

He probably should ask about him, but too much was going on.

Neal said, "I'm kinda tired, Gabe." Claire squeezed her son's hand not moving.

"Sure, Buddy. But you're looking better every day."

"Thanks, Gabe."

So he stepped into the hall. He was just standing alone in a hospital corridor with no idea what he should do next and not trying to listen to their conversation.

Neal said, "What did Scott say?"

Claire said, "He denied everything. Which is always his first line of defense."

And Gabe wandered away. He thought he was hungry. He got in his car and drove around Salisbury until he found a burger place.

Charlie was probably right that he should get his own lawyer for the money laundering stuff, but he didn't know any criminal lawyers except Max, and there was the slight difficulty of being totally broke.

So Scott was lying to Claire. Big surprise. Scott said he had been sucked in by Rachel's friends, which was believable. And Scott might have hired Mia to get the ledger, but even so, he couldn't believe that Scott would hire somebody to kill his little brother.

But maybe he, or Rachel, had hired Chuck to take out just Eric, and never bothered to find out that Chuck didn't take direction well? That would be like Scott, but online customer satisfaction ratings for contract killers were probably hard to find?

His phone chimed.

"Bergeron."

Ellie said, "Steele wants to see you."

"So?"

"So, you should come talk to him." Her voice sounded funny like she was talking through gritted teeth.

He hung up on her.

It was childish. He was so ashamed.

He counted to thirty and called her back. "So where is the Glorious Fourth?"

She said, "Senior Special Agent Steele is at the hospital."

"Talking to Neal and Nagy?"

"At the hospital."

"I'm on my way."

Chernov and Murray were seated outside Neal's room. Gabe smiled and sat next to them. "Good to see you guys. How are you feeling, Chernov? Should you be out of bed?"

Chernov had a much smaller bandage across his nose, and he had two black eyes besides his actual black eyes.

Chernov shifted carefully in his seat. His left arm was in a sling, but he was mostly dressed. "Shut up, Bergeron."

Murray's face was red; even the backs of his hands were sunburned. "How long were you in the sun, Murray?"

"Too long."

"Where's Reed?"

Chernov said something in a language not English, and Murray smiled.

"I'm supposed to meet Steele? Any idea where he is, Guys?" Neal's door was closed so Steele was probably inside. He leaned over and sniffed Chernov. "You know that cologne is starting to grow on me."

Murray grabbed Chernov's good arm.

The Pale Wraith cast a baleful gaze upon him. "Either shut up, or he's going to beat the crap out of you and probably set his recovery back."

"Right. Got it. But one thing: is Steele here?"

Murray said, "Yes, Bergeron."

He sat back and rested his eyes, but that got boring quick. He went and got coffee; three cups.

He thought Chernov was going to refuse or dump it on his head, but Murray took his, and Chernov accepted the cup with a grunt.

They sipped, all comrades for the nonce.

Reed arrived. She smiled and kissed Chernov's cheek. The special agent suddenly resembled nothing so much as a granite sculpture of himself.

She said, "It's okay. Bergeron knows, Cherny."

"I know he does." Cherny pointed at the closed door. "But

Steele doesn't, and I'd like to keep it that way."

Gabe smiled at the special agents. "Steele will never find out from me. He could torture me for days, and I would never reveal a single detail of your passionate yet illicit romance."

Murray smiled again.

Reed shook her head at Chernov. "Relax, Special Agent. You know you should go home."

Chernov said, "I want to see this through, Lynda, and I'm okay."

And the door opened, and Ellie emerged like a butterfly from a chrysalis; a somber, blue-eyed butterfly in FBI black and gray.

Steele and Max were on opposite sides of Neal, who was sitting in a chair surrounded by pillows like a Ming vase being crated for shipment.

Steele and Max smiled professionally and shook hands. Steele handed Max a letter, which Max read slowly and carefully.

Steele said, "It's all there, Nagy."

Max said, "Yes, it appears so." He nodded. "And I'm sure you'll find the ledger very helpful, Senior Special Agent Steele."

"We'll see." Steele smiled. "You're just lucky that Tyson slipped up again and didn't find it."

Steele shook hands with Claire and Neal. Everyone was smiling, the sun was shining, and it was a glorious day. Except for Ellie.

Steele ignored her as he walked down the hall with Max, chest thrown out like the leader of the free world watching the Berlin wall being torn down.

Where was Steele going? He started to follow, but Reed said, "Stay, Bergeron."

And Chernov grabbed his arm.

So what exactly did Steele want with him? And where was this freaking ledger? He was starting to think it was a magic book that only special people could see.

Ellie went back into Neal's room and slammed the freaking door. He was getting tired and cranky. Messing with Chernov was fun, but he was about done.

"Chernov?"

"What?"

"Am I under arrest?"

Chernov actually looked at him. "No."

"Then I can walk away?"

Chernov said, "Yeah."

He got to his feet, but Reed said, "But you might want to stay."

"Why?"

"Ellie will tell you."

"No, I don't think so. It's been a unique experience, but if you'd like to contact me again, please call my attorney."

He would make up a name, if they asked for one.

But Murray smiled. "Don't you want to know where the ledger is?"

He wanted to know.

He really did.

They were all smiling at him, because they knew he wasn't going anywhere.

Wednesday
4:00 pm

The door opened. Claire said, "Come in, Gabriel."

So he waltzed in; Neal and Claire looked happy. "So you handed over the ledger?"

"Soon. Max said I should."

He hoped Max knew what he was doing. "So where was it?"

Neal gave him a big smile. "It's at the post office in Crisfield. I mailed it to Gabe Bergeron, General Delivery."

"What?"

Neal was still smiling. "So if you could do me just one more favor, Gabe, and please go with Ellie to Crisfield to get it? Please?"

Gabe glared at Ellie. "Can't the mighty FBI get it?"

Claire said, "They'd need a court order. You can simply ask for it."

Neal said, "Please, Gabe."

"Okay, I'll do it, but I don't like it."

Claire said, "Thank you for everything you've done, Gabriel. The doctor said Neal may be able to go home tomorrow or Friday."

"Great. Okay." Ellie was glaring at him, obviously impatient to get the freaking ledger.

He wasn't going to tell Neal that he'd never see Ellie again once she had it. The poor guy could figure that out for himself, or Claire could tell him.

Ellie gave Neal a token smile and left the room.

Neal said, "Be nice."

"Sure." But he didn't think he could do that. He really didn't. He stepped out and closed the door behind him.

Reed had disappeared.

He smiled at Ellie. "No way I'm going anywhere with you."

She glared at him. "I'll take you there in handcuffs if I have to, Bergeron."

"Nope. I'll go with Murray or not at all."

Ellie wanted to punch him in the face, but she shrugged, spun about, and marched off.

Murray and Chernov exchanged secret FBI smiles. Murray stood up but Chernov said, "I'll take him."

Murray looked Chernov over. "Sure about that?"

Chernov nodded and rose to his feet carefully, manfully assuming a terrible burden. "But no talking, Bergeron."

Gabe may have dared smile and wink at Chernov.

They walked out to a black SUV. The parking lot blacktop was radiating heat like a barbecue grill, but a lovely wave of cold air enveloped him when he opened the passenger door.

Chernov groaned when he climbed into the driver's seat. "Don't get pissed, but I could drive if you don't feel like it?"

Chernov snorted. "Over my dead body."

"Be that way. I didn't want to drive anyway." Which was actually true.

They motored down Salisbury Boulevard.

"How long have you been an agent?"

Chernov said, "Shut up, Bergeron."

"Of course. May I turn on the radio?"

"No."

"I need a distraction."

"Are you three years old?"

He sat as quietly as he could until they passed Princess Anne. He didn't consciously decide to start singing.

"'Nobody knows the trouble I've seen. Nobody knows my sorrow.'" His voice wasn't nearly deep enough. James probably had the voice for it.

Chernov turned on the radio and cranked up the volume. It was a country western station. He didn't know the song, but that didn't stop him from singing along.

The post office was on the corner of 4th and Main Streets.

It was a brick edifice with a cupola, marble stairs, and a wrought iron railing. It had handsome Palladian windows and a faded, Fifties, fallout shelter sign.

Chernov parked the SUV in front. "Stay inside."

Chernov scanned the adjoining buildings for snipers, but eventually waved for him to disembark.

He followed Chernov inside to find marble floors and wainscoting, wrought iron grills, thirty foot ceilings, and brass post office boxes; all lovingly maintained.

Chernov was scanning the interior, but the threat level was low since the only living things were Jace and Chloe and the auburn haired, postal clerk. He'd seen her somewhere, but he couldn't remember her name.

Jace had a package to mail. It was a box big enough to ship a lawn mower. He hadn't sealed the top or put an address on it.

Chloe said, "Bill said to include an invoice."

Jace smiled at her as the clerk handed him a piece of paper.

Jace said, "Thanks, Donna."

Heather's cousin Donna.

And Jace began to hand write the invoice. All of Chernov's deadly looks bounced off like rose petals.

Jace put the invoice inside, and then he and Donna spun the box round and round as they used enough tape to mummify it for all eternity.

Jace said, "Thanks, Donna." And he hugged Chloe and they moseyed on out of the post office, a smile on their faces, a song in their hearts, and nary a thought in their heads.

Chernov shoved him up to the counter.

"I'm Gabe Bergeron."

Donna smiled. "Yes, I know."

He could feel Chernov tense up.

Donna said, "We met at Samantha's party. And then I saw you in the boat with the new park ranger when that young man was arrested. Did he really murder the yacht guy and Lonnie?"

"And more. Bodies piled high across three continents."

She smiled. "Heather said you were a trip."

"Thank Heather for me. I believe you have a package for

me?"

She nodded and retrieved it from a shelf. "Sent to general delivery. We hardly ever get those. If I could see a photo ID, Sir?"

He showed her his Pennsylvania driver's license, and she handed over a book sized package.

He looked at Chernov. "It would be really funny if this is a photo album of Neal's baby pictures."

Chernov said, "I'd shoot you both."

And then Cindi Lou came in.

It seemed odd for her to be in the Crisfield post office, and maybe that was why it took Gabe a really long time to identify the big object in her little hand.

"Shit."

Cindi Lou used her courtroom voice. "Don't move! I will shoot you if I have to! Nobody move!"

Chernov was going to move. Gabe could see it in his eyes. "Don't, Chernov. Please."

Cindi Lou came up behind the special agent and shoved the long barrel of the big gun into his back. Based on his extensive knowledge of firearms, he didn't think this was a Glock.

Cindi Lou said, "Don't be stupid, Agent. Bergeron, get his gun and put it on the floor. Very carefully and slowly. Do it!"

Chernov was very, very unhappy, as Gabe reached inside his jacket and drew the Glock out of his shoulder holster.

Gabe had never held a gun before; it wasn't nearly as heavy as he'd expected.

"On the floor!"

"Why are you doing this, Cindi?"

"Shut up! Kick the gun away."

He had sandals on so he did a shuffle board maneuver to send the gun sliding across the floor. It gently rebounded from the wall and came to a halt.

Her face was cadaver white again. "Now, the package! Put it on the floor and slide it over to me. Now, Bergeron! Or I will shoot you both!"

"Okay. No problem. Sliding the package. But really, Cindi, why? This goes way beyond stuff a lawyer does for her client."

"Shut up!"

The package didn't slide as easily as the gun, but it made it alongside Cindi Lou.

And then Jace came through the door.

And Donna ducked down behind her marble counter and scooted away, screaming like all the banshees of Ireland.

And Chernov went all FBI and spun around.

Cindi Lou was bent over with one hand on the package, but she managed to get a shot off.

The bang echoed off the marble and rattled the windows.

Chernov fell down.

It was very quiet for a tiny fraction of a second. And then Donna screeched again.

Cindi Lou snatched the package from the floor and ran.

She ran into Jace.

Jace was still processing what had happened and was currently happening, but he had been brought up to be polite and instinctively tried to get out of the lady's way.

Cindi Lou and Jace did a brief pas de deux which ended with both of them falling to the floor.

And Cindi Lou dropped her very big gun.

She got to her knees still clutching the package with her left hand. But as she reached for her gun, Jace extended a long leg and kicked it across the post office like a Brazilian soccer star.

It came to rest next to Chernov, and Cindi Lou bolted.

Chernov was groaning but he said, "Shit! Get my gun, Bergeron!"

He slid across the floor and retrieved it for the special agent.

Chernov was on his knees.

"Stay down, Chernov. You've been shot." Blood was dripping down his right arm.

Chernov shook his head. "Help me up!"

Chernov gritted his teeth as he hauled the guy to his feet. And then the agent grabbed his gun and gamely gave chase or gave hobble.

A disembodied Donna voice said, "I called the cops!"

"Thank you, Donna. Jace, hold onto Cindi's gun."

Jace said, "Yes, Sir."

Cindi Lou had parked in the vacant lot across the street. "The black Caddy!"

Chernov fired two shots as Cindi Lou spun out of the parking lot heading down 4th Street.

Chernov ran for the SUV.

"We're going to chase her?"

Chernov snarled as he tried to get his keys without putting the gun down. He finally stuffed the gun in his sling.

"You can't drive."

Chernov snarled some more; there were foreign words interspersed with animal growls.

"You have a bullet in your right arm." Blood was dribbling down his sleeve. "I can drive."

Chernov shook his head. "You! No freaking way, Bergeron!"

"Be that way, but she's getting away, and you have half an arm. At best. While I am able bodied."

He gave Chernov a double biceps pose. He flexed as hard as he could; he needed to go back to the gym.

Chernov threw the keys at him.

They sailed past his outstretched hands, but he retrieved them. Jace and Donna were watching from the doorway. He gave them a thumbs up and jumped into the driver's seat. Jace waved and smiled.

Chernov got on the radio to the local police as he did a u-turn and then roared after Cindi Lou.

Chernov used his injured left arm to wrap his tie around his also injured right arm, gritting his teeth all the while.

They could see the Caddy rocketing down 4th Street. The SUV had a big engine, and they were gaining on her as they shot past the marina.

Cindi Lou swerved left at an intersection and then right at the next one. They followed.

Chernov said, "My grandmother can drive better than you!"

Which was probably true but hurtful all the same.

The road curved left, but when they rounded said curve, Cindi Lou and her big, black Caddy had vanished.

Chernov punched him in the arm with his left fist and moaned.

There was a school and an intersection ahead.

Chernov yelled, "There! Turn! Turn!"

Cindi Lou had somehow made a hard right and was vanishing down Calvary Road.

He had to brake and back up.

Chernov was banging on the dash with his left fist.

The road was narrow and had a ditch on the right large enough to swallow the SUV whole.

He went a lot faster than he wanted to go. It wasn't nearly fast enough for Chernov.

But they saw Cindi Lou ahead doing roughly a hundred fifty on a road designed for fifteen.

Gabe was following at a slightly more genteel pace and falling behind, but then he remembered driving on this road.

Chernov was talking on the radio again with the Crisfield police. "They say they've got the road blocked up ahead somewhere."

"Excellent. Hold tight, Special Agent."

Chernov looked at him. "Why?"

"Bump ahead." He cinched up his seat belt as Chernov did the same.

The bridge over Jenkins Creek was neither very high nor very long, more of a moon bridge, but it was not meant to be traversed at a hundred miles an hour. Cindi Lou couldn't have slowed down if she'd tried.

She roared up one side and sailed over the other. She landed in a shower of sparks as the back end of the Caddy scoured the blacktop. Cindi Lou swerved into a s-curve that led into a marsh.

Gabe looked over at Chernov as they went airborne.

Chernov had closed his eyes.

He still stuck the landing.

And then he looked back to Chernov and laughed in triumph.

The tide was very high, and the road was very low.

The flooded road had been reduced to a center ribbon of blacktop; marsh and water formed a seamless border on either side.

Cindi's Caddy was spraying water like a speedboat as it

plowed ahead. Cindi did not let off the gas.

He started laughing again.

Chernov said, "What the Hell is wrong with you?"

Twin jets of water were shooting from the SUV tires as they followed her. He slowed down.

Chernov said, "You dumb bastard! What are you doing?"

"Cindi Lou doesn't know the road."

"And you do?"

"Yep."

Chernov was deeply skeptical.

Ahead of Cindi Lou, the road seemed to disappear into the marsh, and by the time she realized that it actually made a sharp left turn, it was much too late.

The sheer momentum of all that American steel carried her into the marsh until an enormous wave of water and mud covered the car, and Cindi Lou's voyage came to a damp and ignominious end.

Gabe braked to a stop, tires still on the submerged road.

Chernov unbuckled his seat belt, but he didn't try to get out of the SUV. He wasn't looking too good. "The ledger, Bergeron."

He nodded to Chernov. He jumped out, opened the back, and retrieved a tire iron before wading into the marsh.

The passenger side door wouldn't budge due to the bottom quarter being buried. He smashed the window.

Cindi Lou was leaning over the steering wheel. Her antique vehicle seemed to be lacking certain safety features like seat belts and air bags. She had hit her head on the steering wheel, and blood was trickling down her face. She was crying softly.

The ledger was in the floor, and the good ship Cadillac seemed to have sprung a leak, but he grabbed the ledger and held it close.

"Why?"

"Give me the ledger!"

"So Layla hired Chuck?"

"Layla did nothing! She's completely innocent. I did it. But he was supposed to get the ledger before he did anything to Eric."

"Yeah, about that; Chuck is a little crazy."

Cindi grabbed for the book again. "Eric deserved to die for what he did to her."

"And what is that?"

She glared at him. "He was a cheat. In marriage and in business. Like all men. She could have gone to prison because of him."

"She still could."

"No! She's innocent. I told her not to marry him. I told her that I...."

"That you loved her?"

"Go away and leave me alone!"

"Right. Leaving now."

He waded through the water to the road. He lost his left sandal in the mud. Chernov had the door open, but he hadn't tried to get out.

Police cars were coming from both directions.

He waved at them and handed Chernov the package.

Chernov tore off the damp wrapping paper.

The Anarchist smiled.

He had a nice smile.

Wednesday
6:00 pm

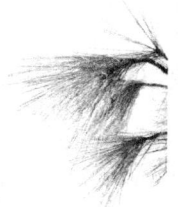

Chernov had refused to let go of the ledger and had refused to get on the gurney until Reed arrived.

Cindi Lou was already on board the ambulance, securely handcuffed. Ed, the paramedic, said she seemed okay.

Chernov was still sitting in the open doorway of the SUV as Ed and Bud tried to stop the bleeding. They and their gurney were ankle deep, or wheel deep, in the water.

Reed shook her head at Chernov as she took the ledger. "Get on the freaking gurney and let them put you into the freaking ambulance, Special Agent."

Chernov smiled at her.

"Now!"

Ed and Bud loaded him on board. Reed jumped in, and the ambulance slowly motored away as the local police cleared a path through the gawkers.

Murray was looking at him shaking his head.

"What?"

Murray said, "Talk to me, Bergeron."

"Okay. Sure. But we should go back to the post office."

"Why?"

"To get Cindi Lou's gun."

Murray was looking down at his nice shoes marinating in salt water. "Yeah. Let's do that."

Jace had surrendered the gun to the local police, and he and Donna were giving eye witness accounts to anyone who'd listen. Chloe was floating nearby.

Murray took charge of the gun, Jace and Donna, and the crime scene.

And Gabe Bergeron sat on the post office steps just replaying the chase in his head and realizing that he and Chernov were lucky not to be dead.

Murray sat beside him on the steps. "Can you drive Dave's SUV back to Salisbury for me?"

"Wait. Chernov is Dave?"

Murray smiled at him. "What were you expecting?"

"Vladimir. Sergei. Pavel. Boris. Rasputin."

"Nope."

"Well, that's disappointing. So tell me your name?"

Murray said, "Kaleva."

"Really?"

"No, Bergeron, but it could have been. That's what my father wanted; his parents were from Finland, but my mother insisted on Carl."

His mother had messed up; the Pale Wraith didn't look like a Carl. Or a Murray.

"Thanks for your help in getting the ledger."

"You're thanking me?"

"I am. Something I would never, ever have believed would happen, but you did good, Gabe."

And Murray slapped him on the back and handed him Dave's keys.

He parked Dave's SUV and reclaimed his Fiesta. He didn't feel like talking to anybody, but he called Claire and reported that the FBI had the ledger.

And he needed to tell Great-aunt Flo that it was finally over, and that he was sorry for worrying her.

The gold and cream Itasca RV in her driveway was a shocker.

He parked and ran across the lawn. Great-aunt Flo's car was missing. Maybe she and Ms. Gutierrez were safely away from home? Or maybe they weren't.

He slipped into the greenhouse, but the only weapon-type thing he could find was a shovel. He headed for the side door.

He tip-toed through the kitchen. A pot was simmering so

Aunt Flo and/or Mrs. Gutierrez weren't gone for long? He climbed the stairs. He heard Kev's voice and headed for the parlor.

Aunt Flo and the Sanduskys were seated across from one another on the matching leather sofas. The conversation faltered when they spotted him and the shovel.

Good ole Kev was totally relaxed, long legs sprawled across the floor. His shirt was unbuttoned to display that furry chest. "Going to whack me with that, Gabe."

"That was the plan. Why are you here?"

Kev didn't move a muscle, but Barb pulled a gun from her purse. Kev was smiling at him. "Put the shovel down and have a seat, Gabe."

Kev pulled a gun from the back of his shorts and rested it on his hairy thigh. The pistols were a matched pair, both silver and bigger than Ellie's Glock but smaller than Cindi's cannon.

Aunt Flo patted the space beside her. "Please sit down, Gabe."

She had a odd-shaped pot holder or something in her lap, and a bag of yarn beside her.

Which was strange since Aunt Flo didn't knit.

She said, "You don't have to aim that gun at my Gabe, Mrs. Sandusky."

Barb laughed. "No? He doesn't look very happy to see us, Mrs. Barnes."

Aunt Flo said, "Why would he? But he isn't going to do anything. Isn't that right, Gabe?"

Which was also strange since Aunt Flo had never called him "Gabe" in twenty years.

Kev said, "So where is it, Gabe?"

"It? I don't know what you're talking about, Kev."

Kev stopped smiling. "Don't bullshit me. I don't have time for any games today. Where is the ledger?"

"What ledger?"

Kev leaned close. "Eric's ledger." Kev slapped him hard. "Hand it over, or things are going to get very unpleasant." Kev slapped him even harder. "For you and Mrs. Barnes."

"Sorry, Kev. I don't have it."

Kev shook his head. "Listen, Asshole. You aren't as tough as you think you are, and I could get off on beating you." Kev parted his lips to display his brilliantly white teeth. "But I don't have time. How would you feel if I started slapping your poor old great-aunt here? Would you like that, Gabe?"

Aunt Flo said, "Oh, please don't hit me."

He said, "So you and Barb are friends with Rachel? And the three of you roped Scott and Eric into this money laundering scheme?"

Barb smiled at him.

Kev said, "Nobody roped Scott into anything. It was his idea."

"Scott's not that bright."

Kev said, "And didn't we find that out pretty damn quick! But Eric took over, and things would have been fine if Scott hadn't gotten greedy and tried to take on some clients on his own."

Gabe shook his head. "Now that sounds like Scott. So how did Eric join your merry band, Kev?"

Barb said, "That's enough talking, Bergeron. Where is it?"

Kev turned to her. "But we still don't know who hired the psychopath who killed Eric, Babe?"

Barb said, "And you think Bergeron knows?"

"The nosy bastard might?" Kev looked at him, not smiling at all now. "Eric was my cousin. He was a good guy."

Eric was no such thing. "Sorry, Kev. I can't help you."

"Come on, Bergeron, we need to know."

Barb said, "Forget about Eric."

The grandfather clock in the hall chimed three. Which was stranger still, and not because it was almost seven, but because the clock hadn't run for years.

Aunt Flo said, "I really have to get that clock fixed. I keep meaning to, but I'm so forgetful lately. Isn't that right, Gabe?"

"It sure is."

Kev slapped him again. "Shut the Hell up about clocks. Where is the ledger?"

He was about to tell ole Kev that the FBI had it, when Aunt Flo said, "I think you should get it for him, Dear."

"I should?"

"Yes, he's desperate. They both are, and who knows what they might do." She tittered nervously. "It's in your car, isn't it? I think that's where you said it was?"

"Okay. Sure. Anything for you, Auntie Florence."

She tittered again. "Just give it to him. Don't do anything silly."

"Right."

Kev pulled him to his feet. "Come on. Show me, Asshole." Kev looked at Barb. "Stay here with the old lady. If you hear anything funny, shoot her."

Barb smiled and aimed at Aunt Flo, who managed to look frightened and befuddled.

Kev shoved him along as he strolled across the lawn heading for his car. Kev could see that there was nothing on the seats.

"It's in the trunk."

Kev said, "Then open it. Quit stalling, Bergeron."

He had thought that Aunt Flo had a plan, but he wasn't so sure now. And where the Hell was Mrs. Gutierrez? Not that there was much she could do.

He smiled at Kev as he fumbled with the keys. "So all that crotch rubbing was just for show? You and Barb weren't hot to get it on with me?"

Kev smiled. "No, that was real enough. But it's probably just as well that you pussied out, Bergeron." He laughed. "You wouldn't have been able to keep up with Barb and me."

He didn't want to open the trunk. Ole Kev was not going to be pleased. "So how did you find out about Aunt Flo? Rachel or Scott?"

Kev pushed the gun barrel into his gut. "Shut up! You don't have it, do you?"

"Sure I do." He opened the trunk.

Kev jabbed him with the gun again. "Stupid, lying asshole."

"Easy, Kev. It's under the spare tire."

Kev said, "Bullshit."

"It is. Just hold on." He lifted the cover as Kev hovered over him.

Ole Kev was peering at the baby tire when Raúl slipped up behind him and shoved a supersized revolver into the spot where the spine and skull fuse.

Raúl said, "Take his gun, Gabriel."

Kev thought about resisting, but Raúl jammed the gun into the base of his skull like a pool cue. "Go ahead. Try something."

Gabe pried Kev's gun out of his hand and aimed at him.

Raúl smiled. "You and Mrs. Barnes heard the clock?" He nodded. "Good. Can you keep this one here, Gabriel?"

He certainly could, but he wasn't going to. "I'm going with you." Raúl shook his head. "She's my aunt, Raúl."

Raúl said, "And him?"

He said, "Get in the trunk, Kev."

It wasn't a very big trunk, and Kev was ever so reluctant.

Kev smirked at him and started to get in. He tried kicking Raúl, which was a mistake. Raúl whacked him across the head and shoved him in the trunk and slammed it. Kev's foot was still outside.

Kev groaned. Raúl smacked him again before making sure all of Kev's limbs were inside before he slammed the trunk again.

The house was a long way from the lane, but it was very quiet.

Raúl started running for the house. He might be big and scary, but Mrs. Gutierrez' "nephew" wasn't very fast, and one Gabe Bergeron got to the door first.

It was too quiet.

They tip-toed up the back stairs to the second floor.

And then they heard Mrs. Gutierrez coming up the main stairs singing. Gabe had never heard her sing before, and it was obvious why she didn't.

She called out. "Mrs. Barnes, do you want some tea?"

She reached the second floor and saw him and Raúl. She waved them back and headed for the parlor. Her right hand was at her side partially concealed by a flowered apron.

"Mrs. Barnes?"

Barb said, "Stop right there! Don't move! Where is Kev?"

He crept to the door. He could feel Raúl's breath on his neck. He peeped in.

Barb was aiming at Mrs. Gutierrez. "I said where the Hell is

Kev?"

And then Aunt Flo pulled a Glock out of her knitting. "Put the gun down, Mrs. Sandusky."

Barb laughed. "You aren't going to shoot anybody, Lady." She looked at Aunt Flo. "But I will shoot her if you don't drop that gun."

Mrs. Gutierrez didn't have a pistol under her flowered apron. He wasn't sure what an Uzi looked like, but it was probably something like the firearm Mrs. Gutierrez had trained on Barb.

Barb was still turned toward Aunt Flo. She laughed again. "Your maid isn't going to shoot me."

He could have told Barb that Mrs. Gutierrez did not like being laughed at, but she found out for herself as Mrs. Gutierrez fired a burst of lightning and thunder into the sofa like an angry Zeus. Or Hera? Could Hera hurl thunderbolts too?

Barb dropped her gun and curled into a ball as sofa innards and the odor of cordite floated around her in a cloud.

Barb was sobbing.

Aunt Flo looked like Winston Churchill during the Blitz, if Churchill had been female and pixieish and eighty.

Mrs. Gutierrez yelled something in Spanish as she grabbed Barb by the hair and dragged her from the parlor.

Aunt Flo looked distressed over her sofa. "Raúl neutralized Mr. Sandusky?"

"He did. I helped."

She smiled and stowed her Glock back among her skeins of yarn. "Of course, you did. We should see to our guests, Gabriel."

"Okay."

Raúl had tied up Barb. He dragged Kev from the trunk and tossed him on the ground next to his wife. Kev was bleeding a little but conscious now.

Aunt Flo said, "He's bleeding, Ezmeralda."

Mrs. Gutierrez shrugged, but she went and got something to stop the bleeding.

Aunt Flo said, "Thank you, Ezmeralda. And thank you, Raúl."

Mrs. Gutierrez and Raúl were focused on Kev and Barb.

Great-aunt Flo said, "The Scott you mentioned is Neal's

brother?"

Gabe leaned on the shovel. "Right. And these guys were co-conspirators with Scott and Rachel and Eric in the money laundering."

She nodded. "And Scott told them about me?"

"Must have."

Great-aunt Flo said, "Did they also hire the hitman to kill Eric? And Neal and you?"

Kev said, "Hell, no!"

Barb said, "Look, we had nothing whatever to do with that. We just wanted to get Eric's ledger, and we thought Bergeron could get it for us."

Aunt Flo looked at him. "And do we believe them, Gabriel?"

"It so happens that we do. Completely." He told her about the lovelorn Cindi Lou.

She nodded. "That does simplify things, Gabriel."

"It does? Wait. Are you okay?"

She smiled. "Excellent. It was amusing."

"Which part?"

She smiled again. "Listening to them trying to interrogate a frail old lady. They couldn't know, of course, that I've been interrogated by experts."

"You have?"

"Ask Mrs. Gutierrez."

Mrs. Gutierrez flicked her black, almond-shaped eyes at him. Like she would tell him.

He knelt beside Kev, and slapped him in the face. "Just not too bright, Kev. You did all this for nothing."

Mrs. Gutierrez laughed and said something in Spanish, and Aunt Flo giggle-cackled. Kev was bright enough to know he was being dissed.

Barb said, "What do you mean?"

"I mean that I personally placed Eric's stupid ledger into the hands of Special Agent Chernov just two hours ago."

Kev said, "Bullshit."

"No, Kev. Neal had it all the time."

Kev said, "No, he didn't. We searched everywhere."

"Wrong again, Kev. Not everywhere."

Great-aunt Flo smiled at them. "So there is no reason for our guests to stay any longer."

Mrs. Gutierrez and Raúl were still giving Kev and Barb a hungry look.

Mrs. Gutierrez said, "The river?"

Great-aunt Flo said, "No, Ezmeralda."

Mrs. Gutierrez frowned. "The garden then?" She glanced at him. "Gabriel has the shovel. He can dig."

Kev and Barb were finally realizing just how serious an error they had made in trying to strong arm this particular old lady.

But he was not going to bury Kev and Barb. He looked at Aunt Flo, and she started laughing at him. "Come with me, Gabriel. Don't do anything to our guests, Ezmeralda."

"Maybe no. Maybe yes."

Aunt Flo took him into the garden. He said, "We aren't going to kill them. No way. Not happening."

She said, "Of course, we aren't. We're going to let them go."

But that was a bit too much turning the other cheek. "We are? How about giving them to the FBI?"

She shook her head. "No, Gabriel. That isn't a good idea. Please don't ask why."

Because it would bring attention to his elderly aunt and her devoted housekeeper and her visiting nephews.

Great-aunt Flo was smiling at him as he slowly worked it out. "You see?"

"I see nothing, but I see enough."

Mrs. Gutierrez and Raúl escorted Kev and Barb to their RV.

Mrs. Gutierrez said, "Don't come back."

Kev and Barb nodded, delighted not to be fish food or worm food. They roared away as fast as their massive RV would go.

Gabe went back to the parlor and sat across from Aunt Flo. The knitting and the pistol had disappeared, and one of her cats was sniffing the bullet holes in the couch.

"Was that a Glock 22?"

She smiled. "I didn't think you knew anything about guns, Gabriel?"

"I don't, but Ellie has one just like that. And Chernov."

Aunt Flo nodded. "Standard issue for the FBI." She shook her head. "Well, that was very exciting, but my couch is ruined."

He nodded. "Yeah. Sorry, and sorry for getting you into the mess."

"Not at all, Gabriel. Please stay for dinner?"

"Sure. Maybe you can tell me a little about Mrs. Gutierrez and Raúl? And yourself?"

"Maybe yes, maybe no."

"Where were you all those years?"

She smiled. "Cuba, mostly."

"Wasn't it illegal for an American citizen to visit Cuba?"

"It was."

"What were you doing there?"

"Living."

"Okay. And?"

She smiled as she entered the dining room; Mrs. Gutierrez and Raúl were already there. "I got married, widowed, married again, and divorced. And I had several careers. A lot can happen in thirty years."

"Children?"

"No. I'm not sure if I'm happy or sad about that."

"What kind of careers?"

She looked at Mrs. Gutierrez who smiled at her. "Exciting careers, Gabriel."

"Going to share any more than that?" He looked at Mrs. Gutierrez. "How about you? So you're Cuban?"

Mrs. Gutierrez said, "Yes, Gabriel."

Aunt Flo said, "As for the rest, Gabriel, that is a discussion for another time."

And that is all she would say, but they had a nice meal, and she insisted he stay in his old room, the turret room on the third floor, which was also very nice.

In the morning, Gabe said his goodbyes and promised to visit more often. He called Neal who was on his way home with Claire. He told him about his trifling adventure with Cindi Lou.

He explained about Kev being Eric's cousin, but he didn't tell

Neal about Aunt Flo and the redoubtable Mrs. Gutierrez. Or the Uzi.

He didn't think Aunt Flo would want him to.

He got back to Philly and took a taxi from the airport.

His own car, which was a piece of money-sucking junk, was sitting dead and withered in front of his apartment building, where he'd left it eight days ago. He missed the Fiesta already.

Mr. Boghossian, his landlord, was tall and dark and made official Murray look as happy as one of Santa's elves. "Is this going to be a thing with you, Bergeron?"

"What?"

"The FBI showing up with a warrant and searching the apartment?"

"What? They did?" Which wasn't surprising really.

"Sorry, Mr. Boghossian. Mistaken identity. Why would the FBI be interested in little old me?"

Mr. Boghossian was deeply skeptical, but he ran up the stairs before his landlord could ask any more questions.

He hunkered down in his apartment for two tranquil days before he got bored. It was definitely time to find a job, any job. Mr. Boghossian would throw him out if he missed the rent payment by so much as a day.

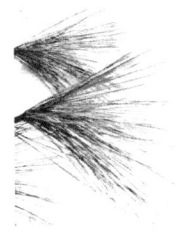

Thursday
Weeks Later

Gabriel Henri Bergeron hadn't thought he'd be walking into the Summer Nights Cafe so soon, or possibly ever again.

Heather rushed over to give him a big hug. She was gussied up in her pink dress again.

"Gabe! How are you, Hon? You look good."

"You do, too. Thanks for helping set this up."

There was a banner that read "Congratulations" hanging from the lights, and the place looked as swanky as linen tablecloths and a buffet could make it. A three piece band was playing a slow song. He had sprung for champagne too. It had taken his last dime, but it was a celebration.

"Are they here yet?"

She smiled. "Not yet. How did you manage it?"

Charlie said, "Yeah, how?" Sergeant King was resplendent in his dress uniform. "You wore them down, didn't you?"

"I don't know what you mean, Charlie. I may have called, emailed, and visited with the Maryland Park Service superintendent and the Department of Natural Resources secretary a few times. The first week was devoted mostly to getting past the feeble roadblocks their staffs tried to throw up, but eventually we came to a meeting of the minds."

Charlie shook his head.

"People tell me that I'm relentless, but I don't see it myself."

Heather giggled and disappeared into the kitchen.

Charlie said, "This is a nice thing, Gabe."

Young Luke, big blue eyes sparkling, was heading for them

smiling. Officer Stevens was very fetching in his uniform regalia.

"I figured I owed Kurt and Sarah. After everything, Charlie. I mean I didn't burn down the cabin, but I was responsible for other stuff." He smiled. "I think you deserve an award too, but the Natural Resources Police awards aren't until later in the year. I checked."

Luke said, "He does, Gabe!"

Charlie shoved a big paw into his face. "No, Bergeron. Do not annoy the powers that be. Do not. Are you listening to me?"

"I hear every word, Sergeant King."

Luke said, "I say go for it, Gabe."

Charlie threw up his hands and stomped off.

Luke traversed the floor with a bounce in his step to the table of a very pretty young lady. "Want to dance, Mira?"

It appeared she did.

Heather popped out of the kitchen. "Gabe?"

"Yes, Ma'am?"

"The champagne is chilled. The cake is ready. Anything else, Hon?"

"Nope. Everything looks A-okay, all systems go." She smiled. "So what happened about Zeke? And the suspension?"

"The OAH reduced it to ten days, thank the Lord. Without Mr. Jerry's lawyer."

"That's good, Heather."

And then Rangers Hobbs and Sharp entered to applause. Sarah was glowing, but Kurt looked embarrassed.

Sarah extended a hand. "Thank you, Mr. Bergeron."

Kurt shook his hand too, and then hugged him hard enough to squeeze the air out of his lungs. "I never thought you were serious."

"I'm always serious, Ranger Hobbs. Well, some of the time I'm not. But some of the times people think I'm not, I am. So let me see them?"

Kurt said, "They're in the car."

"So go get them, Ranger."

Sarah said, "I told you he was going to want to see them."

Kurt fetched their Maryland Park Service Valor Awards.

He wanted a picture, and Sarah insisted that he be in it so

Heather snapped a photo of the three of them holding the awards.

He would have to remember to email it to Wendy; he'd already updated her about Chuck and Cindi Lou. And thanked her.

He shook his head. "Maybe a nice frame will help. I know they aren't the medals I promised you, but give me a few more months...."

Kurt put a hand over his mouth. "Shut up, Bergeron. They're very nice, and we are very pleased. And grateful."

Sarah said, "And we get to keep our jobs."

Heather and her helpers brought out the bubbly and the cake, and they all ate slices of chocolate Smith Island cake and made toasts. He didn't drink alcohol, but this was a special occasion so he was a little tipsy when Chernov, Reed, and Murray showed up.

Gabe hugged them each and every one, and a recovered Chernov didn't body slam him to the floor.

"How are you guys? Thanks for coming." He hadn't really thought they would come when he'd sent the invitations.

Murray said, "We wouldn't have missed it."

Chernov said, "This is nice."

Murray smiled. "It is, Gabe."

"Thanks. Help yourself to food. And drink." He hugged Chernov again. Pressed against his chest, he gripped those flaring back muscles while inhaling a noseful of that cologne. "Are you really okay, Chernov? Dave?"

Special Agent Dave certainly felt fit and strong again.

"I thought you were going to bleed out after Cindi Lou shot you, and you insisted we chase her."

Chernov still didn't punch him. "I'm fine, but do not hug me again, Bergeron."

"Okay." He hugged Reed instead. "So how is the case going?"

Reed had let her black hair down, literally, but not that far. "We can't discuss the case, Mr. Bergeron. Not even with you."

"Really? That's okay. We had fun, didn't we?"

Chernov said, "Hell, no."

"Right. Sorry, Dave. There were some bad moments." He threw his tie over his shoulder and unbuttoned his shirt. He traced the scar across his chest with a finger. "See? Chuck tried to kill me.

And he tried to stab Kurt too. And he kicked you, Dave."

Gabe reached out to touch the scar that ran across Dave's nose, but Dave locked onto his wrist and wagged a finger in front of his face. He smiled at Dave. "Sorry. Chuck isn't a nice man."

Murray said, "But Mr. Szymanski has agreed to testify against Ms. Parker."

"Good. Excellent. She can't wiggle out of that. Wait. That was Chuck's real name?"

Murray nodded. "Nathan Szymanski."

"And besides that, me and Jace and Donna saw her shoot you, Dave."

Chernov said, "I remember."

He said, "What about Layla?"

Murray said, "She's also been indicted."

"I don't know if I'll be able to hold back my tears."

Reed giggled. "You really don't like her, do you?"

"I don't know what you're talking about Special Agent Reed."

He already knew from Claire that Scott, Rachel, Kev, and Barb had been indited.

Murray said, "You should get an award too, Gabe."

"Me?"

Murray said, "You drove Dave's vehicle in a high speed chase. You grabbed the ledger before it got wet."

He had done that. He smiled at them. "That's right. I did."

He was very happy, but he wasn't feeling just right. "Okay, I shouldn't ask...."

Reed said, "But you're going to."

"Right. What about Ellie?" They stopped smiling at him. "What? Did something happen to her?"

Murray said, "No."

"Then what?"

Reed said, "She applied for a transfer, and it came through earlier this week. She's in Los Angeles apartment hunting."

Shit.

Neal hadn't said a word about her. Which was understandable.

And it was probably good that she was a continent away from

Neal. Gabe wasn't going to be petty. "Well, she got away from the Glorious Fourth. So good for her, I guess."

Chernov smiled at him. "Okay. You should get a medal for that, Gabe."

"What?"

"For annoying the Hell out of Senior Special Agent Steele."

"You think so? I mean I tried my best, and his cheeks did get these red spots, but I wasn't sure."

Murray smiled. "Definitely. Like no one who has gone before you."

He would have basked in their approval a while longer, but he had to run to the men's room.

He threw up cake and champagne.

He knew there was a reason he didn't drink alcohol.

He splashed water on his face and went back to the party. Everybody seemed to be having a good time.

He found Kurt and shook his hand. "Congratulations again."

"You aren't leaving?"

"Yeah. I have to go back to Philly."

Kurt followed him outside. "Thanks again, Gabe."

"Sure. You deserved it, and I had fun doing it."

"I'll bet you did." Kurt smiled again. "If you get a chance, come back, Gabe. You really are welcome."

"To the park?"

"Correct."

"I'd like that." He hugged Kurt again.

He drove back to Philly and slept until noon. He woke up feeling a little better. He was supposed to meet with Claire at four.

Claire and Richard's house wasn't the biggest in their ritzy neighborhood, but it wasn't the smallest either.

Claire said, "Come in, Gabriel. I have news for you."

"Good news?"

She nodded. "Yes. Come into the library." She smiled at him. "The portrait is yours, Gabe. And copies of all the family genealogical materials that they have."

"Portrait? The lawyer just said a painting at the reading of the will. Whose portrait?

"Sit down. Coffee?"

Claire had the very best coffee he'd ever tasted, but he didn't even take a sip after she poured him a cup.

Claire said, "You do remember that Leanne was an artist?"

"No. Not really." But then he had this flash of his mother cleaning a handful of paint brushes. He couldn't make out her face, but it was her. She had a paint smudge on her cheek, and she was standing at a sink and laughing.

Whenever he thought of her, the only image that came now was the one from a photo, taken before he was born.

"Wait. She painted this portrait?"

Claire said, "Yes, she did. It's of your father."

Memory was a strange thing; it wasn't anything like a video. He remembered flashes of his fifth birthday party, the new flash of her cleaning the paint brushes, and of her being dead on the floor. Not much of a haul for ten years, but maybe his brain knew best?

Claire said, "I thought you knew, Gabriel."

"No. I don't remember much before coming to live with you and Neal.

She said, "Is there anything you'd like to ask me?"

He took a slug of coffee. "No. I don't think so."

He couldn't unknow something if Claire told him now. His brain would never let it go a second time, so he buried that gnawing curiosity as deeply as he could.

Claire handed him a slip of paper. "This is the number for Marie Murphy, your cousin. She said to call her any time to arrange to pick up the portrait."

"Thank you so much, Claire. Send me a bill."

"Don't be silly, Gabriel. I'm retired, and I don't bill friends. And I will always think I could have done more for Leanne."

He didn't know what to say to that.

The front door opened.

Scott yelled, "Mom!"

Claire closed her eyes. "In here."

Scott barged in. "I'm going to prison!"

Claire nodded. "I'm sorry, Scott, but it is minimum security. How long?"

"You knew?"

She said, "They were never going to agree to no jail time."

"You could have done something!"

Claire's face shifted and locked up, but Scott didn't pick up on it. Gabe Bergeron hadn't either when he'd first come to live with them, but he'd learned.

She said, "I wouldn't have done anything even if I could."

"What?"

"You've been getting away with things for too long, Scott. Maybe this will get your attention."

Scott was truly shocked. "What are you talking about?"

"I could give you a list, but it's been a long day. Richard and I have bailed you out, literally and figuratively, over and over. And you let Neal get involved with a criminal. You knew what Eric was, and you said nothing."

"Always so worried about sweet, little Neal."

She said, "I worry about both of you. Now, go upstairs to see your father, Scott. He isn't very well."

Scott spun around and walked out.

Gabe wanted to hug Claire, but he'd never done that. "I'm sorry, Claire."

She sipped her coffee. "You have nothing to be sorry about, Gabriel. Nothing at all. Neal's coming for dinner. Join us?"

"If it isn't too much trouble?"

"No, of course not."

Dinner wasn't as somber as he'd expected. Neal had to know about Ellie going to Los Angeles?

After clearing up and loading the dishes, he and Neal took a hike from the kitchen to the media room.

Neal dropped onto the sofa. "I have news for you, Gabe."

"Yeah? Good news?"

"There's a job for you if you want it?"

He wanted a job so bad. "Doing what? Exactly?" Who was he kidding? He would take almost anything.

Neal smiled at him. "Accounting, Doofus. At Garst, Bauer, & Bolton."

"Really? Okay, who did you blackmail to get me a job at

Good, Better, & Best?"

Neal shook his head. "First, never ever call them that again. Second, I found the opening, but Mom called somebody at the firm."

"Shit, Neal. Are you serious?" He may have been bouncing up and down on Claire's sofa.

"Yep. Want it?"

"I'll have to look over the employment package; health care, 401K, partnership options...."

Neal punched him in the arm. "Ow!"

"Do you want it?"

"More than life itself. Well, not really, but almost. Wait. Do they know about Eric? And me getting fired?"

He nodded. "Mom talked to them."

"So I call them?"

"Tomorrow. Ask for Mr. Bauer."

He hugged Neal as hard as he could. "Thank you, thank you, thank you."

"Get off me, Bergeron." Neal turned on the TV and from five hundred channels summoned a rugby game.

"Explain the rules to me again."

Neal shook his head. "No."

"Come on. I promise to pay attention this time."

"Not happening, Bergeron."

The guys were running up and down a big field. He said, "Hey, Claire got my inheritance straightened out."

"Yeah? So are they keeping the painting?"

"No, they had a change of heart, or she threatened them with fire and brimstone and perdition, and they caved. Anyway, I'm supposed to call my cousin, Marie, to pick it up and some family history stuff."

"Great." Neal spared him a glance. "That's great, Gabe."

He watched minutes and minutes of rugby with Neal.

"Okay. I know I shouldn't ask, but I'm going to."

Neal started laughing. "I'm shocked that you waited this long."

"You know Ellie's gone to L.A.? Right?"

Neal nodded, staring at the big men chasing each other and

the ball. "Yes, she called me."

"I'm really sorry, Neal."

"You knew all along, didn't you?"

"No, I didn't know anything. I'm just a skeptic and a pessimist, and I always expect the worst." And his track record was worst than Neal's.

Neal said, "I should have seen this coming, but this one time I didn't think about all the things that could go wrong."

"Which is a good thing."

"Is it?"

"Yes, you loved and lost, and I'm sorry. Very sorry. But you'll find somebody else." Somebody who wasn't a cross between Genghis Khan and Lucretia Borgia.

Neal shook his head.

"And you had lots and lots of killer sex."

Neal smiled at him. "You heard? In the cabin?"

"Mr. Bear heard...in the next cabin over."

"Sorry."

"Then quit smirking. Bastard."

"It was amazing, Gabe."

He held up a hand. "I'm happy for you, but I don't want to hear."

"Are you sure? She did this thing...nobody has ever done anything like it before. She got on top...."

"No!" He shuddered as disturbing, unwelcome images appeared in his brain.

Neal was still smiling as the rugby players piled on top of each other for no apparent reason.

Friday
A Week Later

A taxi conveyed Gabe out to a quiet street in Schaumburg, Illinois.

A teenage boy with floppy, incandescently-red hair answered the door of a modest home. "Yeah?"

"I'm Gabe Bergeron."

He took out one ear bud, and said, "What?"

"I'm Gabe Bergeron."

"So?"

A woman's voice said, "Who is it, Caleb?"

Young Caleb said, "Some guy."

A pretty woman in her forties rounded a corner. "Caleb, I swear you are a barbarian. You're mine, I think, but you are a pure barbarian."

She stopped. "Are you Mr. Bergeron?"

"I am. Marie Murphy, I presume?" Her hair was more muted than Caleb's but lovelier for it.

She smiled. "I lost track of time. Come in. Caleb, get out of the way, and let the man in."

Caleb put his ear bud back in and slouched off.

"Do you have children, Mr. Bergeron?"

"No, and please call me Gabe."

"You are so lucky. Call me Marie. My father is Bob Sullivan, John's younger brother."

"Right. I met him at the lawyer's office."

She blushed. "Dad told me. Sorry about that. Donnie has a temper."

"No, I understand. I could tell that it was a total shock."

"It was. Aunt Rhoda should have warned him."

"She knew?"

"Of course. And Aunt Amy and Aunt Brenda. Come in and sit down. If you have any questions, I'd be happy to answer what I can. About the family."

"Thank you. More than anything I'd like to see a picture of him?"

"Of course." She grabbed an album. "These are all yours. Caleb made copies. He made digital copies on a thumb drive thing too."

"Does he know who I am?"

She glanced at him and then smiled. "He wasn't rude because of who you are. No, indeed. I did tell him, but sometimes I wonder if he knows who I am. This is Uncle John...your father."

John Teague Sullivan was about twenty in the photo and very handsome. If he said so himself.

She had pictures from baby in the cradle to sick man in the hospital bed. He didn't want to tear up, but he couldn't help it.

She was kind enough to ask, "Would you like some coffee?"

"Yes, please."

And she left him alone to pull himself together as he leafed through six decades of a stranger's life. He didn't know most of the people in the pictures.

Marie came back and told him who they all were.

It was bizarre.

Marie said, "These are Dad's parents, David and Grace...our grandparents. They're both gone. And this is Aunt Amy and Aunt Brenda, Dad's older sisters."

"Yes, I saw them at the lawyer's office."

"And this is Uncle Ryan; he's Dad's fraternal twin. They're three years younger than Uncle John." She turned to a family photo. "And this is the whole clan."

He could see the grandparents, David and Grace, and their five children and their grandchildren. "Wait. How many cousins are there?"

Marie smiled at him. "You make an even dozen, Gabe."

"You mean I have eleven cousins?"

She smiled. "You do. You don't have many relatives on your mother's side?"

"My great-aunt Flo."

She waited for him to go on, but when he didn't, she patted his arm. "Then this must be really odd for you."

"A little bit."

She said, "Well, if you want to, Dad would like to get to know you. And Aunt Amy and Uncle Ryan. Aunt Brenda needs a little more time."

And presumably, his new half-brother. "I'd love to get to know them too."

Marie said, "I'll write down their numbers. Dad goes to Baltimore on business all the time so it wouldn't be hard to arrange a meeting."

"Thanks, Marie."

He called a taxi to go back to the airport. Marie offered Caleb as a chauffeur, but he valued his life more than that.

"And here is the portrait that Uncle John wanted you to have."

It was wrapped in brown paper and string and was very heavy.

"Thank you, Marie."

"You're very welcome. If you have questions about the family photos, call me. Okay?"

"I will. Thank you."

Marie and Caleb were standing in the doorway. She didn't look very much like John Sullivan, but Caleb did. Except for the hair.

Gabe walked out to the taxi.

He told the driver to take him to O'Hare and settled back.

He should have waited until he got back to Philly, but he was curious. He ripped a strip of paper away.

The face staring back at him wasn't John but his mother; young and smiling and so alive.

She had done a self-portrait for her lover, for John. He wondered where John had kept it during all the years of marriage to Rhoda?

And there was the companion portrait of John. That's why

the package had felt so heavy. John was young and smiling just like his mother. Claire said that he had John's smile. He wanted to see it, but he wasn't sure that he did.

He hugged the portraits and ignored the driver's funny looks as they sped toward the airport and home.

As soon as he could, he set off to visit Aunt Flo to show her the portraits and the photos of John and his family.

She and Mrs. Gutierrez were in the kitchen. He set the portraits on the counter, leaning against the cabinets.

She stepped back and examined them. "Gabriel, they're wonderful. Wonderful and brilliant. Of the things that I've seen, these are the best that Leanne ever did."

Mrs. Gutierrez said, "She was inspired by her love."

And for just a split second, Gabe could see the young Ezmeralda and not the dumpy, middle-aged Mrs. Gutierrez.

Aunt Flo said, "I'm very happy for you, Gabriel."

"I'm happy for me too. I didn't know she was an artist."

Aunt Flo smiled at him. "You didn't remember?"

"No. I don't remember much of those years."

"Did you ever look at the paintings in the back bedroom, Gabriel?"

The back bedroom was on the third floor down a dog-legged hall from his turret bedroom. "I've seen them?"

Aunt Flo smiled at Mrs. Gutierrez. "Come with us."

Mrs. Gutierrez opened the curtains and let in the light. The paintings blazed to life.

He looked at each one. Most of them were by the same artist, but he couldn't make out the signature. But one was by Leanne Bergeron.

It was a nude woman standing in a claw foot tub drying her long brown hair.

"She painted this."

Aunt Flo said, "She did. When she was eighteen. You know who it is?"

He was a grown man, and he wasn't going to blush.

Aunt Flo smiled at him. "She was very beautiful, Gabriel."

She was, but she was his mother. "How did you get it?"

"When I came back, I was too late to find her, but I found this painting. And I found you. She had sold it to a gallery before she died."

He focused on the other paintings. "And who did these?"

Mrs. Gutierrez snorted.

"I can't make out the signature." But the first name started with an "F." "Are these yours, Aunt Flo?"

She smiled.

"Really? They're wonderful. You never said." Like so much else.

"It was one of my careers."

There was another female nude, a couple of abstracts, and a portrait of a young, Hispanic man with long black hair and a cap.

Aunt Flo said, "The lady is me, Gabriel."

"Right. Thought so." He nodded and scooted out of the bedroom. "They're really wonderful."

Her voice floated down the stairs to him.

"I was quite something. In the day."

He wasn't going to tell his eighty year old great-aunt that she had been hot.

Aunt Flo and Mrs. Gutierrez thought his blushing was so funny, and he guessed it was. Still.

On the drive home to Philly the next day, he had thought about the portrait of the Hispanic guy. He had looked familiar, but it was only months later when he saw a kid with a Che Guevara t-shirt that he had figured out why.

Author's note

So ends the first Gabe Bergeron mystery. I hope you enjoyed it!

If you did, there are lots more books with Gabe running amok, or at least talking amok, to check out.

And if you'd like to keep up with what's happening in Gabe-land, please visit/subscribe to the M G Lewis Books blog:

www.mglewisbooks.blogspot.com

Blogs showcasing new books, short stories, special offers (free stuff!), and background details of Gabe and his world will be posted semi-monthly.

Made in the USA
Columbia, SC
22 October 2025